Fierce by M J Tennant

Published by M J Tennant

Barnsley, S71 5SH

https://mjtennant.weebly.com/

eBook formatting by KDP

ISBN: 978-1-7394295-9-1

Contents

One 4

Two 24

Three 42

Four 61

Five 77

Six 90

Seven 102

Eight 115

Nine 127

Ten 140

Eleven 153

Twelve 169

Thirteen 183

Fourteen 198

Fifteen 209

For James xxx

One

Fierce

adjective

having or displaying an intense or ferocious aggressiveness.

It was one of *those* nights.

I had broken down and was stuck in my car, thirty minutes from home and out of *all* the people God could have sent to *save* me. It *had* to be *him.*

Noah Savvas, my nemesis, *my* Voldemort. The one boy who had tortured me through high school. More like Noah Bloody Savage.

A chord of recognition strummed painfully inside me. Why couldn't the past remain in the past? And what the heck was the big guy in the sky thinking? Was this a reckoning? Had I done something to upset him, and *this* was his punishment? Either that or a cruel twist of fate? If it was fate that had intervened. It certainly had a warped sense of humour.

My brain flooded with mindless panic, which *always* occurred when faced with this particular individual.

I watched him from the corner of my eye as he loomed outside my car door; he was still too good-looking for his own good. A walking, talking temptation. Although maybe strike the talking bit. That part *wasn't* attractive; what came out of his mouth was nasty at the best of times! But the sound was like a sinful caress. A throaty rich rumble, a tone that liked to touch.

A coil of tension snaked through my body.

I continued to immerse myself in my seat, shrinking from the threat and praying that he would climb back into his stupidly large truck and drive away. I had *no* problem with him leaving me stranded in the middle of nowhere. Part of me would have preferred that even sitting there in the darkness of my car.

If I accepted his help, I'd owe him one. A thought I certainly didn't relish. I would rather have chosen to sleep there than be indebted to the—NO! I barely managed to stop myself from swearing. Noah wasn't worth the damage foul language did to the soul. I didn't use curse words. I had way too much self-respect for that.

I jumped in my seat, unease hitting me in the belly as his fist *banged* on the window again. Noah had always been overly physical, larger than life, and *impossible* to ignore.

Well over six feet tall, with a toned muscular body. Noah boasted huge biceps, washboard abs and corded thighs; physical masculine perfection at its best. His dad was from Cyprus, so he had that Mediterranean olive-toned skin that constantly glowed. His hair was dark and inky and his eyes, although appearing black, were actually chocolate brown with green flecks in, let's not forget the flecks. They were usually partly hidden behind thick, sooty eyelashes that I'd always thought a bit long for a boy. He was a hulk of a man. To put it bluntly, the guy probably drank testosterone with every meal of the day. Physically, he was blessed.

Over the last couple of years, I had attempted to block him from my every waking thought but unfortunately, Noah Savvas was breath-taking *and* annoyingly unforgettable. A perfect specimen of manliness.

To some girls, he had the *whole* package. As far as I was concerned, he could keep his package to himself. I ignored the fact that every female hormone in my body was still standing to attention.

"You OK Miss? I'm from the garage, I took your call. Are you coming out?" he barked through the glass, that deep baritone, punching through my chest. It was the same voice used by the devil when he spoke to me in my nightmares.

I wracked my brain, attempting to come up with a plausible excuse as to why I couldn't open the door. I came up with nothing.

Why on earth had I called a *local* garage rather than the RAC? I felt so cross with myself that I hadn't recognised his voice on the phone.

During the split second that he'd climbed down from his truck, my mouth had dropped open. I'd heard Noah worked as a mechanic for the army, so how the heck was he now standing beside my car; like a vengeance demon?

I was being tested, I *had* to be. *Nothing* else made sense.

I finally found my voice, "I'm fine now!" I replied in a pitch that was surely dogs-only-high. I did attempt to change the sound slightly as when he recognised me; my composure would be smashed to smithereens.

As I nervously gnawed on my bottom lip, a thought occurred to me. Maybe he wouldn't remember *anything* about insignificant little me. The girl he had been horrid to for at least three years of school. We hadn't exactly moved in the same friendship circles.

Wrinkling my nose, I thought back to how pathetic I'd been at school. You'd think that there are only so many things you could do to a person before they fight back, but in my case, the list was endless as I'd *never* fought back. At school I was a pushover, even my friends had thought so. Standing up to people just wasn't in my nature. When things got tough, I walked away.

When I was little, before my mum left us, she taught me to ignore those that picked on me. Advised me that bullies usually got bored if you didn't give them the time of day. But it hadn't worked; Noah Savvas had *never* gotten bored. He had the resolve of a rhino and skin just as thick. He just bounced back, *every* time.

I knew my ill feeling toward him was not right, I should have moved on by now and adopted my Christian forgive-and-forget approach, but I just couldn't do it. I batted the thought to one side. I'd deal with the shudder of shame I felt about that later. When it came to Noah, I had filed away God's call to 'love thy enemy' years ago *and* padlocked the cabinet.

Noah stepped back before slowly prowling around my car like a jungle cat, assessing the situation. He then returned to my door; eyeing me through the glass with an unfathomable expression.

There was an awkward beat of silence.

"You have a flat," he said bluntly, stating the obvious like I didn't already know that. My hands started to itch, something that happened when I was nervous and I felt thoroughly aggravated by it.

"It's fine. I've called for help," I squeaked again, my body mirroring my tyre, I too was almost flat in my seat, my head level with the steering wheel of my Mini.

"That's right sweetheart and *he's* here. *I'm* the help."

Give me strength. I felt sick with nerves.

Breathe. My muscles were clenched so tightly that they physically hurt.

He pounded the window again, that aggressive-looking tattoo on the back of his hand swinging back and forth. He'd had it done whilst we were at school; after which the head teacher had preached about tattoos in assembly, but of course, Noah had never been taken to task for his.

My head almost retracted into my neck like some type of demented turtle as Noah placed his hand on the roof of my car. My heart skipped a beat as he leaned down and peered into the vehicle with squinted eyes, his expression suspicious. Thank goodness I had turned off the internal light when I'd seen his car pull up. It was dark outside and so hopefully he'd struggle to see in. At least I hoped he would, but who knew, didn't demons have eyes that could see clearly in the dark or something?

"You need to open the door Miss. You're safe. I'm not going to hurt you. I'm here to help."

He released a sigh of frustration before adding, "You've got a spare I assume?"

I'm not going to hurt you. Yeah, like I believed *that* when that's *all* this guy had done during school.

"Go away," I bit out dismissively, take the hint.

"Not going to happen. You called *me*, remember?" Noah released a sigh of frustration and lowered his hand.

"Look, you can open the door or I—" he stopped suddenly, pushing his face closer to the driver's door, straining. He really was determined to see inside and then to my absolute horror, the penny dropped. Drat!

He swore under his breath. I noticed that he had just the right amount of stubble on his face. It gave him that, rugged virile look of the jaw-dropping variety.

"That *you* Red?"

BOOM! I snatched in a breath as chaos came calling in all its monstrous glory! The fact that he used his annoying nickname for me made me want to run him over with my car. Again, not a thought my church would appreciate.

I remained silent, silly things left my mouth when I was in the company of this guy. Refusing to turn myself in, I moodily folded my arms. From my periphery, I saw those full lips stretch and the white of his teeth. The guy had a smile that could have been used to sell toothpaste.

He now appeared slightly amused by my presence *and* predicament. That killer grin of his just lit up his face, adding to his beauty; *everything* about the guy invited you in; on the outside of course. The inside was a different story and not one that belonged in any of the books I read. No, thank you.

The deep gruffness of his voice boomed out again. *Nothing* about him was small and understated.

He suddenly looked lost in thought, "I heard you were back from University. Little Lucy Meadows. What's it been? Two years? My God, you haven't changed at all—oh sorry. I take it you're still into all that bible shit?"

The man put the 'I' in 'inappropriate'.

I decided to apply my right to a vow of silence, praying he'd get bored and go away.

That quiet stretched between us.

He continued to loom there like a terrifying apparition, knocking on the window with his knuckle; now more of a tap, tap, tap than a thud; like something a serial killer would do. The sound was eerie in the extreme and did all sorts of crazy to my insides. I so wasn't ready to climb out of the car and face him. I almost laughed aloud hysterically, 'face him' was a bit ambitious considering I was only five foot one.

"Come on, open up. I can't jack the car up with you sat in it," he pointed out with a huff. I understood what he was saying but it still made me feel like an elephant.

I found my voice. "Why would you want to help me anyway?" I bit back in the iciest tone. One I rarely used. I actually scared myself a bit. My backbone continued to do that crumbling thing.

I ran my hands down my woolly tights feeling cold now the engine was off. My toes were already curled in my boots but not from the weather.

"It's my job for a start. Surely, you're not still sore about school? That was *ages* ago. Aren't you happy-clappy sorts supposed to turn the other cheek and all that shit?" Noah questioned, mirroring my earlier thoughts, reminding me of my shame. And of course, he would; this guy had *always* made me feel I was in the wrong.

I shot him the stink-eye but he carried on regardless. "Forgive and forget; isn't that your motto?" he translated in one of those voices you used to speak to people who were a bit thick. He was obviously desperate for an answer to his annoying question.

I felt like saying, 'Yes, but not with a nasty so-and-so like you'. Instead, I went with.

"Go away, Noah." My pulse thudded like an off-kilter drumbeat.

I accepted the fact that my comeback was lame, but I was past caring. I just wanted him to leave me alone. The guy summoned the worst memories from my hardest years at school.

Deep down I knew I was being ridiculous, if he did drive off, I'd be sat there all night. Either that or I'd be walking home in the dark, another idea I did not welcome; especially having recently watched An American Werewolf in London. A movie that had terrified the crap out of me. No way, I was far too jumpy.

The demon started talking again, now carrying an expression of extreme disbelief.

"You really think I'm going to leave you on your own with a flat in the middle of nowhere?" He shook his condescending head slowly from side to side. "Sorry, can't do it sunshine. I couldn't live with myself. You'll have to open the door."

"I'd rather die thank you," I put in quietly like a proper drama queen, but of course, he heard. The devil also had good hearing I'd read.

His next words were much more forthright and they forced a shiver to lick up my spine.

He folded those *massive* arms over his chest, all bristling, demanding male. "Open the door Red, or I'll put the window through and drag you out; your choice."

My heart fell into my stomach. Yeah, and what a great 'choice'' that was. Wowzer, give me a minute to think about it. The guy was still deranged. He'd probably do it too; I'd witnessed his man tantrums at school.

Like most big, burly country guys, Noah Savvas had a problem with authority and not getting his own way. Pretty much *every* guy at school had been scared of him and that included some of the teachers. He wrote the book on how to be a bad boy. Boys wanted to *be* him; girls just wanted to *do* him. He had been a typical player, a renowned man-whore. There'd also been a rumour at school that Mrs Clark had given him a blowjob in her office. The thought made me want to bleach my brain.

Noah was a treat-them-mean-keep them-keen type; and 'keen' they were. He constantly had girls crying over him at school. I'd heard that his sexual appetites were not easily sated. These facts alone had only made me want to keep my distance even more.

"I'll give you to the count of five Red," he threatened in a silky voice.

I pushed up in my seat and shot him a pained look through the window. "You wouldn't dare?" I knew I shouldn't have uttered *those* words as they were a challenge. And if there was one thing this guy got off on, it was facing that.

Noah grinned that cocky smirk I remembered only too well. It made my fingers curl into my palms. He then dropped his arms and took a step back from the car, glaring down his perfect nose at me, "I totally would and you *know* it," he growled with a wolfish smile.

I had *never* met anyone who could unsettle me like this boy, strike that, man. As I looked him up and down through the glass, he was definitely not a boy anymore. To be honest, he hadn't resembled one at school; he'd looked more like one of the teachers than a pupil. And he still *oozed* animal magnetism. I pushed that annoying re-occurring thought of what he'd now look like shirtless from my mind. It had been pretty damn amazing at school. All the girls who had taken art had begged to sketch that chest.

He was impressively highlighted by the beam of his truck's headlights. I could now see every contour on that strong, sinfully good-looking face. Physically, the guy of every girl's dream stood *right* there, for a certain type of female of course. My resolve against sinfully attractive men was much too strong.

"I mean it Red, don't push it."

"Fine," I bit out between clenched teeth before unlocking the car, knowing that I would only regret it. Like people who overindulged in alcohol when they knew it would give them a headache.

He yanked open the door and offered his massive hand to help me from my car. No thank you, I'd rather grab a nettle. I blew at some rogue strands of my hair, as I eyeballed him through my lashes. He was such a large person: I don't think I'd ever met anyone as tall or as stacked as Noah. I eyed his hand warily. Who knew where *that* had been; probably working its magic down some girl's top!

His face was dipped toward me; he appeared sickeningly pleased with himself that I'd done as he'd instructed. He was even better looking up close even in spite of the smug look.

I knew I wasn't being very accommodating but I couldn't help it, this boy brought out the worst in me. And in all honesty, there wasn't much of that. I was a pleasant, sweet girl, I didn't do angst or temper. I helped out at charity shops and assisted old ladies across the road for goodness' sake. I was the epitome of nice. *Everyone* in my church thought so.

I wrinkled my nose at how un-Christian I was behaving before scowling up at him. At the end of the day, God had done little to intervene in this tormenting situation and so, I decided to shelve his expectations for at least one night.

Noah's strong fingers shot out and curled around my hand anyway, my tiny paw was swallowed by his. He tugged me out onto the pavement and up close to his towering body. My head barely reached the guy's shoulder and I almost had to snap my neck to look up into his face. He was so unacceptably gorgeous and my tummy fluttered; unwanted lust trickling into my pelvis. Great, now I'd have to pump out an extra prayer that night; an apology for my un-pure thoughts.

He looked down at me with a lazy smile, all six foot four of him. Those rock-hard abs sitting well below my eye line. All the girls at school had loved to run their fingers across his toned stomach, and at the time, I didn't get it. I *hated* the fact that the urge to do so now powered through me.

Our gazes were tangled and I allowed myself a brief moment to take him in without the obstruction of my streaky car window.

Noah had eyes that could reach into your soul and extract your darkest secrets and those lips; his mouth was full and crafted for wickedness (although usually set in a smirk) and his nose was spirit-level straight. The guy had so mastered the art of looking down it on those less fortunate. Me being part of that club. He also had that 'I answer to no one vibe', a definite rough diamond. Even now he appeared unkempt, with his six o'clock shadow and his take-me-as-you-find-me attitude.

No matter which way you sliced it, Noah Savvas, in the flesh was *physically overwhelming*.

His name had also always bugged me, as there was *nothing* biblical about him. Nope, not an Ark in sight. Noah was an all-out atheist and proud of it. He probably owned one of those T-shirts with 'Science; Making Religion Look Stupid' printed on it.

I tugged my hand free and stepped to the side to close my door, not wanting to lose what little heat was left in there.

Turning back toward him, I shook the skirt of my dress down, which had risen up whilst I had been sliding around my seat. Noah watched the movement with a guarded expression; missing nothing; I suddenly felt exposed and tugged my duffle coat further around my body. Luckily my bobble hat covered most of my head. I had long, wavy ginger hair and freckles, and my skin was extremely pale to the point where you could see some of my veins. My colouring had always been a source of amusement to this person. The contrast between us couldn't have been more different. The tone of our skin wasn't the *only* difference thank goodness.

Noah's eyes roamed over me like he was hungry and I was a McDonald's.

His next comment made me feel rather frail-looking, but I'd always felt small in his company, in more ways than one. "My God, Red. I'd forgotten how tiny you are." Did he say the lord's name on purpose *just* to annoy me, I imagined that he did; the obnoxious non-believer.

I wrinkled my nose again; I knew it wasn't a good look on me as it matted my freckles together into a blob, but I was past caring.

"Really, well I haven't forgotten a thing about you, so if you don't mind getting on with it *without* talking to me, I'd appreciate it."

I boxed my ungrateful response along with that twinge of shame I'd experienced earlier, I'd deal with apologising for those another day.

He shot me a lopsided smile and my breath seesawed through my chest.

"So cold Red, considering I'm here to save your pretty arse," he pointed out. "Talking about being saved. You didn't answer my question."

He then stabbed a finger toward the sky, "*Are* you still worshiping The Almighty?"

Here we go, I felt a migraine coming on.

"Pardon?" I huffed, staring up at him with wide eyes.

"God and all that shite," he grunted, shifting further and getting into my face. I almost fell back against the car. Noah had always been one of those types of people who invaded your personal space.

I felt a flare of irritation. I know not very Christian, but I wanted to thump him in his too-confident face.

"Yes, and I would appreciate it if you didn't disrespect that." I felt a twinge of annoyance at how prim I sounded.

Noah snorted before saying. "Last time I heard, He was worshipping me."

My eyes narrowed. "Funny. Isn't that a line from Black Adder?"

His eyebrows shot into his hairline in surprise.

"You actually watch TV? Is that even allowed? By your people I mean." A small smile graced his lips. He was grimly amused.

"What does that mean, *your* people?" I shot back with a grimace.

Noah quirked his head at me. "You know, people of the cloth and all that."

Yep, the guy was moronic. I swiftly changed the subject, motioning with my hand.

"My tyre?"

He ignored my attempt to divert, his eyes roaming over my entire body.

"I think you've shrunk actually," he deadpanned. I didn't appreciate it and glanced down, noting how I wasn't standing on the curb. I moved forward and stepped up to the level he was stood on, but he still towered over me like a giant. I was five one to his six four, what can you do? Noah had *always* used his height as an intimidation tactic.

His mouth split into a wide smile; he was clearly amused by my gesture.

"*That* made a difference," he drawled out with a smirk, his eyes dancing with humour. I was surprised my palms didn't start to bleed from the imprint of my nails.

Noah's eyes tangled with mine again and I twisted my head to the side. Uncomfortable with his all-seeing expression. He was a menace, but an *extremely* attractive one. Temptation wrapped in attitude.

I took a moment to compose myself before looking back up into his annoyingly alluring face. He was definitely the serpent in human form, he was probably armed with the forbidden fruit in his back pocket!

A heavy moment of silence passed between us before he piped, "Pop the boot," with a flick of his head. His hair was so dark, like a blackbird's feathers.

"I don't know where the lever is," I said quietly. Feeling like the worst cliché of a helpless female.

Noah rolled his eyes and motioned for me to move out of the way with a flick of his fingers. He then opened the door of my car before successfully finding the latch to release the boot in one swift motion. He shot me one of those annoying, know-it-all looks.

My eyes narrowed as I watched him slowly walk to the back of my Mini.

"So, you didn't become a nun I take it?" Noah shot over his shoulder.

I huffed.

"No, and I was *never* going to be a nun, only in your warped imagination."

He opened the boot and rummaged inside and I pulled my coat even closer against my body, now quite cold. The November air was *biting*. Not one car had passed us in the time we'd been there either. I certainly needed to re-plan my route from work. Maybe one less desolate. I hadn't been back long and the last time I'd lived here; I didn't drive. I needed to familiarise myself with the roads.

I realised Noah was still speaking and attempted to retune into what he was saying. He was still going on about the nun thing. When had I *ever* announced that I wanted to become a nun? That was something that was made up by the idiots at school. Those who picked on me for going to church and because I was small and ginger and had freckles. For goodness' sake, girls *draw* them on now. It's just a shame that they weren't trendy when I was fourteen.

"Was it due to the celibacy thing?" His voice suddenly cut into my thoughts, velvety smooth.

I snorted. The guy hadn't got a clue.

"Nope," I replied with a pop of my lips. Yes, the migraine was well on its way.

He kept rummaging around. I hadn't the foggiest as to what was taking him so long.

"So, if you didn't go for the nun thing. Did you eventually put out and lose it to Paul Kettering?"

His words were not welcome and I tutted and planted my hands on my hips. The cheeky sod. I knew he was just saying it to get a rise out of me but I couldn't help but retaliate. And Paul Kettering, no thank you! The thought of Paul was about as thrilling as a wash with a cold wet flannel. There was a rumour at school that he'd been with so many girls that his thingy had dropped off. Yes, he'd been all over me like a rash but I'd soon shot that one down into the fires of hell.

"Absolutely not! And this is *not* a conversation I want to be having with you Mr Savvas."

He moved away from the boot of the car and approached me with an unimpressed glower. "Mr Savvas, who am I? My old man?"

His comment caused me to drop my arms and shuffle nervously on my feet.

I cleared my throat as he came to stand before me and stated in a hard voice.

"No spare." Noah crossed his massive arms again. He wore overalls but they'd been pulled off his torso and were gathered around his waist, the material bunched up. The short-sleeved T-shirt he was wearing revealed his bulging biceps and I noticed part of another tattoo peeking beneath the sleeve on one arm. I tried not to stare, but it was difficult. Didn't the guy feel the cold? Probably not, another trait of the devil.

He watched me with a hooded gaze. His whole being screamed menace.

"So, who *did* you lose it to in the end?"

My brow creased. "What?" I spat, aware that he'd just spliced two different comments together

"The v-card?"

I exhaled noisily, shaking my head and ignoring that question. "No, what did you say *before*, about the spare?"

He snorted. "There isn't one. You've been driving around without a spare tyre. Good job you didn't get pulled. That would have been three points on your license and a hefty fine. I wonder what your God would have thought about that. Little Red with a criminal record."

He was such a snarky sod.

"Surely points on your license wouldn't make you a criminal?" I responded with a frown.

He snorted. "If you say so. I reckon it would still be frowned upon by the church though."

His tongue flicked out to moisten his lips as he continued to give me a hard look.

How dare he lecture me about the church? I imagined what he knew about the bible could have been written on a napkin.

"So?" he prompted, motioning with his hand for an answer, to what, who knew. Until he reiterated.

"The v-card?" he repeated. His question offered another blow to my equilibrium. I answered him, as I knew he wouldn't back off if I didn't.

"Not that it's any of your business, but no one," I replied flatly. I wasn't ashamed to be a virgin.

He didn't flinch but shifted on his feet, rocking back, eyeing me thoughtfully.

"*No one*, you still have your virginity at twenty-two?" I felt like thumping him, Noah had probably been born *without* his.

"As I said, not your concern, and I'm twenty-one actually. You were above me remember?" I pointed out matter-of-fact.

Noah slowly lowered his arms; his eyes glistening with a steamy ingredient.

"I certainly *wanted* to be Red," he purred in a husky voice. His tone sent a pool of heat between my legs and I pushed my thighs together to try and stop that outrageous sensation from spreading.

"How the hell can you look like you look and *still* be a virgin?" He was genuinely dumbfounded.

"You think I'm attractive?" The question shot out of me before I could stop it. I so hoped he didn't think I was fishing. My self-confidence in the presence of this person usually dive-bombed pretty easily.

"You *know* you are, you've always been stunning," Noah stated, before adding "although, growing up, you were probably too busy polishing your crucifixes to look in the fucking mirror."

I took in a sharp breath, only too aware of his compliment. It was odd, as his words made me feel a bit giddy, nice almost. I batted the thought aside. The devil also played mind tricks I reminded myself. Sins of the flesh and all that.

Noah was now looking at me with his, 'trying to figure me out expression'. He used to do that at school and it would turn me into a bag of nerves. Like he was digging beneath the surface, trying to find an answer to a Red-specific mystery.

He was still shaking his head. "Still a virgin. I just can't believe no one has taken it yet."

I shot him a tight smile. "That's the thing you see. People aren't allowed to just *take* it, Noah, that's called assault."

"Indeed."

He rubbed a thumb across his bottom lip, his expression was now thoughtful. The movement was deliberate and it drew your attention toward his mouth.

"I think you still have it because you're saving yourself for me," he whispered thickly, lowering his head toward me. Moving back another step, I almost pancaked my back against my car. I rolled my eyes so hard it hurt.

"Then that must be it," I remarked sarcastically. God, the guy was annoying.

Noah's eyes moved to focus on my lips and that heat *down there* increased. I clamped my thighs together so hard I almost fell over. I'd be crossed-legged soon.

His voice dropped to a purr. "I remember how you used to eye-fuck me across the cafeteria."

Shame heated my skin as I recalled all those times when Noah had caught me watching him.

"I did *nothing* of the sort," I lied, my voice cracking.

"I doubt you'd be able to take me anyway. You're such a delicate little thing." Noah observed, smirking down his perfect nose.

My pulse raced and I felt a blush spread across my entire face. My body appeared to enjoy his smutty comment.

There was a beat of silence before I shook my head with feigned disgust.

"I wouldn't touch you even with the protection of a hazmat suit. Parts of me would probably start to drop off."

My little remark bounced off his hide and he released a smothered crack of laughter, clearly enjoying our banter. I knew his sexual innuendoes were fake, he was just doing that thing he did. Trying to get a reaction.

"You really did think that you were too good for us all, but I still remember our kiss. To say you were such a meek little thing, you lit up like a bonfire. To think that the fire in your hair actually burns right the way through you. Yet you try so hard to hide it."

His words forced me to close my eyes and my tongue ran along the seam of my lips on impulse.

It had been my first kiss and I had *never* forgotten it, or the sinful thoughts it had aroused; even now.

This guy was just so not good for me. I needed to keep my distance. I couldn't understand how I could be attracted to someone I despised. He'd bullied me relentlessly during my last few years of school, and I would *never* forget that. I knew I would eventually have to forgive it though. Forgiveness was part of my makeup. But not now; I wasn't ready to draw that line just yet.

"I remember it too. You took the kiss without my permission as I hazily recall. That's not really acceptable in polite society Noah."

His expression twisted from playful to stone-cold serious. "Well, we both know I'm far from polite and you shouldn't have goaded me Red."

"How on earth did I goad you? You were the one behaving in an inappropriate manner."

He drew himself up to his full height, suddenly looking tall and daunting.

"You hit me, so I retaliated. That's what happens when you yank the tail of the tiger sweetheart. Turn the other cheek and I don't share the same *fucking* planet." He paused momentarily and his eyes narrowed. "You'd do well to remember that."

Something stirred in my gut and I didn't understand my reaction. His comment was mildly threatening and my body seemed to *like* it. What was I turning into? Some type of masochist; a sexual deviant?

"I wouldn't say I hit you, I *slapped* you and I'm surprised you even felt it. I wasn't the strongest of people and you were *huge*, even back then."

A dark wistful look skittered across his features and he pinned me with slumberous eyes. "Oh, I felt it, Lucy." The way he spoke those words and used my actual name suggested he had enjoyed it. I shouldn't have been surprised really. He probably got his jollies from any type of confrontation, even if he was on the receiving end of it.

I leaned back against my car and looked up at him through my lashes, now feeling a bit more in control after my initial shock at seeing him.

"Well, thanks a bunch for the warning but I don't need it, as after tonight, I don't intend *ever* seeing you again."

He pushed a strand of my hair behind my ear and my skin hummed at the contact.

"Really?" he drawled, the breeze caressing his own hair.

"*Yes really*?"

He laughed with startled appreciation.

"Well, that's where you're wrong Red. I also moved back to the village; *permanently*. A couple of years ago actually."

My face dropped and I felt confusion snake up my spine.

"But I thought you were in the army?"

"Not anymore."

I snorted and questioned meanly, "What were you, a deserter? Wouldn't surprise me."

He leaned back and narrowed his eyes, now pushing his large hands into the pockets of his overalls. He then quirked an eyebrow at me. I took it as a threat.

"A word of warning Lucy. Remember what I said about provoking me. The last time you escaped with just a kiss, but I was a boy then. I'm a man now and the repercussion would be much more grown up." His eyes burned into mine.

My nipples hardened and it had nothing to do with the cold. I so needed to have serious words with my body.

"Great, so you're here to rescue me on one hand and attack me with the other?" I huffed haughtily.

He grimaced.

"I wouldn't *attack* you. If I laid my hands on you, you'd want it, beg me for it," Noah drawled out with sexual assurance. He was such an arrogant sod.

Awareness flickered across my skin and I diverted my thoughts grunting, "It will be a cold day in hell before *that* happens."

"We'll see," he husked, his expression full of challenge. Me and my big mouth.

There was a moment of silence before he totally changed tack. "Is your brother still an absolute twonk?"

Noah had always hated David.

I dashed a hand across my face, shooting him a withering look. "I'm not really sure what a twonk is, but David is fine, thank you. He's the Vicar of our church now, took our dad's job when he retired."

Noah barked out a laugh, it wasn't a pleasant sound. "Of course, he did."

I directed the discussion away from his leading comment. “Anyway, I’d rather not talk about my family thank you.”

He gave me a fluid shrug and then nodded his head in agreement. “Me neither, I’d rather talk about us.”

I exhaled noisily before pointing out. “There is no us.”

He tilted his head, regarding me thoughtfully. “Oh, there’s definitely an ‘us’ Red. And you *know* it.”

I almost tripped over my tongue in my haste to respond. His words touched a nerve and twanged that familiar chord inside me. Reminding that part of my body, that I *wanted* this boy, even though my head was yelling never! I had always been at war with myself where Noah was concerned.

“That’s absolute rubbish, I *hate* you. I have always hated you.” I accepted that the way I blurted these words out sounded over the top. They were also obscenely un-Christian. I suddenly felt ashamed and his grin widened as he shot me a knowing look before tutting.

“What would the good lord think of that?”

Yep, the guy was definitely the devil. Fraught didn’t even begin to describe how this man made me feel in his presence.

Attempting to make a point, I checked my wrist even though I knew I wasn’t wearing a watch; like a *proper* loser. We’d been standing there sparring for way too long and my mind was almost mush. I needed to move things along quickly.

“What are we going to do about my tyre?” I said, feeling tired and cold. Going too many rounds in the ring with this guy was *exhausting*, he had the strength and tenacity of a bear. I was more of a sparrow myself, one with a chapped beak; my lips suddenly felt *really* dry.

Noah’s eyes caressed my face. “You still sulk like a little girl.”

I looked away, biting my lip before Noah added, “Look, I’ll take you home and arrange for the tow truck to collect your car in the morning, sound good?”

Drat, that meant I’d have to sit in his truck, in a small space with him. I’d probably choke on all the testosterone.

I nodded, suddenly feeling like a mean girl.

“Yes, thank you,” I replied in a small voice.

“See that wasn’t so hard, was it brat? It appears I don’t have to teach you some manners after all. Ladies first,” he said, motioning me toward his truck. His comment about teaching me some manners gave me goose bumps. How would he have done that? I shelved the thought, as it created all sorts of foolish, naughty emotions to thump inside me.

I dragged open the door to my car and grabbed my bag before closing it again. Pressing the fob to lock it as Noah went back to slam the boot, butterflies fluttered in my chest: frenzied, like they were attempting to escape a net.

I held back my groan. Noah Savvas was back in my life and I knew I'd have to wave my sanity goodbye.

The cab of his works truck was fairly clean inside which was a surprise. I pulled the door closed and waited for Noah to join me.

As he negotiated his large body into his seat, I forced my face forward. Determined to keep eye contact and conversation to a minimum. Luckily, I wasn't that far from home.

"So, I heard you're back and staying with David and your dad?"

Noah's arm muscles flexed as he started the engine and shoved the car into gear. His head almost touched the roof and he made the amount of space in the cab seem tiny. The guy dwarfed everything to the point where I wanted to fully roll down the window in spite of that cold night air. I felt annoyingly conscious of the strength that sat beside me.

I pulled my bag further against my chest, almost like it was a security blanket.

"Yes, we kept the parsonage when David took over the position."

"So, David is the Pastor at All Saints now?"

"Vicar," I corrected him.

"Whatever. Is that where I'm taking you now?"

I nodded.

"Cool," Noah replied before lifting a hand off the steering wheel and taking out his mobile phone from a pocket in his overalls. "Here, put your number in and ring it."

I shot him a horrified look and he rolled his eyes, explaining, "In case there are any complications with your car."

Drat, I so didn't want to give him my number but I knew I had no choice. I did as he asked before handing him back his phone and then saving him into my own. I listed him under the name SATAN.

His attempt at normal chit-chat forced me to behave myself and I returned the question, knowing it was only polite to do so.

"How about you, are you back living with your mum and Natalie?"

He cleared his throat as he concentrated on the road before shooting me a glance.

"No, I live above the garage now," he explained.

I pulled a face. That certainly didn't sound like the nicest place to live. Above a garage? He must have read my puzzled body language as he added, "I own it. The business. I'm a mechanic. I also cover break-down, hence why I'm here."

Great. If only I had known then what I knew now. I batted the mardy thought away, noting how proud Noah sounded about his trade.

"OK. Well, good for you," I said being the bigger person. I was impressed that he'd done something good for himself. Quite a few kids in the village either sponged off their parents or were on benefits.

That's why I went away to University, to train as a medical secretary so I could get a job and become independent from my family. I disliked this boy immensely but we had history and so I was pleased he was building something up for himself. Unlike the over-privileged Lane boys, who would probably live with their parents forever!

Noah indicated and turned onto the road where my cottage was, again speaking about his home.

"You should come and visit sometime. We could catch up; fill in the blanks about what we've both been doing over the last two years. I have a great space there. Excellent sound system, seventy-five-inch TV, and a king-sized bed fit for a king; *and* queen. He shot me a suggestive look; reverting back to wind-up mode. There was no doubt about it, Noah loved pulling my strings.

I huffed before replying and my answer was swift and brutal, "I'll take your word for it, Noah."

A slashing grin curved his mouth, "You're so cute. Scaredy-cat."

I shot him one of my too-sweet-to-be-true smiles as he pulled the truck up outside my house. The cottage was in darkness.

My unwanted rescuer then undid his seatbelt and turned toward me. "Are you sure your family is in, looks pretty dead to me?" he put in with a frown, nodding toward the house.

"No, it's fine. They're probably in bed. David has an event at the church tomorrow."

"You want me to walk you to the door?" Noah questioned, his eyes roaming over my face. His watchful gaze and thoughtful words warmed my stomach. He could be nice when he put his mind to it. I suddenly felt guilty for my earlier treatment of him and my bad manners. Maybe he had changed?

"No, I'm fine and thank you for the rescue."

He smiled.

"Don't mention it. I'll get your car in the morning and tow it to mine. I own Victoria Garage on Cudworth Lane. You can pick it up any time after noon.

"OK, great but I'm working so, could I come after work? It would probably be just after five?"

He nodded and a strange energy filtered into the cab.

"Where do you work?" he questioned.

"I'd rather not say."

He looked startled by my comeback. "I'm not going to fucking stalk you," he shot out; frustrated.

"Fine. I work on reception at Wade and Sons. The vet's in the village."

"I know it," he delivered smoothly, his expression now quite odd.

Noah was staring at me intently and it forced out my following words. I bit the inside of my cheek before saying, "Thanks again. And for fixing my car so soon. I need it tomorrow night as I have a date."

I wasn't sure why I had felt such a strong need to tell him about the date but the words were out before I could harness them. Maybe this was my attempt to prove I wasn't a square or wrapped up in Noah. His virgin comment still needled.

A dark look swam into his eyes and his chest heaved. I wasn't stupid, I could see that this information unsettled him. He was watching me closely, looking for a sign of insincerity.

"Really, a date? Are you allowed to date?"

"Of course, I am. As I said, I'm not a nun."

A mask dropped in place. "And would I know the lucky man?"

We stared at each other for a long time, almost silently communicating, it was strange.

"Thomas Wade," I replied on an exhale.

He pursed his lips, suddenly looking less concerned.

"The boss's son. Interesting. Well, see you tomorrow then." I found his throwaway comment about Tom being my boss's son worthy of note and filed this away.

"Yes, night…" My voice trailed off into vapour and I stabbed my fingers through my hair.

His eyes followed the movement. The guy had always been obsessed with my locks. "Sleep well little Lucy Meadows," he whispered, his face part-lit by the street light which sat outside our cottage. It gave him a mysterious, roguish look.

I unclipped my seatbelt and jumped down from his car, panicking that he'd attempt to steal a kiss. His eyes said that he wanted to but he'd remained in his seat thank goodness. I told the twinge of disappointment to take a hike!

As I walked over to my house, I felt impelled with the urge to turn back. Like an invisible string was attaching us. Odd, when I was usually desperate to get away from the guy. I ignored that pulling feeling.

As I placed the key into the lock and undid the door. Noah fired the engine and slowly pulled away.

I thought back to the way Noah had looked at me. That silent message.

And now he was gone; why did I suddenly feel a sinking sensation?

Two

My mother ran off with another man when I was sixteen, breaking my dad's heart and throwing our family into turmoil. What she left behind *never* fully recovered. My father became a tormented soul and my brother just got angrier. If I had to sum it up in one word; 'complicated' is how I would have described my home life.

Whenever I thought about my mother, I felt empty inside. I'd tried to contact her so many times but there is only so much rejection a person can take. I didn't understand why she had decided to cut us all out of her life. When I'd questioned my father about it, he'd been extremely vague, muttering something about mum struggling with her mental health. I'd found this revelation odd, as I'd never seen *anything* like that growing up.

During the months that followed her departure, she'd messaged me a few times, saying how she had to get things straight in her head and that I needed to give her time. She'd messaged me some contact details, stating how I wasn't to share them with my father or David, which I'd found odd to say the least. The last time I'd emailed her, my message had bounced back as undelivered.

That had been during my first year at University and I hadn't reattempted any more contact since then. I was *devastated*, but for my own sanity, had decided to bury my feelings and concentrate on my studies and living away from home. Maybe one day she would ask to see me and put things right, give me that explanation I craved. That is what I hoped for anyway, I needed closure. We had never been a close family, but she was my mother.

Where my family was concerned, I was a realist. We were far from perfect; although my brother tried his hardest to project to everyone that we were. David had taken over from our father as the Vicar at our local church, and those who regularly attended his services believed him to be an honest, well-rounded, twenty-six-year-old young man. I was the only one who saw his darker side, that part he kept hidden.

Don't get me wrong, I loved my brother, but I wasn't blind to his faults. He could be demanding and unreasonable, closed off, and even cruel at times. But only with me.

My extended family was also on the thin side, both sets of grandparents had died years ago but my aunt and cousins, on my mother's side, still sent cards on special occasions.

Recently, out of the blue, we'd received an invitation to the evening party of my cousin's forthcoming wedding. Definitely an olive branch type of situation, but I still didn't know if we would all go.

The lights were off in the living room which suggested David and my father had gone to bed. Sliding my key into the lock, I pushed the kitchen door open and stepped inside. It was eerily dark, apart from a shaft of light from the moon which bled in through one of the windows.

Totally on autopilot, I closed the door and searched for the light switch, dropping my bag by the radiator.

Awareness that I wasn't alone suddenly pooled into my stomach.

"Where have you been?" David's voice sliced into the room, quiet and calm and I turned toward the sound; his sudden presence was like a physical slap and my breath ballooned up in my chest.

"*David!* You *scared* me," I burst out agitatedly.

He didn't answer me immediately and I frowned. "Why are you sitting in the dark again?"

The standing lamp by the window clicked on and light flooded the room. I squinted, waiting for my eyes to become accustomed to the amber glow.

David was sitting in dad's reading chair under the lamp. Anyone else would have thought it strange, having their brother sitting in the dark, *waiting* for them, but this type of behaviour was becoming the norm for David. It appeared the element of surprise thrilled him; unsettling I know, but true nonetheless. That threatening migraine from earlier came back at the thought of having to deal with another 'tricky' situation.

Since I'd arrived back from Sheffield University a few weeks ago, if I was late back home, David would wait up. You could have seen this as the actions of a concerned relative, but I knew this was more about control.

Shooting him a brief glance, I bent to retrieve my bag and hooked it over one of the kitchen chairs which sat around the dining table. A table we *never* ate at, not all together anyway. That would be too much like a *real* family; we were far too dysfunctional for that.

As usual, the kitchen was a mess. Pots and pans were still on the side and cups were left strewn on the table. I used to love spending time in this particular room, it was small and cosy and was decorated with farmhouse-type units. Very traditional. It also used to be the warmest place in the house, but not anymore.

When David didn't answer, I purposefully filled the silence.

"I thought you'd both be in bed." I chuntered, positioning myself beside the head of the table. David remained in the chair with his face half-shadowed.

"How could I go to bed without knowing where you were?" The cold tone of his voice wrapped around me like rope and I suppressed a shiver.

Pursing my lips, I replied, "I got a flat tyre and had to wait for the recovery guy." I purposefully maintained my cool. It wasn't difficult to upset my brother, he was the opposite of unflappable. I withheld the fact that the recovery guy was in fact Noah Savvas from high school.

His face creased. "You should have texted me. I would have come for you. You shouldn't be riding in cars with strange men," David lectured. His face was a mask of relaxed indifference, but his hands were fisted on his lap. He was still dressed in the cream chinos and the navy jumper he had been wearing that morning. He didn't appear to have his phone and there was no book close by. He'd just been sitting there, *staring* into the darkness. Again, this type of conduct was not that unusual. David certainly had a strange side. I put it down to him being overly protective as my dad never noticed me. David had, in a fashion, taken it upon himself to play the role of parent.

At the end of the day, I was mom's spitting image and so my father spent most of his days avoiding me, whilst wallowing in his own self-pity.

David cared about me, he just did it in a weird way, but I knew my brother was just looking out for me. That's what I told myself anyway. What else could you do? I was back, this was my home and there was no escaping it. Not until I could afford a place of my own and let's face it; I needed a better paying job. Man does not live by bread alone and all that.

I pulled my coat further around my body and removed my hat, hooking it on the chair opposite my bag. As I said, the kitchen used to be the warmest room in our cottage. We had an AGA cooker that used to heat the room beautifully, but dad had stopped cooking months ago, David had said.

"Why is it so cold in here?" I questioned whilst clearing the dining table of dirty cups.

"We're saving money. You need to do the same too, in your room. Now you're back, we need to keep the bills down."

His comment made me feel like an inconvenience, but I nodded my head in agreement as I stacked the pots in the sink.

There was a three-beat silence before David said, "Mrs Haunch said she saw you out with Thomas Wade the other day."

And there it was. My brother's beef was usually boy related. He had a deep-rooted issue with relationships in general, I imagined this was due to my mother leaving. I didn't overanalyse his thought processes though; David Meadows was a mystery that would *never* be solved.

"Yes, we've been out a couple of times," I replied carelessly, drying my fingers on a tea towel.

"Is it wise to sleep with the boss's son? Couldn't that jeopardise your job?" His words were totally uncalled for. I'd seen Tom *twice*. David was blatantly spoiling for a fight.

"I'm not *sleeping* with him David, as I said, I've been on *two* dates. Mrs Haunch should mind her own business." If there was a Queen of the Nosy-Parkers, Mrs Haunch would be it.

"So, he's not who you were with tonight then?" David questioned with a lick of doubt.

"No, as I said. I've been sitting in my car for the past hour."

Our eyes locked in a silent battle. "I can easily find out if you're lying."

I exhaled sharply. "I'm not *lying* David." My breath whistled through my clenched teeth. "Look, it's late, I'm going to bed."

He stood, the shadowed side of his face now appearing in the pool of light from the lamp. "Aren't you going to kiss me goodnight?"

I rolled my eyes, throwing the towel on the table, my heart thumping in my chest.

As I approached, David stood waiting with a strange expression. Guarded almost. His hands were by his sides and they were still fisted. He was obviously upset, but surely it hadn't anything to do with the fact that I'd seen Tom? As I said, my brother was hard to read.

He twisted his head, offering his cheek and I raised up on my tip toes and popped a brief kiss there. I was slightly taken aback that he'd steered me toward his face, but I acted on impulse. I usually kissed the back of his hand, like the other churchgoers. As a sign of respect.

It felt slightly odd, but it didn't make me *overly* uncomfortable, it wasn't like I was kissing his mouth or anything.

I pulled back and he looked down at me, his expression was cryptic, his eyes roaming my face like he was looking for something.

"Goodnight David," I said, drawing my gaze away, a churning feeling in my belly.

"Goodnight sister," he replied in a flat voice.

I grabbed my bag and hat off the back of the chair, and left the kitchen, mounting the stairs to my room, taking them two at a time. I briefly checked my phone; I had a text message from SATAN. Great, now he could torment me from anywhere on the fricking planet!

Goodnight Red, sleep well x

I deleted it without responding.

My thoughts flashed back to David. That strange panicky feeling starting to snake along my spine.

Not wanting to sound like a broken record, but I hated conflict of any kind. When I got to my room, I pushed the old peeling door closed and turned the key in the lock.

Something I did *every* night since I had been back, and something I would *always* do whilst living in that house.

* * *

I had been working at Wade and Son, a local veterinary practice for a few weeks now. The owner's daughter Ella Wade (also Tom's sister) had shown me the ropes and I was almost up to speed. Tom was currently working as a trainee vet at the practice. He was nice and sweet, but I still wasn't sure about him, having only been out a couple of times.

When I got to work the next day, it was quite frantic and I hardly saw Tom, which was a relief. He'd taken to buzzing around reception on a regular basis and had started to become a bit of a nuisance. He didn't need to really as I'd already agreed to see him again.

I had decided to take it slow and give him a chance, he was a nice boy and treated me with kindness. I didn't feel that spark that everyone talked about, but I'd never had a boyfriend and so how would I recognise it? I suppose when it happened, I'd just know.

An emergency was brought into the surgery after lunch, a dog that looked like it had been attacked. It had puncture marks around its neck and was bleeding heavily. It had been found by a dog walker in a hedge in my village of Sinnington. Marcus, the lead vet was in between clients and so I rushed it through.

After what had turned into a heavy day on my feet, I started regretting the plans I had made with Tom for that night. I really wanted to go home and sit in the bath, but I wasn't the type of person to let someone down. I also had to collect my car from Noah's. Another job that I could have done without.

Marcus thanked me for my hard work and I left for the bus stop. I knew exactly where Cudworth Lane was and luckily the number seventy-nine went straight past it. I imagined Noah had bought Mr Robinson's old garage which was where my dad used to take his car for its MOT years ago.

After a short wait, the bus arrived and after around twenty minutes, I pressed the bell for my stop. I could see a smattering of shops that were still in business but appeared to be closed, and I exited the bus, pulling my coat further around my body. I'd changed at the surgery so I didn't have to go out in my work uniform.

I'd chosen a pretty navy dress, with dark tights and brown boots. I hadn't wanted to be too dressed up as Tom had said he was taking me for supper to a local pub. I had brushed my hair and left it loose and it fell across my shoulders in soft waves. I'd also added some lipstick which wasn't unusual for me. I did wear makeup, just not much. I preferred subtle.

The garage unit was quite large with a forecourt section where several cars were parked. Mine sat there too in all its shabby glory. From where I was standing it looked like the tyre had been changed.

I eyed the signage thoughtfully, Victoria Garage. The door was closed but the large shutters next to it were open. It was a wide area, big enough to allow cars through. I slid under the metal and entered the unit.

I concentrated on putting one foot in front of the other. I was nervous as the place looked like it had been abandoned. Noah *had* to be there though as he hadn't locked up.

"Noah?" I shouted into the dimly lit area. I could hear a faint whirring noise and one of the strip lights that was suspended from the ceiling was buzzing. My heart thudded, almost painfully in my chest. The beat reminded me of the theme tune from Jaws.

I was surrounded by a variety of cars that appeared to be in the process of being worked on, or had been during office hours; most of the bonnets were still propped up and there was one raised high above me on a ramp. Workbenches and cluttered tool racks were everywhere and there were several items of machinery, I wondered fleetingly what they did. As I scanned the area, I saw stairs leading to another mezzanine type level.

Making my way in between the vehicles, I noticed a section at the back where some tyres were stacked. It was cluttered, but *organised* chaos I would say. The smell of oil and rusting metal lingered in the air.

“About bloody time,” Noah shouted from behind me and I turned to see him leaning in the doorway to a room, possibly an office. He had one strong hand placed on the doorframe above his head. Dark and devastating; his arm muscles were mouth-watering.

“I said it would be after five,” I pointed out flatly.

His gaze was steady on my face and he lowered his arm, pulling out an oily rag from his pocket and wiping his hands without breaking eye contact. He was again dressed in those pulled-down overalls. His tee was tight against his muscled body, like a second skin. The guy had one of those bodies that could sell postcards.

After cleaning his hands, he took off the baseball cap he’d been wearing, threw it behind him, and ran a hand through his messy, black hair. As he turned back to face me, his eyes appraised my appearance; starting at my head and then travelling down the entire length of my body. If anyone else had looked at me like that, it would have been considered rude. But of course, Noah got away with it somehow, probably because I let him.

He looked hot and sweaty and had a dirty streak across one cheek. It made him look even more sinfully attractive. Dirty, in more ways than one.

I shook off the thought and yanked my bag further onto my shoulder. The impact this wretched guy had on me was annoying to say the least.

Noah pushed off the doorframe and started to pace toward me like a jungle predator; his steps were determined. I withdrew my purse.

"How much is it please?" I questioned, pulling out my debit card. I got straight down to business. I didn't want to encourage any more unnecessary conversations. My head was still spinning from last night's discussion.

He came to stand before me and looked down at my hand before shaking his head. Again, he stood *way* too close. "Sorry, I should have said. The card machine is down and so I can only take cash. It's sixty-five."

Drat, I didn't have any money on me. My face dropped and his eyes narrowed.

"Tell you what, you can have it on the house, for old times' sake."

"For old times' sake?" I volleyed back with raised eyebrows.

"Yes, for me being a dick to you at school."

I pursed my lips thoughtfully. Yeah, like one fricking tyre would make up for the years of torture he'd put me through!

Telling myself to stop overreacting, I questioned him. "So, you admit you were horrible to me at school then?" I knew I shouldn't push it but couldn't help myself. If the guy was admitting he was aware he'd bullied me, maybe there was hope for him yet. And then again, maybe not. Everyone knows a leopard never changes its spots.

"Absolutely. But you did ask for it," he drawled, a devilish glint in his eyes. He was trying to draw me into an argument. Same old, same old.

Ignoring him, I changed the subject. "I could post you the money," I suggested, looking up at him from beneath my lashes.

He slowly nodded his head from side to side as he pinned those dark, deep eyes on mine. "No, it's fine. It's on me."

I felt like releasing the groan I was holding back. I so didn't want to be indebted to this man in any way, shape, or form. He was the type of person who would probably call it in, one day. And his request would no doubt be unreasonable, like a blow job or something else as hideous.

"OK, well; thank you, Noah." It still felt like I had just made a deal with the devil.

He handed me my keys and I pushed them into the pocket of my coat and dropped my purse into my bag.

"She's out front," he explained with a flick of his head.

I nodded my thanks, and made to walk around him, but he blocked my path. His huge body was like a potent threat. My chest tightened. Now what?

"You know there are other ways you could thank me," he said suggestively in a teasing tone. I could feel his breath on my face, it was warm, with a hint of mint and aromatic coffee. Here comes the unreasonable request!

I shot him a withering look. "I'm not going to sleep with you for a tyre Noah." Deep down I knew he was joking.

"Your loss," he fired back with a cheeky wink.

"Anyway, I have to go. I have a date remember," I replied.

Realisation spread across his features and his eyes flickered over my body where my coat had fallen open.

"Of course, the date. Nice outfit," he drawled, rudely looking me up and down again; his snarky tone betraying the fact that he thought the opposite. I tried to settle the nerves that were now rioting like a gang of thugs inside me.

Taking a deep breath, I scrunched up my nose and swished back my hair, my neck actually hurt from attempting to retain eye contact; he loomed when he was close.

"I would say thank you, but I imagine you're being sarcastic." No matter how cross or unstuck he made me feel, I was determined not to show it.

He quirked his head to the side, regarding me thoughtfully. "There's nothing *majorly* wrong with it. It just isn't the type of thing I'd expect a girl to wear on a date. Tom Wade, wasn't it?" His gaze ran over me tauntingly.

I managed to hold off tutting and briefly glanced down at my dress. "Yes, and why not?" My question was out there before I could stop it. Why on earth was I giving this guy the rope he needed to hang me with? Or tie me up. Where the heck had *that* thought popped from? I appeared to be turning into a pervert.

Noah's hand rose to his face and he slowly ran his thumb across his bottom lip. He seemed to do that a lot, it was sexually provocative. I was inexperienced but I wasn't stupid. It had the desired effect and my tummy flipped.

"Unless you're wearing it with a strategy in mind," Noah added, his face full of contemplation.

The lines of question on my forehead must have stood out a mile. I so didn't know where he was going with his comments, but I knew it wouldn't be nice.

Biting back a caustic reply I glared up at him. "Strategy?"

His lip curled. "To stop your date from trying to cop a feel of course."

My fake smile was digging grooves into my cheeks now and I blew out a nervous breath, not really knowing how to deflect that one. "And how would this outfit stop him from doing that?" Not that I could ever imagine someone like Tom 'copping' anything.

Noah snorted as he dropped his hand, stating with insulting ease.

"No guy wants to touch a girl that dresses like his mother."

I exhaled sharply. "Indeed. Well, thank you for that tip on fashion Noah."

His voice dipped and he tilted his head slightly. "Or a buttoned-up virgin. Take your pick."

I stifled the urge to slap his face. His grim determination to unsettle me should have been applauded really.

"Are you this mean to everyone or is it just me?" I questioned, my palms starting to itch again.

He raised one winged brow, staring down his perfect nose at me.

"Don't let your halo get too bent out of shape. I'm not being mean, I'm being honest. I couldn't be overly harsh to you Red. It would be too much like kicking a kitten." His words were totally at war with his actions. This guy so got off on being nasty to me.

I rolled his reply around my head. "Your, not-so-subtle point being that I'm weak?"

His dark eyes danced. "*You* said it. You haven't toughened up at all since school. And to think of all that hard work I did, trying to get you to stand up for yourself."

I choked out a laugh.

"So, you were trying to *help* me by *bullying* me? I must say I'm not sure I agree with your methods."

Pushing an unsteady hand through my hair, I cleared my throat, adding. "We can't all look like a walking talking steroid Noah," I muttered, my eyes fluttering over his powerful, sun-darkened physique. The guy was built like a mountain; all muscle and not a hint of fat in sight.

His lips twisted. "Strength comes in more forms than just the physical sense, you know that,"

"So, I'm weak-minded too?" My hands were now fisted by my sides. Why on earth was I still standing there having a conversation with him? It was like my feet had grown roots. Although he *was* blocking my path, I'd have to physically move him out of the way to get by, and the chances of doing that were of course, zero.

"In a fashion, no pun intended," he chuckled, motioning toward my dress again.

A determined look hardened his eyes before he carried on with his attack. "Not necessarily weak-minded, you were intelligent enough. You just never stood up for yourself. You were a proper coward and blanked anyone you saw as a threat to your quiet, painfully dull existence. I remember you with your nose in the air, lording your virginity over half of the rugby team, like a *proper* tease. No one was good enough for you were they princess?"

I was totally unprepared for the offensive attack and my pulse twitched with annoyance. I would *not* cry in front of this guy and I swallowed down the looming lump in my throat. I needed to shut this down. He had the sensitivity of a butcher when it came to my feelings.

I crossed my arms, trying to shield myself from the pull of the past. "I see. Well, thanks for that detailed evaluation of my character, and whilst I always thoroughly enjoy our little chats Noah, I need to go, Tom will be waiting. Excuse me please."

His eyes flared briefly as I mentioned Tom's name, but he remained *exactly* where he was, still blocking my escape route.

"So polite Red. And there it is, right there. Running away, like a skittish little girl. Stand up to me, tell me to fuck off. Did you not hear all the things I just said to you?"

I huffed. "Your opinion is your opinion Noah and I don't care, so please step aside. I don't have time for this unpleasant walk down memory lane." My tone was sharper but of course, it still lacked confidence and strength. Two things I had *never* felt in this boy's company.

His reply was firm, no-nonsense. "I did you a favour with your tyre, the least you could do is stay and talk to me for a minute."

My automatic reaction to his refusal to move out of my way was odd. My skin fizzed, it was as if my body craved the physical nearness that my head was attempting to avoid.

I took a deep breath before pinning him with my best-unimpressed glower; which was probably still fairly pitiful. So, what, I didn't like attention or confrontational situations, so sue me.

At high school, especially when I'd started to physically develop at fourteen, I'd drawn all sorts of unwanted interest, especially from the boys. Some of those being Noah's rugby friends, unfortunately. I had *hated* it and so had ignored them and attempted to blend in, to become more of a wallflower type. I'd failed of course. But I hadn't given them the time of day, and that was when the bullying started. Macho boys did not like to be ignored, especially the big guy who was standing before me.

Their egos had all been huge and none of them had expected rejection from the unpopular, prim little church mouse. So they'd punished me I suppose.

I huffed out a breath, replaying his last words before I said, "Five minutes then, but I don't want to talk about school?"

If I'd had any illusions that there was a nice guy in there somewhere he smashed them away with his next revelation.

Noah rubbed a hand across the roughness of his jaw.

"Why not? Having all those boys panting after you must have made you feel good. You pranced around school like you were above us all. Charles used to have a major crush on you. Did you know that? Matty did too." His lips twisted into something that no sane person could ever call a smile.

"Yes, I knew," I replied with a sigh, feeling tired from digging up the past. Noah's best friend Charles had asked me out several times but I'd steered clear. His interest in me had only made Noah much meaner. Noah had said he was horrible to me to toughen me up, but I knew he'd treated me badly after I'd offended him and his friends. They had been such a tight-knit group.

He raised both his eyebrows and shot me a questioning stare, flicking a hand at me.

"And you were *never* tempted?"

His comment was rich, considering.

"You made it perfectly clear that I wasn't to go anywhere near any of your friends so no, of course not." My reply sounded wooden even to my own ears.

Noah's methods to antagonise me were outrageous but what could I do? I couldn't exactly shove him out of the way, I'd probably crack a finger bone or something.

"You were untouchable," he stated.

"It wasn't like that at all, I just wanted to be left alone. I didn't appreciate being pawed at."

My eyes shot helplessly around him toward the doorway and as I went to move again, Noah stepped sideways, purposefully blocking my retreat again with his *huge* body. I almost walked into him. He wasn't overly threatening, but his behaviour was still appalling under the circumstances. I couldn't believe that he was actually keeping me there against my will.

"What about Matty? Surely you fancied him?" Noah said, mentioning the captain of the rugby team by name again. A boy whom almost every girl at school had panted after. Apart from me of course.

"Well?"

His sharp prompt wiped away my recollection and I delivered what I hoped was one of my best haughty looks. "Not particularly."

An idea suddenly occurred to me. "Have you been drinking or something because your behaviour would suggest so?" I challenged. See, there was a bit of fight in me, even if it was just a smidge.

Noah laughed; it was a guttural sound. He then folded those large arms over his chest, causing his biceps to bulge even more. The guy had strength in spades.

"I'm stone-cold sober baby. We're only talking about the past, surely that's what old friends do. Catch up," Noah muttered thickly, the light glinting off his ebony hair.

"We're not old friends Noah, you treated me appallingly. If anything, I'd say we were enemies. At school anyway."

"It wasn't like that. I was just trying to toughen you up. Surely if you pull the kitten's tail too many times, she eventually bites or scratches. Aren't redheads supposed to have a temper?"

I released a ragged sigh of frustration, "You're going to make me late Noah. Please move before I say something I'll regret," I bit out, refraining from stamping my foot like a frustrated kid.

He took a deep breath before saying, "Oh, I so wish you would. Go on, give me your *best* shot."

"You're insane. Your behaviour is mental Noah. You shouldn't be speaking to me in this way. Maybe I should give you the number of my cousin, she's a therapist." My cousin Katy, the one who was due to be married, worked with mental health patients. Noah's middle name was probably nut-job.

"I want you to move out of the way. Your behaviour is unacceptable."

He uncurled those arms before motioning toward where I stood with a flick of his wrists. "So do something about it. Tell me where to go, fight back."

All six foot four inches of muscle and forceful will towered above me. His mood was now dangerous, he was probably pissed off about the therapist comment, but I wasn't afraid. If anything, my heart pumped faster and my blood was singing. I blinked. "Are you mad, I'm *half* your size?"

His eyes soften although only slightly. "I don't mean *physically* I mean with words. Get mad; get even."

Something burned inside my chest, an emotion that I didn't recognise. I so wasn't in the mood to play these types of games with him but I couldn't move, it was like I was paralysed.

Glaring up at him I said, "I could slap your face again, how about that?" Yeah right, I totally didn't fancy my chances of survival if I did that. I recalled what had happened the last time I'd done that. My thoughts switched back to that day when Noah kissed me. That earth-shattering kiss at school and the cat calls and whistles of encouragement from his friends at the time. I still hated the fact that I had enjoyed it so much. But I knew with every part of my being that it had been wrong. That hadn't stopped me from wanting him though. Hence the distance I put between us. My body's hunger for Noah was a weakness I would *never* feed.

"Well?" I huffed.

He chuckled, his voice deep and throaty. "You could try brat," he said with taunt emphasis.

Noah angled his strong jaw toward me, provocatively *daring* me to hit him. Turning my head away, I relaxed my stance. "No thank you. I've lost the element of surprise now," I really did sound like a sulky child.

The atmosphere crackled between us and I turned my face back toward him. Invisible daggers must have been shooting from my eyes.

His cocky expression made me want to claw at his face with my fingernails. Again, I was experiencing out-of-character thoughts; something that occurred often when in this boy's presence. He pushed buttons that I didn't even know existed.

His mouth was now curved into a wide smile. Unashamedly highly amused by my response. "But surely lashing out would make you feel so much better. Don't you *ever* want to smash stuff?"

"No, I don't. That's not who I am."

"Whatever, you've been brainwashed by the bullshit of your religion."

"It's got nothing to do with the church, I don't generally hit people Noah. Well, apart from when they deserve it," I responded, having of course hit Noah at school. But we were teenagers then. Surely now we were adults, it should have been different between us.

He pursed his lips as he took in my response before saying. "That's probably for the best."

He suddenly appeared much larger as he straightened and took a step toward me. I managed to stand my ground although he was so close. I could smell his heady scent; Noah was all male.

"As you are more than aware, there'd be consequences to your actions." The way he said the words suggested more than a kiss as retaliation.

My brow scrunched in alarm.

"What, you'd hit me back or something," I panted disbelievingly. His threat shouldn't really worry me as Noah would never lay a hand on me in anger. He wasn't that type of guy.

His reply was charged with sexual energy and I didn't care for that one bit.

"You look like a terrified field mouse. No of course I wouldn't hit you, but I'd definitely put my hands on you," he flared provocatively, something undefinable in his eyes.

I managed to stifle my gasp.

"You really are a brute, aren't you? If you don't move, I'll scream, how about that?" My voice must have jumped up a whole octave. Why I was giving the guy warnings as to my possible means of escape was *beyond* me. My anger was now mixed with incredulity.

"I doubt anyone would hear you out here. Apart from me of course and then I'd be forced to shut you up."

My eyes widened, probably like a heroine in a horror movie seconds before she was attacked. My legs wobbled.

"You look like you're about to faint, Red, but you can relax. I'm not a serial killer or an abuser of women. Even ones as provoking as you. My method of shutting you up would bring you pleasure, *not* pain. I don't hit girls." he replied slowly, drawing my attention to his mouth.

Although I attempted to stop it, lust pumped hot and strong into my body.

"Noah. Please." I now did sound pathetic which is *exactly* what he had accused me of being.

He lowered his head. "*Beg* me and I'll think about it," he whispered silkily against my ear, his lips so close. Noah had the resolve of a Rottweiler and could probably be just as fierce.

I eyed him moodily through my lashes. I could see from his expression that he was thoroughly enjoying lording his control over me. He must have had a boring life if he had to do this to get his hoo-hars.

"You're still a pig and I think I hate you," I replied in a quiet voice, almost to myself. I felt like I was wasting air attempting to make him see sense. He just wasn't listening.

A muscle ticked in his jaw.

"No, you don't, you don't hate anyone. You're too pure and God-fearing. That's part of the problem. You believe all that shit your father and brother spout. They have complete control and you're terrified of being true to yourself, scared of stepping out of line."

I raised my hands in a gesture of surrender. "I've had enough. Stop toying with me and let me go." The guy was a monster in disguise and I was his personal punching bag, but that was the way it had *always* been.

Noah lifted his hand and pushed a lock of hair behind my ear and I jumped slightly as his roughened finger touched the soft skin of my face. They were hands that belonged to someone who did manual labour; callused and rough. Would they feel that way against my body? I swallowed the slutty thought. My soul was heading for the gutter it appeared.

He drew back and directed his hooded gaze onto my flushed face.

"There's a fighter in you somewhere Red, I know it. You just need to find her and let her out. You act like a robot, but you're a flesh and blood female, not a fucking doormat. You need to learn how to stand up for yourself and be the real you. Not this starchy nobody." Noah paused momentarily, watching me intently for my reaction to his words. "Maybe I'm the guy to make you realise that by toughening you up. Dragging you out of that shell you've trapped yourself in."

Copying his earlier movement, I crossed my arms across my breasts, suddenly feeling exposed.

"I don't generally find myself in a position where I have to. Apart from when I'm with you. I dislike conflict of any kind thank you very much."

Noah took a step back and perched his backside against the bonnet-less car behind him. "But conflict is a part of life Red, unavoidable. *Everyone* has to deal with tricky situations from time to time. It's important that you know how to manage them. Take your brother for instance." Noah's strong face hardened. He was so agonisingly male.

Nervous knots started to twist in my stomach. "What about him?" I replied tightly, again not sure where he was going with his new line of attack.

Noah's expression darkened as he watched me. "After your mother left, he walked all over you. I remember the way he used to treat you; like you were his little pet. I imagine nothing has changed. It's fucking twisted Lucy and it used to wind me the fuck up. It always has done. Your dad was no better. Grow a backbone and stop allowing them to mould you into something you're not."

Shock reverberated through me. "I don't know what you think gives you the right to psycho analyse me or my family, Noah. You don't *know* me, I haven't seen you in years."

"Our history together gives me that right."

I rolled my eyes, "Our history together is like a bad, twisted version of a Greek tragedy Noah. And I would prefer it if you wouldn't bring my family into this personal nightmare of yours. I don't need *fixing* thank you. I didn't then and I don't now."

His constant jabs were starting to get to me. Especially when he referenced my brother's treatment of me.

"You were just such a lost cause, and I like to fix things. That's why I do what I do. I'm trying to help you Red, even now after all these years."

"By being horrible to me and making me late for my date with Tom?" I questioned, totally confused about how those actions were teaching me anything apart from how much I really disliked him. Maybe he wanted me to hate him?

"In order to help you, I first have to establish what makes you tick. I'm a mechanic, first in the army and now for myself. I have to work out what the problem is before I mend it."

His macho power play was draining. So he saw me as some type of jigsaw he needed to put together.

"I see, so you've decided to label yourself as my saviour in some way and first you need to get into my head?"

He dipped his dark head and whispered. "I can safely say, I *definitely* want to be inside you, Lucy." The look he gave me was primitive and raw. He said my name like he was saying a sex word. It made the situation feel much more serious and intense.

I attempted to avoid the staggering heat of his gaze. A strange feeling pooled in me but I ignored it. Annoyed that my body had decided to respond to his smutty comment again!

If there had been something within reach, I would have thrown it at him. I knew his suggestive words were purely for show. To get a rise out of me, to see me lose control. It appeared Noah's mission to knock me off balance was still the same as it had been at school.

My memory burned with bitterness. I couldn't believe that he dared to state that he bullied me with my best interests at heart. What a load of bull poop.

I almost said a rude word but managed to stem it, going with, "Still as crude as ever. You really are a horrible man, Noah." My breath rattled in my throat.

He shot me a lopsided smile, his lean features taunt with satisfaction. "You have no idea," he asserted roughly before he moistened his mouth with his tongue. Unwanted sexual awareness curled within the pit of my stomach again. My body had once again betrayed me.

There was a beat of silence. My cheeks flushed hotly as I tried to process what was happening.

I couldn't tear myself away, it was like Noah was attempting to give me a glimpse into another world, *his* world. A place that was full of mystery and hidden promises; *risks*. But did I really want to be part of it, leave the safety of what I knew and throw myself into the unknown? Absolutely not!

"So, enjoy yourself with Tom. Try and let your hair down, you might even enjoy yourself for once."

"I'm looking forward to it actually," I replied in a 'so there' tone.

"*Whatever*. Do you know what 'seize the day' even means? I bet you haven't even kissed him yet."

I rolled my eyes and pushed past him.

"I would say behave yourself, but I know you will."

Those parting words resonated as I left the building on legs that felt like they were tied on with elastic.

As I climbed into my car, the truth rotated like a windmill. The man had the power to turn me into an emotional wreck. He also stirred up other unwanted feelings, but I was determined to beat those away.

Noah Savvas was not and never would be my boyfriend and so *those* types of thoughts needed to be buried deep. I shook off the ludicrous thought of Noah and me together.

I would *not* allow my body to dictate my behaviour or control my life.

No way.

Three

My date with Tom went well, but I felt self-conscious. At the end of the day, he was my superior at the surgery. Yes, he was still in training but as far as pecking orders went, he was well above me. I was at seed level being a receptionist.

From the outset, I'd had the intention of giving it a chance, but I just wasn't feeling it. Something was off. My brother's words about sleeping with the boss's son also kept tunnelling into my head, tainting the experience.

We'd met at a pub called The Crown, it was in the next village from mine and I'd parked my Mini next to Tom's Volvo. I'd driven past the place but had never been in, I wasn't really a pub person, even when I was at Uni. I remember I'd buried my head in a book during fresher week when everyone else was partying and getting obscenely drunk. A 'bonding exercise' Melanie, one of my house-mates had said. No, thank you.

During our meal together, we spoke about a variety of subjects, family being one of them. I didn't go into too much detail as my home life was slightly embarrassing, but I did tell him that my mother left us. He was one hundred percent the gentleman and hung on my every word, watching me keenly over the table. Tom only glanced away briefly as he focused on cutting into his huge steak.

Tom still lived at home with his parents and his sister Ella, with whom he had one of those typical types of brother/sister relationships. They were close, but they wound each other up. I felt slightly envious, considering the train wreck that was my relationship with David.

Tom's mum didn't work and sounded pleasant enough. He said she was the busybody of their village and if there was any gossip worth knowing; his mother was the font of all knowledge. I already knew that Tom's dad owned the practice.

At the end of the evening, as he walked me to my car, I toyed with the idea of letting him down gently. I wasn't really sure I wanted to date anyone as I was still getting used to living at home again. My intention of giving the guy a chance at the beginning of the evening slowly decayed with each mouthful of food. And my lasagne had been cold in the middle, adding further insult to injury. I'd spent part of the meal eyeing up Tom's plate; how I wished I'd chosen the steak.

To be perfectly honest, my cousin's wedding was playing on my mind. If I stuck with Tom for a while, maybe he could be my plus one. I doubted my dad and David would go and I totally didn't relish attending a party on my own. I knew this could have been considered as me using Tom, but I batted any guilt about that to one side.

At the end of the day, boys complicated things and there was allsorts to consider now I was back home again. I dreamed of finding myself a flat to rent but I was stuck for now until I made more money.

"So, you fancy coming to a party at the weekend?" Tom suddenly announced as we stood beside my car. It wasn't late, but it was dark and thankfully the area was well-lit by flood lights. I didn't like the dark.

There was a definite smell of the country in the air. It teased my nostrils. My senses had obviously forgotten that smell after being away for so long. I was more used to diesel fumes and the essence of the city now.

Tom looked so desperate, I felt like I couldn't say no. My thoughts darted back to what Noah had said and his 'seize the day' comment. His words and behaviour from earlier still niggled. He'd made me feel like the dullest person on the planet. Wretched man.

I hated to admit it, but maybe Noah was right and I should go. Step out of my comfort zone.

I refocused on Tom. I didn't have any plans for the weekend and so it couldn't hurt. Plus, I was only twenty-one, yes, I was a bit of a square but shouldn't I try and let my hair down like Noah had said? The sly remarks he'd made, had really started to get me thinking. I felt like I now had something to prove all of a sudden and not necessarily to Noah; but to myself.

"Where is the party?"

A whoosh of pleasure highlighted Tom's face; easy on boy, I hadn't said yes yet.

"It's at Nathan and Ryan Lane's house. It's a pool party, as in swimming pool, not snooker pool," Tom confessed, running a hand through his mop of locks.

My face dropped as he gave me the names of whose party it was. Everyone knew those boys were trouble. Silly, privileged rich boys. I'd heard that Nathan Lane had once crashed his car whilst drunk driving and had gotten away with it. They were one of those families that had friends in high places.

"A swimming pool party? In *this* weather." I couldn't keep the horrified element out of my tone. Tom grinned at my response.

"It's indoor and it's heated. I take it you've heard of the Lane's?"

"Who hasn't? I'm not sure I should be associated with them either. If David found out he'd be cross."

"David?"

"My brother, he kind of runs the family."

"But you've been away at University, and you're twenty-one, surely independent of all that overprotective brother nonsense. Ella doesn't listen to a word I say."

The fact that I was being preached to by someone as straight-laced as Tom, ruffled me. Like I was the boring one. I suddenly felt as dull as tombs. This thought did not sit well with me, Noah's comments swam in there again and this forced my decision.

"Yes, I'll come. Why not."

I was surprised Tom didn't jump up and down on the spot and clap his hands he was that delighted.

"OK. Cool. I'll pick you up. You can have a drink then."

I wasn't a drinker, but I had to be more interesting than Tom, surely? I batted the mean thought away. He was a nice boy, and surely the Christian in me *wanted* nice? Noah's face bounced back in there. What the heck, he was the polar opposite of nice. I felt annoyed that I'd let his words resonate with me for most of my night.

I pecked Tom on the cheek before he could lean in and kiss me. I wasn't the type to kiss on the mouth on a third date, nope. For me, that was more of a fifth or sixth-date thing. If at all, to be honest. I'd usually lost interest by then. Either that or my brother ensured I did. Whenever I had come home for the holidays, he'd meddle where he could.

As Tom set off for his car, I released the lock on my Mini, briefly checking my phone. I had a message from David asking me to get some milk. I also had another text from guess who; SATAN.

How was the date?

Scrunching up my nose I thumbed in. **None of your business. Go away.**

Did he get to first base? My guess is not.

Deciding against replying again, I pocketed my phone, batting off that urge to google 'first base'. I'd heard of it, but didn't know what it entailed. His text made me want to stomp my foot in annoyance. Noah Savvas probably had the ability to irritate me to death.

Climbing into my car, I hated the fact that Noah was right. I *was* a prude. Drat, the man, he now appeared to be glued into my thoughts, his image swirling around my head like a repetitive church chorus. I'd hardly thought about him when I was away, but I suppose out of sight out of mind and all that.

I started my car and jammed it into gear feeling annoyed. Why had what Noah had said stayed with me? He had no real power over me surely; did he?

* * *

The rest of the week went by without too many dramas at work. Another injured dog came in and was assessed by Tom. From the size of the wounds to its neck, it was diagnosed that the animal was also attacked by another dog. Unfortunately, the creature was in such a bad state, that it had to be put to sleep.

From the whispers at the surgery, foul play was suspected. Something was going on with these dogs and there had been suggestions of dog fighting for profit. The thought chilled my blood.

Marcus, being the most senior vet had told me to call the non-emergency police number and log an inquiry. The woman on the phone was cold and unhelpful and didn't seem to care. She tried to push me in the direction of the RSPCA. She didn't even give me a case reference number.

Finally, it was the weekend. Tom had been going on about the party for most of the week at work. He'd also tried to fit in another cheeky date beforehand but I'd already had my excuse in place.

The pool party at Nathan and Ryan Lane's house was an afternoon event. Tom said their parents had banned them from any more parties in the evening, due to Nathan trashing their house in the past. I preferred it, to be honest, I could then avoid David clock-watching until I came home.

I put my swimming costume on under my clothes, not wanting to end up in one of those situations where I had to change in front of strangers. The showers at school still haunted me. I wasn't overly conscious of my body, yes, I was petite and a bit on the thin side but I knew I had a nice enough shape. I just hated people staring and I didn't like to show myself off. I wasn't allowed to be vain; vanity being one of seven deadly sins and all that.

Tom parked the car and unclipped his seatbelt before twisting toward me. "You look nervous," he said, his forehead crinkled. I undid my own seatbelt and curled my hands around my sports bag like it was some type of weapon. I'd packed fresh underwear, a towel, and a jumper in case it was cold. Tom had said that the pool was heated but what about the rest of the building; I wasn't taking any chances. I hated the cold. Plus, if I felt uncomfortable in my swimsuit, I could put my jumper on over the top. I'd pulled my hair into a ponytail and wore no makeup. I probably looked like a fifteen-year-old. What can I say, I had a youthful appearance.

My eyes rounded, "I'm fine. I am a bit nervous. This is probably the first party I've ever been to," I confessed, shooting Tom a whimsical look.

Tom squared his shoulders and asked, "Didn't you go to any parties at Uni?"

"No, not really. I was too busy studying. I bet you think me boring."

His face scrunched up. "Not at all. I don't think you're boring. I prefer books to people myself. You don't need to be nervous. We'll stick together."

His kind words reassured me. Tom was definitely one of the nice guys, unlike some. I pushed thoughts of that particular person to the back of my mind. Although the thought of the possibility of him being there lingered. I imagined Noah would know the Lane boys well, they all moved in that same pretentious circle.

A thought suddenly occurred to me. I remembered Noah said that he knew of Tom, but did Tom know Noah? I shook off the thought. It didn't really matter if they were the best of buds, I knew that anything romantic with Tom was probably short-lived.

I thanked Tom for his 'sticking' together comment. He'd put me more at ease.

We both climbed out of the car and then it hit me just how rich the Lane family was. Their estate was *huge*. Tom and I had been talking when he'd pulled in through the gates and so I hadn't been looking out of the window. My eyes roamed appreciatively around the yard. There were several outbuildings surrounding a large stone-built mansion. Units with shutters were on one side of the house and a set of three garages at the other with a selection of expensive-looking cars parked outside. There was also an annex built onto the side of the mansion that almost looked like another house. The curtains were closed and there was a black, shiny sports car parked outside it with one of those private plates. Reading the lettering, it had to belong to Ryan Lane; so he *was* also a poser, that didn't surprise me after everything I'd heard.

It appeared the family was *extremely* wealthy; you could have fit our entire cottage into the main house several times over. When Tom had told me about the party, I had assumed the swimming pool would be in one of those outhouses, like a purpose-built greenhouse made of glass or plastic. Something that had been erected over the pool as an afterthought in case it rained, which of course it did all the time in Yorkshire. My expectations in respect of the afternoon tripled.

Tom directed us down the side of the house and through some wrought iron gates which had been left open. The padlock still had the key in it. I briefly glanced into the house through the windows, wondering what it would look like inside but you couldn't see much really. Now I knew what 'how the other half lived' meant. The Lane family were certainly not on my half, that's for sure.

The pool was located at the back, an extension from the main house which must only have been built a few years ago. The stonework had been matched up but it was newer, less weathered. There was not a crappy greenhouse in sight. Windows ran all the way around it so you could see straight through, but the glass was misted in areas; condensation from the pool I imagined. I could see clusters of people in there, lots of half-naked bodies, some in the pool, others sitting on the side or on the sun loungers which were dotted around the deck. There was a huge splash as one guy bombed into the water. I could hear the dull thud of music, laughter, shouting, and general conversation. Anxiety bubbled in my chest. I told myself I could do this.

As we entered the building through some glassed doors, there was a large hallway, I could see through an archway into the section where the pool was. There must have been over thirty people there and the atmosphere seemed friendly enough. Everyone was just having fun and I felt myself relax slightly. Under one of the arches was a well-stocked bar. A couple of people were getting drinks and one girl was sat on a bar stool, her shocking pink bikini rather risqué. I thought about my boring yellow swimsuit, it wasn't even a high-legged one. I'd look like a total square compared to her. I was glad I hadn't brought my swim cap.

In the hallway, there was a corridor and Tom showed me where to change in one of the many rooms, I wondered fleetingly where they all led.

The place Tom took me so I could get ready was cluttered and small. It was probably a storage area as there were loads of boxes and other people's bags and coats. The door had a lock and I twisted it.

I took my clothes off revealing my swimsuit underneath and found a spare corner to shove my stuff. Pulling my towel out of my bag, I then went to find Tom. Considering it was cold outside, the pool room was really well-heated and I didn't feel chilly at all.

Most of the girls were wearing bikinis and all looked quite normal, with no fake boobs or strange lips; just average people with varying body shapes. It was a relief as I had part-envisaged loads of pretty people like on that old show Baywatch.

Tom was waiting for me by the bar where there were now several people all engaged in different conversations. He wore bright red swimming shorts, his skin almost whiter than mine and he was tall and skinny. Next to the toned body of the guy on the other side of the bar, his beanpole-ness stood out even more. He smiled, those cute dimples appearing at the side of his mouth as I approached. He then introduced me to the host, Nathan Lane, who was actually the man standing at the other side of the counter.

He was tall, muscular, and *astoundingly* good-looking. He had a scar running through one eyebrow, making him appear dangerous. His grin was cocky as we approached.

"Fuck me, Thomas Wade, in the flesh." The guy's eyes flickered over Tom's white, thin body with an amused expression. "I think you need to join us in the gym mate."

I thought his comment a little cruel, especially as I was standing right there but Tom didn't bat an eyelid.

"Sup Nate," Tom replied as they bumped fists. Nathan Lane then turned to look down at me, before shooting Tom a surprised look. His eyebrows inched up to his hairline; his hair being as black as Noah's. Why Noah's face had just popped in there again, was anyone's guess. I flicked a brief glance around before resting my eyes back on our host.

"So, *this* is Lucy?" Nathan said with a confident smile, his gaze roaming appreciatively over my small frame.

"Lucy, this is Nathan or Nate. He's rich and useless and not worth your time." Tom's words surprised me. I knew he was joking but they were still a bit below the belt when I didn't know the boy. "He's also a renowned player and so please do keep your distance."

Nathan's grin widened and he released a whistle as he said, "Cocky fucker aren't you. Showing off in front of the girlfriend. At least you can stop stalking girls on Tinder now." He crossed his muscled arms over his wide chest. Poor Tom, it was like a boy in a face-off with a man. I did a double take as I processed that he'd just called me Tom's girlfriend. Tom didn't correct him either. I wasn't having that.

"We're just friends, aren't we Tom?" I said in a high-pitched voice.

Tom shot me a glance and grinned. “For now.” He added a wink and I smiled back. He was charming, in a wooden type of way.

“So, Lucy. What can I get you to drink?” Nathan said, shooting a knowing look between us.

I looked at Tom for some guidance, not really sure what to say. I didn’t really need anything alcoholic but I also didn’t want to appear buttoned-up, Noah’s words coming back to taunt me.

“Any recommendations Tom?”

Nathan cut in before he could reply. “Why don’t I make you one of my specials?” he offered. The stranger beside me grunted and I shot him a look. Did I imagine the ‘don’t do it’ stare?

I pursed my lips, thoughts of date rape drinks circling me like a bad smell. At the end of the day, I was with Tom and I trusted him one hundred percent. The guy in front of me, not so much.

“Not too strong though Nate, she doesn’t really drink,” Tom put in. He then grabbed a coke which sat in a basin of ice on the surface of the bar. As Nathan mixed my drink, I slowly started to unwind.

The two boys chatted between themselves briefly and I continued to glance around the space. Tom said something about Ella and Ryan, but I didn’t catch Nathan’s reply. I found it interesting that he linked his sister’s name with Ryan. Did he mean Ryan Lane, surely not? He had to be thirty odd. I tucked away the thought.

Nathan handed me a tall glass before he went on to serve someone else. I eyed the odd-coloured liquid thoughtfully. I couldn’t even begin to describe the colour, but it tasted nice and was fruity. Tom said I didn’t need to worry as he had decided not to drink due to the amount of studying he had to do over the weekend. I wished I’d known that before I’d opted for Nathan’s ‘special’. The liquid was probably taking the enamel off my teeth with every sip.

We walked along the wet pool deck toward the water. I felt a few eyes follow me and saw a couple of people I used to go to school with. Max and Kyle Walker were sitting in a Jacuzzi that was set into the ground; they briefly acknowledged my wave. We went to the same school but I didn’t really know them. I remembered Max more. He was known for his lack of brain cells and was a class clown of sorts. A girl was with them, she sat on the side and had her legs in the water. Her face was familiar but I couldn’t quite place it.

I spent some time in the water and was included in several different discussions. Everyone was quite welcoming. Tom and I spoke with a girl called Sophie; she was a hairdresser who worked in Scarborough and she kept complimenting my colouring and saying how I should *never* dye my hair.

It wasn't until I saw Natalie Savvas, Noah's sister that an anxious feeling started to radiate through me. Natalie had also gone to my school but I didn't really know her either. She was in with the popular crowd and probably didn't even know I existed. She was teetering on the edge of the pool, in a bright red bikini when a guy pushed her in. He then jumped in after her and after a frenzied splashing war, they started to kiss. I averted my gaze; tuning out of what Sophie was saying to Tom.

My skin prickled and I suddenly felt the need to cover myself with my towel. If Natalie was there, it was possible that her brother was too. Drat. I so wasn't in the mood to be faced with that fly in my ointment. The thought of Noah seeing me in my swimsuit started to churn my insides. No doubt he'd say something horrible. I remembered him corning me in the changing rooms at school once and making fun of me because I was the only one in my year that couldn't swim. He'd found this out *after* throwing me in. At least he'd had the sense to save me. I eyed the water warily. I still wasn't that strong a swimmer. That was also the day he stole one of my gran's romance novels I was reading from my school bag. He'd held it above his head and taunted me in front of his friends, asking me if I used it to rub one out. I hadn't known what he meant at the time but had still been mortified. It was only later when one of my friends explained it that I'd moved onto crime novels from that point onwards.

With the memories of Noah's torment fresh in my mind, I scanned the entire room, looking at all the strangers. It was odd really; apart from the last two years, I had lived here my entire life. Yes, I'd heard of the Lane family but I'd never met them, and apart from Tom, and the others I went to school with; I didn't know anyone else. The villages in this part of Yorkshire were close-knit. A place where everyone knew everyone usually. I suppose that's what they meant about different circles. As I certainly hadn't moved in the ones these people had. This crowd knew how to let their hair down and have fun. Not the type to go to church and from some of their expensive-looking swimwear, I imagined they'd be from families that had money. Even Tom's parents had a huge house.

Tom and Sophie appeared to be getting along famously, I felt a bit forgotten about. I checked my palm, someone had obviously spilt their drink on the side of the pool and I must have had my hand in it as my fingers were suddenly sticky.

Wrapping my towel around my body to cover my costume, I excused myself, saying I was going to the loo.

A girl at the bar pointed to where the toilet was. Nathan was still there, now talking to a big mean-looking guy with tattoos all over one muscled arm. They both had a bottle of beer in their hand, Nathan was openly laughing and the other guy was doing what must have been *his* version of a smile; he looked like he was mildly in pain.

Nate sobered as I passed, his eyes watchful and the big one turned to see where he was looking. I offered them both a shy smile but only Nathan returned it. The other guy just narrowed his eyes at me with a scowl. Rude much? He was insanely good-looking with dark chiselled features. Aggressive waves seemed to radiate from him.

After washing my hands and re-securing my towel, I left the bathroom and went to make my way back to Tom and Sophie. As I was just about to turn the corner into the archway where the bar was located, a strong arm encircled my waist from behind and I was dragged back against a solid, rock-hard chest. As my lips parted with a half-gasp, half-yell, the sound was muffled by a firm hand covering my mouth. Air *whooshed* down my nose and confused panic flared as I was lifted off my feet and dragged backwards with the offending body. The guy who held me shouldered open one of the doors at the back of the hallway and I was carried into the room. My heart was thumping at a manic speed. He held me so tightly I could hardly even struggle.

It didn't take long for me to realise that it was Noah. I could tell from the size and feel of his body as I'd never met anyone as big or as solid. He released me and I spun around to face him, my damp ponytail plastered against my neck. Blood thundered in my ears and my chest was heaving.

I swayed on my feet but managed to catch my balance. Noah looked wolfish as he leaned back against the now-closed door.

"For the love of... you *scared* me, Noah!" I yelled breathlessly up into his annoyingly satisfied face. "That *wasn't* funny."

He raised an eyebrow. "You *knew* it was me," he said in a matter-of-fact tone, folding his massive arms across his naked chest as he regarded me with that smirk. He really was one to break the mould in men. He actually thought that by me knowing his identity meant it was OK to grab me. I suppose in the weird world of Noah, that would be the case.

"That's not the point. And I couldn't breathe, you're so rough!" I complained, smoothing back my wet ponytail which had fallen forward.

"You have no idea baby," he drawled out slowly in that sexy voice that I hated so much. I wanted to scratch his face for scaring me. Yes, only for a split second but it was still there. The thought of marking his skin gave me an insane amount of pleasure. There was now no denying it, this man brought out the worst in me.

Once my heartbeat slowly returned to normal, I then saw him properly and sweet baby Jesus and the orphans. There was rather a lot of him. My *entire* body warmed at that display of manly flesh and I felt a visceral kick. OMG, Noah Savvas in black swim shorts stood in front of me *bare-chested*.

He looked like he'd been sculptured by God himself. His pectoral muscles were as well-defined as his stomach, and a full-on six-pack stared forward, the chiseled bumps jutting out toward me. Now I understood why girls at school loved to run their hands over *that* area, I hated to admit it, but at that moment, I too felt that urge. His crossed arms highlighted that tattoo I had seen when we were by my car. It covered the top of his bicep and shoulder, the image tapering off toward his back. I wondered fleetingly what the full picture would be of. Beelzebub maybe?

Tattoos were popular with country guys, and like most village boys, Noah also appeared to enjoy people drawing all over his body with needles.

I was speechless, my mouth opening and closing like a fish, my ravenous eyes, feasting on his body like a starving person. I was so going to hell in a handbasket. I just hoped I wasn't drooling. I was usually very apt at controlling my saliva when in the presence of this guy. But right then, I was toast.

He tilted his head and regarded me through narrowed eyes. "You're looking at me like you've never seen a guy with his top off before Red," Noah determined as his eyes roamed up and down my body. I was so relieved I wore my towel, as it was like body armour to me at that point. My skin appeared to be singing, desperate to be closer to him; the invisible pull determined.

I dragged my reluctant eyes off those perfectly formed man-nipples. Noah's chest was smooth and I wondered if he shaved it as his legs were covered with fine dark hairs. Again, legs that were corded with muscle. I pushed away the thought. *As if* he'd shave his chest; Noah was way too manly for that level of grooming.

I snorted. "Don't change the subject. Why am I in here?" I glanced around taking in 'here', which appeared to be another room full of boxes.

"You're just too easy to abduct Red. Like a pretty, helpless rag doll. I've been planning on kidnapping you for the last twenty minutes," he stated confidently without a hint of regret. The guy was a law unto himself. Surely normal guys didn't go around dragging women off into rooms. Arrogant ones like Noah obviously did. The guy did what he wanted and played by his own rules.

My eyes flickered to his strong chest again. I sure hoped my tongue wasn't hanging out. I bit the inside of my cheek as a distraction and pulled my gaze back to a safer place; his face (although only slightly safer). Gosh he was gorgeous.

Noah's expression suddenly became inquisitive, "I must admit, I was surprised to see *you* here. Not your usual crowd. And out with Tom Wade *again*?"

I placed my hand against the dislodged towel near my chest to stop it from slipping further, totally aware that I was alone in a room half-naked with Mr Testosterone himself. The guy was magnificently male and I suddenly felt extremely girlie and vulnerable.

"Yes and it's going really well actually," I lied, jutting my chin out as if to say, and what of it?

"He watches you with a serious case of raper face. Don't you find that disturbing?"

"What? He doesn't do that. And anyway, we're friends really. We're taking it slow," I pointed out. Not really sure I agreed with Noah's description of how Tom looked at me.

He shook his head and said sarcastically, "You'd have really bland children." Noah was of course fluent in sarcasm.

I winced, my lips twisting. "We've only been out a few times Noah, I don't think we're at that stage yet," I pointed out coyly.

His expression became clouded and hard to read, "Has he put his mouth on you yet?"

Clearing my throat, I crossed my own arms over my chest; mirroring his stance. Stand up to him, stand up to him, my backbone chanted; replaying everything he had said to me, accused me of being or not being.

"I don't think that's any of your business really." My reply was tart.

He quirked a brow at that one and then his voice became firmer, "What if I've decided to make it my business?"

I swallowed as Noah unfolded his arms and shoved his hands into the pockets of his shorts, drawing my attention to *that* area. I quickly pulled my eyes away but I couldn't stop the thoughts of what he would look like, *down there*.

Straightening and miserably trying to appear taller, I glanced behind him at the door, almost willing the thing to open. Surely Tom would be wondering where I was?

"And why would you want to do that?" I sighed. Why had I asked *that* question?

He gave a careless shrug, rocking his back against the surface of the door.

"Maybe I feel sorry for him. He has a right to be happy," he said flatly. I totally didn't get where he was going with that. The guy couldn't have been more cryptic.

"What and going out with me would make him unhappy?"

He removed his hands from his pockets and rolled his huge shoulders. The guy couldn't stand still for two minutes. "Yes, when he found out the truth and realised how you'd wasted his time."

I did feel a twinge of guilt, but I ignored it and shot a look at the ceiling of the room in a 'give me strength' motion.

"And what truth is that?"

"That you're into someone else," he said, again with that matter-of-fact tone, pushing off the door and taking a step toward me. That charged energy between us crackled and more awareness pooled into my body.

My heart leapt in my chest. Here we go again. "And I suppose that's you is it?" I now knew *exactly* where he was going. I used my words as a delaying tactic as I attempted to control the sudden desire that raced through me.

There was a moment of silence.

"That's right. Me. And I'm very territorial," he said with a sexy curl to his lips, his gaze scouring my face.

Shaking my head in denial, I unfolded my arms and dropped them to my sides, again eyeing up the door.

"As I said the other night Noah, you're deluded." I so wanted to force-feed this guy my sour grapes. My mind did anyway, my body wanted him to feed on something else entirely. I knew my nipples were hard, probably attempting to catch his attention. They certainly had a mind of their own at that point.

Lust crashed through my core as he said. "I could prove you wrong. I only have to touch you."

His gaze narrowed as it travelled over my breasts before resting on my face again. Our eyes tangled.

"I bet you'd cum really prettily."

His last comment forced a jet of heat between my legs and I immediately recognised the kick of lust. I should have been accustomed to his indecent remarks by now but I wasn't. The chaos of my emotions in this man's presence just made no sense to me. Everything was all of a jumble. He had the subtlety of a sledgehammer and yet he spoke to my lady parts like a pro.

"Do you touch yourself when you think about me?"

My stomach dropped, like being on a rollercoaster. "I'm not going to answer that," I gasped, feeling totally unprepared.

"What? It's a natural question for a man to ask?"

"Whatever, look, I need to get back to Tom." My voice cracked and I knew he'd heard it. Everything seemed to be out in the open and I had nowhere to hide.

I watched as his tongue flicked out and ran along his bottom lip.

His head dipped and his eyes were now hooded.

"Take the towel off and come here," he instructed, crooking his finger. I swallowed and my pulse jolted, almost stalling, yet the blood in my veins pumped faster.

My brain struggled to process the command and I did the opposite and took another step back. Running from that challenge in his voice.

"No thank you, I'm fine here." There was a catch in my throat as I answered and I watched him, feeling both timid and strangely excited. Tension pounded in my temples.

He shot me a look of measured impatience, "You still don't appear to understand how the male mind works. *Do it* Red before I do it for you," his voice was now a sensual demanding whisper and it did funny things to my tummy.

'Do as he says,' a little voice urged inside of me.

Taking a small step forward, I raised my chin. I'd show him that I wasn't pathetic, that I could stand up for myself and do some 'seizing'.

There was a definite sexual pull between us like we were attached in some way. My body wanted to follow his lead, but I needed to keep my cool.

Noah continued to watch me in smouldering silence and I was unable to drag my gaze away.

"What?" My voice was unbelievably calm.

I twitched as he shoved off the door and closed the distance between us, wrapping his fingers around my upper arms. Noah slowly turned my body and manoeuvred me so my back was against the door. Catching me off guard.

"Next time, drop the towel when I ask you to," he whispered, whipping said item off my body and slinging it behind him; like I was a doll to be undressed. I shivered beneath his stare as his dark eyes roamed over my body. It didn't matter that I wore a one-piece, I felt naked under his gaze. I couldn't meet that intense glow and I twisted my head to one side. His domineering behaviour thrilled me, how could it not? This man cornered the market in bossiness.

Noah's finger traced the skin on my bare shoulder. My whole body was on fire. He too cocked his head to one side with an expression full of lustful intentions.

"Nice suit."

He paused momentarily as he caressed an area of exposed skin. "Do you have these all over your body?" he questioned; his deep voice thick with emotion.

I glanced back toward where he touched a small cluster of freckles on my shoulder. "Yes," I panted. My control was severely starting to fray around the edges. Let's face it, the guy was lethally attractive and had probably been breaking hearts from his cot.

His breath was warm against my neck and I lifted my head further; his eyes were dark and heavy; full of silent promise. The woodsy scent of his skin with the slight twinge of chlorine lingered between us.

"One day," he drawled slowly, his forehead dipping to mine, "I'm going to count every single one of them.

The thought of Noah's eyes honing in on my most intimate areas caused another delicious sensation to stir in me.

I sucked in a breath; you could almost taste the sexual tension, "That's ambitious. They're pretty much everywhere," I replied on an exhale.

His tone became deathly serious as he lifted his head. "And one day I'm going to touch you and see you, *everywhere*."

Through those last few years of school, Noah had made me suffer but at that moment, I didn't care. I *wanted* his hands on me. My head and my body were now aligned and heavily invested at the moment.

Noah was so close, his naked chest now at my eye level and as I stood there looking up at him, my senses were whirring. Although he'd released my arms. I couldn't go anywhere. I was pinned between his rock-like body and the door.

Noah lifted one of my hands and placed it on his chest near his heart. His skin was smooth; solid and warm. He inhaled sharply as my fingers made contact. He then lifted my other hand and exposed the skin of my wrist to his dark gaze before drawing it to his mouth. His tongue gently swept across the skin over my pulse and I gasped with pleasure, my whole being burning with need.

Noah's lips curled as he noted how my body was responding. I was melting like an iceberg in the sun. His eyes smouldered against my upturned face and I was breathing quite heavily, but he appeared *totally* calm. I swallowed again nervously, my eyes silently pleading for him to let me go whilst my body surged toward the strength of his torso. Excitement flowed through my body like a river of fire.

A whimper fell from my mouth as Noah released my wrists and moved his hands to cup my jaw, tilting my face up toward him with his thumbs. He then lowered his head and crushed my mouth with his. An emotional explosion went off in my chest and my eyes fluttered closed.

I was lost.

His tongue pushed between my lips, entering my mouth, stroking and tasting, his hands tightening against my jaw. I leaned up into him, savouring the feeling and his kiss became more demanding. That feeling of excitement was consuming and my legs wobbled. I raised my hands to his biceps, enjoying how his skin there felt against my fingers; that tattooed section covered by my hand. He growled in triumph and my breasts pushed against the hardness of his chest. I was literally coming apart, my control in shreds.

One of Noah's hands moved to tangle around my ponytail and he tugged gently, forcing my head back, exposing more skin. This movement separated our mouths and Noah buried his face in my neck, kissing the column on my throat and I moaned as he nipped at it with his teeth; the slight pain was pleasurable. I then felt how hard he had become. The large length of his sex was against my stomach and a jet of unease shot into me like the lethal injection.

OMG, what on earth was I doing? I moved my hands to his chest to push him away and he released me instantly, putting much-needed space between our two bodies, lifting his head. He was also breathing heavily with desire-fuelled eyes and I placed a shaking hand to my lips, searching his face, my own breath coming out in soft pants as I attempted to claw my way back to reality.

Unsaid words hung in the air between us and the atmosphere was so thick; it throbbed. I felt for the door handle behind me, I needed to get some self-respect back.

Once I was certain I could escape, I stepped forward and slapped Noah hard across the face. His head was knocked to the side with the impact before he turned back to look at me, irritatingly unperturbed and I twisted; pulling open the door, making my escape.

Shame at how I'd behaved pounded through me. Remorse, regret, embarrassment. I had to fold my arms over my chest to hide my hardened nipples, having left my towel behind.

He didn't try to stop or follow me as I shot from the room. I did cast a glance behind me but Noah must have remained there. Probably until he had himself under control. Yes, I was inexperienced but I knew all about the birds and the bees; I'd felt it against my stomach!

Nathan Lane grinned at me from behind the bar and his buddy also turned to look. Both wore cocky, self-assured expressions. I dealt them both a haughty glare. Goodness knows what they thought. Had they seen Noah drag me into that room? Adrenaline pumped through my body. They probably thought I'd just had sex; my entire body was flushed with arousal.

I lowered my legs into the water next to Sophie and some of my newly found colour slowly drained away from me. They hadn't even noticed I'd been gone! Great. Now I felt like a pathetic loser; as well as a whore.

Shock channelled through me at my loose behaviour. Shock, entwined with a dose of giddiness. I was surprised I hadn't passed out with excitement.

Nodding my head at what they were saying, I attempted to look like I was joining in. After around five minutes I turned away, looking for Noah. He was now with Nathan Lane and the moody, mean-looking guy by the bar. They were all fist-bumping, a motion that was starting to annoy me and within seconds there was a swarm of girls around them, flirting like their lives depended on it.

The amount of interest shouldn't have surprised me really as they were all absolute hunks. Each one of them held that same, aggressive, bad-boy vibe that girls just seemed to gravitate towards. At the end of the day, the bible states; a person is known by the company he keeps.

I watched warily from under my lashes so it wouldn't look like I was staring at him. Noah's broad muscular back was then facing me, revealing the tattoo I'd glimpsed earlier. Most of his back was covered, the artwork unique; possibly something to do with his heritage. The mean guy didn't look as terrifying with Noah standing next to him.

I rolled my eyes at myself and then pushed off into the water. Submerging myself completely, before coming up and standing next to Tom. I needed to wash Noah Savvas off my body. The chlorine from the water made part of my neck twinge and I placed my hand on a sore bit that stung slightly. Checking my fingertip, there was a dash of red. Noah had actually *pierced* the skin when he'd bitten my neck; although I had to admit, it was more of a nibble. Lust crashed into my pelvis again at the thought that he had marked my skin. *Branded me.* It appeared I really was a masochist.

Sophie explained that she needed to get dry as her dad was due to pick her up and I turned to Tom with a look that said I'd like to leave.

"You feeling a bit wrinkly, cos we can go now if you want?"

I smiled. The guy read me so well. I wondered if I kissed him whether it would be the same as it was with Noah.

"Yes, please."

Tom helped me from the pool and we padded barefoot, dripping across the pool deck. A few people had left and I could see Natalie starting to tidy up which was a surprise. She'd never come across as helpful at school.

I moved closer to Tom as we needed to pass through the archway by the bar to get to the rooms to change. I'd left my towel in the room Noah had dragged me into and I didn't want to leave it there.

Tom nodded a 'hi' to the group and we almost made it. He blatantly did know Noah.

Said annoyance stepped out in front of us, his eyes *burning* into me. He was holding my towel. My heart skipped a beat as Tom shot me a questioning look and the two other boys watched the scene with annoying smirks, like they were sharing a secret.

"Your towel brat," Noah said with a lopsided smile, the girl next to him darted a glance between us. Carnal energy crackled at the word brat; Noah had that maddening ability to make even the most horrible nickname seem sexual somehow.

The guy was amoral and perversely proud of it. I wondered if the girl almost climbing up his body was his girlfriend. A thought which tasted significantly bitter.

Recovering Tom said, "Ah yes, you guys know each other from school. You said so in the pub the other week." Delivering the last sentence at Noah.

I snorted. "Yes we went to school together, but I wouldn't have said we know each other, not really."

My nose wrinkled at how much I sounded like a moody schoolgirl.

Noah was watching me with deceptive idleness and my eyes widened as he tested his jaw with his hand, moving it from side to side before rubbing it. A silent message in reference to my slapping him. His message that he was looking forward to getting payback was clear

He flexed his fingers, before lowering his hand. "Whatever you say, Red," he drawled with a taunting smile. I snatched the towel from his hand without a thank you and shot back over my shoulder to Tom, "I'll be out in five minutes Tom."

As I walked away, I could feel everyone's eyes on my back; but only felt truly scorched by one set, those belonging to Noah Savvas.

Later on, as sat on my bed, I received a text.

Sweet dreams gorgeous. N x.

It was from Noah.

I decided to reply. **Goodnight Noah.** I left off the kiss on purpose.

I can still taste you in my mouth. After reading this several times, I put my phone on silent and pushed the offending item under my pillow. My tummy continued to jitter.

Noah bloody Savvas. My head's worst nightmare, my body's wet dream.

Four

Over the next couple of weeks, I didn't receive any more annoying messages from Noah. Maybe he'd gotten the message after the slap and my being unresponsive to his last inappropriate comment. At the end of the day, the boy was no good for me and I needed to keep my distance. I would *not* give into the madness of this thing, *whatever* it was; infatuation, insanity?

I found my feet at the surgery and was really enjoying my job. The building was always bustling; there just wasn't time to get bored. I also loved the ethos that came with being a hospital for animals, the clients were always so appreciative. Pets were family at the end of the day.

There were six staff in total; me, Marcus, the lead vet, one in training (Tom), two vet nurses, and the cleaner, Abi. Jonathan Wade, Tom's father was rarely there. I saw him briefly from time to time.

When I'd originally accepted the position, I had done so on a temporary basis. My training was as a medical secretary and the pay for that would be much higher than that of a veterinary receptionist. The harsh truth of the matter was that I needed money and *fast*. I was *desperate* to save so that I could find a flat of my own and remove myself from the toxic situation that was home life.

One day, Jay, one of the vet nurses allowed me to assist in preparing a cat for surgery. The experience was nail-biting but so rewarding; especially when the procedure went well and the owner came by to collect him. The pet belonged to a little girl and she was full of excited chatter and cuddles as they'd left the practice.

Jay was super friendly and encouraging, with blonde curly hair and a huge grin that appeared to be permanently fixed on her face. She had the most amazing sneeze, it went on forever, 'que, que, que, que'. It sounded like someone trying to start a car when the battery was flat. I'd actually caught Tom jigging along to the noise; like the sound created a tempo that forced you to dance. Odd, but funny.

Now that I had successfully completed my course at Uni, I had seriously been thinking about my next steps career-wise. My original idea of becoming a medical secretary had changed. I loved my time so much at the practice working with the animals and so I decided to look at the possibility of training to become a vet nurse myself. Jay was really inspiring, saying that the course I had already studied would at least be helpful as medical lingo could be hard to grasp. When the reception wasn't so busy, she started giving me pointers and allowing me to observe more procedures.

Things with Tom and I had cooled off. He had started to see Sophie from the pool party. It didn't upset me as my focus had been more on work and I was happy that he'd met someone. I just hoped it went OK for him. Jay had said that Tom hadn't had much luck with girls in the past. His sister Ella also wound him up about it, saying how he needed to get laid. I'd also heard her call him a virgin a couple of times.

It was a cold morning in December and the weather was miserable; the temperature had dropped radically. The practice was extraordinarily quiet and a couple of appointments had been cancelled, so Tom had sent Jay home at lunchtime, leaving just the two of us to finish up.

I was just in the process of hanging up the phone after making an appointment for a cat to be neutered the following week; when Noah *burst* in through the glass doors. The receiver rattled along with my nerves as it crashed into the cradle of the phone.

His broad chest was pumping with exertion and my eyes narrowed with concern. He was carrying an animal of some kind wrapped in a sheet. Whatever was under there was thrashing around, the sounds it made were muffled, between a growl and a whimper I would say.

I shot around the side of the counter and rushed toward him, my sixth sense kicking in. He needed help and fast, whatever he was holding was strong *and* aggressive.

Noah's face was pulled taunt as he struggled to hold onto the animal, I could see a tail poking out and guessed it was another dog. He lowered himself to his knees, continuing to battle with his energetic burden. His mouth was curled into a snarl and I felt a curious swooping sensation in my stomach. I noticed how Noah's expression was lined with pain and his pallor was dull; he certainly didn't have his usual golden glow.

"Noah, what do you need?" I panted, my breath whooshing between my teeth. The burst of raw panic in my chest was almost painful.

His hard eyes clashed with mine, "Get Tom, now. Tell him to get a shot of sedative, quickly," he ordered in a strained voice; his eyes pinned to mine.

Exam room one to the side of the waiting rooms was open, but it was empty and so I pushed to my feet in order to find Tom; shouting his name. As I rounded the corner toward the door of his office, I burst in without knocking: uncaring if there were any clients in there, this was an emergency type situation. Tom looked up from the paper he was studying, shocked at the intrusion. Luckily, he was alone.

I almost tripped over my tongue in my haste to blurt out the instructions, "Noah's here and he has an injured animal, a dog. He says it needs sedation and he's struggling to keep it still."

Like a true professional, Tom was on it. I watched with admiration as he shot to his feet, spinning to the cabinet, withdrawing a syringe and a vial of drugs. He didn't stumble or choose the wrong drawer, he was calm and collected, and *fast.* To be honest I had *never* seen him move so quickly. Tom in professional mode was a miraculous sight to see.

We both rushed back to Noah, who was luckily still subduing the animal. The sheet almost covered it entirely and I saw there was now blood on the floor and on Noah's hoodie.

"It's bleeding," I announced, pointing out the obvious.

Meeting my concerned look, Noah shot out, "That's my blood."

I was horrified, "What?" I said in a panicked voice. Fear at the thought of him being hurt jetted into me; my own blood starting to chill. Considering my mixed feelings about Noah, which bordered more on the negative, I was shocked by the power of that emotion; my level of concern.

Tom dropped to his knees beside him and lifted part of the sheet to find the skin of the animal so that he could administer the shot.

"The fucker bit me," Noah's grunted in between tussles, his scowl deepening. My mouth gaped open in shock. How badly was he hurt? The thought made my breath come quicker.

Tom drew back and stood before walking into the empty exam room and expertly disposing of the needle in the 'sharps only' waste.

"It should start to take in a minute, just keep holding him," he shouted over his shoulder. "Where are you bleeding, Noah?"

I was now also on my knees, crouched in front of Noah, frantic eyes searching him for injury. His jean-encased legs seemed fine.

Lifting my gaze to his face, I felt another twinge of worry, "Are you OK?" I questioned sincerely. I experienced a raw need to touch his face with my palm and comfort him. What the heck was going on with me? I batted the thought to one side, no matter what I thought about Noah, he was a human and in pain. *That's* why I was so worried, I convinced myself. *Nothing* more.

The bundle, if you could call it that, started to relax as the sedative kicked in and Tom brought over an animal carry crate so he could move it into the examination room.

"Noah?" I repeated, realising he hadn't heard me.

"I've been better," he replied truthfully, a bitterness I didn't like seeing, entering his features.

I noted the sticky rivulets of blood which stained Noah's hand and surmised that the injury was most probably to his arm. As if hearing my thoughts Tom put in, "Give me a minute and I'll look at that arm Noah," he promised.

Once the animal was completely still, Tom, with Noah's help, removed the sheet and carefully placed the unconscious animal into the carry crate.

It was a grey, speckled Staffordshire Bullterrier type and its leg was bent at an unhealthy angle. Again, it looked like it had been fighting and was badly scared, but the injuries were not fresh. It also had one ear missing. My heart squeezed in my chest, the poor little thing.

It was then that I saw Noah's injury in full as he lifted the sleeve of the hoodie he wore, his eyes pinned to the area. There were four puncture marks above his wrist on his forearm and blood was slowly running onto his hand.

"Oh, my God! Noah," I didn't care that I'd taken the lord's name in vain. I shot to my feet to get the first aid kit. On my second day at the surgery, I'd been sent on a first-aider course and so I knew I needed to stop the flow and clean the wound.

Tom had taken the animal through to room one and I urged Noah up onto one of the chairs in the waiting room. He was so large, he basically had to straddle two chairs.

Tom came back to stand beside me and looked down at the wounded. "I need to leave the sedative to fully take before I can assess the animal. What happened Noah?"

Noah's head came level with my chest and I gently took his injured arm and raised it up to reduce the flow of blood to that area, standing between his strong thighs.

As I gently cleaned the wound with an alcohol-free wipe, the bleeding slowed and my stomach turned over. I told myself to get a grip, if I was going to be a vet nurse, I'd see blood from time to time.

The only way you knew that Noah was in pain was the occasional twitch as I dabbed at his injuries. The holes looked fairly deep, probably a hospital job and you could see scoring marks from the dog's teeth as Noah had most probably yanked his arm out of the beast's jaws.

"I hit it with my truck, it came out of nowhere, it was definitely running from something," he informed us with another wince.

"What else, its wounds don't look that fresh at first glance," Tom replied with a frown. He was in full-on efficient vet mode as he watched me clean the wound with an interested expression.

I concentrated on my job and even though I wasn't looking at Noah, I could feel him studying me.

"It wasn't moving so I got out to check, it may have a busted leg or something. It went for me and I managed to get my arm free. It didn't run away though and I could see it was injured, which is probably the reason it bit me. I got the sheet and wrapped the fucker in it before coming here. I couldn't leave it there."

So, there was a softer side to him. I was surprised Noah didn't run the thing over with his truck, considering the damage it had done to him. Those were Noah's words after all, that he didn't ever 'turn the other cheek'. This obviously wasn't the case and this proved that there *was* another side to him, a caring one. The thought made me feel warm inside.

"There's a dog fighting syndicate in the area, there *must* be. The fucker was escaping I'm sure of it and it's pretty messed up if you look at it. Injury wise."

"You probably did some of that when you hit it with your car?" I suggested, not wanting it to be true about the suspected dog fighting thing. Although unintentionally, my tone suggested I was portioning some type of blame on Noah. Which was so not the case.

I lifted my eyes as he yanked his arm away, helping himself to one of the bandages, taking matters into his own hands. He started to haphazardly wrap the wound in gauze before shooting me a dark look.

"Well, I didn't knock its fucking ear off with my truck did I genius?" His voice dripped with disdain and I felt like bursting into tears, hurt vibrating inside me. Not necessarily due to the harshness of his tone, but the whole scenario. Some vet nurse I'd be. I couldn't even handle one emergency.

Tom scratched his chin thoughtfully as he drew Noah's arm further forward to inspect it. The difference in the sizes of their limbs would have been comical under any other circumstances.

Crossing my arms over my chest, I hooked my chin at Noah, "Does it hurt?" I stupidly asked. Not knowing what to say and feeling like a petulant child that had just been told off.

Noah's temper flared again. "No, it feels amazing, what the fuck do you think Lucy? Hurts like a bastard," he growled, holding his arm with his other hand. His look shot daggers at both me and Tom. It appeared Noah did not handle pain well, but I suppose who was graceful when they were hurting.

"I was only asking, you don't have to bite my head off," I put in defensively. I was infuriated beyond endurance.

The way he spoke to me with such disrespect and contempt hurt; and probably more than it should. We'd had our ups and downs in the past but this was the first time Noah had genuinely lost his shit with me. I didn't like it.

Before I could analyse my feelings, I pulled my face away and eyed my fingers which were covered with Noah's blood. To think he was trying to save the dog, even though it had injured him was impressive. He had always been incredibly brave, nothing seemed to faze him.

Tom was still assessing the injury but he shot a look between us both. The atmosphere was electric and not in a good way.

"So, you wrapped it in the sheet to stop it going for you again?" Tom perused, partly to himself; helping Noah tie off the bandage that was already starting to turn red.

"Yeah, I'd seen it done with vicious cats on TV," he said in a softer tone. Shooting me a strained look. Did I hear a trace of regret in there, did he realise he'd almost taken my head off?

"When was your last tetanus shot?" Tom put in suddenly and I stepped further back.

Noah grunted, his eyes snapping briefly to Tom, "Fuck knows." His bad attitude was basically orbiting the room around us, his voice like a hot whip.

"Well, you're going to need one. The wound also needs cleaning and dressing *properly*. So, it's the hospital or I do it here," Tom informed him with a commanding edge to his tone. It was refreshing to see, Tom in take-charge mode.

I turned toward him. “Why don’t you take him into room two and I’ll clean up out here?”

Tom pursed his lip before nodding.

“What shall I do with the patient?” I questioned, causing Tom’s brow to furrow. “I mean the furry one?” I explained, jerking my chin toward the other exam room.

Noah released a groan of frustration and leaned his head back against the wall behind him, closing his eyes. I so hoped he wasn’t going to pass out, as I doubted Tom and I would be able to stop him from crumpling to the ground.

Tom’s eyes narrowed at Noah’s movement, obviously also concerned.

“The dog’s fine, he’s crated for now. Let’s sort Noah out first. Believe it or not, he’s the priority.”

“Is he?” I said moodily which resulted in a flying scowl from Noah. His moody eyes on me again.

Tom glanced between us before he said, “And that’s coming from a guy who prefers animals to humans,” attempting to joke. I almost snapped out he isn’t *my* priority. Feeling like I’d also been bitten, but mine was a human bite; travelling all the way to the bone.

Tom cleared his throat, jamming hands in the pockets of his white lab coat, “Well Noah, what’s it to be? Me or the hospital?”

Noah groaned, now in a ‘give me strength’ fashion, and pushed to his feet.

His nostrils flared, “*You* better do it. I don’t do hospitals. But if you cause me any more pain, I’ll knock you the fuck out,” he threatened and I believed him too.

Tom rolled his eyes in a ‘whatever’ fashion obviously confident that Noah wouldn’t hit him. After the big guy’s change in mood, I wasn’t so sure.

I left them to it and went to get the mop, my hands shaking. Noah’s blood was smeared on the floor and I washed the vinyl before cleaning myself up. It was past closing time and so they’d be no last-minute visitors thank goodness. It had looked a bit like there had been a massacre with the blood-stained floor.

After around ten minutes, both men walked out of room two, Noah had removed his hoodie and stood there looking like he was back on his perch again. I noticed he wore his work boots and that he now clutched the blood-stained hoodie in his hand. The tight green tee he wore was plastered to his muscled physique, I noted it was printed with the logo of his garage.

“All, OK?” I said as brightly as I could through my misery.

He shot me a dark look, favouring his bandaged arm, "I think things are pretty far from being OK Lucy," Noah pointed out moodily as he walked into the waiting area. It was like I couldn't say *anything* right and his presence made the room feel so much smaller. The guy just had an attitude so much bigger than everyone else's.

He now stood at his full height, without any drooping of the shoulders, once again a tower of strength. I imagined someone like Noah would *never* want to show any degree of weakness. That was probably why he had been so testy with me. That's the excuse I tried to convince my misery of anyway.

I had thought I hated this guy; I couldn't understand why his being so angry at me hurt so much. I was losing the plot big time.

Tom appeared and smiled reassuringly at me, "Noah's just upset because I gave him a numb arse."

Noah snorted, "And you can be fucking careful how you repeat *that* line, Wade." I knew exactly what he meant. Back to being Mr Crude; yes, Noah was fine. I found it mildly amusing that he second named Tom. Talk about a bear with a sore head.

"Right, Lucy, you take him home. I have to see to our four-legged friend in there and Noah won't fit in my car anyway as it's full of stock," Tom said with a twist of his head.

"He probably won't fit in mine," I echoed honestly a twinge of defiance weaving through me.

Tom and I were facing each other, totally ignoring the looming mood swing next to us.

After a muffled curse Noah barked, "You guys do know I'm standing *right* here?

He looked enraged with his hands on his hips; well and truly affronted. Wowzer, he really did hate not being the sole person in control of a situation.

Tom and I continued to talk about him like he wasn't there and he growled something under his breath, possibly in Greek. It wasn't English anyway and I knew it would be rude, Noah only knew the bad words.

I turned toward the towering inferno, all bristling with angst. Standing there as if the world owed him one. My eyes roamed over his hulking body and I hesitated before saying, "I'll get him in mine somehow don't worry."

Noah took an agitated step forward, casting a shadow over me like an eclipse. He outmatched any red-blooded heterosexual man on the planet.

"I can drive my fucking self!" he boomed down at me; it appeared the injection had not numbed his temper.

Tom was full-on Mr Authority, it was quite attractive. Being bossy suited him.

"You can't drive home Noah, your injury is on your gearstick hand and if you think I'm going to allow you to fuck up what I've just done, I can tell you now, that's *not* going to happen." Wow, that had to be the first time I had seen Tom assert himself.

The look Noah gave us both could have cut glass. He wasn't happy at all and clearly didn't deal with taking orders well. Maybe that's why he had been thrown out of the army. His issues with authority. I pushed my frenzied speculation to one side. Yup, I was definitely still smarting from the way he'd spoken to me. I much preferred the version that wound me up and was mean to me in an *annoying*, sarcastic boy type of way.

I said goodbye to Tom, who still of course had the dog to deal with and after grabbing my bag and car keys, I went out to my Mini with a disgruntled Noah following sheepishly behind me. He was deathly silent and I didn't know if that was a good thing or not. Should I try to clear the air between us *before* we got into the car or leave it? I decided against it as I wasn't sure I'd be able to be polite. I was still smarting from his cutting tone.

When we got to the vehicle, I turned and said, "You'd better not bleed in my car."

Noah rolled his eyes as I opened the passenger side. I could see he was still in pain and I wondered how he'd feel sitting on his bottom, considering the injection he'd just had. Part of me hoped it hurt like hell.

Like Elvis, the Christian in me had totally left the building.

What happened next was quite comical. Noah lowered himself carefully into my car; he almost had to contort his body to fit into the seat. He swore under his breath as he hit his head on the roof. As I then tried to shut the door, I almost closed it on his bad arm and he grunted, shooting me a 'what the hell are you playing at' expression. Drawing his injury toward his chest, as if I had just thumped him on it.

The door wouldn't close due to his bulk, and I had to lean my bottom against the metal to try and secure it against the solid muscle of Noah's shoulder (which was jutting out and therefore stopping the door from clicking shut).

I reattempted, rocking back against it again and again.

"Are you trying to kill me, woman!?" Noah belted as I heaved.

I lost my own temper. Something I hardly ever did.

"Well, what do you *expect* me to do, you *bloody* giant? I said you wouldn't fit. BMW *obviously* didn't manufacture this car with guys like you in mind, did they!" I revelled in the sweet recklessness of losing control; it was a new feeling for me.

He shoved the door off his shoulder and shot me a sneering glance, "It's a fucking Mini. The answer is in the name Lucy!"

I stared down at him with my hands on my hips (my attempt to be challenging).

"We're going to have to go in yours. Give me your keys." I said, pulling the door open and placing my hand out flat in front of his face.

He eyed my fingers with distaste, clearly troubled by my suggestion. "There is *no way* you're driving my Navara."

He exhaled noisily, clearly frustrated with the situation.

"Here, try now," he commanded, twisting so he was half facing the driver's side.

I swung the door closed and it shut. Lowering my face, I bit out through the glass. "See, you can be accommodating when you want to be."

Noah scowled and flipped me the middle finger and I shot him an evil look before stomping around the front of the car. My stomach was still swirling.

The journey to his place was tense. Steam was surely coming out of my ears. I was so cross with him.

I turned the radio on to drown out that tense silence. Unfortunately, it was playing a particularly depressing song, which wasn't really any more beneficial at that point.

I attempted to concentrate on the road as one strong hand lifted and turned down the volume.

He was the first one to break the silence as I pulled onto Cudworth Lane.

"I'm sorry," Noah said quietly, shooting me a pensive look. I must admit, his words of contrition surprised me. I was so annoyed at that moment; 'love thy neighbour' could do one, as far as Noah was concerned.

"Sorry?" I volleyed back, pretending not to know what he was talking about.

"I'm *sorry*, about how I spoke to you. Back there at the practice."

I sniffed, roughly changing gear, and the gearbox groaned.

"Really. When? I didn't notice anything different. You usually talk to me like crap Noah," I pointed out in a snippy voice.

Noah exhaled again sharply, his nostrils flaring, I could see his exasperated expression from my periphery.

“I was out of order. And I *am* sorry. Please *forgive* me.” His voice was actually sincere for once. “I’ll make it up to you I promise.”

I left it a few beats and didn’t respond until I pulled the car up outside his garage.

Make it up to me indeed, my brain started to catalogue all the different ways he could do that. In the end, the catalogue fell short.

Deciding against taunting him I replied, “Fine. And *yes*, you will make it up to me. You really upset me, Noah.”

He lifted his hand and palmed the back of his neck. “I know, but I was in pain, OK? I don’t handle pain well, believe it or not.”

“Yes, well so was I, in a fashion. Fuck,” I sighed, feeling some of the stress at the situation slowly drain from my body. I rolled my shoulders, dragged on the hand break and turned off the engine.

Noah’s face changed and a smile broke out across his features. His eyes danced with humour. My goodness, his mood was so quick to change; like an annoying set of temporary traffic lights, that lets out only two cars at a time.

My nose scrunched and I narrowed my eyes back at him. “What?”

“You just said fuck,” he revealed with a toothy grin. “I can honestly say I’m shocked. I don’t think I can be dealing with any more surprises today.”

I shook my head, “I did not.” Guilt forced me to interlock my fingers in my lap. Had I really said the word fuck?

“You did.”

I puffed out a breath. “It appears we’re spending too much time together then. You’re rubbing off on me.”

I held a hand out to ward off the obvious smutty comment which I saw flit behind his eyes. He was such a dirty-minded sod.

Noah leaned back against the door, his face becoming serious again as his eyes roamed over my clothes.

“I like a woman in uniform,” he drawled, that sexy look back as he scanned my seated body.

Pulling a face at my work gear, I huffed. The uniform really was quite bland and did *nothing* for the paleness of my skin.

“Anyway, we’re here,” I replied, ignoring his comment.

“Thanks for the lift and again, I really am sorry, I didn’t mean to shout at you.” His tone after such rabid (no pun intended) anger, was a relief and I felt partly soothed.

I awarded him with a half-smile.

Begrudgingly I felt the sudden flare of need to offer him some support.

"Well, you have my number, so you can call me if your arm falls off," I pointed out, in an even tone, absent of upset.

Light danced in his eyes. "I think I'll struggle if my arm falls off."

I raised my eyebrows pointing out, "You have a spare."

"Indeed," he volleyed back.

The mood was lightened and we shared a look. At the back of my mind, I knew something had shifted between us.

"Anyway, don't forget you owe me one. I'll hold you to that," I stated in a firm voice.

Noah's brow scrunched, "What about your free tyre?"

"That doesn't count as that's in the past," I shot back with a definite tone.

He snorted, shooting me a look of mock incredulity before his shoulders dropped.

"Well surely the way I treated you at school shouldn't matter either then, *that's* in the past."

I shot him a look that could have frozen lava.

"That's *not* the same thing at all, you bullied me for years and so there was a build-up of wrongdoings. That can't just be forgotten so easily. And before you go on about Christians and forgive and forget. I *will* forgive you one day, I'm just not ready yet."

There was a pause as we watched each other in silence, our eyes glued together.

He conceded. "OK, I owe you one. The question is, what is it you want? You could come upstairs with me and we could discuss it? Fine-tune the details."

I tutted, "Nothing like that you raging perv. It has to be something that will make you think twice about being mean to me. Something that will knock you out of your comfort zone maybe." I paused for thought. "I'll sleep on it."

He tilted his dark head and regarded me thoughtfully before nodding.

"You do that, but don't push it," Noah agreed.

Before he left the car, he shot me one last heated look.

"Are you sure you don't want to come up? Kiss it better maybe?" Noah said with a cheeky wink.

A twinge of heat fizzed inside me. He looked like a little boy who wanted to open his Christmas presents early and my mouth broke out into a full-on smile, I even laughed. I don't think I had ever or would ever meet someone like this man, one who made me feel things I knew I shouldn't be feeling. But it was difficult, when Noah turned on the charm, it actually did make my knees go weak. In my subconscious, I knew he had always had power over me and now, I was gradually starting to understand why. Sexual chemistry just flowed between us. Natural. It should *never* have come to that, considering how he had treated me at school; but I only had so much control. The body really did have a mind of its own.

"I think I'll pass Noah. Goodnight and don't get that dressing wet."

His eyes dropped to my lips and he suddenly looked like a drowning man.

"Goodnight Lucy," he whispered softly. My own gaze was drawn to the softness of his bottom lip.

Noah didn't try and kiss me. He unclipped his belt and then negotiated his *huge* body out of the car. It was awkward and cumbersome and he cursed as he hit his head on the roof again whilst climbing out. I bit my lip to suppress my smile.

My eyes rolled of their own accord at the disappointed thrum I felt by the fact that he didn't try to touch me. But why would he, I was just another in a long line of females drowning with lustful thoughts about him. The guy would have his pick of girls; I was getting ahead of myself if I thought I would *ever* be one of them. And did I even want to be, no of course not.

I thought back to the girl at Nate's pool party. He'd probably had sex with her that very evening.

I drove back to my house with a million unanswered questions in my head and a craving feeling in my body, that I knew only one boy could feed.

* * *

When I got home, I felt exhausted. It was dark, even though it wasn't that late, winter weather and all that.

I entered the house and took off my coat. My dad was sitting in his reading chair and I kissed him on the cheek, his skin was ice cold and I pulled the throw across his knees and further up his legs.

We had a brief conversation, but I didn't go into detail about what had happened at the surgery. Dad had this habit of not looking at me when I was talking and I found it upsetting.

When I got upstairs, a jet of alarm shot into me. David was in my bedroom!

Anxious adrenaline burst through my chest. What the heck?

"David, what are you doing in here?" My tone was firm, and of course, it needed to be when dealing with my brother.

He didn't look guilty for being there; he just stood with careless indifference. He knew he wasn't allowed in my room after that last time. I swallowed at the thought.

I pushed my door wider. He was standing beside my bed and he turned at the sound of my voice. As he saw me a strange expression twisted his face and my heart started to pump faster, like it was trying to break free from behind the cage of my ribs.

"David?" I shot out again, planting my hands on my hips. My palms started to itch.

My last words knocked him out of his trance.

"I'm checking your radiator, to see if it's off. As I said, no more heating on in the bedrooms."

He was *lying*, I could feel it, and he was standing *nowhere* near the bloody radiator. Something was wrong and I felt unease race through me, but what could I do? In his current state, my dad would be no help.

"OK, well. As you can see, I turned it off as you asked.

He ignored me, nodding toward my stomach, "What's that?"

"What?" I glanced down.

"Is that blood?"

There was a dash of Noah's blood on my tunic, "Yes," I confirmed, not wanting him to be worried.

His face scrunched up. "Is that animal blood?"

Of course, he wasn't far wrong, Noah could be considered an animal. I twisted my reply slightly.

"Yes, I helped out today with another injured dog." It wasn't a total lie and so I knew I wouldn't need to repent. To be honest, I couldn't remember the last time I had. Life seemed to have become too hectic to focus on religion lately.

Batting off the thought I focused on my brother.

David appeared intrigued by the news and his look became thoughtful. "Colin Kettering said something at church that there appeared to be a flurry of injured dogs turning up. Foul play maybe?"

I nodded and dropped my hands to my sides. "Yes, we've had a few at the surgery," I replied honestly.

David dashed a hand down his jaw.

"I'll say a few words on Sunday, ask everyone to be vigilant. I know there have been puppy farms in the area before."

"That would be good, thank you, David."

"Are you coming on Sunday?" David asked, a strange, half-pained expression twisting his features.

"Yes, of course," I replied, giving him the answer that he wanted. I usually enjoyed church, but at that moment, the thought of going to service was like a looming headache that no pill would fix.

His question reminded me of my cousin Katy's forthcoming wedding. David hadn't given me a solid answer as to if he and dad intended to go yet. I was pretty sure that they wouldn't. Our families had drifted apart when my mother left us; Katy's mum was her sister and it got a bit awkward after that. David and Katy had also never *really* warmed to each other. I blamed David of course. As I said, my cousin worked with people who had mental health issues. She'd probably secretly psychoanalysed him and didn't like what she'd unearthed.

To be honest, I still wasn't sure that I would go, I still had no plus one and *nothing* to wear either.

David took a moment to answer before he said, "Dad isn't going, so I probably won't bother. We never really got on. I'm surprised she invited us to be honest."

So, dad was a no; too much risk of running into his sister-in-law who like me, also looked like my mother.

"We'll I may go, show my face. It's nice that they've made the effort."

David remained silent, adding to the oddness of the atmosphere.

"Anyway, thanks for checking the radiator."

He nodded before reluctantly leaving my room.

I listened to the sound of his footsteps as he went downstairs before doing what I always did; closing the door and locking it.

Throwing myself onto my bed, I pulled out my phone, scanning through a couple of messages I'd received from my Uni friends on our WhatsApp group. I keyed in a few replies here and there. As I was about to place my phone on the bedside table, SATAN flashed up.

Thank you for looking after me today and sorry for being a dick.

My lips tugged into a smile.

You're welcome. How's the arm?

'SATAN is typing…' appeared. I briefly toyed with the idea of changing my nickname for him to Noah and then decided against it. Yes, my feelings had softened toward him but he was still the source of all evil.

Still hurts like a bastard. He replied. I was becoming numb to his colourful use of language.

Well, take care and don't do anything taxing. I thumbed back.

Like a sad case, I waited, a little too eagerly for his response.

Thank fuck it's not my wanking arm. I almost fell off the bed and an automatic giggle left my lips. The guy had no filter at all.

I know you're just trying to shock me, Noah.

An image of Noah 'bashing the bishop' as my friend Melanie would say, shot into my thoughts. OMG, I so hoped he wasn't doing *that* whilst he was texting me.

When the time comes, I'll do more than shock you Red.

A flare of lust jetted into me. It appeared I was turned on by a text message conversation. My body really was letting the side down.

I held off replying to that one; I needed to shut this down. SATAN is typing appeared again and I actually held my breath.

What are you wearing?

And that one did the trick and I cut him dead. **Goodnight Noah.**

I still went to sleep with the meatiest of smiles, my thoughts and dreams well and truly taken over by SATAN himself.

Five

Being a Good Samaritan, the next day, I decided to drive over to Noah's place to check on him. It was the weekend and I imagined the garage would close at noon. I purposefully timed my arrival so that I wouldn't be interrupting anything. Not that I thought he'd be able to do much work with his injury anyway.

As I pulled up and parked my car, I made my way over to the entrance where a boy was in the process of closing the shutters. He wore garage overalls; obviously one of Noah's sidekicks.

As I approached, his eyes swelled and he did that looking-you-up-and-down thing boys did when they were interested.

He introduced himself as Alex and was actually quite charming. He was outrageously flirty to the point where I must have blushed to the roots of my hair. He made me feel attractive and feminine. It was nice.

His tall frame was quite gangly and he had blonde hair, blue eyes, and boyish features. I imagined him to be younger than me, possibly still in his teens.

Just before I could ask where Noah was, that booming voice I knew only too well roared out from within the belly of the unit; he definitely had the voice of a demon.

"Alex, are you closing the fucking shutters or what?" Noah's voice was ruthlessly commanding.

My walking tormentor then appeared at the entrance, clearly surprised to see me. He looked fit enough to eat, drat the man. Why did he have to be so attractive, even when he'd been working with oil and rust? It just wasn't fair. Shouldn't he look like a big, sweaty mess?

"Red? Can't keep away can you," he drawled. This time his overalls were fully up and fastened, covering his torso. How did he still manage to look so beautiful in such basic work gear? Noah was like a dark terrifying angel that destroyed any willpower with just one look.

I ground my teeth and stepped away from Alex.

"I was in the area," I lied with a smile, sounding thoroughly unconvincing.

His eyes narrowed and he directed a glance between me and the younger man, who was in all truth, standing way too close to me. Noah's dark eyes hardened and his mouth compressed into a thin line. He looked thoroughly ticked off.

Alex suddenly looked really guilty; his eyes pinned to his boss's face. As if he knew he'd stepped on some toes or something; which was of course a silly notion. It's not like Noah was my boyfriend.

"Fuck off then. Go home. I'll lock up," Noah blasted hotly with a flick of his head. His deep voice reverberated through his chest.

Alex jumped to attention. I was surprised he didn't salute. "K, see you Monday Boss. Laters Lucy," he responded respectfully before disappearing.

"Little shit, I take it he was all over you like a rash?" he questioned with a not-too-pleased look on his face. It was odd really, how could he be jealous? Although on second thoughts, Noah probably viewed me as his personal plaything; a toy; his own doll to torture.

"It's OK. He was just doing what most members of your sex do around me," I replied, not wanting to get the boy into trouble for harmless flirting. I scrunched my nose at how conceited I must have sounded.

"He was quite charming; I imagine he has a talent for attracting the ladies," I added, trying to suggest that Noah wouldn't have a clue how to behave around a lady.

He didn't like that and his face darkened, his expression bleak.

He cocked his head, staring down that perfect, judgemental nose. "Oh, he has a talent all right. The guy can belch the entire alphabet," he declared, his face twisting into a smirk.

I shook my head with a 'whatever' look; there was little comeback to that one.

Alex drove passed us and waved, and not being rude, I returned it. Noah shot him the deadeye before turning back and unashamedly checking me out, or at least what I was wearing. Something I didn't recognise flaring in his eyes.

"Laura Ashley's still doing a roaring trade I see," he announced with an amused tone.

Again, he made fun of my clothes and I felt a throb of annoyance. "Very funny. I didn't come here to trade insults with you."

"No? What did you come for?" There was a glint in his eyes; I was starting to see the 'tells' of this boy's cards much quicker now. I thought back to that article I'd read in a magazine that men thought about sex around seventy percent of the day; as far as Noah was concerned, that was probably an accurate figure.

"So, do you want to come up? See my man-cave? You know, *do* stuff?" His voice dripped with sexual innuendo.

A strange feeling kicked into my gut as I responded, "No, I didn't come here for *that* either and you need to get those types of thoughts out of your head."

He rolled his shoulders and then cracked his knuckles.

"Or what? What are you going to do if I don't? What if I decide to kiss you again?"

Everything was about a challenge with this guy. He was the most argumentative person I knew.

I blinked before pointing out, "Well, you know what happened last time," I said tartly, reminding him that I'd retaliated. He'd accused me of having no backbone in the past but I'd lashed out, surely those actions had proved him wrong.

"Oh yes, I had forgotten about that," Noah answered as he leaned against the doorframe; one hand massaging his cheek thoughtfully. I never thought for one minute that he'd forgotten about it.

"I must admit, I was quite surprised. The little mouse can roar. You high-tailed it out of there quite quickly though," he drawled.

"Of course I did and I won't say sorry, you deserved it." My voice shook slightly as a strange light appeared in his eyes. Thoughts of retribution maybe? I glanced around, it was quiet, but at least we were *outside* and not in his building. I could easily walk to my car if I needed to. The fact that I didn't want to, slightly bugged me.

Noah shoved off the frame and came to stand inches away. We were so close that I could see the tiny lines at the corners of his eyes. Wise eyes that had seen and done things I could only have imagined. My thoughts drifted to his time in the army and I wondered fleetingly again why he'd left.

His next comment dragged me back.

"I don't *expect* you to say sorry. I'm glad you did it, it's been long overdue," he admitted.

I almost swallowed my tongue. "Well, *that* wasn't the response I expected."

He wasn't listening, his eyes were roaming over my face before coming to rest on my lips.

"I accept that I go too far sometimes, I'm not totally ignorant."

My eyes widened in shock at that one; was that his way of an apology, as let's face it; as far as sorrys went, it blew.

His eyes were now zeroed in on my mouth and I felt a frisson skate over my skin. Something pulsed and blazed between us. My reaction was difficult to hide. The guy was sex on legs, he knew *exactly* how much power he had over the fairer sex and I was no different. I just had to keep telling my head to keep my body in line. It would be so easy to let go with this guy; irrespective of how part of me still disliked him.

Before I could stop my thoughts which I appeared to be overly processing; I wondered how many girls he had been with. Probably tons. I strategically positioned this thought to the forefront of my mind, maybe this fact would help with my restraint

Suddenly, my meanderings were smashed away as Noah lunged forward and grabbed me by the arm, hauling me toward him. My breath whooshed from my lips with surprise and my mouth dropped open.

He held me in place, his grip strong around my non-existent bicep. I noted he held me with his uninjured arm.

Noah lowered his head and spoke down into my face; his voice was relatively soft which was a contrast to how roughly he held me.

"You still taste as sweet as you look. I knew you'd come apart for me. Your tongue remembered mine, Lucy."

A little tremor of excitement ran through me and I placed my free hand on his chest to steady myself.

"You were out of control, Noah."

He moved his gaze from my mouth to my eyes, before announcing, "Actually, you're wrong. You're lucky I'm a restrained kind of guy. At least kissing is done to instil pleasure, you wouldn't believe the number of times I've wanted to shake you until your teeth rattle."

A cocktail of excitement and alarm shot through me.

"I don't understand how I can generate that level of emotion when we don't even know each other, not really."

"You're just one of those girls that needs fucking Lucy, to pound some life into you. And you enjoyed my kissing you, your head can lie, but your body can't."

"You're outrageous." I was flustered now.

"Shall we put it to the test?"

Here we go again. My nose twitched with irritation but I ignored his shaking threat, "You force-kissed me without my permission again and you just can't do that," I said a little breathlessly. I could feel pockets of heat all over my body. That memory of his mouth against mine was replaying in my head; and oh lord, what a mouth it was.

Noah released me suddenly, almost throwing my arm away from him.

After a moment of silence, he folded his arms again and gave me a steady look. My hand dropped to my side and I resisted the urge to rub my skin where his fingers had been. He hadn't hurt me but it tingled.

"You give me permission to touch you, *every* time you look at me," he whispered, his eyes locked on mine.

My reaction to these words was pure heat and I purposefully lowered my head; closing my eyes. "As I've said before. You're deluded." My tongue sneaked out to moisten my lips which were suddenly warm like his mouth had only just been there. I remembered how steady his heartbeat had been within his chest when mine had been thumping like the hooves of a racehorse.

"You keep saying that, but your body is blatantly at war with your head. Your nipples are hard, even now and it's nothing to do with the fucking temperature. You come alive when I'm near you. You want me, you just don't *want* to want me."

He was right of course and I *hated* how well he read my response to him. I'd come to see him with good intentions but it appeared my body had not.

"You're wrong. I'd have to be mentally impaired to fancy you," I lied, suddenly feeling flustered again. The tone of my voice was brittle.

He ignored my insult and his nostrils flared like he could smell something; probably burning, as my pants were surely on fire.

"You know it isn't good to store up all that pent-up sexual frustration, it could make you go blind," Noah preached cockily.

"You seem to do just fine," I pointed out, my thoughts darting back to the girl at the party.

"I don't have any pent-up sexual frustration, Lucy. I deal with mine in the shower."

And my tongue fainted.

Noah actually managed to lower the tone even further. If there was a ruler of the dirty-minded people, Noah would be it.

I moved back slightly, I needed space. My face must have been bright red.

Noah continued to look down at me, his head dipped. "Just admit it, Lucy, you've always had the hots for me."

Sucking in a sharp breath, I then choked out a laugh, "You're mad. You're rough and uncivilised. Not exactly things a girl wants in her dream man and I think I do hate you actually," I pointed out with a definite tone of my own. Again, another lie. I didn't hate this man, had probably *never* really hated him, but there were certainly parts of him I didn't like.

His pupils widened and he tutted. "Why? Because I'm honest?"

I suddenly felt tongue-tied as I knew *I* wasn't being honest. There had always been something between us but I'd preferred to bury it. I knew I needed to do that again really as nothing could come of it. Nothing apart from what happened in my dreams and let's face it. That was all physical stuff, coming from that part of my brain that I couldn't control.

His eyes narrowed at my silence. "Be careful now, you don't want to hurt my feelings. What would your little church think of that?"

Here we go again with the church stuff, I shot him an unimpressed glower and snorted.

"I doubt a ten-ton truck could hurt *your* feelings. Yours has to be one of the toughest hides I've ever had the misfortune to meet. You're like a rock. Impenetrable."

"Oh, you'd be surprised. I have a softer side," he went on, totally not offended.

"You do? Well, I think I'd prefer that version to this one. You make me□—" I cut myself off from what I had been going to say. I didn't want to admit that he knocked me off-kilter, made me question myself; *forced* me into a state of confusion.

Noah lowered his head, his face so close to mine, I could feel his breath in my hair.

"□—What? What do I make you Lucy?" he whispered gruffly. The air felt charged and heavy.

Sighing, I shrugged before squaring my shoulders.

"I don't know, so many different things, but believe me when I say, *none* of them are good." I stabbed my hands through my mane of hair. My naughty thoughts were *not* good for me, so I wasn't lying.

"But at least you feel *something*, which is better than walking around like you're half asleep all the time," he delivered with insulting ease.

Luckily, I managed to refrain from stamping my foot like a toddler.

"I do *not* walk around like I'm half asleep thank you very much. Where do you get off saying that to me?" The guy had hit a nerve.

"Yes, you do. Like I said before like a robot and the person who programmed you is your *fucking* brother. He yanks your chain, and the church, in turn, yanks his."

A headache was now approaching and I started to regret my decision to visit him. I hated talking about David, it brought all sorts of unpleasant feelings back.

"Please leave David out of this… this…"

"What? This thing between us?" he supplied with a provocative look. The guy was arrogant beyond belief.

I dashed my hands down my face. The man could frustrate a saint.

Tilting my head, I drilled him a look. Hoping my words would penetrate his thick skin. "For the last time. There is no 'thing' between us." Of course, at the very back of my mind; that place I kept my secrets. I knew I was in denial.

"And that's where you're wrong Red, there's definitely a 'thing'. Stop playing hard to get and accept that." His determination should have been applauded.

Noah shoved his hands into the pockets of his overalls before rocking back on his heels, staring down at me thoughtfully.

"Am I the only one who has ever touched you?" he questioned; his tone now quite serious; that voice rough and raspy. I felt like I'd just come off a roundabout in a kid's playground. "You certainly taste like it."

"What do you mean?" I said weakly, not appreciating the fluttering in my chest his words evoked.

"Am I the first man to kiss you, touch you? Sexually I mean?" Noah reached down and idly wrapped a curling strand of chestnut hair around his hand. Rubbing it through his fingers as if needing to feel its softness.

My frame stiffened into defensive mode.

"That's *none* of your business really. We hardly know each other and that's not something I'd share with the boy who used to pick on me at school. You'd probably just end up using any detail to your own advantage."

He grinned, a tell-tale sign in his eyes. "That's a yes then."

I released a puff of air before rolling my eyes, "OK, yes. You're the only one. So, what. It won't be that way forever, so you can take that smug look off your face."

He drew his bottom lip into his mouth with his teeth before stating.

"We'll see. What if I intend to keep it that way? Maybe I'll decide to tell the Tom Wade's of this world to back the fuck off."

Grimacing, I stated in a fairly steady voice, "I don't think I gave you permission to play the possessive boyfriend card. And besides, I'm not seeing Tom. He's with a girl called Sophie now. They met at Nathan Lane's pool party of all places."

Noah's grin widened. "When he was supposed to be with you? Ouch, that must sting?"

I pursed my lips.

"It doesn't bother me actually. We were never really a thing or anything, he didn't even kiss me."

Noah was pleased by the news.

"I'll let him live then," he said with an air of finality.

I narrowed my eyes, "I should think so. He pretty much saved the day yesterday."

He yanked his hands from his pockets and rubbed at his face like he was suddenly trying to wake himself up.

"He stuck a needle in my arse, Lucy, I doubt he'll get the fucking medal of honour," Noah bit out abruptly. He was obviously still sore about that in more ways than one.

"You are so ungrateful," I tutted, shaking my head, my hair falling down my chest.

He watched the movement before taking another chunk and this time, he brought it to his face and inhaled. Not in a Hannibal Lector-type of way. His eyes closed for a second as he took in the scent before he released it and looked down at me.

"Did you just smell my hair?" I attempted to sound like I thought it odd behaviour and he had the sense to look slightly ruffled.

He motioned toward me with a flick of one wrist, "Well, what do you expect? It's all coconutty and shit," he replied with a tone.

I raised an eyebrow. "Right on the first ingredient, not so much the second."

His eyes widened and he shot me a look of surprise. "So, you *do* have a sense of humour."

Noah folded his large arms again.

He was such a smug sod. I decided to try and annoy him, see if I could knock him off his perch.

"Anyway, maybe I want someone like Tom? Predictable, calm, and safe. Someone who's nice to me for a start."

"Sounds about as exciting as a fucking tomato. Is that *really* what you want in your man?" Noah growled in a deep, thick voice. A muscle started to tick in one of his exotic cheekbones.

It suddenly felt like someone was beating my nerves with a hammer.

"Well, I don't want someone who is overbearing and stomps all over me either," I shot back, motioning toward him with my palm.

My words took him aback and he frowned.

"I don't do that. Not really. As I said, I'm trying to help you. You lost your way, Lucy, ever since your mother left. You need dragging out of that shell you've locked yourself away in."

Noah hit another nerve by bringing my mother up.

"I would ask you to leave my mother out of your assessment of me, thank you very much." I wasn't really *that* upset. I only felt a heavy numbness when I thought of her now.

His eyes narrowed before he carried on regardless. "My point is that there is more to you than meets the eye and once all that locked-up fire inside of you is released, we're all in for one hell of a ride."

I watched as Noah unfolded his arms and ran his fingers down my arms. I suppressed a shiver as he added quietly, "And I personally, am looking forward to the firework show."

Shaking myself out of that dangerous zone where I allowed Noah to lure me, I remembered the main reason I was there and it wasn't idle chatter. My meaner side kicked in and I suddenly had an overwhelming desire to mess him up and ruffle some man feathers. Surely, we all had at least one thing that drew us out of our comfort zone. Noah's own personal nightmare popped into my head; *religion*, the church!

Pushing my clever idea to one side temporarily, I said. "If I were to bare my soul with anyone, I cannot imagine it would be to you, Noah. Anyway, this is a pointless conversation." I quickly changed the subject before he could comment. "How's the arm today, any better?"

He drew said area up to his face and flexed his fingers. "It's sore but I'll live. I've had worse."

"What you need is to rest it, Noah."

"What I *need* is some rough angry sex to take my mind off it," he contradicted tersely.

I rolled my eyes, here we go again. "I don't think *that* would be a good idea at all."

His eyes were locked onto my face, his expression suggestive; like I was the other party involved. The guy must be sex-starved if he was imagining rough, angry sex with me. Before I could stop it, an image of what that might look like popped into my head. I tried to ignore the treacherous excitement that gushed through me.

I redirected my kinky thoughts. "Have you heard anything from Tom about the dog?"

He blinked, shaking himself out of his own probable perverted reverie, "I'm going to call Tom later to see how it is. I wonder if he's been able to save it."

His empathy should have been refreshing, but I was too engrossed in my sudden decision about how to make Noah pay.

"Anyway, if your arm starts to ache or anything, maybe pop to the practice on Monday, so Tom can change the dressing," I suggested helpfully.

He shot me a twisted look. "I suppose you think I belong at the vet's instead of the doctors, me being so uncivilised; like an animal."

"If the cap fits," I said with a grin, challenge in my eyes.

"Sammy Smith from school said you were an animal in bed," I pointed out with a slight kink in the middle of the sentence. Why I was going *there* was anyone's guess.

"Did she," his voice was a purr and I cleared my throat.

I ran my tongue over the seam of my lips to moisten them, they suddenly felt dry. Noah's gaze flickered, watching the movement before his mouth curled into a sexy smile.

"You're such a prick tease," he said, his eyes narrowing slightly.

He wasn't upset, he was turned on. The silence stretched between us like we were sharing a moment before the atmosphere switched. Refusing to accept that there was anything special between us, I changed the subject.

"Anyway, on that note, I've decided to call in the favour you owe me." I thought back to all his nasty comments about my church. It was time to reap some karma.

He quirked an eyebrow. "Already?"

"Yes, why not."

He shot me a pained expression and splayed a large hand across his chest, rubbing his hand across the area in circular movements.

I straightened my shoulders and delivered the news. I had chosen one of the things I knew he would *hate* the most. It appeared I did have a bit of the devil inside me after all.

"I want you to come to church with me tomorrow."

And BOOM, after all his talk about fireworks. Noah himself lit up like a rocket and I turned on my heel and headed for my car, my back against the fallout. He swore several times, again not in English but you could tell they were curse words.

I actually enjoyed it as he shouted that he'd 'rather die than set foot in my church.'

"Come on Noah, you might like it," I shouted back, facing him over the roof of my Mini.

"I seriously doubt that," he returned dryly, his voice raised slightly to be heard across the yard. He just stood there *glaring* at me with his hands on his hips and his feet apart. His stance screaming his annoyance. I was surprised he hadn't come after me to be quite honest.

"There's a chance you can be saved; we could make you into a better man," I suggested, thoroughly enjoying myself.

"Going to church *once* is *not* going to make me a better man Lucy, so why attempt the impossible? I am who I am. This is me. *I'm* not the one pretending to be something I'm not."

Noah continued to glare back at me and I grinned cheekily.

"Whatever. You're so full of it. You're scared, admit it."

He nodded. "Yes, I am scared; *terrified* of dying of fucking boredom, listening to the rantings of a bunch of easily led morons," he belted.

"I dare you."

And the gauntlet was laid. I knew at that point that he'd come. There was *no way* he could walk away from a blatant challenge. It just wasn't in his nature.

And my last words were…

"Pick you up at nine in the morning and please wear something other than those bloody overalls." And I blew him a cheeky kiss before throwing myself into my car.

His face suggested that he wanted to drag me back by my hair.

The triumph I felt as I drove away felt awesome. I could see him in my rear-view mirror holding two fingers up and it made me laugh even more.

I was actually having fun at someone else's expense and it felt great.

Had little old me got one up on the big bad wolf? It appeared so.

* * *

After leaving Noah, I decided to nip into Scarborough to do some shopping. Although it had taken me a while to come to a decision, I would go to Katy's wedding and I needed a dress.

Whilst I was checking the racks in one of the more expensive boutiques, Natalie Savvas appeared. It was a shock at first but it turned out to be a pleasant one.

She was *really* friendly, explaining that she was working there temporarily to cover the Christmas period when the store was at its busiest. There were two other people in the shop, but she appeared to give me her undivided attention.

Natalie immediately knew who I was from school, which was refreshing, and she was so different from what I remembered. Super nice. She'd have to be, of course, me being a customer. But she even engaged in small talk and I didn't feel uncomfortable having to talk about my dress size or anything. She complimented my figure several times and made me feel at ease.

We spoke about school briefly and I tried to stay away from any conversations about her brother, but the plan failed when she said.

"I remember Noah used to have it in for you," she confessed unashamedly.

I took the dress she passed me to try on through the curtain of the changing room.

My voice came out as a croak. "Yes, he wasn't the nicest."

"I hope you didn't take it personally. He was twat to most people at school. His friends were the same," Natalie said as I removed the black gown off the hanger.

"I saw you guys talking at Nate's party. I take it you're on better terms now?"

I almost blew a raspberry but managed to stop myself.

"Not really. Could you help me with the zip please," I asked, hoping to change the subject. Natalie pulled the curtain back and secured the dress for me.

We both looked at my reflection in the mirror before Natalie shook her head in denial.

"Nah, that's not right. The black makes you look like Casper. You're too pale to wear black."

I totally agreed with her and she turned me around and helped me with the dress before closing the curtain again.

The long blue dress she'd given me earlier still sat on the hanger. It wasn't the type of number I'd usually go for but I tried it on anyway.

"Take what he says with a pinch of salt. He's been a moody sod ever since he left the army," she said, her voice distant, suggesting she'd moved away.

I saw my opportunity. "Why did he leave?"

There was a beat of silence before she said from outside the curtain again.

"All I can say is that he *had* to leave. You'll have to speak to Noah for the whole story. It's not really for me to say."

I appreciated her loyalty toward her brother. She spoke about him like they were quite close. How I would have liked to have had a close, *normal* relationship with a sibling. What I had with David was like a car crashing in slow motion.

After trying on several dresses, I went for the first dress Natalie had chosen. It was backless and not something I would usually have dared wear but she was so encouraging. Wearing it would certainly be up there with me doing some seizing again.

Noah's comment about me dressing like someone's mother and the Laura Ashley gibe swam around my head whenever I was standing in front of my wardrobe.

I thanked Natalie for her help and bought the dress.

As I stood in my bedroom later that night, I wondered whether to ask Tom to be my plus one, but wouldn't that look pathetic, considering he sort of had a girlfriend now? The thought of going to a party alone gave me a sick feeling. Then thoughts of Noah popped in there, but I shooed them away. He probably didn't even own a suit.

And anyway, I wasn't *that* desperate, was I?

I buried the thought. Nope, going with Noah wouldn't do at all. I certainly didn't want to feed that pull I felt toward him.

Nothing good could *ever* come from it.

Six

Considering it was winter, it was a bright crisp Sunday morning and fairly mild.

After showering and washing my hair, I left it loose, applied a minimal amount of makeup, and then pulled on sheer tights and my favourite dress. It was a wool wrap-around dress in dark green that tied at the waist. It had a slashing neckline which revealed a hint of cleavage (still respectable enough for church), falling in an A-line just below my knees. I loved how it complemented the smallness of my waist and accented my boobs (but not too much) and the contrast of the colour against my red hair was spot on.

My father was at the table eating breakfast when I walked into the kitchen. Kissing his cheek, I pinched a slice of his toast and explained that I was going to David's service. He didn't even look up from his coffee.

When I got to Noah's, he was standing outside on the pavement looking sorry for himself and I couldn't hide my smile. To be honest, I was surprised I didn't have to bang on the door and prise him from the building.

My heart stammered in my chest. He had scrubbed up and was wearing, black chinos and a dark maroon jumper. The work boots were gone and, in their place, a pair of brogues; it even looked like he'd polished them. He still didn't look like anyone I knew who attended church, but he looked tidy and handsome and I was pleased he'd made an effort.

As he approached my car, I noticed the shadows beneath his eyes. He looked tired but still drool-worthy. I couldn't seem to erase my attraction and I wondered fleetingly if he did have a girlfriend. Who was I kidding? He probably had a different one each week, if my memory of school was anything to go by.

Noah clambered awkwardly into the car, favouring his bad arm. I didn't have my coat on and I saw him flash a look at my body, but he didn't comment on my dress. I wasn't sure how I felt about that as I had worn it with him in mind.

"I can't believe I'm actually doing this, and on a bloody Sunday," were his first words which were grunted out. His eyes were fierce and his jaw set like stone.

As I pulled the car away from the curb, I shot him a smile. "You never know, there may be a place in heaven for you yet, Noah?" My tone was playful but he still shot me down with a scowl, shrugging nonchalantly.

“I imagine hell is way more fun,” he replied with a twist to his lips. “And if you’re trying to save my soul, let me tell you; you’re too late. Especially considering what I’ve been doing all morning,” Noah added with a wicked look. I knew *exactly* what he was referring to.

“Nice,” I replied flatly which encouraged a further saucy look.

We drove in silence for a while before he asked. “How long is this thing anyway? I need to go back to bed, I’m knackered.”

“I’m not surprised if you’ve been doing *that* all morning,” I replied grimly.

My comeback surprised him.

Rolling my eyes, I answered his question. “The service usually lasts around half an hour. How is your arm?”

“Still hurts like a motherfucker,” he said but I didn’t flinch.

“You should have texted me. I’d have understood if you’re not feeling right.”

“No, I’d rather get it over with,” Noah said in a muted tone.

“Maybe I should take you to the walk-in centre so they can check you’re bandage?” I suggested.

“No, it’ll be fine,” he huffed whilst readjusting his seat belt. He really was a fidget. The guy couldn’t sit still. I could smell a slight twinge of aftershave. It was extremely masculine and heady and it tantalised my senses. I glanced across at him, he was such a huge person. He took up most of the space in my car.

“You do know I’m only doing this to score brownie points with you,” he suddenly said, his tone less moody. I saw him glance at my legs. My tights were flesh-coloured instead of the usual black. I wondered if he liked what he saw.

“Brownie points? Is that your way of telling me you were in the brownies? Isn’t that a girl’s only club?” I grinned as I changed gears.

“You know what I mean,” he replied in a flat voice. He wasn’t his usual jokey self and I imagined this was due to no sleep and the looming visit to church. Even tired and grouchy, I was still attracted to him.

My goodness, the ladies going to church that morning had a treat in store. The old biddies that attended David’s Sunday service would probably pass out when they saw Noah in all his manly glory. Old women were the worst when it came to good-looking men.

“So, you have a game plan. You’re trying to get into my good books by agreeing to come to the service, is that what you are saying?” I flung back, translating his code.

He shuffled in his seat again, staring out of the front window. "Not necessarily to get into your good books. I'd prefer to get into something else," he stated bluntly. He delivered the words in a suggestive tone and without any awkwardness; just like he was speaking about the weather.

My chest heaved as the thought of twisted sheets and sweaty limbs surged into my head. I suddenly couldn't get the mental image of us together out of my mind. Bearing in mind we had *just* pulled up outside the church, his comment couldn't have been more inappropriate, but I batted the scolding to one side. If he knew how his words affected me, he'd just become cruder. Noah Savvas liked to shock, there was no doubt about that and I *refused* to give him any more ammunition.

"Can I please ask you to be on your best behaviour?" I stated in a 'don't mess with me voice'; well, my version of one, which was of course still mild and insipid.

"You can ask," Noah began recklessly and then his expression changed. "It's fine Lucy, I have been in a fucking church before you know," he shot back in frustration. My goodness, he *was* in a mood.

"Really?" His confession surprised me.

"Yes *really*, for family weddings and shit."

Ah, of course. I hadn't thought about that. I turned off the ignition and we both climbed out of the vehicle.

As we walked side by side, I saw the little glances he stole my way. I was carrying my coat and had purposefully not put it on. The last time I'd worn this particular dress to church, Mr Haunch and several of the other men had outlandishly leered at me. I knew I looked good in it. I so wanted Noah to compliment me due to all the horrible comments he'd made about my dress sense in the past. But, just my luck; *nothing* apart from the sneaky looks.

The churchyard was busy, lots of elderly, salt-of-the-earth churchgoers, and a handful of grandkids were dotted around, some chatting, others making their way inside. We weaved through the bodies and I said the usual hellos and engaged in small talk here and there. Noah just loomed beside me like a spare part, a tight uncomfortable smile on his face. I noted he also kept fiddling with the collar of his jumper, forever Mr Fidget.

Sheila Simms, a church regular was all over Noah. She was always caked in makeup and wore her bleached blonde hair up in a severe bun. Sheila was a well-known flirt and I managed to successfully steer Noah away before one of her ovaries exploded.

As Noah and I filtered in through the large wooden doors of the church, David was standing inside the archway that led into the nave, greeting people as they came in. A lump appeared in my throat as I remembered how Noah felt about my brother and what he'd said about him. I swallowed hard, I hadn't thought about that when I'd come up with the plan.

Pushing aside thoughts that were now pretty useless I decided it would be OK. We were in church with an audience at the end of the day, how bad could it be?

I smiled up at my brother before reintroducing them, you couldn't not really.

"David, you remember Noah, from school?"

My brother had just finished shaking hands with little Meryl Fredericks. An elderly lady from our village who always smelt like soup. As he turned, his attention moved off me and onto Noah and his face dropped.

"Yes of course, how could I forget? Hello Noah, welcome." David offered Noah his hand.

"David," Noah replied through tight lips, glancing down his nose at David's raised arm. I could see his own hands were still fisted at his sides.

"I must say I'm surprised to see you here," David said with a loaded expression. My heart rate accelerated unevenly as he dropped the hand that Noah had made no move to shake. It was like I wasn't there, my brother paying me no attention at all. He was transfixed on the much bigger man who did actually cast a shadow over him. The fact would have been amusing under different circumstances.

Tension fizzed between them as Noah replied, "That makes two of us," with a smirk. I didn't miss the dangerous undertone. My stomach lurched. There was no mistaking the significant level of dislike that fired between them. I suppose I should have expected there to be some type of atmosphere.

My brother suddenly looked awkward, and considering we were in earshot of several members of the church, his next words surprised me.

"Maybe you'll actually learn something Noah," David said recovering his disposition after the other man's snub, his expression passive and at war with his tone. I felt Noah stiffen beside me and he lowered his head toward the smaller man. There was no comparison between them, David being tall and thin with strawberry blonde hair and Noah, being big and macho with thick black hair.

Noah's laugh was a sharp dismissive grunt before he said, "I *seriously* doubt that David," before stifling a yawn. The atmosphere between them turned my stomach and I suddenly thought Noah was going to walk out and leave me there, so I grabbed his hand. Both David's and Noah's gazes flew down to where I touched him, but before either could comment, I steered us away. I felt Noah's strong fingers stiffen against my palm.

We walked partway between the pews as I usually sat toward the front, but Noah stopped near the back and turned to look down at me.

"I'll sit here. There's no way I'm sitting up front with the little old ladies watching your brother like he's some type of messiah," he said with a flick of his head, a shadow falling across his face. I thought about arguing but decided against it. He was there and that was the point. Of course, he wouldn't want front-row seats.

"Are you sure?"

"Yes, you go. I'll *pretend* to listen from the back."

I nodded, toying with sitting beside him but I could see Mrs Browning waving me over with an urgent expression; like she was worried I'd miss the start. She sat twisted in her seat next to Mrs Haunch, whom I managed to stop myself from sticking my tongue out at.

"OK, I'll see you in a bit." I then watched as he lowered his large body into one of the pews. At least he had space at the back, as no one ever really sat there. I couldn't imagine Noah surrounded by old ladies anyway. The guy couldn't blend in if he tried. He sat there with a pissed-off expression, looking like a Roman gladiator that had been asked to 'sit this one out'.

It was odd really as although I'd blackmailed him to come as a punishment, I was glad he was there. I was also happy that he'd pushed my brother's nose out of joint.

I walked down the aisle, briefly turning back to check he was OK, which was ridiculous really.

I took my seat, attempting to shake off that looming feeling of dread. He was in church at the end of the day, what was the worst that could happen?

* * *

I inhaled sharply, sweeping a glance around the room. Partway through the service, a strange noise emerged from the back of the nave. At first, I'd thought it was coming into the building from outside, maybe one of the tractors working in a distant field, but it wasn't. The noise was coming from a person.

David was delivering the main part of his speech and the sound started to get gradually louder.

Someone was snoring.

It did happen from time to time, one of the elderly men usually, but this sound was different, deeper, and throatier.

At one point, from his position by the lectern, David had to stop speaking and he squinted down the length of the church with a frown, trying to establish where the interruption was coming from. As a particularly loud snort was emitted, David actually dropped his prayer book and a few people in front of me turned with bemused expressions.

As several pairs of eyes appeared in front of me, I also turned; squirming in my seat, partly confused, part mortified. My mouth was hanging open and my eyes were wide like saucers.

Heat crept up my throat. My worst suspicions were confirmed as my eyes landed on the guilty party. It took a moment before my brain registered it was Noah.

He was asleep and snoring, *loudly*; the sound not that dissimilar to said tractor. His head had rolled to the side and he was slouched at an awkward angle in his seat. I spun my head back to the front and bit my lip, David's expression was *murderous* as he continued speaking, now much louder into the microphone. The sound of my brother's drone-like voice and Noah's rattle was a strange combination, it almost sounded like the microphone was feeding back.

Then something totally out of character occurred. The giggles kicked in.

I got the most *overwhelming* urge to laugh, a wave of full-on belly laughs threatening as Noah's rattling pipes echoed around the building. I had to bite my lip to stop myself from releasing that rising flood of humour. I placed my hand over my mouth as my shoulders shook gently, betraying the fact that I was silently amused. The situation was so funny, comical really. Yep, I was definitely going to be banned from church. A couple of kids in a pew across from me started to point at Noah, aka sleeping beauty. The guy had said he was tired earlier.

I toyed with the idea of sliding out of the pew and waking him, but luckily hymn one-two-nine saved me. Everyone stood in preparation to sing and the organ blasted out with gusto. Luckily the noise drowned Noah out.

I smiled as I stood, Mrs Browning allowing me to share her hymn book. As I glanced briefly back at Noah, he was now wide awake, thank goodness. He was sat up, wearing a confused expression, like he'd zoned out and didn't know where he was.

The rest of the service went without hiccups, no more human tractor noises but as everyone was leaving the church, Noah caught his bad arm on the side of the pew and he yelled. "Jesus Christ!"

His blasphemy rained over the churchgoers as he hopped around the aisle clutching his injured arm, blatantly in *excruciating* pain. The groan spewed from my mouth as aghast shocks and disgusted exchanges echoed around us. Talk about fire and brimstone.

Needing to salvage the situation quickly and at least attempt a dignified retreat, I helped Noah down the aisle and ushered him into the churchyard as fast as possible. His face was bright red and his body tense. I could see he was angry, his arm no doubt, still throbbing.

As we got out into the sunshine, he turned on me like a storm cloud and I grabbed his good arm. I certainly didn't want to start arguing in front of everyone. We were already the centre of attention.

"Not here. Whatever you have to say to me can be said in the car," I shot out, my expression probably resembling a schoolmarm. Noah tugged his arm away and he stormed off in the direction of my Mini, his broad back flexing as he stomped away.

A flutter of nerves shot through me at the looming man tantrum fast approaching.

I glanced briefly back at the church doors, where people were streaming out like ants. My eyes briefly met David's. He was upset. His lips were pulled tight and they lacked colour. I turned away, knowing that I'd also have to deal with the fallout from *that* later.

As I got to my car, Noah was leaning against it with his large arms folded across his chest. His brooding expression darkened as he saw me. Anger harshened the fine features of his movie star face.

I replaced my syrupy smile with an 'I want to punch you in the face' look.

"Well?" I cut in before he could blast at me. You could see his annoyance on every taunt grove of his face. He'd hurt himself and he needed to take it out on someone. And yes, I was the one in the firing line.

Noah's eyes narrowed. "I assume that's a rhetorical question as you don't really want to know what I think Lucy. But I can tell you now, you won't *ever* get me in that church again," he stated between tight lips.

"I wouldn't want you there, for once we agree with each other. You do realise you fell asleep and were snoring your head off?" I said, with a touch of sass. Yes, I had felt an uncontrollable urge to laugh, but it had still been embarrassing.

"Like I give a shit," he snarled down at me with undisguised fury. I ground my teeth together.

My voice almost failed me as I couldn't understand why he was so cross. I shuffled nervously on my feet and shot a look behind me. "Calm down Noah. Do you want me to look at your arm?" I offered, which was extremely nice of me considering how obnoxious he was being.

"Why, are you a *fucking* nurse now," Noah huffed stormily. His mood was dangerous but I wasn't scared. Those words still stung like a slap. Or how I could imagine one feeling, having fortunately never been slapped.

I opened my mouth to fight back but nothing came out. Jamming my hands onto my hips, I felt the neckline of the dress part and his eyes moved to that area. A glint of something else appeared in his gaze and he dragged his focus back to my face. He was obviously too angry to go *there* right now.

I dropped my arms again and pulled the fabric of the dress closed. I couldn't have him looking at me like he wanted to ravage me when I was telling him off.

"I'm trying to help and you don't have to yell at me."

I refrained from moving closer and poking him in the chest. Any physical contact at that particular moment would not go down well.

His gaze now smouldered, those dark eyes roaming over my body.

"Right now, I want to do more than yell at you Lucy," he threatened before motioning behind me with a flick of his head. "You're lucky we have an audience."

I swatted the looming feeling of disappointment away. "Well thank goodness for small mercies. You're not to touch me again Noah, in any way. I won't allow it," I replied semi-breathless.

"I could make you eat those words and you *know* it. If I were to take your mouth right now, you'd be *desperate* to feel my hands all over you. And then who knows where it could lead?

He glanced fleetingly at the front of my car. "I quite like the idea of taking you over the bonnet of your car. *Especially* in front of your silly little church."

Heat flared inside me.

"You're disgusting," I choked out.

His voice became sultry. "You'd so want it too," Noah said, now looking at my lips.

The images his words invoked were X-rated. He was mostly right of course, my willpower around this man appeared to crumble every time we were together. My body *did* crave his, I just had to run as far as I could away from that fact. Keep a level head and remind myself how much of a pig he'd been in my company. All those nasty things he'd said at school.

"You're so full of yourself." I practically groaned the words.

He shoved off the car with an animal-like grace and barked. "Get in the car before I change my mind." My stomach was in knots and I felt turned on by his commanding tone.

"Has anyone ever told you you're really bossy?" I huffed with a click of my tongue and he shot me a look of relaxed indifference.

"Frequently. Now get in the car," he repeated sharply.

I exhaled noisily before I shot back. "Shouldn't that be my line, it's my car."

As I unlocked it and set off around the bonnet (which I refused to look at now for obvious reasons), he yanked open the passenger door, glaring at me over the roof. I was surprised the door didn't come off in his hand.

"*Don't* start with me. I'm not in the mood," Noah warned, his eyes narrowing dangerously before he lowered himself to climb in.

"Fine. And please try not to tear my door off?" I shot out before nibbling on my lower lip, nervous knots twisting in my stomach.

In response to my request, he *slammed* it, *really* hard. The whole car shook.

We eyed each other through the window of the driver's door in a clash of wills and I could feel an unfamiliar throb of temper, but I refused to allow it to consume me. I reminded myself, I was always nice and calm. Even when dealing with the Noah Savvas's of this planet. Reluctantly, I climbed in next to his tense, massive body.

The journey back to Noah's was unnervingly quiet; the atmosphere tense as he pretty much sat there like a stiff sulking giant. Why on earth did it feel like I was in the dog house when Noah had made such a spectacle of himself? His profile was resolute, his lips compressed. Gosh, he was a moody sod. His pride had obviously been knocked when he'd injured himself.

As I pulled up outside his place, he unclipped his belt and shot me another dark look. “That's it now, the debt is paid in full,” he said now much calmer. I scanned his face. He really did look tired.

There was a loaded silence between us before Noah said with a tilt of his head, “Did I really fall asleep?” I couldn't stop the smile that spread across my face, but I tried to hide it.

He looked unconvinced. “Why are you smiling, didn't I embarrass you in front of your flock?”

I bit back the chuckle and his expression relaxed.

“I was slightly embarrassed, but it was funny and to be honest. I enjoyed how much it annoyed David.” I replied, that half-hidden smile now tugging persistently at my lips.

Noah rolled his shoulders and flexed his arms. Obviously not comfortable in such a small space. “So, you're actually happy I pissed off your brother? That's rich.”

“Yes, I was actually. Nothing usually fazes him when he's up there. It was refreshing to see him ruffled.”

“See, there is a bad girl in there somewhere. Told you,” Noah said with a smug look and I rolled my eyes, before saying.

“David was *really* cross. He probably thought you were doing it on purpose and as I brought you, no doubt I'll pay for it later.”

A dark look shadowed Noah's features as he digested my words, a frown marking his forehead. “What do you mean by that?”

I shrugged but still replied. “David, he'll be angry. I was the one who brought you after all. No doubt he'll take it out on me as he always does.”

He shot me a steady look. “And *how* would he do that?”

His response puzzled me. “Well, you know, the usual way.”

Noah dashed a hand across his jaw. “No, Lucy, I don't fucking know, what's the *usual* way.”

“He'll shout, you know, *raise the roof* and all that.” I couldn't understand his reaction, there was a cocktail of emotions flickering from the depths of his eyes. We were so close I could see those green flecks.

His gaze was drilling. “And that's it?” Noah said with a twist of his head.

It then dawned on me what he was thinking. “Yes, of course, he isn’t violent if that’s what you’re getting at.”

Yes, David was the proverbial odd-bod and a control freak but he wasn’t aggressive, not really. Cruel rather than violent, I would say.

There was another beat of silence in the car before Noah said in a deep, thick voice.

“*Every* man is capable of violence Lucy.”

I eyed the hard set of his jaw. “Not David.”

He looked at me like I was as thick as a plank before his eyes roamed over my face like he was looking for something. “If you say so.”

His throwaway comment made me feel defensive but before I could question him, he spoke again.

“My bloody arm.”

Noah flexed his fingers, a pained expression crossing his features.

“You knocked your arm pretty hard in church, maybe you should take the bandage off and check it?”

“I’ll be coming into the surgery at some point as I want to visit the wounded. See if the dog I hit is OK.”

My thoughts wafted to the crazy dog situation going on. David mentioned the injured dogs during his speech, asking everyone to be vigilant and to keep an eye out.

“OK, well. I’ll see you at the surgery then. I’m glad you’re getting help,” I replied.

Clearing his throat, Noah said, “Talking of help, you have my number now and if you ever need me, you can call me, anytime. You know that don’t you Lucy?”

His offer to watch my back should have been unwelcomed after his recent behaviour, but I found it strangely reassuring and kind.

“Yes, of course,” I whispered my reply.

Noah was watching me with weird fascination and I suddenly felt his hand touch the back of mine where it was resting on the gearstick. Curling his fingers over my skin he then lifted my hand to his mouth, planting a soft, tender kiss on my wrist. My breath caught in my chest. The skin fizzed where his lips touched and he was watching me, *drinking* me in almost.

A heatwave of pleasure danced up my spine as we sat there in silence, the tense atmosphere from before gone, and the air was now charged with a different element.

I wanted to snuggle into him, suddenly feeling safe and noticed; a catalogue of other emotions I couldn't name spiralled around my insides

Noah's gaze flickered briefly over my body, lingering on my neckline before he said. "Nice dress by the way." My face lit up into a full-on blush and I lowered my eyes as he shot me one last penetrative look before he climbed out of the car.

I drove home with a thousand questions in my head. My morning had been so very different than usual and the emotions I had experienced were mixed and confusing. The one thing I did understand was how my feelings had radically started to change toward Noah.

The truth of the matter had been unspoken as our eyes had tangled. Noah Savvas had gotten under my skin and there was *nothing* I could do about that.

My resistance against him was continuing to slip.

Seven

I woke up around four in the morning and couldn't get back to sleep. The land of Nod just didn't want me there and so I decided to go to work early. The need to check on the dog that Noah had brought in was at the front of my mind. Tom had said she was gradually recovering and considering she was an ex-fighting dog, she appeared relatively tame and loving. 'He' had actually turned out to be a 'she'.

It was still dark outside and I unlocked the front doors of the practice and entered the building. As I switched on the lights and walked further into the waiting area, something was off. The place was much colder than it usually was and I had one of those feelings of not being alone.

Panic flared up in my chest as I heard glass smash, fight or flight kicking in and I hopped from foot to foot, my reflexes in a muddle as to what to do next.

"Hello?"

Nothing. Only silence.

I twisted back to the glass doors which were perfectly intact and were, in fact, the only way into the surgery. Was one of the animals free? I started to doubt what I'd heard as I stared down the corridor into the eerie quiet.

I bumped my hip on the edge of the reception desk as I moved further into the building.

"Hello, is anyone there?" I called out again, my eyes watering. The corridor was long with examination rooms on both sides but the door to the storeroom was ajar. I stopped walking and peered nervously into the room. The light was off but there was a window in there so I could see fairly clearly.

The atmosphere was thick and tense and my chest lurched as a shadow fell across the medicine cabinets that lined one wall. Ice cascaded down my spine.

A burst of adrenaline snaked from my stomach to my chest. Someone had broken into the building! Fear threatened to consume me as full-on panic kicked in.

I rammed my hand into my Tardis-like bag searching for my phone before realising I'd left it on the seat of my car.

I was frozen to the spot, like my feet were stuck with glue and my mouth dropped open, a gasp forcing my lips apart.

"I've called the police!" I lied, my voice quivering, revealing that chill of fear which sat thick in my gut like some type of disease.

The practice phone was around the other side of the reception desk and hearing whoever it was move; there was no way I'd reach it in time.

I forced a swallow.

He then appeared, larger than life in front of me and my breathing accelerated. A strange man with a chilling smile. My hand clutched my chest as real terror jetted into my veins like a fatal dose of heroin, I suddenly felt like I was trapped underwater and someone was dragging me downwards. My throat dried up and I couldn't scream.

The man was tall with a commanding height and he stared across at me with an expressionless face which was scary in itself. My eyes dropped to his hands where he clutched several vials of drugs. OMG, he was a drug addict. I felt a flare of recognition. Did he look familiar to me or was he just the perfect example of the junkies you saw in dodgy dramas on TV?

His huge body shadowed me and through the fog of my horror, I tried to take in as much as possible about his appearance as I dared.

He took a frightening step toward me, his stormy eyes colliding with mine and I raised a hand out to try and ward him off.

"Don't come any closer." Another jolt of fear zapped through me.

My whole body started shaking, anxiety plucking at me.

"Have you really called the police or are you lying?" he said with a sneer, he spoke with a thick, Yorkshire accent. His face was craggy, he had dark hair and scruff on his face and his nose appeared bent out of shape. His eyes were levelled at me like one of those red sight lasers on a gun.

My legs started to wobble and tears gathered in my eyes as we stood there, almost squared off. Which was ridiculous, the guy could crush me like a bug.

My feet felt like they'd been covered with clay.

He pocketed the items he held and moved closer toward me and I gasped as he grabbed my upper arms, shaking me once; hard. "You say *anything* about this and I'll find you," he snarled down into my face. His breath was rank.

I shook my head, pain shooting up my arms from his angry, vice-like grip.

Snatching in a stark breath I panted. "I haven't called them and I won't say anything. Please don't hurt me," my voice sounded like it was coming from miles away.

His grip tightened even more and he dragged me against his body, towering over me like a large threatening monster. I was helpless. My breath was leaving my body like it was being ripped from my lungs by force. My heart thundering in my chest.

"Remember what I said. If I see any police sniffing around here, I'll come for you Carrots."

His mouth tightened and he roughly shoved me away. I almost fell over before he stepped back and regarded me with an odd expression. I couldn't say how long we stood there, staring at each other, but the level of relief I felt as he moved away, escaping through the front doors was euphoric.

My whole body was almost fitting and my arms throbbed from where he had held me. I can honestly say that I had *never* felt fear like it.

Once he was out of the building, I ran around the reception desk to the phone. I called Tom and thankfully he answered after a couple of rings. I bit out what had happened through chattering teeth. My distress was palpable.

After hanging up, I padded around into the waiting area and slumped onto the floor, waiting for rescue. Shock pulsed through my cotton wool-like limbs, making me feel weak. Pressing my back against the reception desk, I pulled my knees up to my chest and sobbed; my breath struggling to exit my lungs.

A silence beyond any silence I had witnessed crept into the building.

* * *

Tom's car screeched into the car park and he ran into the building and dropped to his knees before me. My heart continued to fluctuate.

He pulled me in for a hug, then became all medical-like, checking me for injury. My arms were red from the man's hands but there was no bruising yet. The red welts looked angry against the pale whiteness of my arms.

I explained briefly what had happened as Tom assessed me for further damage before directing me over to one of the chairs in the waiting room, I was still shaking but had managed to stop blubbering. I felt so weak and useless, but what could I have done? The guy had been huge. A massive towering beast. The thought of what he could have done to me chilled my bones.

The shock continued to power through me as Tom started asking me a variety of questions.

“What’s going on?” Noah’s voice suddenly bled into the room, but it sounded like it was coming from a distance. Relief shot through me that he was there. He knocked me out of my comfort zone on a regular basis, but he *always* made me feel safe. I almost ran into his arms, only *just* managing to restrain myself.

Something I had never dared to think, let alone speak aloud became apparent; I suddenly *needed* Noah. Like a flower needs the rain. Gone was the vengeance demon. At that moment he was like a celestial being sent from heaven.

I must have looked a complete fright and I glanced up, the dampness from my tears still there. They stung my cheeks like acid.

Tom put out a hand to stop Noah from rushing forward, but he brushed it away and marched toward me, lowering to his haunches, so we were almost level. His eyes searched my face before he took my shaking fingers in his. Running his thumbs over the backs of my hands to soothe me. I felt some of my earlier fear slide away at the touch. Right now, I needed this guy like I needed the air in my lungs.

Noah’s eyes roamed my face and his jaw tightened.

Tom put a calming hand on Noah’s shoulders. “Everything’s fine, Lucy’s just had a shock.”

My face was burning.

“What type of fucking shock? She’s white as a sheet! What the hell happened?” He thundered up at Tom with raw aggression.

“Please Noah, calm down. I’m still trying to get the facts myself. Some guy broke in and threatened her,” Tom delivered, his rapid voice wavering slightly. “Why the hell are you even here?”

Without turning back to Tom, he lifted his bandaged arm briefly, it must have started bleeding again as there were dashes of red against the gauze. Tom nodded in understanding and continued to watch us silently.

Noah dropped his injured arm, all thoughts of it forgotten about and he moved his face closer and shifted one of his hands from mine, pushing back my hair. The motion was mollifying. I could see he was struggling to control his temper.

After a beat of silence, he quickly assumed a mask of complete control, although it was short-lived.

“Red, Lucy. Tell me what happened. Are you hurt?” he encouraged, attempting to coax the answers he wanted.

I suddenly saw him then, properly. His outraged dark eyes drilled into mine.

"Noah," my throat felt dry as I breathed in a raw undertone.

The look on his strong bronzed profile lifted as I spoke and he attempted to smile reassuringly.

"I'm here, you're safe. What happened?" His deep voice brimmed with authority.

Once he dropped his hand from my brow, I shot forward into his embrace and pushed my arms up around his strong shoulders, burying my face into his neck. He almost fell backwards, obviously not ready for my weight but he straightened and dragged me up with him so we were both on our feet. One arm wrapped around my waist. Noah then lowered his body to allow me to keep my head cradled against his skin.

And the floodgates opened again.

I full-on sobbed against him, blaring as both his arms encircled me, pulling me tighter against his body.

"That's it, just let it out. You're in shock."

And I did just that. In between sobs, I could faintly hear the two men talking over my head. I'd closed my eyes, still sick from that threat of violence.

"Where's the fucker now?"

"We don't know. I don't even know if it *was* Wallis. I didn't see him, she called me and I just found her like this," Tom replied, his own voice still slightly shaken.

"Did he touch her?"

"No, I don't think so. He took some meds."

"Do you think he was a druggy?" Noah questioned.

"No, he took Enrofloxacin. It's an antibiotic to treat dog bites."

"Fucking K9 meds? So, there *is* truth in that dog-fighting shit. He probably needs it to reanimate his fucking champion. Wallis must be the one behind it all. Do you have CCTV here?"

"No, my dad never bothered."

I pulled away and Noah glanced down at me with level dark-as-night- eyes. "Better?"

I nodded, only too aware that I needed to blow my nose, it had definitely been running.

Lowering my arms, I tugged back gently so that Noah released his hold on me. I then moved over to grab a tissue from the reception desk.

I'd never seen Noah look so enraged; his temper even topped that day he'd been bitten. Although he was both angry *and* confused, like for once he didn't have all the answers. Well, that made two of us. It felt like a wrecking ball had gone off in my head and nothing made sense anymore.

Blowing my nose, I threw the tissue into the wastepaper basket and turned toward the two men. I had myself under control now and that strength, that fight Noah continuously tried to evoke, flooded me like a tidal wave in the harshest of weathers.

"Whoever it was, I've seen him before, in my village, recently. He has *something* to do with the injured dogs, I'm *sure* of it," I said, wiping at my cheeks which were still damp.

"It must be happening near my village, we've had two dogs now that were found in Sinnington."

Noah swore under his breath and even Tom looked angry. It came as a surprise as I had *never* seen anything but placid on his face, even when he was pissed off with Ella.

"Describe him again, Lucy," Noah said with a dark look. Starting to pace, now all business.

"He was slightly shorter than you, with dark hair, and a rugged face. I would say he'd had his nose broken in the past. He also had a tattoo on the back of his hand."

The two men exchanged a look before Noah said. "So, he had ink? Can you describe it?"

I wracked my brain, digging back into my memory. "I'm not sure, an insect, like a scorpion or something?"

"That's Wallis," Noah replied, his body set at an aggressive stance.

"As in, Moses Wallis. The guy who used to run a fighting syndicate in town," Tom said, partly to himself.

Noah turned to glance at Tom, before twisting back to me. "So, what everyone thought was Wallis's version of the movie Fight Club, is *actually* a dog fighting club," Noah fumed, temper bouncing off him in waves. He exuded pure masculine power from every pore.

"It would appear so," Tom said, shaking his head in disgust. He looked shattered but of course, he would, animal welfare was his passion, his life.

Noah shot me a compelling look that held me captive, "So, what happened Lucy, don't leave anything out. Do you need to sit down again?"

Noah was so protective and warmth bloomed in my stomach. The feelings that had been developing over the last few weeks were just getting stronger and I could no longer fight them.

I swallowed and firmed up my spine, shaking my head, feeling better on my feet. I did have to lean back against the desk to steady myself, before telling them everything that had happened.

I explained about hearing the glass smash and seeing Wallis come out of the store room, stealing the medicine. Part of me wanted to tone down the bit where Wallis had grabbed me, as I knew Noah would kick off but there was little point leaving it out, my arms were starting to bruise.

Noah took a step forward and inspected the tops of my arms; my skin now wore purple marks.

He battled with his rage, his entire body almost shaking before he released me and jabbed a hand through his hair.

"Motherfucker, I'll kill him." His tone was riddled with pure venom. If you would have heard the way he said it, you'd have believed him. He was ready to commit murder and all because I was hurt. My heart swelled larger in my chest, even amidst the chaos of the situation.

Noah started to pace again before Tom cut in with his thoughts. He was so intelligent and sharp.

"Right, well, we'll need to call the police. Report the break-in and tell them about our suspicions," he suggested.

Panic licked up my spine.

"No, please don't. He said he was watching the surgery and that if he saw any police, he'd come for me. Now I feel sure that I've seen him in Sinnington. He may know I'm connected to the church, where I live even."

"Going to the police is the best thing to do Lucy, for everyone," Tom preached provoking another flare of worry.

There was a beat of silence before Noah interjected. "No."

"*No*, what do you mean *no*? We'll *have* to report the break in any case. We'll need a crime number for the insurance. He smashed the window in the storeroom to get access and the shit he took isn't cheap," Tom returned with a deep frown.

"No. Lucy's right. We need to think about this. The police have about as much finesse as a tank. If this shit is going down where I think it is, they'll go in there, all guns blazing, and the fuckers will get away. We don't even know for definite if they are using Crabtree's old farm. I say we deal with this ourselves."

My ears pricked up at Noah's words as he clearly knew more than he had been letting on. He saw my expression and cast me a look. "I've been doing some digging ever since that mutt tried to tear my arm off."

"Lady Lamb Farm near me? That deserted place?" I put in, taking a step toward the two men.

At my words, Tom looked like he was going to be sick.

I inhaled, mentally coaching myself to say my next words.

"I agree with Noah. We need to handle this quietly, get some facts, and find out *exactly* what is going on. Then when the time is right, we could bring the police in so they can catch them red-handed. The police will need evidence."

Tom and Noah both looked down at me and I saw a hint in Noah's eye; like he was proud of me. My pulse raced at the feelings this thought generated.

It took a little while to convince Tom, he was worried about the crime number and not being able to claim for the damages but he agreed to state it was an accident. His father was visiting another surgery further up North and he was away until the following weekend. That would give us time to tidy and board up the window.

Noah said he was going to involve his friend Connor and I was totally on board with that suggestion. Two big burly guys were definitely needed, especially considering the size of Wallis.

After Tom had re-bandaged Noah's arm, he left, saying how he'd been in touch. Tom and I then opened the surgery for business. He did tell me to go home, but at that moment, I couldn't think of anything worse.

* * *

Later that week, Noah arrived at the practice with a group of his friends, just as I was about to lock up. Tom had been called to one of the local farms to attend to a horse going into premature labour and Marcus was meeting him there.

Noah had been so caring and had texted me every day to check how I was.

The group entered the surgery through the front doors, having parked their cars in the car park. Noah was in the lead and I held one of the double doors open to allow them in.

"I thought you were going to come yesterday for Tom to check your dressing again?" I questioned as he moved to pull the other door wide.

He shook his head, staring down at me. "To be honest it seems fine now. How is he, the dog I mean?" Noah questioned with a flick of his head toward the back of the surgery.

"It's a she?" I informed him.

There was a beat of silence as he drank my comment in.

"That explains it then," Noah said with a smirk.

"How so?" I shot back as the others shuffled into the waiting room.

"Bitches fight dirty," he said with a cheeky grin. This encouraged my own mouth to curl.

Noah and I closed the doors and walked over to join the others. The big guy Connor from the pool party was there as was Nathan Lane. The girl I assumed to be Connor's girlfriend was with them, she walked by his side like she was attached to him. I smothered the pang of envy as she was outrageously beautiful.

She was a similar height to me, slightly taller, and jaw-droopingly gorgeous. Pale, flawless skin, white blonde hair, and clear, bright blue eyes. She was probably the prettiest girl I had ever seen. Perfect. A definite Eve.

She was introduced as Harlow. Such a sweet name too, it suited her. Connor and Harlow were also actually stepsiblings which I imagined must have made things difficult if their parents were together.

We all spoke over each other at first during reintroductions, before switching to possible options on how to deal with what we knew so far. Noah was the most vocal, a definite leader of the pack.

"So, how's this going to work? Bearing in mind, our history with Wallis?" Connor announced in a deep voice. Those huge arms were folded over his chest; his sleeve of tattoos looked as aggressive as their owner. Harlow was standing to the side of him, wearing an expression of adoration.

Noah had said that the boys had been involved in an incident a year or so ago with Moses Wallis and his tribe. So, they all knew of each other which made it tougher for the boys to scope the place out namelessly.

Finding my voice, I decided to pitch my own idea. Noah's had sounded way too dangerous.

“I think we need to avoid any possible trouble. Maybe Harlow and I could drive to the farm in one car and pretend we’re lost or something. You could follow us and park outside in case we needed you. We could see if there is anything at the farm to suggest it’s in use.”

The was a beat of silence as everyone exchanged glances as if trying to identify each other’s thoughts, before revealing their own.

“That’s if you want to, of course, Harlow?”

She smiled and nodded her pretty little head, “I’m up for anything. I hate animal cruelty.”

“Well, what do you think?” I said, directing my question at the boys. They were all looking at me like I’d suddenly grown two heads.

“That’s shit,” Nathan burst out in a monotonous voice.

I forced myself not to react. Gee, thanks, please do say what you mean; don’t sugar-coat it.

Noah’s brows were clamped with fierce concentration and he shuffled uncomfortably beside me and said, “It doesn’t happen often but Nathan’s right. Your plan blows Lucy.” He then flexed the fingers of his bad arm and I wondered how it was healing.

Batting off the unearned sympathetic thought, I planted my hands on my hips.

“Think about it. Two girls pulling up in a Mini, they won’t suspect a thing. If we do get caught, we could flirt and stuff, get them onside. Make them think we’re after a bit of fun or something.”

“So, not happening,” Connor bit out through gritted teeth, roaring to life, his expression bleak as he shot a glance at Harlow.

Her brow scrunched, “I can speak for myself, Connor. I think it’s a good idea, and I’m in,” she said in that melodic voice of hers. We exchanged a smile of understanding. You go girl; my insides screamed.

Connor released a sound, a half grunt, half laugh thing. “You’re not in,” he said, doing that quotation marks with his finger’s thing at the word ‘in’. “Not even *slightly*. In fact, I don’t want you involved at all.”

The proud jut of her nose turned into a wrinkle. “But I want to help,” she responded, looking thoroughly offended and slightly embarrassed by her boyfriend’s dictating behaviour.

"You're not going anywhere near Wallis, Harlow." His gaze was electrified and could have been considered terrifying, but she wasn't fazed by it.

His tone brooked no argument but she had a go anyway and I was impressed by her resolve (even though it was short-lived). She was almost as small as me, but her backbone was obviously twice the strength of mine. I shot Noah a look from beneath my lashes. He also looked impressed and it annoyed me.

Connor watched her as if she *belonged* to him with a stamp of ownership that screamed mine! I experienced a spasm of envy that bled into my disapproval of him. He obviously cared deeply for the girl.

"Connor James Barratt. You're not the boss of me," she shot up at him, her jaw titled at a challenging angle. Yep, he totally was. I found it interesting that she second named him. The girl obviously meant business. "If you go in there all muscle, you'll just end up fighting and that won't help anything."

He stared down into her face, his expression now amused and there was a glint in his eye. Like he was enjoying her attempt to stand up to him. It lasted a few seconds and then the scowl was back. The guy's moods could give a person whiplash.

"Get in the car Harlow," he commanded.

I thought she'd stamp her foot but after a beat of glaring at him, her shoulders slumped. She opened her mouth to argue but Connor cut her off.

"Get in the car, or I'll put you there myself."

She exhaled her frustration, puzzled hurt in her eyes.

"Now."

"*Fine*. Sorry Lucy," she whispered and did as she was told. Well, at least she tried. I couldn't imagine many people standing up to Connor.

I wondered fleetingly when he'd actually moved to Yorkshire. He didn't have a Yorkshire accent but he *definitely* behaved like a guy from the village; rough, outspoken and so sure of himself. A no-nonsense attitude. To be honest, they were all pretty much the same; village mentality and all that; country boys weren't the most subtle of breeds.

I realigned my thoughts on the issue at hand before I said bravely, "OK then, I'll go. Scope it out and then report back." I suddenly felt very aware that I was standing before three huge blokes bristling with male aggression. I probably looked like a jumped-up puppy.

Noah released a frustrated groan and leaned back against the wall. "Fucking hell," he groaned, shooting me a look of ironic disapproval. "You pick your moments to grow a pair, Lucy."

Wasn't *he* the one who said I needed to toughen up?

Batting off the observation, I went with. "Well? What do you think?" I noticed Connor was watching me with a look that sat somewhere between mild fascination and boredom.

Noah shook his head to signify his no. "You're not going alone. I forbid it. Plus, the fucker has seen you now. If you appear there out of the blue, he'll be suspicious." Authority was now oozing out of every pore and I wanted to kick him in the shin.

"If it even *was* this Moses guy," I said with a pointed look.

"It has to be Wallis or at least one of his," he replied, narrowing his eyes.

Noah's words made my insides twist as quite frankly, I never wanted to lay eyes on the guy again. What he said next was marginally worse.

"Lucy's right. We need to find out if we have the right place first. I suggest me and Lucy drive over in my truck. If we see anyone, we make out. Simple. You guys follow and park outside as backup, for if the shit kicks off. I could do with Lucy there to point him out, as you say, we can't be one hundred percent sure that it was Wallis who broke in here."

My cheeks felt like they were on fire. So, our cover story was that we were there to have sex, great.

The boys all appeared to agree with this suggestion and I was outnumbered.

"Great. So, I have to play some type of hussy that gets it on with her boyfriend in the back of his car. Classy," I grumbled, feeling thoroughly short-changed.

"What's the hell is a hussy?" Nathan frowned, quirking his head.

"A slag," Connor informed him with a twist of his lips, "or a slut, take your pick," helping to bring my comment into contemporary language these twits would understand. Realisation spread across Nathan's face and I felt like I belonged in the fifties. Great.

Noah turned, his gaze tracing over me. "We can do it in the front?" he said with a cheeky wink.

"What?" I asked, losing the plot for a nanosecond.

"It doesn't have to be in the back, we can make out in the front," Noah mocked me recklessly and I wanted to thump him. I could feel the eyes of our audience and they were thoroughly entertained. How could he look so angelic when he was such a devil?

"Noah," I said in warning.

He scratched a hand over the bristle on his jaw whilst eyeing me thoughtfully.

"It's the best plan. I don't want you on your own, these guys are bad news, Lucy, you have *no* idea," he explained in a hard voice before it softened. "And we can practice a bit beforehand, you know, like an audition," he taunted. Did the guy ever take anything seriously?

"Funny. That isn't going to happen. The first time I have sex will *not* be in a car," the words were out before I could hoist them back. Further embarrassment whooshed through my chest like a tsunami. OMG, I had just admitted I was a virgin to a couple of strangers.

Noah came to life, drawing the heat off me, thank goodness. Did he do it on purpose to shield me or not, there was no way of knowing. I tuned into what he was saying.

"That's the plan then. So, we'll head over to the farm on Friday evening. You guys follow us and park close and we'll see what we see. Scope the place out."

The boys nodded and grunted.

"Take your crappy truck Connor, not Nathan's, all the world will see you coming in the Porsche."

"What the fuck does that mean?" Connor volleyed back, folding his huge arms across his chest with a menacing look.

"Your piece of shit Ranger will blend in," Noah explained with a grin.

Connor bristled moodily, thoroughly offended. "What the fuck, piece of shit? Let's hope your baby doesn't break the fuck down when you need to make a fast getaway."

I rolled my eyes. Men were idiots. They spoke about their cars like it was a family member or something.

So, that was the plan, and I got it.

What I didn't understand is why I felt so disappointed that I had to wait until Friday to put it into action.

I experienced a dart of astonishment. Did the idea of making out with Noah have anything to do with that?

Absolutely. And my body won the battle, again.

Eight

The rest of the week crawled by at a snail's pace and the surgery was fairly quiet, considering what we believed was going on with the dogs.

Our one-eared patient, Vincent, as I had decided to name her (after Vincent Van Gough) was improving as each day passed by and she was *such* a sweetie.

Noah came by a few times to visit and a definite bond was developing between the two of them. I was surprised as I'd always thought of him as the grudge-bearing type. Evidently not when it came to animals. He hated the name I had given her, saying how it was a boy's name and shortened it to Vee.

On Friday, Noah texted my phone to say he'd arrived outside my house; I'd purposefully told him not to knock on the door. I didn't relish the thought of him and David crossing paths again so soon after the incident in church. Something David had gone on and on about to the point where I thought my ears were going to drop off.

As I pulled on my boots, David was leaning against the doorframe which led into the living room, watching my movements with narrowed eyes. I purposefully told him not to wait up, knowing he probably wouldn't listen to me. I was still reeling from the mouthful he'd given me after the incident with Noah. He'd also attempted to forbid me from seeing him again in *any* capacity, but I'd ignore him of course.

I left the house, leaving my dad cooking supper and I asked him to save me a plate for later. He didn't question where I was going or even look up from the saucepan he was stirring.

I'd decided to wear tight skinny jeans and an oversized grey jumper. I left my duffle coat at home as I also had a T-shirt on and didn't want to be too hot and trussed up.

As I climbed up into the truck, Noah's eyes ran over my legs.

"Tight jeans, very nice. I think it must be the first time I've seen you in jeans," he said, starting the car.

He looked edible, in baggy jeans and a black hoodie that was stretched over his huge mountain-like shoulders. A flush of awareness crept up the back of my neck.

He squeezed my leg and an electric current seemed to flow through his fingers into my skin.

"You have seen me in jeans, I used to wear them to school on non-uniform days," I pointed out as he pushed the car into gear.

He shot me a look, one eyebrow arched, "Not *tight* jeans, those things you used to wear to school were oversized and baggy. I used to imagine them falling down."

I grinned. He had a great sense of humour.

It lasted seconds before he ruined my good thoughts of him with a smutty aside.

"How easy are they to take off?"

I shouldn't have been surprised as Noah had *always* been unbelievably frank. Sexual energy now fizzed freely around the cab of the car. Trust him to change the mood without even trying. I felt my heartbeat stutter.

"Where are the others?" I questioned smoothly, rubbing the area where his fingers had been to erase that delicious feeling.

"Behind us." Noah's voice was low and husky.

I turned in my seat to look out of the small window of the cab to see what I assumed would be Connor's headlights.

"Are you nervous?" Noah asked as I twisted back. I noted how strong his hands were on the wheel and wondered how they'd feel against my body.

It was starting to become extremely difficult to change the direction of these types of thoughts. The more I saw this guy, the further he wedged himself under my skin.

"Not really. Irrespective of school, I do feel quite safe with you Noah," I admitted.

He briefly turned his attention from the road, his eyes tangling with mine. "Maybe you shouldn't speak too soon."

His words dripped with silent promise and that look in his eyes had been lined with need. Need for me, for my body. This thought made my cheeks heat further and I turned to stare out of the front windscreen.

Noah chuckled beside me, thoroughly pleased with himself.

Katy's wedding swam back into my head. I had decided to ask Noah to be my plus one, why not. I'd make sure he knew I was asking him as a friend.

"So, I wanted to ask you a favour." This got his attention and he jammed the car up into the next gear with a huff. Briefly checking the rear-view mirror; probably to establish Connor had kept up.

"Fuck off. I've still not fully recovered from the *last* favour," he barked, making reference to his visit to church. I managed to withhold the disapproving tut that wanted to push its way between my lips. The jury was definitely out on whether his behaviour that day had actually repaid anything. In my opinion, that was a big fat no.

I went in for the kill.

"Well, actually. You still owe me one really. Zonking out and blaspheming in church *certainly* wasn't a 'making things right' move. David kicked off at me later that night and is *still* going on about it. You are even deeper in his bad books now and so yes, I think you do still owe me one."

"I think you're taking the piss, Lucy."

"It hasn't got anything to do with the church this time, I just need you to take me somewhere." My words encouraged a leering smile to spread over his perfect features.

"Go on. You have my attention."

I remained silent for a moment, re-evaluating whether asking Noah to the wedding would open up a whole new can of worms. Did he even know how to behave at a formal function or would he do something to show me up? I must admit, Noah didn't appear to be teasing me half as much over the last couple of weeks, but that didn't guarantee he wouldn't say something to embarrass me.

I continued to roll that thought around. Bottom line, we would be going as just friends and so how could it hurt?

Sod it, you only live once and all that. I certainly didn't want to go alone and so my options were limited.

"I have a wedding to attend next Saturday and I need a plus one," I explained, my voice sounding overly husky. Probably because it felt like I was asking him out. I wondered if my face had gone red.

Noah echoed my thoughts and my lips parted in surprise. "So, you need a date?" His tone was mildly amused and I wanted to thump him on the leg, even though I'd probably shatter some cartilage.

"Nope, I need a *friend*," I delivered with a surprising measure of calm. I emphasised the word *friend* on purpose. Thinking of Noah as my date made me feel wibbly inside.

"So, we're friends now?" Noah imparted with one of those shit-eating grins.

I thought about it for a moment or so. "Yes, I suppose in a weird way we are."

"*Good* friends, that do each other favours and stuff?" he said hopefully.

I pushed myself back into my seat with a huff. "In a fashion," I replied. "Let's not get too carried away."

"You do realise where all of my dates end?" he questioned smugly. I resented the tug of jealousy this caused.

"No, not really and I don't care," I lied.

"Well, to sum it up I'd say… horizontal?"

I bit my lip. I hated how rotten this thought made me feel. Why couldn't I go back to hating him again?

There was a three-beat silence before he said.

"OK, I'll take you." His words forced a tremor to run through my body.

I felt a bubble of relief at how quickly he'd said yes, "I take it you own a suit?" I cringed at how rude my words sounded once they were out there.

Noah glanced at me briefly, "Yes, I don't live in my work clothes, Lucy. As I said before, I have been to weddings and shit. My family on my dad's side is fucking massive. There's always something going on."

It was the first time Noah had mentioned his dad to me. Pushing the thought aside I reassured him.

"Anyway, it's just the night do, so you won't have to be bored through the wedding service or anything like that," I pointed out.

"Good. Thank fuck for small mercies," he returned somewhat dryly.

My goodness, the guy swore, a lot.

"And not a church in sight!" I promised.

"Even better."

We drove the rest of the way in silence but the atmosphere between us was fairly friendly. We appeared to be making progress with our relationship all the time. We were still in an 'I love to hate you' scenario but we were *definitely* closer. I decided not to over analyse the lust factor. That was way too scary.

The farm was only ten minutes away from my house and Noah turned off the headlights as he drove through the old battered gates into the yard. One of the gates was hanging off; the place having been left empty for quite some time.

It was deserted and there were no cars there which suggested there wouldn't be any dog fighting going on. At least not at that moment.

The area was quite sparse, with just a few pieces of old rusted farm equipment, piles of litter, and scattered hay bales. Some of the outbuildings were damaged and one of the roofs was missing. The grand farmhouse which sat in the distance was obviously derelict. The crumbling stonework of the half-encased ivy-strewn house was sad to see. I remember it had once been so pretty.

The other boys didn't follow us into the property and so I imagined they had parked on the road outside; following Noah's instructions.

Pulling the car further into the yard beside one of the large barns, Noah tugged the handbrake on and turned off the engine. We both undid our seat belts.

It was dark outside but the yard was highlighted by the full moon. We probably should have brought a torch. I had a light on my phone and that was it.

Shooting a glance toward Noah, I raised my eyebrows. He was watching me with a curious expression.

"What?" I questioned.

He slowly inhaled and his pupils dilated.

"Nothing. Just thinking about how nice you smell."

My eyebrows then knitted, "Oh, OK. Thanks, I suppose."

Noah continued to look at me like I was an apparition.

It was difficult but I managed to sever that connection between us by saying, "So, what now?"

His expression switched to thoughtful, "We wait," he replied.

Casting my eyes beyond him through the glass, I searched the silence outside feeling puzzled.

"What for?"

Noah briefly shot a glance beyond the windscreen, copying my gesture, "To see if anyone's actually in there."

Releasing a sigh, I straightened in my seat and cast my eyes forward. Taking in the sad little farmhouse.

"What shall we do whilst we wait?" I questioned, even though I knew my comment would probably draw some filth from Noah. He didn't let me down.

"You could straddle me?"

The chuckle burst from my lips and I twisted my head, giving him a grin. "You really are a pervert, aren't you?"

His eyes glittered with boyish amusement but he didn't smile. He just sat there looking sexy. "Not at all. I'm a realist. What guy could sit in a parked car with a pretty girl and not want to make out? It's human nature."

My lips twitched and I wondered how he'd react if I behaved out of character and did as he'd suggested. I didn't of course, that would have been way too out there for me.

Clearing my throat, I replied in my primmest voice, "I think I'm fine here thank you."

"Spoilsport," he said under his breath, rubbing his thumb over his plump bottom lip. He seemed to do this when he was having sexual thoughts. The action made my nipples harden against the lace of my bra. Thank goodness I had a jumper on. If Noah Savvas found out just how much he *did* affect me, there would be no stopping him. I knew that now.

Changing the subject, I suggested.

"I think we should get out and have a look around. We could hold hands, make it look like we're looking for a place to—well, you know," I stuttered, my mouth unable to form the actual words.

He cocked an eyebrow. "A place to have sex," Noah filled in for me, without blinking an eye.

I fell silent for a moment, the way he said the word sex sent a jet of heat between my thighs and I crossed my legs.

Noah's eyes narrowed in on the motion and he gave me a knowing smile. Gosh, the guy missed nothing. Did he know that I was actually a little damp down there?

"Yes," I replied, running my hands down my jean-clad thighs.

He pushed off his seat and leaned closer, appearing to expand further in the small space.

"You can't even say the word," he husked.

I moved back a little, the door biting into my shoulder, "I can, sex. There see."

He made me feel like a schoolgirl again.

I fell mute as he cocked his head, his eyes roaming over my face, as if the answer to a question may be written there.

"Haven't you ever been tempted?"

Shaking my head I explained, "No, not really. I've not met the right man yet."

Noah snorted and moved back against his seat, resting his hands on the steering wheel.

"Oh, you've met the right man, you just refuse to accept it.

He was still watching me, those dark eyes intense.

"Maybe I should force the issue," he whispered but I heard the words as clear as a bright Yorkshire morning.

My face twisted and I shot him my best-unimpressed face, "I don't think so Noah. You know what *that's* called."

His whole body oozed sexual confidence as he said, “It wouldn’t come to that. You’d melt like butter. Actual brute force wouldn’t be necessary.” His tone was so matter of fact and yes, it turned me on, but I still wanted to yank some of his hair.

“You’re such a big head and so full of yourself,” I batted back with some exasperation. They definitely broke the mould with this guy.

His lips twisted sexily and he wiggled his eyebrows to highlight his next point.

“You could be too, full of me I mean.”

I mirrored his earlier snort before pushing my phone back into the pocket of my jeans, the movement forced my jumper to slide off one shoulder. “You’re so crude.”

He gave me a cheeky grin. “You love it.”

Another one of those silences snuck into the cab as he eyed my naked skin. Feeling conscious, I dragged the material back in place which knocked Noah out of his trance.

“Come on then.”

I frowned. “What?”

His eyelids flickered. “Let’s go and poke around, I need a distraction from this hard-on,”

Laughter burst from my lungs like an iron ball from a cannon. Noah Savvas was a law unto himself.

I purposefully twisted away, ignoring my urge to check out the area he was referring to. Was he being serious? Had he been sat in the car with a stonking erection without even touching me? The thought did crazy things to my inside and I filed them in the bottom drawer of my mind. The place I had started storing the naughty lustful thoughts I was now experiencing on a daily basis. It appeared I did have a dirty mind and Noah was the man who had unleashed it.

We climbed from the car into the semi-darkness. As the place was deserted, there were no lights; just that glow of the moon.

As I moved around the truck toward Noah, he started to fiddle with his phone. A moment later, a beam of light hit me in the face and I held my hand up to shield my eyes.

Noah had switched on the flashlight on his iPhone and then had proceeded to try and blind me with it, it appeared.

“Noah!” I scalded and he lowered the offending device.

“Sorry,” he apologised, switching it off and re-pocketing it. “I just wanted to check it worked, we’ll need it to see inside.” Of course, by all means, ‘let there be light’ but not in my fricking eye!

“You’ve probably melted part of my retina,” I complained in a moody voice.

He grinned, his white perfect teeth flashing.

“You good?”

I blinked and nodded, shuffling to stand before him.

My pulse kicked as his fingers closed around my own and he tugged me along.

“Let’s do this Nancy Drew,” he whispered with a smile.

To say I wasn’t the most adventurous of people, the excitement of the unknown wound itself through my chest.

Noah and I walked hand in hand over to the large beaten-down barn, the one that still had its roof intact. There was definitely a feeling that we weren’t alone.

As we approached the door, the gravel crunched under our feet and Noah strained against the large rotten entrance into the building. There was a faint glow of light and then I heard the shuffle of something, feet maybe? It was only slight, but Noah heard it too.

My heart thudded and blood roared in my ears as Noah swung me around and backed me up against the wall of the barn.

Our eyes met and tangled, we were totally in tune and knew what needed to be done. I did the only thing that made sense and followed Noah’s lead.

I inhaled sharply as he took my wrists and drew my arms above my head, pinning them against the barn before his mouth took mine with *aggressive* possession.

My pulse took off and I was soaring, the feel of his lips delicious as they moved demandingly against mine. My mouth parted and his tongue drove inside, filling and feeding me. It was hot, carnal, and *deeply* moving, so much so that I felt my legs go weak.

The moment forced all rational thought from my mind as I succumbed to the immense pleasure my body was experiencing. I didn’t care if we got caught, everything felt so right.

I needed to be even nearer and I tugged my wrists free of his hold and they dropped to his shoulders. Noah lowered his hands and curved them around my backside before lifting me against the surface of the wall. His fingers were firm and my legs parted around him as he shuffled further into me.

I braced my hands over his shoulders, my fingers clawing his back. My breasts were crushed against his rock-hard chest. We fit together perfectly this way, our difference in height smashed away.

Noah lifted his head briefly, “Wrap your legs around my waist,” he instructed in a passion-fuelled voice before taking my mouth again, and I did *exactly* that. That solid part of him was pushed against my core, creating chaos with my sex, I was suddenly *soaking wet*.

The long jumper I wore was almost up to my waist. I could feel the air against my bare back above my jeans, but I didn’t care.

I couldn’t say how long we were like that, with me back against the wall with my limbs wrapped around him, but I *never* wanted it to end. The fact that there could have been danger close by, was also *thrilling*.

Noah’s hardness which he’d referred to in the car, was now pushing into my core and I wondered how he would feel inside me. I tightened my thighs, which ground that bundle of nerves between my legs against him and a wave of pleasure darted through my loins. I sucked in a breath, gasping at the feeling that friction was creating. Noah growled into my mouth, his hands tightening on my bottom and drawing me closer still, and again another burst of pleasure, this time *stronger* than the first, more intense…

“Can anyone join in?” a voice suddenly bled in from beside us. It was like being doused with cold water.

Noah dragged his mouth away from mine and twisted his head toward the sound. His breathing was laboured as was mine and my vision was slightly blurred.

He grunted and slowly lowered me to the ground, carefully. Attempting to catch his own breath.

As my feet touched the floor, I pulled my clothes straight. My legs were jelly-like and Noah put out a hand to steady me as we both turned toward the stranger.

I was panting and semi-confused with the strength of the feelings I had just experienced. That sensation was still there, but gradually fading and I understood for the first time in my life, what sexual frustration felt like. I had been close, close to experiencing that peak of sexual excitement that everyone talked about, and now it was gone.

Noah and I shared a moment, his eyes searching my face with such tenderness before he masked it and turned toward the man who had interrupted us and shattered that magic.

Thankfully, it wasn't the man from the surgery. It was a younger guy, he looked between us with a slightly amused expression. I suppose amused was better than suspicious.

"You're trespassing you know?" he said before Noah could answer.

Noah seemed to grow in height beside me as he stared down at the smaller man.

"We could say the same to you," he pointed out, giving *nothing* away.

I slowly started to get my breath back and pulled myself together, allowing Noah to take the lead again. His fingers wrapped around mine and he held my hand again, pulling me slightly behind him. We must have looked like a regular couple, in the middle of nowhere, getting off with each other. A strange cocktail of excitement and fear whooshed through me. Had I just behaved in such a licentious way?

"I'm security actually, I'm just doing the rounds," the stranger informed us. I could tell he was lying. He didn't look *anything* like a security guard.

"Really? Where's your car?" Noah questioned, releasing my hand and folding his arms across his huge chest.

I felt no fear for my safety in this boy's company. There was no comparison between the two men. I would have put the stranger in his mid-twenties, he had piggy eyes and his hair was shaved short. He still looked as rough as a dog; no pun intended!

"I only live around the corner," he said flatly.

"I see, well I guess we better get going then." Noah's tone was still disbelieving as he unfolded his arms and motioned for me to head to the truck.

I did as I was instructed, ignoring the leering look from the stranger.

As I moved away and climbed into the car, Noah and the guy were still talking, I couldn't hear what they were saying and I pulled the door closed cutting off the sound completely.

After a few minutes, Noah shook the man's hand and moved away. He joined me in the car and started the engine. The 'security guard' stood with a guarded expression zoomed in on the truck.

"So?" I questioned, wanting to know what I'd missed.

"He says I'm a very lucky boy," Noah taunted with a lewd expression.

"Noah," I warned, not in the mood for one of his games.

He cleared his throat before saying. "We were right, this is the place they are using," Noah's voice was deep and firm.

"How do you know? We didn't even see inside."

I eyeballed the stranger warily as he stood watching the car; waiting for us to leave.

Noah shot me a look as he put the car in reverse. "Didn't need to. That guy is definitely involved in something. I remember him from Nate's party last year."

My heart lurched in my chest. "Did he recognise you?"

"No. I dragged Wallis out with Connor and wasn't involved in the other shit that went down, but I remember that fucker trying it on with Natalie." Noah paused for a minute as he pulled the car out onto the road. "He was definitely with the same group as he left when the others were kicked out."

Noah drove out of the gates, turned left, and pulled the car up alongside Connor's truck so the side windows were level. They had parked further along the road by some tall trees. Nathan was in the passenger seat and he lowered the window, Noah doing the same.

"This is it. It's not happening tonight though. Follow me back to mine. I need to drop Lucy off first."

I silently huffed. Great, and now I was being left out.

My eyes sought the clock on the dashboard, it wasn't *that* late. "But I want to come too, I want to be involved," I said, leaning forward my eyes catching Connor's. He was sat with his hands on the steering wheel, looking beyond Nathan.

Noah twisted back toward me with a terse expression. "Your involvement in this finishes here."

Squaring my shoulders, suddenly feeling prickly, I questioned. "How do you know it's definitely the place or that he's involved? Just because he knows this Wallis guy?"

There was a moment's pause as Noah announced his disturbing deductions.

"The back of his hand was scarred, he had what looked like a blood stain on his jeans and he had a dog lead draped around his neck. I'd say that puts him at the top of our shit list. He was preparing the area, ready for a session. He's probably the money man. We'll have to leave it for a few weeks. From what I researched, fights usually happen every two to three weeks and we'll need to catch them at it."

A car's headlights appeared in the distance, forcing Noah to move his truck as we were on the opposite side of the road, parallel with Connor.

"See you back at mine," he shouted as he slid the window back up and accelerated the car.

There was very little chatter on the way back to my house. Noah seemed to be in some type of trance. He was probably planning their next move; one *without* me it seemed.

Thankfully, Noah didn't say anything about what had happened between us. We spoke briefly about the wedding and I told him I'd text him the address. I'd decided it would be better for us to meet there instead of him picking me up. I certainly didn't want to spoil my dress in his truck. Yes, it was fairly clean inside but it was still a work vehicle.

Noah was fine about it and to be honest, I did wonder if he'd heard a word I'd said.

As I made my way up to my room it was still fairly early. David was nowhere to be seen thank God (sorry).

The only thing on my mind was the memory of how Noah had lifted me against the wall and the feel of him between my legs. The truth of the matter was, that if we hadn't been interrupted, he would have brought me to climax.

Physically we worked. He complemented me in ways I could never have imagined and I wondered how it would feel to have someone like Noah as my first.

After tonight I knew the answer, euphoric.

Nine

The following week was fairly uneventful at work. I kept in touch with Noah via text but he didn't really have anything further to report.

He came into the surgery one day, but I didn't see him to talk to as I had a queue of clients at the desk.

At the end of the week, I noticed Vee was no longer with us and I wondered fleetly where she'd been taken. Stray dogs usually went to one of the rescue centres but as she was an ex-fighting animal, they didn't always take them. I made a mental note to ask Tom about it. I knew Noah would be upset, as he'd become quite attached to her.

The day of Katy's wedding had arrived and I spent most of the morning getting ready. Dad had always been a definite no and David couldn't make up his mind so I booked a taxi, having arranged to meet Noah at the venue. If he showed up. Knowing my luck, he'd turn up in his work overalls in an attempt to make some type of irrelevant point. I thought back to how insulted he'd looked when I'd asked him if he owned a suit.

The hotel was magnificent; a large Georgian building with ivy draped across parts of the weathered stonework; elegant and traditional. I'd driven past the place several times but had never been to any events there.

I paid the taxi driver and climbed out of the car.

The lobby was huge with an ornate sweeping staircase down the middle of the room. It was the grandest of features and I imagined a perfect backdrop for wedding pictures. I wondered how many bedrooms were up there.

There were a few guests dotted around but they were all dressed casually and so didn't appear to be there for Katy's party.

I smiled at an elderly man who was attempting to convince his grandson that sliding down the banister of the staircase, was not a good idea.

My high-heeled sandals clicked against the shining marble floor as I crossed the lobby; curious to take a peek at the room we would be in. The wedding breakfast had been held in another part of the building earlier that day.

I hadn't minded that I'd only been invited to the evening event. I hadn't seen Katy in years and was surprised to get an invitation at all to be honest.

One of David's colleagues had married Katy and Mark in a ceremony at a church in the next village from mine. It wasn't a shock that Katy hadn't asked my brother to do it; they'd never been close, even when we were children. I felt a twinge of sadness. We use to see my uncle and auntie's family loads back then. Of course, when my mother left, everything changed; mum's abandonment had made things awkward. Dad couldn't even look at my auntie Jo, who was again my mother's spitting image.

David had found out through the local clergy that only close family and friends had been invited to the service and following wedding breakfast; with a larger guest list for the evening. I imagined this would have been to keep the numbers down as weddings were expensive. Part of me wondered whether David would suddenly turn up and the other half of me hoped he wouldn't. Not very sisterly of me I know, but I had Noah to consider now.

The grand ballroom of the hotel had been beautifully decorated. My cousin Katy had commissioned Ella Wade, Tom's sister to design the entire collection of flowers and she had done an *amazing* job. Tom had told me on one of our past dates that his sister was a gardener and was into all things green, as well as being a 'pain in his arse' (his words not mine).

My eyes scanned the area, drinking in the beauty. Bunches of white lilies, carnations, and chrysanthemums were arranged all around the room.

There appeared to be around twelve tables that were set out for ten people dotted around a wooden slatted dancefloor and the large head table sat in the middle at one end of the room. The centrepieces on each table were also stunning and the tables were beautifully laid with crisp white cloths. The chairs also had white covers, each one set with a gold gauzed ribbon tied into a bow.

The atmosphere in the air was charged with excitement and happiness and the scent from the blooms complimented the whole package.

A lady in a business suit was zipping here and there around the room, readjusting chair covers, tweaking flowers, and ensuring the right cutlery was laid and I imagined her to be the wedding planner Katy had engaged. She looked a bit like a bee buzzing from flower to flower.

Walking back into the main lobby, I checked the time on the large grandfather clock which sat beside the huge mahogany reception desk. I was early and possibly one of the first to arrive. My eyes searched the area; three members of staff were busy behind the counter, taking calls or typing on their computers.

I glanced over to the large rotating double doors, now *willing* Noah to appear. Would he let me down, was he the type of man to break a promise?

My feet suddenly felt hot enough to melt the glue of my shoes and so I lowered myself onto one of the large chesterfields close to a crackling open fire. I was careful of creases and smoothed down the material of my dress with my fingers.

With Natalie Savvas's help, I'd chosen a floor-length, sleeveless silk gown. It was sapphire blue and clung to every curve of my body; the neckline was high but the dress was backless. The opening revealed most of my back and skimmed the top of my backside. It was probably one of the most revealing dresses I had *ever* worn, but I felt like a film star. Natalie had been so encouraging at the store and I'd finally given in. I was so pleased I'd caved. I had chosen minimal jewellery, just a simple bracelet on my arm and I had a bag of the exact same colour as my dress; a lucky find from a charity shop in Scarborough.

My hair had been fashioned to fall down my front over one shoulder, so as not to hide the main backless feature of the dress. The red of my hair shone brightly against the blue. I felt *amazing*.

After reapplying my lipstick, I popped it back into my bag and as I raised my head, Noah materialised before my eyes like a Greek God; tall, dark, and commanding. I swallowed a number of times as he approached; his appearance almost knocked me off my seat. I was pleased to see him; the reaction was so strong it almost winded me.

He looked *incredible* in a classic dark suit that fitted him so perfectly it could have been tailored. The white crisp dress shirt had been pressed and he wore a tie a similar colour to my dress. Was it a coincidence or had Natalie been involved? I imagined the latter.

His shoulders were so broad, almost pushing against the material that hugged them and I slowly rose to my feet as he saw me. His gorgeous, model-like features aimed in my direction. He had shaved too, he looked less rugged but still *extremely* masculine. He was still a wolf in sheep's clothing of course.

Noah's dark eyes roamed over my body and I could see by the glint in his eyes that he liked what he saw. This reality caused the heat from my feet to lick up my spine, and my heart did a somersault.

As he came to stand before me, he smiled down into my upturned face before running one finger down my cheek. The touch of his skin almost stalled my heart. My body stirred to life.

The past was well and truly in the past now. I had to admit it, I now felt something and whatever it was, it was gradually getting stronger each time I saw him.

"You look beautiful," Noah whispered. I noted the hint of aftershave. He'd really made the effort and part of me wanted to stretch up and hug him. I refrained from doing so of course.

"Aren't you going to give me a spin, isn't that what you girls do? So, I can see the whole package," he grinned with a flick of his eyebrows. I felt a twinge of nerves for having worn something so sinfully daring.

I took a steadying breath and turned slowly on the balls of my feet. I heard his breath catch in his throat as he noticed the dress was backless and although only brief, I could feel that penetrating gaze against my bare skin. I wondered fleetingly what it would feel like for him to remove my dress, but before I could dwell on it, Noah took the initiative and slid his hand around my waist.

Drawing me to his side he suggested, "Shall we?" as he guided me into the main ballroom. I couldn't do anything but follow, my feet shuffling to keep up with him. I had to walk two steps to his one, his legs were so much longer than mine.

I could feel his fingers on my hip bone, they moved slightly with the sway of my walk. He was so tall and strong beside me and I noted a couple of waitresses ogling him as we passed by. I wasn't surprised, Noah Savvass was stunning; *all man*, confident and more at home in his suit than his usual work clothes it seemed.

Noah directed us both to the bar, like a perfect gentleman. To be honest, my heart started to flutter in my chest at the way that made me feel. This was new to me as I'd never seen this gentleman-like side of him before and I felt feminine and sweet, almost like a princess in his company.

"What would the lady like to drink?" Noah suddenly said, his lips just above the cuff of my ear, the one exposed by my hairstyle.

"Prosecco please," I replied as we stopped by the bar.

The sound of a harp suddenly trickled into the room, adding a burst of romance to the excitement surrounding us.

"We can do better than that. Two glasses of champagne please mate," Noah said to the barman. The fact that he changed (and improved) my order sent a jet of excitement through me. I was obviously all for controlling types of men, and of course, that is *exactly* what Noah was.

This evening, I was that new me I was experimenting with, the one to let her hair down and live the fairy tale. Stepping outside of my comfort zone was becoming a regular thing for me and to be honest, I hadn't thought much about what the big guy in the sky thought at all lately. I'd even missed saying my prayers a few times.

As I eyed Noah's strong profile, I decided to embrace the evening and let go. David wasn't there and so I didn't need to feel uncomfortable. No doubt he'd be watching my every move with Noah. The thought of the atmosphere at the table whilst I sat in between Noah and my brother left a bad taste in my mouth.

As Noah handed me the crystal chute, I decided I didn't care. Maybe Noah was right and I needed to start standing up for myself. No matter what I did, David would be displeased anyway. It was a no-win situation with him.

Guests were starting to come into the ballroom in droves now, a coach or something must have arrived as they all came in at once. Herds of them, all looking thoroughly glamorous, an assortment of colour and style.

I peered through the people for a glimpse of the bride but couldn't see her. I'd need to give them my congratulations. I'd already sent their gift and card in the post to their house, in case I had decided not to come.

Noah took my hand, his fingers curling into mine and he guided us away from the bar where most of the new arrivals were flocking. We walked in silence toward the huge windows. They ran along one wall, boasting a magnificent sight of lush, rolling gardens. The sun was slowly starting to fade; again, a romantic picture.

As we stopped, Noah released my hand and I placed my clutch bag and drink on a side table by the window.

Glancing up, I saw he was watching me over the rim of his glass; his lips were mesmerising as he drank, his Adam's apple bobbing as he swallowed. Was it wrong that I felt a sudden urge to place my mouth there? I eyed the strong, tanned column of his throat; my heart almost spluttered like a faulty engine.

"So, this has to be our first official date," Noah said lowering his glass, his voice deep and husky. He clutched the delicate stem of crystal with his tattooed hand, the contrast of the elegance of the flute being held by something dark and dangerous giving him that extra edge. I longed to trace the image stamped there with my fingertips.

Hoping that my tongue wasn't hanging out, I shot him my best attempt at a sassy look. "This isn't a date Noah, this is a friend doing another friend a favour, remember," I informed him a little tartly. I had only had a couple of sips of champagne but was already feeling a tingle. I was aware that the sensation was probably due to something or should I say someone else. At the end of the day, you'd have to be dead not to notice how attractive Noah was.

"So, is this a friends-with-benefits type of arrangement then? You won't find me complaining," Noah said with a devilish look. Adrenalin shot through my core. He was being blatantly provocative again.

Sexually charged energy seemed to bounce naturally between us. I embraced it as tonight I was the new me, bible free and all that.

"If you think you'll be getting any of those types of benefits from me, you can think again Romeo," I replied, my own voice leaving my mouth with a slight catch. I so hoped he didn't notice.

"Why not? After what happened at the farm, you know we'd be sensational together," Noah drawled with a wolfish smile. He made me feel like a lamb. "If we hadn't been disturbed by that tosser, I'd have already made you cum."

My nipples tingled and I was braless. I needed to calm the heck down if I didn't want to be walking around with the bloody things pointing through my dress. "Yes, well, there will be none of *that* going on here tonight."

He chuckled with a sexy rattle, "None of what? You still can't say it."

The fine hairs on my body stood to attention and I took a deep breath, "Sex." There, I said it (again). Rather loudly too, by accident of course.

"You want what?" Noah boomed out as another couple drifted by us to find their table. I knew he did it on purpose to embarrass me. My heart skipped a beat, he was such a sod and I grabbed my own glass and took a long gulp, my eyes frantically searching those around us to check that no one else heard. My cheeks heated. I must have been as red as a tomato.

I scowled and viewed him through narrowed eyes, "Very funny."

Noah, adjusted his tie saying, "Well at least you think I'm funny."

I picked up my drink, needing to do something with my hands. There was another beat of silence as we both enjoyed our bubbles. The room was quite busy now with some people sauntering around the room, and others sitting at their tables or standing in clusters. The music from the harp was beautiful.

Suddenly there was a ruckus near the doors as the bride and groom entered, followed by a stream of bridesmaids dressed in claret red. You could tell they'd all had a few from the way they wobbled in their heels. Noah and I both turned to watch as an assortment of guests approached the happy couple. I held back, deciding to wait until the herd of people had moved away. Katy looked a little overwhelmed, it was probably best to catch her later. Her dress was stunning; white lace, straight up and down; not a meringue in sight.

"So that's your cousin, Katy, she looks good," Noah said from beside me as we both looked over at the flurry of people.

"Yep, that's Katy."

"What does she do? For a living I mean?" Noah asked before turning to place his empty flute on the table next to my bag.

"She's a therapist, well, at least that's what she used to do anyway, Counselling. We lost touch for a while. To be honest, I'm surprised she invited me."

He nodded his understanding as we faced each other again. It was almost like we were attached by an invisible thread. I shuffled on my feet and smoothed my hair.

Noah's eyes ran over my body like liquid fire, "So, Natalie said you came to her shop and she helped you with the dress?"

"She did. She was really helpful and friendly."

His eyes were now hooded, I was so close I could see those green flecks. Noah had unusual eyes, probably due to his Cypriot father and English mother.

I watched as his nostrils flared. "That would explain the backless element. I can't imagine buttoned-up little you thought about going for something so risqué."

My eyebrows threaded, "It isn't *that* risqué, and it's only my back," I said with a careless shrug.

The look in his eyes suddenly darkened. "Yes, and what a back it is," Noah whispered, dipping his head. His voice was quite drugging and my skin fizzed as he stepped further into my space, sliding a hand around my waist. His fingers were rough as they skimmed against my bare skin. But of course, they would be, Noah worked with his hands.

"Noah," I pretty much exhaled his name, a breathless warning.

"What?" he replied, schooling his expression.

His hand settled at the bottom of my back near the base of my spin and my pulse took-off as he started to stroke the skin there.

My nipples tightened again. It was amazing how my body responded to something so simple. He was stroking me and it felt like a lover's touch, his eyes on my lips. I moistened them with my tongue. I was aware of every part of my body; it was like he'd cast a spell on me and I couldn't pull away.

I saw a mischievous glint in his eyes as he slowly slid his hand further down under the material of the dress, his thumb now resting on my backside next to my thong. A breath panted from my mouth.

Noah inhaled, obviously excited that I hadn't stopped him, but what could I do, if I did that, I'd draw attention and that isn't what I wanted at that moment. I also didn't want him to stop, not really.

Attempting to rein in the raw emotion that was racing through me, I purposefully tilted my head to the side.

"Noah?" I said again as he slid his hand across the bare flesh of my bottom cheek. I gasped as his fingers touched the top of my lace thong.

"This isn't right." I met his gaze with a challenge of my own.

"Feels right to me," he uttered back, his gaze searing mine.

Noah's voice dipped even lower, "I didn't expect you to wear that type of underwear?" The devil said, quirking a brow at me. I pulled a shuddering breath into my lungs before I swallowed and said, "I had to, otherwise you'd see it through my dress," I paused and sighed, "And what the heck I am doing, discussing my underwear with you?" I muttered the last part to myself.

I felt dizzy and totally at war with myself. The new me, was *scary* and I suddenly didn't know how to behave. Pursing my lips, I managed to pull myself together. The vision of me with my legs wrapped around Noah's waist shot into my head, generating extra heat.

"The last thing I will say about my underwear is that you need to take your hand off it."

His expression was defiant, devilish and I jumped as he gently twanged my thong. The friction caused a jet of heat to surge between my legs and he smiled, noticing my reaction. The odd thing was that I didn't feel any shame, even in the room full of people. Yes, we were out of the way, but there was *nothing* to stop people from looking over and seeing us. Was it the alcohol or was I losing the plot? Part of me blamed the dress.

Shooting him a pointed look, I discarded my glass and moved my hand around my back, closing my fingers over his wrist to pull on his hand. He removed it, but only because he'd decided to.

We were now staring at each other in silence, the buzz from the chatter of the other guests purely background noise. I was surprised he couldn't hear my heart pounding against my ribs, it was thumping so dramatically.

He now rested both his hands gently on my hips and I placed my own fingers over his, but I didn't push him away. They just sat there on top.

Noah's face became serious and he tilted his head.

"You want me Lucy and you know it. I can hear it in your voice when you speak to me, your sigh of pleasure when I touch you; even the way you look at me," he whispered in a gruff voice. I could feel heat all over my body, inside and out.

My mouth twisted slightly but it wasn't a smile.

"It doesn't matter Noah, as it's never going to happen. We're too different, we want different things." I was right, we were light years apart in respect of our interests; but who was I kidding? Whatever was going on between us, it was gradually growing; becoming stronger. My mind wandered again over to that thought of Noah taking my virginity.

He shifted his big body again. His nose was now almost touching mine and my head was bent so far back that some of my hair had fallen to the other side of my shoulder, *kissing* my burning skin.

Noah's face was unreadable for a moment before he gently skimmed his nose back and forth against mine.

"I disagree, we both want the same thing actually,"

I blinked in bewilderment before our eyes locked as he drew back. "And what is that?"

His mouth curled and he pulled me against his body, whispering in my exposed ear, "We both want to make you cum."

Flames licked up my spine, heating my flesh. The sensation was so powerful and raw. Lust crashed into my pelvis and I could feel the fire of excitement in my bones.

My mouth fell open and I wobbled slightly but he held me firmly as my knees almost gave way into a full-on swoon. Our bodies were touching but it didn't look out of place, others were doing similar things. Although they were together, Noah and I were not. And I needed to remind him and myself of that; I could feel my resolve slowly melting away. I had *never* experienced temptation that extreme.

"You need to stop Noah and you shouldn't be touching me again," I panted, my hands now flat against his chest. This was so very wicked and shameful.

"But I like touching you and that dress is a blatant come-on, purposefully worn to tease me. Do you really think I'll be able to keep my hands off you all night? It's not going to happen Red. All I want to do is take you upstairs and—"

"And *nothing* Noah, this shouldn't be happening."

"You weren't saying that at the farm when you were basically *riding* my cock," Noah growled.

His colourful language almost caused my heart to stop, "I was playing a part. Acting, remember?"

He shook his head, "Well, they should give you a fucking BAFTA for your performance. If you think for one minute that—"

BOOM! He was cut off as someone tapped a microphone to see if it was on and it echoed into the room to a burst of applause and shocked laughter. I didn't know whether I should feel relieved or disappointed as confusion chewed into me.

"Sorry folks," came the amplified voice. It was Mark, he made a brief announcement to welcome everyone and explained what would happen over the course of the evening. I tuned him out, focusing my attention on the explosive situation in front of me.

Noah's face was now an unreadable mask as he released me, picked up my clutch, and took my hand.

"Let's go and find our table, I need to sit down." I didn't question him, I just followed. I knew my face was flushed. My freckles had probably all joined into one smatter of pink.

As we threaded in and out of the guests, I didn't really see anyone I recognised. The bride and groom were now separately speaking to different groups of people, mingling with their guests.

"Well, fuck me. Check *you* out in a suit?" a deep voice rumbled. I recognised it as Connor's which surprised me. What was Connor doing at *my* cousin's wedding?

Noah turned toward the sound, pulling me around with him. We had just found our table and were about to sit down.

“Wow Noah, you look *amazing*,” a soft female voice cooed. I immediately identified it as Harlow’s.

“All right, easy. He doesn’t look *that* fucking good,” Connor replied with a mild scowl. Did the guy *ever* smile?

He also looked extremely handsome, dressed in a crisp white shirt, and black fitted trousers. The boys did that man-hug thing and slapped each other’s backs in greeting. Harlow gave me a finger-tip wave. She looked *stunning*.

Noah tugged me closer to his side. “Better keep an eye on your date,” he said, playfully motioning to Harlow with a flick of his head.

Both Harlow and Connor swept a glance between us, back and forth; their eyes narrowed thoughtfully.

I smiled my greeting but Connor blanked me and the two boys immediately engaged in boy banter. Thankfully, Harlow placed her hand on mine and moved me to one side so we could speak.

“You look *amazing* Lucy, stunning dress.”

“Thanks, so do you.”

She was like the perfect female package, so pale and pure, her long blonde hair hanging loosely down her slender back. Her skin was so smooth it almost looked airbrushed. She’d outshine any model on Instagram.

I shook off the thought, realising how rude I was being by staring, and said, “I love that colour on you.” She wore a skin-tight red lace dress that accented her soft curves. I imagined it was a designer brand.

“Same. That colour against your hair is perfect.”

Harlow’s smile was wide and full and it made her even *more* beautiful. The girl could probably melt even the toughest of hearts with it; she’d probably make the Pope drool. She must be what the angels looked like. ‘Shut up Lucy, you’ve put the bible away for the evening’, I reminded myself. I also sounded like I had a Harlow-shaped girl crush.

“My apologies for Connor, but everyone knows my boyfriend is a social deviant,” she sang, her voice like a melody. The girl was definitely sent from heaven.

Connor and Noah carried on their conversation, something about the gym and I also heard him mention Vee which was strange. I had forgotten to ask Tom about her. Maybe Noah knew where she’d been sent.

We stood in a huddle for a while with the boys chatting about one thing and Harlow and I talking about Operation Lady Lamb. I explained what had happened and brought her up to speed. She said that she knew the boys had been speaking about it during their workouts but that Connor wouldn't tell her anything. I knew Noah and Connor had created a gym at Harlow's dad's farm and I hated the fact that they were keeping stuff from us.

It appeared we were all sitting on the same table which was yet *another* surprise. There was another couple who had already sat down and they were Roger and Wendy; they introduced themselves as friends of the groom. They were elderly and seemed nice enough. Their presence reminded me to ask Harlow about who had invited her or Connor, *one* of them had to be the plus one. It must have been Mark as I'd never even heard of Connor or Harlow until Nathan's party.

Before I could raise the question, I was distracted again.

"Hey Lucy, I didn't realise you'd come," Tom's sister, Ella suddenly materialised beside me, dropping into the empty chair. The girl had no finesse but she'd dressed up for a change.

"She hasn't yet," Noah whispered crudely against my ear and I elbowed him in the ribs, swallowing the scathing snort that was attempting to push itself out there.

I hadn't realised Tom's sister would be there. I knew she'd done the flowers but that didn't necessarily warrant an invite, did it? I shook off my bitchy thought. Ella looked so different in the dove grey trouser suit she wore. Whenever she came to her dad's practice, she always wore dungarees or baggy jeans. If she was surprised that I was there with Noah and not Tom, she didn't show it. No doubt she'd have met Sophie by now.

Ella introduced her boyfriend and it turned out that it *was* the infamous Ryan Lane, Nathan's brother. He didn't look that old to be honest and they actually looked quite good together. Again, another good-looking chap. He obviously took a *huge* amount of pride in his appearance; *nothing* was out of place.

His suit looked like he'd been born in it, it fit that well and he had a sharp, intelligent face but didn't seem to smile that much. Not even through the introductions. It turned out that pretty much everyone knew each other and I felt a bit like an outsider. The two empty chairs must have been for my father and my brother and I felt annoyed that David blatantly hadn't let Katy know they couldn't come.

Ella and Ryan offered to buy a round of drinks and went off to the bar; leaving me and Noah, Harlow, and Connor (and the old couple who appeared to be keeping themselves to themselves). The catering staff was in the middle of bringing the buffet out and Wendy kept glancing at it, obviously ready to pounce when it was open.

We chatted for a while about the situation at the farm, although it was short-lived as the boys just kept changing the subject. They mostly sparred with each other, making jokes and doing that whole one-up-man-ship thing.

Seeing an opportunity, I turned to Harlow and Connor with a bright look, "So how do you know Katy and Mark? I assume you've come as the groom's guests?" I directed my question toward Harlow. Connor was slouched in his seat, looking like he didn't want to be there, but he straightened at my question. Rolling his broad shoulders as if to remove a knot.

There was an uncomfortable silence and Connor's eyes roamed over my face like he was studying me. I felt like something in a lab all of a sudden. I wondered what I had said that could have offended him. It obviously didn't take much.

Harlow shot a brief look around the table before she replied, "We're actually here for Katy. How about you?"

Curiosity fuzzed my brain.

"Katy's my cousin."

Realisation dawned across her sweet features and Connor dashed an agitated hand across his jaw.

"I see. Cool," Harlow replied looking uneasy. What the heck?

Noah nudged me with his knee as if he was attempting to send me some type of silent message but I was stumped, I hadn't a clue what was going on, there was now an atmosphere and I didn't like it. They were hiding something, it made me feel even more like an outsider. Had they gate-crashed my cousin's wedding? Was that why they were acting strange? I was determined to get to the bottom of it.

"So how do you know Katy?" I repeated my question.

Again, that strange silence before Harlow mumbled, "Connor and Katy work together, well, sort of."

I was about to ask where, as I was sure Noah had said something about Connor being a farmer but before I could speak, Ryan and Ella came back with the drinks. I imagined Ella had been invited as the florist for the wedding but Connor being a work colleague of my cousin just sounded off.

Harlow and I had white wine and the boys and Ella were drinking beer. Ella was definitely one of the guys.

Ryan and Ella got dragged into a conversation with the old couple, something about farming equipment, and that chatter just started to flow.

I sat back and for the first time that evening, relaxed.

Ten

"So, I take it you guys are together now?" Harlow suddenly questioned in a friendly inquisitive voice. Her boyfriend Connor just loomed there with aggressive waves bouncing off of him. His sleeve of tattoos was just visible under the somewhat see-through white of his shirt. The guy oozed that definite bad-boy vibe. They *all* did to be honest, just in slightly different ways.

Physically, Connor and Harlow were like opposites; if she was day, he was night. It obviously worked going on the way she fawned all over him. I batted the mean thought away, blaming number four of the seven deadly sins; envy. She was just so perfect in every way.

I shook off my thoughts, drawing my attention back to her statement. She had obviously formed the wrong impression of my relationship with Noah.

"We're not together, we're just friends," I corrected her with a tight smile, feeling overly aware of Noah's huge frame sitting beside me. My words even sounded ridiculous to my own ears; Noah was fast becoming my unhealthy weakness.

"Yeah right," Connor suddenly bit in, a cocky expression on his face. It screamed 'I don't believe you.'

I waited for Noah to confirm what I said but he just sat there, large and powerful wearing a grin. I wondered what was so funny. There was a definite secretive look bouncing between the two boys. The silent 'boy-code' thing they were doing was frustrating. I hoped Noah hadn't told his friends we'd slept together which would be a total lie. I pushed away the thought, I didn't really think he was that type of guy.

"So, you've come to the party as just friends?" Harlow said with a grin. Did they all know something I didn't?

I cleared my throat and took a sip of wine. Surely, they didn't think our 'making out' session at the farm was real? That had been our agreed cover. OK, I admit, things had become steamier than expected but *they* didn't know that, did they?

"I needed a date, so he's actually here tonight as a favour to me." I realised a little too late that my reply made me sound like a proper loser. I scrunched my nose at how pathetic I sounded.

Having obviously heard what I'd said, Ella's attention was pulled away from the older couple.

"Tom would have brought you if you were that desperate," Ella pointed out, totally unaware of how rude this sounded; Noah being sat *right* there.

"Ella," her boyfriend Ryan shot in, his voice like a slap on the hand.

She shuffled in her seat, "Oh, sorry, Noah. No offence."

Noah shot her a sardonic look, "None taken."

I then made matters worse by adding, "No, it's fine. I know Tom has been seeing someone. Noah was available and I didn't want to come by myself." I had officially made myself sound like a proper sad case. What on earth was my mouth doing?

Ella then tittered but Ryan nudged her and Connor snorted rudely, saying "nothing worse," under his breath. Harlow spoke over the last part.

"So, are we allowed to ask *why* he owes you one? What did he do? Something atrocious I hope."

"Do we *really* want to know Ella? It's Noah, I imagine it's something that shouldn't be aired in public." Ryan said with a smirk.

I placed my wine down and plopped both hands on either side of the knife and fork in front of me. Noah leaned over the table to lift the water jug; filling everyone's glasses. No doubt he wouldn't relish the thought of me telling his friends he'd even been in a church, let alone his conduct that day.

Ella and Ryan who had been talking quietly to each other refocused their attention on me. I looked around the table, uncertainty pumping within me.

"Inappropriate behaviour," I replied, my tight smile turning genuine as I shot Noah a sideways glance. His face was a mask now; giving nothing away. He was so lucky I was such a nice girl; I could have easily thrown him under the bus.

"Oh, do tell," Harlow cooed with encouragement, not wanting to leave it there.

Noah smiled with a feral edge, "You don't want to know Harlow; it's way too hardcore for your pretty ears," he said with a private grin. I hoped he wasn't referring to the other night.

Harlow wasn't offended and grinned back at him as Connor came to life beside her.

She had her small hands on the table and I watched as her boyfriend lifted one and brought it to his mouth, kissing the inside of her wrist. There was no doubt about it, they were a tight couple.

I noticed how flawless and perfect her fingers were against his. Connor's knuckles appeared to be badly scarred with dark red grooves. What the hell had he done to his hands?

He must have seen where I was looking and lowered his hand but kept his fingers wrapped around Harlow's. It was sweet to watch, they really were adorable together even if he was a grumpy sod with mashed-up hands. Maybe she had him under her thumb and not the other way around. She was an angel, after all, I imagined most boys would bend over backward for her. They'd have to get past the Hulk that was Connor first of course.

"Noah could write everything he knows about hardcore on a fuck—, on a napkin," he mocked without shame.

They were doing that thing that close friends did. Winding each other up. I'd always thought it thoroughly immature but these guys seemed to do it in a fairly sophisticated way. I noticed that Connor had been about to swear but thought better of it. It appeared being in his girlfriend's presence had forced him to remember his manners.

"Blow me, and at least I can write dipshit," Noah bit back with a smirk.

Connor gave him the middle finger and the two boys exchanged knowing smiles. Harlow pulled her fingers out of Connor's other hand and elbowed him in the ribs. He grunted, lowering his rude finger gesture and shooting her a sheepish look.

"He's got a point Con," Ella joined in.

"I don't think you should get involved in this one Ella, high school reject that you are," Connor returned, now cradling his beer against his chest.

Ryan shuffled beside her and she grinned shooting him a look to say, 'Back off, I'll deal with him.'

"I finished high school actually."

"Yeah, and look where it got you, digging in other people's gardens. At least your parents have one child they can be proud of," Connor said with a sneer. I knew from what Tom had said that Ella had a chip on her shoulder about equality between her and her sibling; that she thought their parents favoured him in some way.

"At least I don't shovel animal shit for a living, although you do clean up quite nicely," she shot back, totally unfazed.

"Connor looks amazing in a suit," Harlow grinned, defending her boyfriend.

"So does Ella, although isn't that *your* suit Ryan?" Connor bit back, his eyes dancing with mischief as they roamed over the trouser suit she wore. I knew he was calling her butch.

“Stop being a twat Connor,” Ryan cut in with a roll of his eyes. “You’re just pissed off that Ella has the ability to wear the pants in a relationship, instead of being pussy-whipped.”

Ella laughed and shot her boyfriend a grateful look. Harlow grinned across the table.

“It’s totally fine Ry. And I do agree with you Har, Con *does* look good in a suit. It just goes to show, you can’t polish a turd, but you can roll it in glitter.”

I imagined they treated each other like this all the time, as the others didn’t bat an eyelid. I felt a bit uneasy. I wasn’t very good at playful banter and making fun of people but I also didn’t want to sit there looking like a stuffed owl.

“She’s got you there, farm boy,” Noah said, choking out a laugh.

“You shovel animal shit?” I questioned with wide eyes, now puzzled, only half aware my mouth was moving.

Harlow came to my rescue, “Connor’s a farmer,” she said, beaming up at him.

So, he *was* a farmer; so, unless my cousin had radically changed her career how did they work together? She’d always worked in mental health.

“I thought he worked with Katy— “

Again, that strange feeling around the table, and then the penny dropped and I felt like swallowing my tongue. The big guy blatantly had issues.

Connor was one of Katy’s patients!

I glanced between Harlow and Ella, understanding now written on my face. The elephant that I had invited into the room in my ignorance, sitting right there in the middle of the table.

Connor’s body language screamed ‘not happy’ and from the look around the table, I was right. I so needed to wind my neck in.

“Sorry, it’s none of my business.” I back-peddled.

“You’re right about that,” Connor shot back, placing his empty beer on the table and coming to his feet. “I’m going to the bar. Same again?” Harlow shot me a tight smile and then nodded up at him.

“All right big guy, fucking cool it,” Noah piped up from beside me, his bicep catching my arm. There was a definite tone to his voice.

Connor swung him a grim look before motioning toward the bar with one hand, “I intend to, but you fuckers can get your own.” And off he went. The old couple on our table shot a dirty look at his back, no doubt due to the bad language. I suddenly felt like crying. It was strange as when Noah was mean to me, I managed to remain relatively strong. Maybe because I was used to him. With Connor I sensed a real threat; the guy was darkness encapsulated and it was unnerving. He was a law unto himself.

I felt horrible until Ella chimed in. "Please don't take it personally Lucy, you weren't to know. He's just a touchy fucker." Her words soothed me a little bit but I still felt bad to have upset someone who clearly had real problems.

"His moods change like the fucking wind Lucy. In five minutes, he'll have forgotten about it. I'll have a word." Noah part-whispered in my ear. I played with the cutlery as Noah then stood and followed Connor.

"Your cousin or should I say Dr Dyson invited him here as part of his therapy. He isn't the most social person as you can see and it was suggested he come. Kind of a social experiment. Katy is amazing to invite him to her wedding, but they do have a close bond and she thinks it will be good for him." Harlow informed me, shooting a glance toward where Connor stood at the bar. "I literally had to *beg* him to come. Con's getting better but we've still a way to go. But don't worry, he's not that far gone that he would ruin her wedding or anything."

I hadn't even thought about that.

"I'm sorry, I didn't mean to upset him."

"Honestly, it doesn't take much."

"He'll be fine. The whole of Scarborough knows the guys got anger management problems. To be honest, I'm surprised you haven't heard the rumours, Lucy," Ella said twisting back toward me.

"I've been away at University for the last two years," I pointed out.

Ryan leaned around Ella, "So, you probably moved away when Connor moved onto the farm with his mother. That must have been around two years ago."

A smile spread across Ella's features; I read this to say. 'My boyfriend is so clever,' it was heart-warming but I still felt crappy, I needed to change the subject.

"Have you guys been together long?" I asked Ella and Ryan, they also looked like a solid couple.

Ryan slid his hand under the table, no doubt touching her leg or something. I was rubbish at flirty behaviour, but I could read it well.

"It's complicated," Ella said with the meatiest of smiles and I nodded my understanding. Possibly a story for another time. I imagined it would be quite romantic. Ryan looked so grown up; a proper adult and he hadn't joined in with the playful banter of the younger guys. He behaved much more grown up. I felt happy for Ella.

Ella and Harlow carried on talking about Connor and his anger management issues and I tuned out, a bit fazed.

Noah appeared and lowered himself back into his chair before finishing off his beer.

"You, OK? You don't have to worry, if he attempts to kick off again, Harlow will string him up. He wouldn't chance upsetting her; she stops blowing him if he pisses her off," he said with genuine concern which surprised me. I ignored his blowjob comment of course. I so couldn't imagine that pretty mouth wrapped around anything other than a nice, innocent lollypop. I rolled my eyes, the booze was kicking in.

"It's fine," I replied. He obviously still saw me as the pathetic female again and to be honest, that's *exactly* how I felt.

Connor appeared back from the bar with a round of drinks. He placed down the tray and started to circulate them.

"I've brought a peace offering," Connor stated gruffly, his eyes catching mine. I gave him a shy smile, my 'forgive and forget' motto bouncing to the forefront.

Ella leaned across and took a beer.

"I should think so," she shot out at him before directing the first part of her next sentence my way. "Connor's usually a tight bastard. I think this is the first time you've been to the bar in months."

He lowered his massive body into his seat and slid his arm around his girlfriend's narrow shoulders. "Save it, Ella. Good job your rich boyfriend can pay for your round. Making fuck all doing what you do for a living and all that."

Ryan smiled and Ella stuck two fingers up.

The chat then flowed quite nicely. We spoke about our jobs and where we lived in the village. Connor and Ella continued with the barb-throwing, especially when she was talking about her gardening business. Most of the questions were batted my way as I was the one everyone knew the least about. We also talked about our families, only Ryan was aware of my church and so the discussion around this was fairly short-lived which was a relief. I didn't want them to think me a religious nut. Yes, I believed in God, but I didn't go around shoving it in everyone's faces as my brother did.

We also spoke about Moses Wallis again. I knew that the boys had a history with him after Connor mentioned it that day at the practice.

Ella started to talk about that party where Wallis and his crew were escorted off the premises and said how she got injured, hit in the face. Connor rolled his eyes.

"How long are you going to milk that story, Ella?" he questioned drily and it kicked off between them again, this time with Ryan jumping in there.

"If you keep this shit up Connor, we're going to have words," Ryan threatened in an even tone. It wasn't overly aggressive but held a thread of silent promise.

Connor cocked him an eyebrow and folded his hands behind his head.

"Bring it, rich boy," he replied with a smug face.

"Anytime princess," Ryan shot back. I noted a hint of actual animosity there which suggested that the two boys may not have always been so friendly. In their strange taking the piss out of each other way of course.

Suddenly, there was a surge of people dotted around the tables surrounding us who stood. Wendy shot out of her seat like a bullet from a gun and joined the buffet queue, her husband trotting after her shaking his head. I noted they had one of those chocolate fountains in the dessert section; I certainly wouldn't be trying to take that bad boy on in my dress.

"Shall we, *friend*?" Noah said, offering me his hand and laying the 'friend' comment on thick. I took it allowing him to pull me to my feet and we walked together to the back of the queue.

I must admit, it felt normal being in his company, almost like we *were* on a date. I was no longer the pawn he pushed around.

As we stood in a cluster, I tuned out of what the others were saying, watching the side of Noah's face and appreciating how animated he was with these people.

I knew now that I had misjudged his actions in the past. I appeared to have created a caricature of the real person but why; had I done this to protect myself in some way? A method of self-preservation? My confusion about my feelings toward Noah was off-balancing.

The wine had started to relax me and I knew that it wasn't the right evening to be attempting to psychoanalyse anything, not really.

Taking the plate that Noah offered me with a thank you, I knew that something was happening here. But the main question was, did I really want to know what?

* * *

Roger and Wendy said their goodbyes almost immediately after they had eaten. They had been an entertaining couple to watch, what with Wendy only having a small plate of food and then pretty much stealing most things off her husband's plate.

Once they had gone, the banter at the table became much louder (partly to be heard over the music as the disco had started up) and we were able to speak much more freely, especially Ella.

I felt gooey inside and imagined this was due to a combined effect of the vibe of the party and the three glasses of wine I'd consumed. I didn't usually drink much and hoped that the full plate of food I had eaten would soak up some of that swirling sensation I was experiencing.

As the disco had kicked off, the dancefloor was now almost full. The lights were flashing to the music and they had one of those silver balls that hung from the ceiling, shooting a million stars across the floor. It was pretty.

I monitored Noah's friends in silence from my seat at the table. They were all talking about stuff that had happened in their past again and so I couldn't really join in. I wasn't offended, I was enjoying the opportunity to people-watch.

Connor couldn't keep his hands off, Harlow. If he didn't have his arm around her, he was kissing her neck or touching her leg and her look of sheer joy was almost magical to witness. They were the best-looking couple in the room and were so obviously in love. I felt another twinge of envy.

I caught some of Ella and Ryan's banter, they didn't appear to be as touchy-feely but you could tell they cared about each other. Ella seemed to enjoy winding Ryan up and my goodness, since the old couple had left, she now had no filter. The girl swore in almost every sentence I heard.

Noah and I had been fairly quiet, drinking in our surroundings and I suddenly wanted to dance. An urge that had clearly come out of the blue, as I *never* danced.

A medley of slow songs drifted out through the speakers and some people left the floor as others joined it.

Noah leaned his head toward me saying, "So, I take it I've successfully repaid my debt to you?" His voice was playful.

I shook my head and slid my hands over my hair to ensure it was still gathered at the front.

"No actually, I have one more request," I replied. Was I imagining it or did I just slur? I blinked up at Noah. He looked as sober as a judge. To be honest, I hadn't seen him drink much at all but boy, could the guy eat. He *inhaled* his food. Both he and Connor must have gone back for seconds several times. 'Grazing', Ella had called it.

Noah wiggled his eyebrows in a sexy way, I was surprised he didn't wink. The guy was probably born with a dirty mind.

It was becoming increasingly harder to resist him and I threw caution to the wind, the alcohol giving me that extra bit of courage I needed.

"Dance with me?" My tone sounded quite commanding and I applauded myself. Being in Noah's presence appeared to be slowly building that non-existent backbone he had mentioned several times.

"Of course," he replied, those creases at the corners of his eyes appearing. My pulse accelerated.

Noah took me by the wrist and led me onto the floor, and my hands automatically slid up around his neck. He dropped his fingers to my waist, I imagined he'd probably be able to span the area, I was so narrow and his hands were *really* large. My high heels brought us closer together and I didn't have to crane my neck as much.

We swayed to the music and at one point I rested my head against his strong chest, breathing in his scent. Our nearness suddenly felt so right.

As one track changed into another, I raised my head to peer up at him through my lashes. His face was lowered and his dark eyes probed mine.

He was such a good-looking man; *shatteringly* attractive in fact.

"Don't look at me like that," Noah whispered down at me in a thick voice. It licked up my spine and would probably have done that somewhere else if I had let it. I told myself to be strong. Whatever this thing was between Noah and me; I knew at the back of my mind that it was wrong. Would never work. We were just too different.

"Like what?" I questioned almost dreamily.

The music had been gradually getting quieter as we drifted away from the speakers. I glanced around to see that we were no longer on the dance floor but at the top of a corridor where there were patio doors that led to the garden. I knew Noah had orchestrated it as I'd hazily felt him leading me away.

"How am I looking at you?"

"Like you want me to kiss you," he said into my ear. His breath was warm against my skin and the naked base of my spine tingled.

A courageous feeling suddenly swept through me and I embraced it.

"What if I do, want you to kiss me that is, as an experiment of course? Just for tonight," I stated in a silky tone. It suddenly felt like I was having an out-of-body experience and was watching a different version of myself.

"What if I want more than just a kiss?" Noah returned, flagrant desire raging from the look he gave me. His eyes gleamed and I noted how pale my skin looked against his.

"Well, there's no way *that's* going to happen on the dance floor, so for starters please," I said, feeling like the seductresses I had read about in my grans Mills and Boon books. I was *past* caring. My resolve had been temporarily smashed away.

My chest swelled and I moaned as Noah's hands slid down to cup my bottom, pulling me against his solid frame. I tried to suppress the shiver that ignited my entire body at his touch.

And BOOM! A firework went off inside me. It was carnal and raw.

Noah lowered his head, his lips closing over mine and it felt *amazing*; I pushed myself up onto my tiptoes to cement our mouths closer together, sighing into his mouth. His kiss was gentle at first, exploring the surface before it hardened and became more demanding. His tongue plundered my mouth, diving in and out, like a frenzied version of the sexual act.

Everything got a bit more heated as he drew my bottom lip into his mouth, biting down gently and that heat I'd felt between my legs intensified. I pushed my body further against his.

Noah growled deep in his throat and almost lifted me into him, his fingers splayed over my backside. He ground his arousal into me, it was hard against my belly, branding me and I wanted to touch him, feel him in my palm. Everything felt so natural, and unforced as he hungrily fed on my mouth.

I was too excited to be shocked as he deepened the kiss, his tongue thrusting boldly. At that moment, Noah *owned* me; and he *knew* it and there was nothing I could do to stop it. It was powerful, mind-blowing and I wasn't sure I would ever recover from it. My sanity had left the building along with my resolve.

I moaned softly as he raised his head and put his forehead against mine, his breathing was heavy and laboured, like my own.

"Come home with me Lucy. We'd be dynamite in bed," Noah groaned in a tortured voice. Sexual tension crashed between us in waves, you could almost physically feel it. His words triggered the wildest of thoughts to race through my mind.

And again BOOM! My blood was still pounding, but this time his words knocked me out of the passion fuelled mist. What the hell was I doing? Almost climbing the guy in a public place?

The realisation of my behaviour crashed into me like a truck. I imagined sleeping with Noah would be an unforgettable experience but I needed to get real. There couldn't be a future between us. I needed a Mr Right, not a Mr Wrong. I wanted someone who was nice to me and listened, Noah was probably one of those guys that started texting on his phone when you were talking. Not to mention we were opposites in every way!

Everything we had gone through together over the last few weeks raced through my mind. What happened at the farm was at the top of that list.

I wobbled on my legs, dropping my arms and splayed a hand to my chest, my breath leaving my body in ragged pants. I was like one of those drug addicts at the mission that was going through their withdrawal stage, but I had to get through it.

Noah had to hold me up and I felt the colour in my cheeks rise.

"I take it that's a no," he said bluntly in a disappointed voice and I smiled back at him shyly, now feeling embarrassed.

Rolling his eyes, he wrapped an arm around my waist and led me toward our table. The others were still sitting there talking through the music and they all turned to look at us as we approached in silent question.

Connor's eyes roamed over me in an assessing manner and I felt very aware that my nipples were straining against the material of my dress. My face was also on fire and my lips felt swollen from Noah's kiss. I probably looked *exactly* like the Jezebel I was!

"If you're just friends then I'm the fucking Pope," Connor said hooking a brow at us. I shot Noah a self-conscious look and saw a hint of understanding cross his face.

"We *are* friends as Lucy said, *friends with benefits*." He then winked at me which caused me to choke out a laugh. I so needed to lighten up. So, we'd kissed again? It was a party and we'd had a good time together and that was it. Why did my mind always try and blow things out of proportion?

It's not like it would be happening again. Tomorrow I would go back to being the usual me that was determined to keep this boy at arm's length.

Noah grabbed my bag for me and we said goodbye to the group. Both Harlow and Ella had put my number into their phones and suggested we all hang out sometime. Harlow was staying with Connor at his stepdad's farm until after the New Year and so they'd be plenty of time before she went back down south.

We managed to catch Katy but couldn't find Mark to congratulate them and thank them for allowing me my plus one. I apologised for my father and David not being able to make it but she frowned and shook her head, looking past me around the room as if she was searching for someone.

What she said next didn't sit well with me at all, "I saw David a minute ago, he was speaking to Mark. Haven't you seen him? He should have been on your table."

An alarm bell started to sound in my head and my stress levels went up a notch. David *had* come to the party? I hadn't seen him. Unless he'd just dropped by. But even then, why would he not have found me out? Made his presence known. Had Noah being there put him off?

"What's wrong?" Noah asked as we walked toward the lobby.

I searched the area, wondering if I'd see him. How odd that he hadn't come to find me. I rolled my eyes and batted off the thought, figuring my brother out was like trying to resolve an unsolved case that had been left cold for twenty years.

"Nothing. Katy said she thought she saw David here," I replied, shivering slightly against the night air.

"I didn't see him," Noah responded as he shrugged off his jacket and draped it over my shoulders. I could smell that soft aftershave scent which was now wrapped around me.

"She was probably mistaken, and where are we going?" I questioned, suddenly puzzled as to why I was being herded across the car park.

"I'm taking you home. I have the truck."

"But haven't you been drinking?" I said as we came to stand beside it. The moon bounced off the bonnet. It was a crisp December night but the sky was quite clear.

"Yes, but not enough to make a difference," he confessed, opening my door and motioning for me to climb in.

I raised my brows up at him. In other words, he was over the legal limit but not drunk. Great. Was getting into the car aiding and abetting? To be honest, I was too tipsy to care.

I conceded and climbed in and Noah helped me with my dress before he walked around the front and slid into the driver's side.

"No funny business and you will take me straight home?" I informed him with a pert look.

He looked at me for a long moment with unwavering intensity, before saying, "I'll be a perfect gentleman."

Yeah right.

He stretched, "Besides, our first time *certainly* won't be in a car. I have far too much finesse for that."

I couldn't help but laugh, he was so sure of himself and cheeky. It was funny really, as those annoying traits of his from before were actually becoming quite endearing now.

That reoccurring thought swam around me, I was developing feelings for someone I had always been so determined to stay away from. Now I suddenly felt an unquenchable need; desperate for his nearness. My lips still tingled from his kiss.

It all felt too overwhelming and there was an unfamiliar ache inside me. If I was foolish enough to fall for this guy; I was going to be in real trouble.

As he drove me home, thoughts of David played in my head. I needed to put my mind at ease. Had he been at the party and if he had, why had he kept himself hidden? The whole thing reeked of weird, but where my brother was concerned, *nothing* surprised me.

Eleven

"Do I get a goodnight kiss?" Noah questioned smoothly as I unclipped my seat belt. I shot him my best 'don't push your luck,' face. We were parked outside my house and the thought of David or my father seeing anything was much too chancy.

"I need time to get my breath back before I let you take it away again, so no," I replied honestly with a smile.

He grinned, it made him appear quite boyish.

"Coward," he huffed, mocking my response.

Pushing open the door, I twisted back, "Thank you for being my plus one."

"You're welcome, anytime."

"I enjoyed myself, Noah. Your friends are cool too."

His even white teeth flashed as his lips twisted. "They're not my friends. They're just a group of people I tolerate," he joked.

I hatched a 'whatever' look. Noah had always been surrounded by people wanting to be his friend. It was the same at school. A loner he was not.

"Anyway. Thank you again and I suppose I'll see you when I see you." Why the heck did I suddenly feel that there was a boulder in my throat bigger than the whole of Yorkshire?

My goodbye was seriously lame, but I didn't know what else to say. Noah remained in his seat, watching me with such a deep expression; craven need almost. Should I have kissed him? The fear of sending him mixed messages snaked into my thoughts.

His voice dropped to a whisper and his eyes zoomed in on mine.

"I'll see you in your dreams Lucy."

He was such an arrogant sod but a cute one. After climbing from the truck, I closed the door thinking back to how much he used to annoy me compared to now. My head was a scramble of emotions. The dots just didn't join up.

My heels clicked against the cobbles of our front path as I made my way to my front door, slotting my key into the lock and turning it.

The lamp was on in the kitchen, I could see the faint glow underneath the door. I wasn't surprised as I knew David would have waited up. At least he wasn't sitting in the dark this time.

I closed the door behind me and stepped into the kitchen. My stomach sank to my knees as my eyes met David's.

He was standing there like a still, lifeless statue. And for the first time, I felt *real* fear, the type that chills your bones.

He had his arms folded, his face was flushed red and his lips were drawn into a tight line. His stance was aggressive and ready for a fight. I noted he wore a shirt, trousers, and a tie and this jolted my memory.

So, he *had* been to the wedding. Could the weirdness get any weirder? I swallowed down the lump of anxiety in my throat.

"Katy said she saw you at the wedding. Why didn't you come and find me," I put in, being the first to interrupt that *angry* silence; if silences could be angry that is.

David was leaning against the table and at my words, he unfolded his arms and rested his hand by his sides against the wooden surface. He looked thoroughly pissed off.

"Why would I have done that? You already had a date," he bit out, his voice dripping with barely concealed poison.

So, he *had* seen Noah and me. And what the heck did that mean? Even if David and I had gone together, he wouldn't have been my *date*. The whole thing felt odd, twisted almost.

"You could have joined us, you had a seat at our table," I replied feeling a hint of courage as I took a step forward.

"As if I would share the same table as that Cypriot *scum*, I have standards," David said nastily. "He's always wanted you for himself. Seeing him touching you makes me sick to my stomach."

David's eyes roamed over my shoulders and I realised that I still had Noah's jacket on, his scent lingering in the air between us.

"You even smell of him," David sneered nastily, hooking his head toward the jacket.

"He was being nice. A gentleman. It was cold and I didn't have a coat." A second wave of dread flooded my insides.

"Noah Savvas doesn't even know what the word gentleman fucking means Lucy. He's slept with half the village. Rumour has it, he's done his sister."

An unpalatable shaft of disgust shot through me; there was no way that was true.

"That's *ridiculous* David."

I watched as my brother dashed a hand across his face, he looked troubled; like he was struggling for control and another jolt of panic kicked into my chest. This was different, he was livid. Livid and he had no right to be. The muscle in his jaw ticked. This couldn't be good. I knew in that split second that I should have just left, gone upstairs to the safety of my room and locked the door, but my feet wouldn't move.

David pushed off the table and took a step toward me, glaring down into my face but I didn't step back; I was too confused by his behaviour. His reaction was so much worse the usual. He was almost behaving like a jealous boyfriend. A spasm of alarm swept up my spine.

"How long have you been fucking him, Lucy?" David's voice boomed like an explosion; his tone cracked around the room. It felt like I'd been hit by an avalanche.

I shook my head to deny it but he cut me off, "You slut, you *fucking* slut!" His breath reeked of spirits; an empty bottle of Vodka sitting on the table behind him.

And then, my life as I knew it ended.

The blow when it came felt like I'd been hit with concrete. My entire face *exploded*; my head jarred violently to one side as David viciously backhanded me. I felt my lip split, the metallic taste of blood as I fell, my arms flailing to brace my body against... what? I hit the stone, and another shaft of pain lanced up my back. As my fingers searched my face, I touched my mouth, my fingers were sticky; red. The whole area throbbed. Had I momentarily lost consciousness?

Emotion clogged my throat, but I must have screamed, or yelled; *something* as the door to the kitchen crashed open and Noah stood there, like a tower of strength; his strained face searching the room.

He moved into the kitchen, his hard, angry gaze shifting between me and David before realisation at what had happened infected his features. His massive shoulders lifted and he looked twice the size as he prowled toward David. I attempted to push to my feet, *terrified* for my brother. Noah's face was *murderous* and he grabbed David by the shirt with both hands and rammed him back against the table. The smashing of glass as the Vodka bottle went flying echoed around the room. A hand shifted from my brother's shirtfront to wrap around David's throat as Noah half pinned him to the table.

"Get in the car Lucy," he instructed over his shoulder as his large fist tightened over my brother's neck; his entire body bristling with unfettered rage.

My face was throbbing and I weakly tried to stand but I couldn't make it. I was off balance, dizzy.

Noah had his face pushed into David's.

"If you *ever* touch her again you sick fuck, I will *end* you," he growled between tight lips, his fingers squeezing, causing my brothers' eyes to bulge.

Gut-wrenching panic hit me that he was going to kill him.

"Noah," I said weakly but everything hurt.

"*Do you understand me*?" Noah bellowed.

Through my tears and pain, I saw David frantically nod, his expression one of sheer terror as he stared up at the much larger man.

Around a beat after, Noah released him and he slid off the side of the table and dropped to the floor. The bigger guy standing over my brother's crumpled body.

I watched helplessly as Noah spat on the floor, close to David. "*That's* what I think of your *fucking* church!"

He then turned, moving toward me with such grace and speed for someone so large.

Bending, he pushed his hands under my legs and back and scooped me up into the safety of his arms. Removing me from the danger, taking me away from the misery, the hurt, that menacing proximity.

My family as I had known it was changed forever.

Clutching my bag in one hand, I wrapped my arms around Noah's neck as he stormed toward his car. Misery lanced through me as he lowered me beside it before yanking the door open and assisting me inside. I looked over his shoulder as he helped push the folds of my dress into the cab, my head reeling.

"He didn't follow us, doesn't have the guts. If he does, I will lay the fucker out cold," Noah announced before slamming the door and storming around to the driver's side. He was enraged but in control. That was the difference, David had also been livid but out of control, perversely so.

The engine fired up and the car shot forward and the maelstrom of emotions I experienced was indescribable.

I rested my aching head back against the seat, that sick feeling rotating around my stomach. Noah was gripping the steering wheel so tightly that his knuckles were white. He was angry, *enraged* actually. His temper frayed to breaking point. The atmosphere in the cab of the truck was thick and dangerous.

"Did you hit anything when you fell?" Noah questioned anxiously, giving me a level look.

The side of my mouth ached and I pressed the back of my hand against it, trying to ease the throbbing. "I don't think so. It's just my face," I replied with a croak, feeling my shoulders tremor. I suddenly felt all shivery, my dignity was fracturing fast.

Noah jammed the car into another gear and accelerated; his shoulders set at an aggressive angle. "Do you want me to take you to the hospital, as a precaution?

Shaking my head, I responded weakly, "No, won't they want to know what happened?"

Noah shot me a dark look before refocusing on the road. "Probably, and you need to tell them the truth. You've just been assaulted, Lucy."

I knew what he was saying was right but the thought of telling anyone that my brother had hit me, made that agonising feeling of betrayal tighten. That small thread of trust I'd held through my relationship with David had snapped. It was gone for good. I attempted to sniff the tears back but they lingered in a pool at the base of my eye; a bubble snaked up my spine.

"He's my brother," I said sadly. I knew at the back of my mind that my loyalty was misplaced.

Noah didn't care for my comment and he growled at me, "I don't give a shit who he is. *No one* has the right to do that. He's lucky he's still breathing."

Dropping my fingers to my lap, the pain in my jaw appeared to be spreading.

"But he'll get into trouble."

"Don't you *dare* think about protecting the bastard! Otherwise, I'll turn back and finish what I started," Noah barked at me.

I felt an unfamiliar constriction in my chest and I opened my eyes to study his profile. His jaw was stuck out at a challenging angle.

"Look, can we not talk about this now," I asked in a small voice. The weakness of my words cooled him down and some of the stiffness from his shoulders eased.

There was a beat of silence before he replied. "Of course, sorry. I'm just angry, fuming actually."

We drove in silence as I tried not to replay the ugly event in my head. David's twisted face swam in and out of my thoughts. I knew he'd been drinking. There had been a faint smell of alcohol. Like father like son, it appeared.

The kiss Noah and I had shared must have been witnessed and it had obviously pushed my brother over the edge. I didn't have the strength at that point to portion any blame. I was so confused.

Twisting toward Noah I asked. "Where are we going? I don't have a place to stay." Again, another unhappy truth. What the hell was I going to do now? There was no way I was *ever* going back to that house.

Noah cleared his throat. "You're coming to my place, then we can assess the damage fully. Maybe you should have a hot bath or something." His tone was firm and confident like he had everything already figured out and I realised, that no matter how much this boy unsettled me. He now made me feel safe. It was like a miraculous transformation from our relationship at school.

My lip stung as I attempted to smile.

"Thank you and for coming to get me. How did you know what had happened?" To think I'd spent years seeing this person as a bad apple. I felt a slither of guilt having never had Noah down for the type of guy who would rescue a damsel in distress. But he *was* that guy. Why hadn't I realised that before now?

He pulled the car into the yard of his unit and parked up beside an old Ford. He cut the engine and then turned to me, he was so broad and overpowering in the small space.

"You still had my jacket. I was just about to knock on and heard the shouting. Fuck me, hearing you scream out like that almost gave me a heart attack. I just lost my shit, something snapped."

Noah raised a hand and put a gentle finger to my lip, "That's going to be nasty in the morning."

He lowered his hand before saying, half to himself, "I take it he *was* at the wedding and saw us."

"Yes," I replied flatly, feeling utterly miserable.

Noah shifted in his seat, dark penetrative eyes roaming over my face. "Motherfucker, I swear to God..." Again, he was all attitude.

I raised a hand to soothe him, not ready to deal with any more outbursts of temper, from anyone. "No Noah, please, calm down."

We climbed out of the vehicle, Noah sprinted around the front of the car to help me down. His caring behaviour, made me want to bawl my eyes out even more.

"Are you OK to walk? I can carry you?" he suggested, curling a protective arm around my waist, my skin heated where he touched. I welcomed the contact; it was reassuring and warm.

"No, its fine," I replied as we made our way over to the side door by the shutters.

The workshop of the unit was quite cold and we walked between the cars and made our way over to some stairs. They would of course lead up to Noah's living space and I felt a hum of something unidentifiable fizz through me; nerves perhaps?

"Come on up," Noah invited, releasing my waist and taking the first two steps. His hand was outstretched with his palm facing up and I placed my fingers in his. He held me with his arm behind his back and tugged me gently along.

As I climbed the stairs behind him, I heard a scuffle from above, before a pair of brown eyes and a velvety nose appeared.

Vee!

"Oh, my goodness, you took her? I thought Tom had arranged a shelter," I shot out, feeling *elated* that she was there. Her tail was wagging furiously and as Noah released me, I bent down and stroked her head, her one ear flipped to the side.

"She's the new woman in my life," Noah said with a grin as Vee circled him with her tail wagging.

I straightened and glanced around. The area was open plan, like a mezzanine and it was furnished *exactly* like you'd expect a studio flat to be. Masculine colours, varnished wood, and the walls around the space were part brick part metal. The lighting was provided by a handful of lamps that were set out around the room.

There was an area set out like a living room, carpeted with a huge flat-screen TV, surrounded by old gnarled chesterfield sofas, one large, one smaller, and a chair. The chair carried what appeared to be freshly washed towels which were stacked high. A coffee table sat to the side but was clear of pots. The bedroom area was to the left in one corner where the huge bed sat; the dark grey bedding inviting. There was a large wardrobe and another old chesterfield chair with clothes draped over it. A door on my right led to what I assumed would be a bathroom and straight ahead of me was a kitchenette. The units were fairly modern and a large table sat in the middle of the lino. The rest of the flooring was wooden floorboards which were varnished. I noticed massive speakers and a sound system beside a writing desk which was covered with papers.

“Sorry about the mess,” Noah apologised as he moved the fresh laundry from one of the leather chesterfields.

Glancing around I smiled, “No it’s fine. It looks cosy.”

He dusted down the leather of the chair and motioned for me to sit.

“Here, take a seat. I’ll go and get some stuff to clean you up. Your face is already red.”

Part of me wondered what my face looked like, but the thought of checking the mirror and seeing the damage done to me by a member of my own family was just too painful. The unknown felt better, what I didn’t see, couldn’t hurt right? I also accepted that I would look at my worst right then, and so maybe I could check my face once I’d cleaned it up a bit.

“I just can’t believe he hit me,” I said partly to myself as Noah returned with a damp cloth and a fluffy black towel. Kneeling down in front of my legs, he started to dab the corner of my mouth with the warm cloth. It came away with blood on it, but then I’d known I was bleeding from the mark on my fingers.

As he gently wiped my face, he suggested in a calm, encouraging voice. “Don’t think about it now Lucy. Let’s get you cleaned up and I’ll get you something to sleep in. We can talk about it in the morning, once you’ve rested.”

Noah finished off cleaning my face, eyeing the damage with narrowed eyes and I pulled my face away and glanced around the space. My gaze fleetingly skated over the large, masculine double bed again. I wondered briefly how many girls had shared it. The thought left a bad taste in my mouth and I recognised the flare in my chest to be jealousy.

“Where will I sleep?” I said to distract my thoughts.

He hooked his chin toward his bedroom area and said in a curt voice. “You can take the bed. I’ll take one of the sofas.” My brow creased as I frowned, looking at the three-seater sofa next to the chair I was sitting on.

Noah slowly raised to his feet and I looked up at him as he towered over me. “But you’re huge, you’ll not be comfortable on that surely,” I shot out, worried about putting him to so much trouble.

“Probably not but there’s only one bed.” Noah stepped back and I carefully pushed to my feet. “I rarely have guests and if I do, they share it.”

He gave me a cheeky wink which lightened the mood and I smiled shyly. I knew he wasn't hitting on me. Not really. This was serious stuff and Noah was behaving like the perfect gentleman.

Craning my neck, my eyes searched his face again before I said.

"We could share it?" My tone was calm without a hint of anything inappropriate. It just made more sense. There were two sides after all.

I was standing so close I could see Noah's pupils. They dilated at my words, those grey flecks almost dancing. I watched as he walked away and deposited the stuff he'd used on my mouth on the table in the kitchenette.

Noah's huge body then stalked back over to me almost intentionally slow before he came to stop before me. "I don't think that's a good idea, Lucy."

I could see from his expression that he was *deadly* serious. "Well, I'm injured and I trust you."

At that moment I did trust him. With everything, including my virginity. He wouldn't touch me right now of that I was certain.

Noah recovered from his thoughts and he smiled down into my face. One hand pushing a section of my hair back over my shoulder. I still wore his jacket. "Even so, I'm not sure I trust myself," he said, partly to himself. He touched the curve of my cheek with the pad of his thumb; the skin was slightly rough, again a reminder of the manual work he did.

There was a tiny tense pause before he dropped his arm away from my face and stepped back.

"I trust you," I repeated. And he knew from the tone of my voice that I meant it.

"Maybe you shouldn't."

There was a beat of silence.

"Do you want a bath?" Noah suddenly asked; startling my thoughts. Maybe I'd confessed I trusted him a little too soon. My eyes widened at the way he just put it out there.

His lip curled in a sardonic smile, "You are so delightfully transparent, I didn't mean with me."

I felt fairly comfortable and relaxed and was surprised by my reaction to the bath comment.

"No thank you, I'd just like to go to sleep really," I said with a quiver in my voice.

He nodded his understanding and gave my shoulder a tiny squeeze before he turned and walked away, leaving me to shrug out of his jacket.

Kicking off my heels, I moved over to one of the kitchen chairs and hooked his jacket over the back. Vee came over for another quick stroke before settling in the bed by the kitchen counter.

Noah returned with a T-shirt in his hand for me to sleep in and he motioned to the door which I'd assumed was the bathroom earlier.

"I'll just take Vee out to do her thing. Why don't you use the bathroom?"

I smiled my thanks and went over to where he'd motioned, entering the small space and closing the door behind me.

I could hear Noah moving around in the next room, he was huge at the end of the day and so I imagined he didn't do anything quietly. The bathroom was spotless, which was another nice surprise. I'd always imagined Noah would be messy and it was such a relief. Yes, I was injured and feeling sorry for myself but I also wasn't in the mood to be faced with any boy grottiness.

I removed my dress and stood naked apart from my lace thong. After splashing water across my face, I stood on my tiptoes to allow myself to see into the mirror. It was set at a higher angle, obviously, it had been placed to allow Noah to see into it. I could only see the top of my head and nose and decided that maybe it was better to see myself in the morning. I could then spend the night trying to forget. I noted how puffy my eyes were.

As I left the bathroom, Noah had put a makeshift bed together on the sofa. He had changed into black sweatpants and was topless. Vee appeared to be fast asleep in hers.

Making my way nervously toward him, I shyly skimmed my eyes across the beauty of his flawlessly crafted physique.

His pectoral muscles were so defined and I suddenly had the urge to trace one with my fingertip. Noah glanced down at his chest, following the direction of my interest.

"I can put a top on if it would make you more comfortable," he suggested and I smiled back at him reassuringly. He looked devastatingly sexy as he rubbed the back of his neck, one bicep flexing at the motion. Was it wrong that I wanted to lick his skin even in my battered state?

"No, it's fine." I returned politely. I suppose I should have been thankful for small mercies that he didn't sleep naked.

Noah motioned toward his bed. “The bedding is fairly fresh. Missy changed the sheets this morning which is fortuitous, I think.”

He explained that Missy was his cleaner and I felt a dart of relief, having a moment of panic that he meant a girlfriend or something.

There was a definite heat between us, sexual energy, but of course there would be. The attraction we felt for one another had been ignored but it was blatantly there. Noah was right, I had been in hiding.

“Night then,” Noah said before turning away, breaking that connection between us. Probably purposefully. His tee covered me and fell just above my knee but I was braless and I knew he’d be more than aware of that.

As he climbed onto the sofa, I moved to the bed, ‘Noah’s bed’ and pulled back the sheets before climbing in. It was so comfortable.

“You in?” Noah shot out.

“Yes, thank you.” Even though they were clean, the sheets still held a hint of his musky scent and I drew him in through my nostrils.

Noah clicked a remote he held which must have controlled the lamps as they all went out. I’d left the light from the bathroom on and it allowed a soft glow into the room. I was pleased as the thought of waking up in a strange place in the middle of the night in pitch darkness after wasn’t the most welcomed thought. I didn’t like the dark.

There was silence.

I could hear the occasional shuffling as Noah twisted and turned, trying to get comfortable. Maybe I should have offered to sleep on the sofa, I’d probably fit better.

I could hear the soft sound of Noah’s breathing.

We both must have laid there for around ten minutes before I suddenly got an overwhelming urge to cry again.

“Noah?” I whispered into the part-darkness. The leather of his chair creaked as he turned around to look at me. His face was part-shadowed.

“Yeah? Are you OK?”

Pursing my lip, I nodded slowly; our gazes tangled.

“Please, would you sleep with me?”

“Lucy…” he started to argue before I raised a hand to stop him.

“I mean, beside me. Not to *do* anything, I just don’t want to be alone.” My voice still exited my chest like a welcoming caress.

Our eyes remained entwined before he said. “Are you sure?”

Under normal circumstances I would have been a tangle of nerves but at that moment, I had never been more certain of anything in my life. “Yes.”

Noah climbed off the sofa and slowly walked toward the bed. As he slid into the other side, I wondered if I should ask him which side he usually slept on, but he kind of answered when he said. “And, no I don’t have a side, you’ve seen the size of me, I usually take up the entire space, so apologies up front if I breach any invisible lines. You can just thump me in the ribs and I’ll move back.”

I felt the mattress dip as he lowered his large body under the sheets beside me.

I was laying on my back staring up at the ceiling, feeling very aware of how close he was but I didn’t feel awkward or uncomfortable at all.

“Noah?” I said into the quiet.

He shuffled under the covers, turning to face me and I copied him so we were both on our sides face to face. Noah rested his head on one tanned arm.

“Why did you leave the army?” I decided to bite the bullet and ask the question, if he didn’t want to tell me, he didn’t have to.

It was dark but I could still see his features clearly. He took a moment to answer.

“I was discharged,” he began in a deep voice. The sound resonated pleasantly through my bones. “*Dishonourably* discharged.”

I felt a twinge of shame for what I’d said that first day by my car about him being a deserter. My guilt still didn’t stop my mouth from moving. “Why?”

His eyes creased as he smiled and I felt a shard of relief that I hadn’t offended him by being so direct.

“I hit an officer. Broke his nose,” he explained, his voice now held a trace of stern. I could see from his expression that he was partly reliving the experience from the slight bitter smile he wore.

“We don’t have to talk about it if you don’t want to,” I slid back, not wanting to upset the guy who had basically been my hero of the hour.

Noah’s revelation as to how he was kicked out of the army was quite shocking, but I welcomed the story as it distracted me from my own problems.

Noah had been posted in Iran and was working as a trainee helicopter mechanic. Having only been in the role for eleven months, he had been a fairly junior member of the squad but his work had caught the eye of his superiors. He spoke about the army with such passion and explained that he'd fully intended on climbing the ranks to work his way up to one of the commanding roles.

He explained that there had been a rumour going around his squad about their superior officer, a well-decorated staff sergeant. The basis of the gossip was that the staff sergeant had been involved with several young female civilians; something which was more than frowned upon. Especially considering they were underaged.

Noah had originally decided to ignore the gossip, having wanted to keep his head down but after witnessing how the staff sergeant behaved with couple of local girls, he started to believe the gossip was true. He explained how it was one of those things that just started to eat away at him and the fact that no one else reported the sergeant, really started to stoke his conscience to the point where he couldn't turn his back.

I was holding my breath when he explained how he'd come to punch the man involved.

"I caught them in a storeroom off the mess hall. He was on top of her; she couldn't have been more than fifteen and I just lost it."

A horrible sick feeling hit my stomach at the thought of what that poor girl must have gone through. Noah said that she'd been trying to push him off when he'd grabbed the back of the sergeant's shirt to physically remove him.

"I just went for it, smacked him in the face and he went down like the piece of shit he was. His nose was pretty much spread across his face, I did think I'd killed him at first. Shit myself big time. After that it all kicked off. He blatantly lied about the incident during the investigation and said I'd attacked him on purpose. Said I had anger management issues and wouldn't follow orders. A load of shit basically. The Iranian girl had been too scared and had denied everything to the translator so I got court marshalled and stripped of the one stripe I had. Army career over. Just like that," he explained with a snap of his fingers.

His expression was raw.

A moment of quiet inched in between us as I stared into Noah's eyes. Like I was seeing yet another side to this boy that I'd never seen before. He'd risked himself and his career for a stranger. He could have just walked away. My heart squeezed and I felt an overwhelming need to move into his arms. Knowing where that could lead, I redirected my train of thought.

"Do you regret what you did?" I asked with a frown.

His answer was immediate, “Hell no. I’d do it again in a heartbeat.” And I believed him.

His voice turned grave as he made an unpalatable point, “The sick fuck is still out there though, who knows how many girls he’s torturing. That’s where the regret comes in, the fact that in spite of what I did, he’s still getting away with it. I spoke to a couple of mates in our squad, but they were too chicken shit to get involved. It’s times like that when you know who your real friends are.”

Noah turned onto his back, the covers only part covering his torso as he regained his composure.

And that was it right there, the night I slept beside Noah Savvas, my ex-nemesis.

We moved onto other subjects after that, mainly about our families. I told him more details about how my mother left and how this had affected my father. I didn’t speak too much about David as I felt it too painful after what had happened. My lip was sore, a constant reminder that my own brother had struck me. Something I had *never* thought he could be capable of. I thought back to that conversation in my car when Noah had stated that all men were capable of violence. I guess he was right.

In the morning, I was very aware of Noah’s hard body pressing into my back. As I opened my eyes, he was spooning me. My breathing almost stalled altogether. I knew I needed to pull away, but it felt so nice. The hardness of his skin imprinted against the softness of mine. From his shallow breathing, I could tell he was still asleep and I shuffled slightly before I realised one of his strong arms was across my waist. I could feel his fingers splayed against my bare belly where his T-shirt had risen up. His hand was at the bottom of my breasts but I didn’t care, the contact felt yummy. I needed to bat the urge to play with fire away. One of his strong legs trapped mine.

I laid there, without pulling away for another half an hour or so before Noah started to stir. My knicker-clad bottom was pressed into the v between his corded legs and he tugged me further against his body, his head nuzzling into the back of my head, taking in the scent of my hair. He was still half asleep. OMG did he imagine I was a girlfriend or something? Had he forgotten it was me, I opened my mouth to speak but he beat me to it, his hand flattening against my abdomen. A heady mix of arousal and adrenaline pumped through my body. I felt more excited than I had in years; there was a full of rave going off in my stomach. That flush of desire was intense and need stormed through me.

I drew in a careful breath as Noah whispered into my neck where my hair had slipped forwards. "Since you're nearer my side, I assume you were the one to breach the invisible line, Miss Meadows."

My whole body must have blushed and I resisted the urge to turn and bury myself against him as he slowly withdrew his hand. The level of disappointment I experienced felt like I'd suddenly lost a limb or something. I turned in the bed to face him with a smile. He had that slumberous sleepy head look, he was still gorgeous of course and I wondered what a state I would look with my hair all over the show, a fat lip and a possible shiner.

Thoughts of the events of the night before came flooding back, but I still managed to crack a smile; and crack it did as a twinge of pain needled into my bottom lip.

There was a spark of mischief in his eyes. "My apologies, I didn't mean to take liberties," I began in good humour, although there was nothing to laugh about, not really.

"You can take liberties with me anytime Lucy, you know that," he replied with a wolfish smile.

I knew that was my cue to move, the thought of Noah and morning glory suddenly popping into my thoughts. I couldn't be dealing with *that* right now. I knew most guys got this anyway when they woke but surely when they had a half-naked female next to them, it would be inevitable?

"Do you want me to turn my back so you can get out?" He offered as he pushed himself up to lean on his elbow. Once again full of good intentions.

"No, it's fine. I have underwear on," I said in an 'as if' type of way. Still being playful but with an added hint of flirty.

"Shame," he replied in a smoky voice and a feathery sensation shot up my spine.

Our eyes were locked and I couldn't move away. It was like an invisible thread connected us and I so wanted to lean forward and place my mouth against his. His hair was mussed from sleep.

"You don't have to be afraid of me Lucy. I'd never hurt you."

"I know," I responded in soft voice.

The silence grew between us, a message being shared before he pulled himself together.

"Off you go then, get washed up, before I show you my true colours and do something we'll both regret," Noah drawled in a voice full of sexual promise.

I wrinkled my nose as our gazes remained entwined.

"Thank you, Noah, for not trying anything on. I do appreciate it."

"I should bloody well hope so, I haven't had sex in six weeks; I should get a fucking medal," he ground out in a rough voice.

I ignored that twinge of jealousy. He didn't need to tell me twice and I whipped the bedcovers off.

As I climbed out, I heard his intake of breath as he must have seen part of my thong-clad backside as I climbed out and escaped to the bathroom, running from his threat. I wasn't uncomfortable, it felt nice. At that moment, I welcomed his interest in me. He took away that edge of loneliness that I don't think I had managed to shake since my mother left.

As I went to the bathroom, there was a fresh towel, soap and a new toothbrush on the sink that Noah had no doubt laid out and I gratefully used the facilities, feeling thoroughly cared for.

And then it hit me with more force than my brother's fist.

I was falling for him, the boy from school that I had despised, the one who was mean to me, wound me up, and enjoyed toying with me like a cat did a mouse.

I was falling in love with Noah Savvas with my *entire* being. And yes, I was afraid of Noah, but not in the way he thought. I was *terrified* of how he made me feel. I now wanted this boy with every fibre of my being.

Reality crashed into my thoughts as I realised that Noah was a gift to me that just kept on giving.

My heart was talking to me a lot louder now.

The writing was on the wall; I was falling and falling fast.

Twelve

When I'd finished in the bathroom, Noah handed me some of his joggers; the smallest pair he owned, he confessed with a grin. They were still *huge* and I had to fold the waist over a couple of times so they didn't fall down my legs. I kept the tee on that I had slept in and was very conscious of my bra-less chest as I joined Noah in the kitchen.

He'd made us both some buttered toast; it was the first time I'd shared breakfast with a boy and it made me feel terribly grown up. Not a bad thing I suppose. Vee had sat there the entire time, watching each mouthful. Once we'd finished Noah fed her and took her out for a quick walk. I was so happy he'd kept her. They seem to suit each other.

Even though I had no intention of going home just yet, I needed some stuff. After a lengthy discussion, Noah agreed to drive me over to my house so I could pack some essentials. It was Sunday and the house would be empty during the morning.

"So, you're sure David won't be there because if he is, it's going to get bloody. I'm just warning you," Noah chuntered as he pulled his Navara up outside my house; his brow raised quizzically.

He looked smoking hot as usual, sat there with his huge perfectly sculptured body like a Greek God dressed in black jeans and a pale grey hoodie. The top made his skin look darker.

I managed to stop my tongue from hanging out and replied, "No, it's Sunday. David wouldn't miss service, especially after what happened. He'll need to be in church to cleanse himself in some way. That's how it works when he messes up."

Both my dad and David would be at church which gave me the chance to get in and out quickly without having to deal with anything unsavoury. I knew I'd have to face it eventually and speak to my father about what had happened. Part of me wondered if David would have said anything. Would he even be sorry? I didn't know if I'd had any messages on my phone as the battery was dead and I didn't have a charger.

"What do you mean messes up? Are you saying he's hit you before?" Noah barked out incredulously. Snapping my thoughts back.

I closed my eyes against a sudden, unexpected sting of tears.

"Talk to me Lucy," Noah coaxed, his voice now much calmer.

Something inside my chest began to unwind and I turned to face him and opened my eyes.

Moistening my mouth, I said, "No, he's never hit me, or touched me in any way but he did come into my room one night."

"What the fuck?"

"Please Noah, just listen." In his current state of mind, Noah had little to no patience when it came to David.

He moved his hands off the steering wheel as he shut off the engine and twisted his upper body, his features contorted into a brooding expression.

"Sorry, go on," he muttered, dragging a hand down his face; possibly an attempt to deny his frustration.

I explained how I'd woken up on my first night back from University to find David sitting in my room, watching me as I slept. Noah listened without interruption, regarding me through narrowed eyes. I could see as I told my story that he was having difficulty processing what I was saying. And I must admit, once I'd aired the words, David's behaviour that night seemed even stranger. A shudder wracked my body.

At the time, David had excused himself by saying I'd been yelling in my sleep for our mother. I'd felt strangely exposed, pulling the sheet further against my chest like a shield. Being fuzzy and half asleep, the situation had been difficult to process. At the time, I wasn't totally sure whether David was lying or not but I still remembered the strange expression he'd worn, haunted almost. I'd felt uncomfortable but I'd blamed it on the fact that I was in shock. The whole thing had left a bad taste in my mouth. *That* was the reason I locked my door every night after that.

My mind started to run through David's past unexplainable behaviour and Noah's comments about how my brother treated me. I remembered his words that night by my car. I guess he was right, how could I have not seen that until now? My brain was full of foggy memories.

My eyes remained glued on Noah's face. A muscle in his jaw ticked which was the only evidence that he was angry until he said, "And he's *never* touched you?" His teeth were clenched and his stare penetrative. It was almost like he was drilling into my memory banks to try and draw out any repressed feelings. Dark memories that I may have been unintentionally holding back.

“No, never. He started insisting I kiss his cheek which was odd I suppose looking back,” I explained, holding up a hand to stop him from firing another question before I could explain. “He’s the vicar, it’s either a kiss to the hand or the cheek, a sign of respect.”

My tone should have been convincing as I hadn’t really seen anything wrong with the kiss. Not really.

From the harsh sound he released and the stern set to his shoulders. Noah disagreed.

“The guy deserves as much respect as *fucking* Putin. Its sick is what it is. He needs help Lucy and until he gets it, you need to stay the fuck away,” he bit out with furious resentment.

Shame and remorse engulfed me and there was an uncomfortable silence before Noah drew in a noisy breath, taking the keys out of the ignition.

“I think it’s something to do with my mother. I look so much like her. I know her leaving us really screwed him up. He never used to be like this,” I explained in a small voice. Yes, David had hurt me but he was my brother and I loved him. There had to be some explanation. I certainly didn’t want Noah to hate him.

He rolled his shoulders as he pushed his car keys into the pocket of his jeans. “It doesn’t excuse his behaviour, Lucy. David needs *serious* help.”

My shoulders slumped. “What am I going to do Noah, I’ve nowhere to go.” Another dart of misery jabbed me in the chest.

He leaned across the gear stick and squeezed my knee with one strong hand, his face now full of sympathy. “Talking of mothers. I’m going to call mine. You can stay in my old room at the house. I’m sure she wouldn’t mind.”

“Couldn’t I just stay with you?”

“No. You obviously can’t continue to stay with me Lucy,” he replied in a firm voice.

I knew my suggestion was as ridiculous as my reaction but I felt a twinge of hurt at his words. “Why not?”

Noah’s mouth twisted, looking at me like he thought me stupid. “You’re not room mate material I’m afraid. I’m a guy and it’s you. I only have so much restraint, Lucy. I’m not a fucking saint,” he admitted.

My chest soared at the words ‘it’s you’, they made me feel special, wanted. My voice left me and I swallowed several times but nothing came out.

The fact that he had suggested I could stop with his mother was massively welcomed. I didn't know Elena Savvas that well but I'd heard through church that she was a good woman.

"You would tell me if David had done anything else wouldn't you?" Noah suddenly said again. He was so fierce and protective and I loved it.

And him. BOOM!

The thought just popped into my head before I could stop it and I moved my thoughts along, now was *not* the time to be analysing my feelings. I was probably overthinking things after what had happened, confusing my emotions due to being in such a needy position. That's what I attempted to convince myself of anyway.

I nodded. "No. There's nothing else. Just the weird, possessive brother thing. He's just odd and dad doesn't even look at me, again another piece of weird. I don't know which is worse to be honest."

"The whole thing is screwed up. Your dad should be looking out for you, not *fucking* ignoring you. Look we'll get your shit and then I'll call my mother and get you a place to stay sorted. OK?"

I smiled. The thought again lifted my spirits as there was no way I could afford a hotel long term.

"You're sure no one will be in?" Noah repeated, an edge to his voice. Almost like he'd quite like the opportunity of seeing my brother again for round two.

"Yes, no one, dad will be with David," I said solemnly; feeling a twinge of sadness, I suddenly felt like an orphan.

Noah cleared his throat, unconvinced. "Well, I'm coming in with you. Just grab the basics, we can buy any other shit you need."

I glanced down at myself; I'd need more than the basics. I'd also need my work uniform as I certainly couldn't afford to miss work. Not that I thought Marcus or Tom would sack me for not being in uniform.

I'd cram as much as I could into my sports bag as I didn't know how long I'd be away or if I even ever wanted to go back. It was all still so raw.

We entered the house and I saw there was even more glass on the floor. I carried my bag and my heels in my hand and so carefully stepped over the mess.

"I'll wait here," Noah said as he stood inside my tiny kitchen, looking larger than life and thoroughly unimpressed.

I shot up to my room.

Pulling fresh underwear from my bedside drawers, I then grabbed a few pairs of jeans and some T-shirts, my work uniform, and a couple of dresses. I managed to fit a pair of boots into the sports bag and shoved my trainers into the handbag I used for work. I also managed to pack some essential toiletries and my hair brush.

Changing into black Capri pants, a white tee and blue hoodie, I slid my feet into ballet flats and left my room. I'd transferred my phone from my clutch and shoved it into the pocket of my trousers.

I eyed David's bedroom door as I walked past, the memory of his hand against my face coming back.

As I re-joined Noah in the kitchen, I grabbed a phone charger off the kitchen table and we both set off for the car.

Pulling away from the house, my heart sat heavy in my chest and I drew in a deep, shivering breath.

That was it. The day I left home. It was just such a shame I left under such *tragic* circumstances.

* * *

Being a man and full of fascinating contradictions, Noah was *unbelievable*. Having been my arch nemesis in the past, he was now like my guardian angel. He sorted *everything*. I'd never felt so cared for; so well looked after. He was still in my phone under SATAN and I knew I'd have to change that now.

Whilst Noah steered the car along the winding dirt road that led to his mother's house, I attempted to turn on my phone but there was totally no life left in it. I'd charge it at Noah's mum's house, maybe David had messaged me to say sorry, either that or dad may have attempted to contact me. Wishful thinking and all that.

As I had been gathering things in my room, Noah had called his mother and explained the situation. He was candid with me and told me that he hadn't held anything back. I felt a bit embarrassed, but knew he was right to come clean with them; they'd be more sympathetic with my situation then. I'd seen Noah's mum a couple of times and had only really spent a short time in Natalie's company but staying with them felt right.

On the way over, Noah and I spoke some more about his time in the army, you could tell he missed it. I wondered fleeting what that monster of a staff sergeant would be doing now. My faith over the last few weeks had been radically tested and the results about how I felt about my faith were not yet in. I hadn't said my prayers for the last few weeks either. In respect of my Christianity, I just felt disappointed. Like I was being punished.

Noah's mum's house sat back off the main road and was surrounded by tall trees; they gave the place a gloomy look but I didn't care. It felt safer and more welcoming than home. The building was made from stone and was in keeping with the other houses in the village. It had a large driveway and two garages that had seen better days.

Natalie and their mother Elena Savvas, were waiting outside the front door when we pulled up. They were both so welcoming, Natalie even pulled me in for a hug which wasn't totally awful. She had a sweet, exotic scent and looked really pretty in ripped jeans and a black hoodie. The top was the same colour as her hair. Jet black like their fathers. Their dad Theo worked in Cyprus for most of the year. Elena worked from home and sold beauty products, or at least she had done when we were at school.

We chatted briefly over a coffee and they didn't ask too many prying questions which I was thankful for.

Noah helped me with my stuff and gave me a brief tour before leading me up to his old room.

As I walked into what would once have been the lion's den my heart raced in my chest. I was Lucy Meadows, little Lucy that used to be picked on by this boy and now I was going to be temporarily living in his room, sleeping in his bed. The thoughts caused my pulse to twitch. When did everything get so mental?

The room was much bigger than mine at home and it had a cold feeling about it; an unlived vibe, which of course it would have, considering Noah now lived at the garage.

My breath tripped in my throat as my eyes fell on the bed. It was a double and the sheets were a dark navy blue. The walls were all painted cream apart from one feature wall which had dark blue wallpaper on with a splodgy design on it. There wasn't a wardrobe, just an exposed rack with coat hangers and a couple of Noah's old shirts hanging there. A long unit sat against the wall down one side of the room under the window and there was a chair tucked under a writing section. The rest of the surface was littered with electrical devices; a large screen TV, a turntable, two large speakers and lots of gaming gear. A typical boy set up really. The only thing which stood out as odd to me was the wall which had shelving on and was lined with books. *Loads* of books. I'd never thought of Noah as a reader.

"Well, what do you think?" Noah suddenly said from close behind me, his breath against my neck. Having finished my perusal of the area, I turned to look up at him. He was in my space, no shock there then. The only difference from before was that I now didn't mind it, I enjoyed his nearness.

"I never had you pegged as a reader," I said up at him.

"Yeah, I love books," he confessed, looking a little shy; like I'd guessed a secret or something.

"What's your favourite?" I questioned, wanting to draw more from him. It's like I was learning more about this man every day and what I unveiled, I liked.

"IT, Stephen King. I'm into horror. You?"

Pursing my lips, I ran through the books I'd read over the years before replying, "It has to be Gone with the Wind."

His eyes creased as he shot me a knowing smile. "Of course. Anyway, you should be comfortable enough here. I would suggest you don't go snooping through any of my old stuff though, you may see something you don't want to see," Noah informed me with a wiggle of his eyebrows. To be honest, I was torn. Part of me wanted to go fishing around his stuff and the other side knew it wasn't a good idea. I'd probably unearth a year's supply of condoms or a dirty magazine or something. Not a thought I relished.

I grinned back and shot another glance appreciatively around the space.

"Thank you, Noah, for everything you've done for me," I said.

He stared down into my upturned face. Was he counting my freckles? His expression was now quite intense. I remembered that throw away comment he'd made that day about counting every single one on my body. It made me think of his hands on my skin.

His eyes became hooded. "You know you can stay as long as you want. This is your home for now, OK?"

I watched him from beneath my lashes. I wanted to push myself up onto my tip toes and smash my mouth against those sensual, full lips.

A heat pulsed around us as he took another step forward and pulled my bags out of my hands, throwing them carelessly on the bed. I twisted to watch the movement before coming back to face him.

Unfettered desire was pooled in those dark eyes, the green flecks visible due to the closeness of our bodies.

"This door has a lock too Lucy. I do stop over sometimes, but I usually use my dad's room. The bed's more comfortable," he declared.

Puzzled, I questioned, "Your mum and dad have separate rooms?"

He nodded slowly, his lips twisting, "Yes, my dad snores and so mum regularly boots him out. Not *every* night, just sometimes when he's here."

I thought back to Noah in church, like father like son it appeared.

Noah was still explaining and I drew my attention back. "Dad spends so much time away, mum gets used to having a bed to herself and it takes time to adjust to sharing."

He paused and then his voice deepened into a tone that liked to touch. The hairs on my arms prickled.

"I must admit, I quite liked sharing last night. I got used to it straight away," he informed me; his pitch quite throaty.

Squinting him a pointed look I batted back, "Really? Surely you share your bed with girls all the time?" I was totally fishing and Noah quirked his head.

"Not really. They're never invited to stay the night."

That hadn't been what I'd wanted to hear but I could tell from his tone that he was winding me up purposefully. Was he trying to make me jealous? Absolutely, the rotten sod.

"So, I'm one of the lucky ones then," I replied, tilting my chin toward him with challenge. I managed to keep any hint that his comment had rattled me out of my reply.

"You're more than that," Noah whispered softly lifting a hand to stroke my cheek.

My head automatically moved into the caress.

Noah swiftly withdrew his hand, masking his expression.

"Anyway, as I said. Feel free to lock your door if it makes you feel safer."

Raising my eyebrows and delivering my best suggestive look, I replied. "So, I need to use the lock during the nights you stop over so you don't get the urge to ravage me in my sleep?" I responded, pushing a chunk of hair back over my shoulder.

He lowered his head and gave me a sexy smile. "Abso-fucking-lutely."

I couldn't stop the chuckle, my shoulders shaking before I composed myself and said up into his perfect face.

"Maybe I won't lock it then."

Once the words were out there, they sat between us like an invisible charged challenge; vibrating like an electric current. The shocking thing was that I meant *every* word. I *wanted* to be with this boy, with my heart, body and my soul and now he knew that. I'd bared myself to him, and opened up.

"I see. So, at last, we understand each other."

I allowed a beat or two between us before I replied.

"But that's just it, Noah, I don't understand you, not really. I don't understand why you were always so horrible to me at school. I spent those last two years torturing myself that I'd hurt you in some way."

He strummed a fist across his nose before saying, "You did hurt me, daily. Oh, not on purpose. You had no idea of the effect you had on people Lucy, on me mainly. You didn't give anyone the time of day. It was like you held yourself like you were above everyone else. I wanted you and it wound me up that I couldn't have you."

Although he said it in a fairly pleasant way, his words stung. Had he really misunderstood me so much at high school?

"But that isn't how it was at all Noah. I was shy, I didn't want to be noticed." I took a step back; my neck was starting to hurt from staring up at him.

Noah followed my retreat and moved forward.

"I know that now. I probably knew that then but I was a stubborn fucker. I didn't like to be told no."

My eyebrows scrunched, "When did I tell you no, we didn't even have that type of relationship."

"Every time you looked at me. I could see you liked me in those sly looks you shot my way but knew you'd *never* do anything about it. I suppose I treated you badly as a method of self-preservation, to protect myself. You got under my skin Red, what can I say."

The truth of everything hit me, the misunderstandings; the wires were crossed so much I was surprised we were now at a point of finally being able to untangle them.

"I also hated the fact that you were so withdrawn and I knew that wasn't the real you. Don't forget we were in primary school together, I remembered you then. You lit the place up; like a fire burning brightly. A breath of fresh air."

My nose wrinkled at the memory. I had forgotten Noah and I also attended the same primary school, I remembered he'd been tall and gangly then; he hadn't filled out.

So, in a nutshell, Noah had known me *before* my mother left and then witnessed the aftermath. And he was right, over the last few weeks of being in this *impossible* boy's company, I was gradually becoming myself again. The girl who was so much more fun than the zombie I'd become, especially the last couple of years at high school.

"I think you're right Noah and now this thing has come to a head with my brother, maybe I can move on properly," I whispered, dipping my face.

Noah pulled me into his arms in a solid bear hug and placed his chin on the top of my head. His warm strength enveloped my body.

"Maybe we could move on together," Noah whispered into my hair and my pulse sky rocketed.

I drew back and looked up at him.

"I'd like that, Noah."

His mouth pulled into a full smile before he moved his hands under my armpits and lifted me against him, his mouth covering mine.

He held me off my feet like I weighed no more than a feather, my breasts we pushed against his hard chest. *Everywhere* my skin met his sparkled like a firework that had just been lit.

His mouth moved expertly against mine, his tongue entering my mouth and I met it with my own. The kiss was much gentler and I imagined this had something to do with the slight tear on my lip. It turned out that it hadn't been as bad as the clotted blood had suggested.

Noah growled against my mouth and raised his head before lowering me back to the floor.

"You're mine little Lucy Meadows," he said, his face full of warm fondness; I felt small and pretty and utterly feminine.

"Yours," I whispered up into his face; the strength of feeling I had for this boy at that moment was off the chart.

He bent down and placed another soft kiss on my lips before moving to the door, saying over his shoulder, "I'll leave you to get settled in and I'll pick you up at six."

Before he could close the door, I questioned, "Where are we going?"

He turned to face me, our eyes meeting through the narrowing gap between the wood.

"On our first date."

* * *

Later that afternoon after having charged my phone, I checked it to see I had no messages. My heart dropped, having expected at least a call from my dad. As far as he was concerned, I hadn't come home last night.

Pushing away the horrible thoughts. I stood looking down at the clothes I had packed. *Nothing* seemed to match and I felt annoyed that I rushed it so much. Time had been a huge factor as I'd been terrified of David coming home early. If Noah had seen him again, I knew it wouldn't have been good.

Huffing, I rolled my eyes at the pile of clothes. Noah wasn't really a fan of my usual wardrobe and so I decided to find Natalie to ask her opinion on what I should wear. Would I tell her about the date, considering it was with her brother?

I went downstairs and found Elena. It appeared Noah had told both his mum and sister he was taking me out. She was full of excited chatter when she saw me lingering near the kitchen. She explained that Natalie was in her room and I went off to find her. Noah had pointed his sister's room out during our tour.

I listened against the doorway in case she wasn't alone. Music was playing faintly and I knocked on.

Natalie pulled the door wide with a smile on her face and any tension I had felt disappeared.

"Hi, so… Noah's taking me out tonight and I don't know what to wear," I explained with a shy smile.

She scratched her chin thoughtfully before saying, "So, you're the one to tame the wild beast. I must say, I'm surprised."

She opened the door wider and beckoned me inside; eyeing me in Noah's robe with a meaty grin.

Throwing herself onto her bed she patted a space on the mattress and I reluctantly joined her, curling my legs up beside me. I'd never really done the girl-talk thing and felt slightly out of my element. I hoped Natalie didn't notice how stiff my shoulders were.

"I can imagine you're surprised. I'm guessing I'm not his usual type," I admitted, taking in her bright pink bedspread. The room was splashed with colour but not overly girlie like my room at the cottage.

"Totally. I remember you were so quiet and shy at school. Noah used to come home and rant about you. Guess he liked you back then. That's what guys do; act like dicks to get your attention."

I smiled, "I suppose so. I certainly didn't see it then though and probably unfairly condemned him without giving him a chance."

"It was probably for the best. He was still a dickhead at school. Boys mature at a slower pace than girls.

I nodded, in complete agreement with her.

Sniffing, Natalie questioned. "So, what did you bring with you? What do we have to work with?"

"Not much really. I was wondering if you had something I borrow for tonight?"

Her face came alive and she shot out, "OMG, I love a makeover! Although you're so tiny compared to me."

She paused, her eyes thoughtfully roaming over my body before she climbed off the bed and motioned for me to get up. I felt a bit on display as she calmly walked around me, circling me with a pensive look.

"I may have something from years ago that we could do something with."

I spent the next hour being fiddled with, tugged around, preened, tweezed, you name it. The girl was a menace, but in a good way. By the time she'd finished, the transformation was unreal.

Back in Noah's bedroom, I admired myself in the small mirror.

Natalie had styled my hair into a riot of curls that fell across my shoulders and back like liquid fire, the deep chestnut colour glowing with health. I hadn't a clue what products she had used but I would certainly be buying some for myself.

She had made up my face and although I wore slightly more makeup than usual, I didn't feel overly caked in it. My eyes appeared a brighter blue against the smoky eyeshadow she had used.

Most of Natalie's clothes had swamped me as she was much taller and her build curvier but she'd eventually found a dress at the back of her wardrobe that she'd bought as a teenager. She confessed to keeping it, saying how she'd always intended fitting back into it one day but no such luck. It suited my figure like perfection, as if it had been made with me in mind. It was fitted and dusky grey with a slashed neckline and the hem fell quite high above my knees. The sleeves were capped and I wore it with black tights, heeled boots and a matching cardigan. Natalie had quite small feet and so I borrowed a pair of her heeled size five boots which with an extra pair of socks, fitted my size threes.

To finish off the look, Natalie let me borrow her black leather cropped jacket and a bag to match. I felt *amazing* and I couldn't wait to see Noah's face. The dress wasn't overly dressy but would be fine for either a pub or a restaurant.

I'm taking you somewhere to feed you. Are you looking forward to our first official date? Noah had texted me.

Absolutely. I replied, whilst checking the time on my phone. The afternoon had been swallowed up it seemed.

Good. I'll be out front in ten, be ready for me. I bit my lip; the guy was even bossy by text but I liked it.

Elena whistled when she saw me, she was sat at the kitchen table with Natalie. She pushed to her feet and gave me a key for the front door.

"You look lovely," she said, beaming her approval.

"Thank you," I replied, popping the key into my bag.

Tilting her head to one side Elena stared at me with kind, thoughtful eyes.

"Enjoy yourself Lucy. Noah will show you a good time."

Her question frayed my nerves a little and I wondered how best to respond. It took me a moment to gather my thoughts and I replied with, "Thank you, I think we're going out for something to eat."

Her smile widened and crow's feet appeared beside her eyes.

"He's a good boy Lucy. He hasn't had it easy what with his dad being away most of the time and what happened in the army. Noah had to grow up fast, but he looks after us when his patéras isn't here." I easily understood the Greek word for father.

Soaking up what she was saying, I questioned her. "Don't you miss each other?" Even before I'd ended the sentence, I knew my words were rude. It was none of my business really why her husband lived in Cyprus whilst she remained in England.

Luckily, she didn't appear to take offence.

"Yes, absolutely. But it's been this way for years and you get used to having the space. He comes home every month. When I had Natalie, I decided against moving to Cyprus. I changed my mind. I didn't want to raise a daughter there. Their views can be a bit old school where women are concerned and I wanted her to have an English education."

She paused and looked reflective for a moment before saying, "And to be honest, it makes sense. Theo's business is over there and he couldn't really run it from the UK. We speak most days via Zoom, the time differences is only an hour and when we do see him, we make it extra special.

I saw Natalie shoot me a suggestive look over her mother's shoulder before she called out, "Like rabbits."

I choked out a laugh at what Natalie was suggesting and Elena rolled her eyes. "Ignore my daughter. She appears to have an unhealthy interest in my love life."

I nodded my understanding but I didn't really agree with the long-distance relationship thing. I wondered if Noah ever felt abandoned by his dad, like I did my mother.

"Anyway, off you pop and remember, this is your home for as long as you need. Come and go as you please. Help yourself to anything," Elena said kindly. She had such warm eyes but they were pale, not at all like Noah's.

"I should pay you some rent, to cover bills and stuff."

Elena shook her head. "Don't mention it and don't worry about all that stuff, we can sort that another time."

I smiled and waved my goodbye whilst checking my phone. It had vibrated to say I had a message and I needed to see if it was from my dad or David. It was from Noah.

Get your arse out here Meadows!

In spite of the radio silence from my family, I walked toward the front door feeling welcome and wanted; something I had rarely felt in our cottage in Sinnington. My thoughts shifted fleetingly toward David and my dad again before I shut them away. It was too raw, too painful to think about right then.

Tonight, was about having fun and getting to know Noah on another level entirely. And, I for one, was really looking forward to it.

My misery in respect of my family could wait.

Thirteen

Leaving the house with an unfamiliar spring in my step, I feasted my eyes upon the masculine glory that was Noah Savvas. He was leaning back against the side of his truck, those strong arms folded over his chest.

As I approached him, the gravel crunched under my feet. He was regarding me with one of those customary self-assured expressions of his, surrounded by an air of impatience. My heart thundered like the hooves of a racehorse in my chest.

He looked like a film star and my tongue suddenly felt twice the size in my mouth. I was so nervous, my entire body vibrating.

Noah was wearing dark blue jeans, a checked shirt and a black leather jacket. His shoes were the ones he'd worn to Katy's wedding. He hadn't shaved, but the roughness enhanced that vibrant animal magnetism, he was so handsome. I felt my blood pressure sky rocket; just the sight of him was giving me jelly legs.

I tugged Natalie's jacket around my frame, the night air was chilly.

Noah's gaze roamed over my outfit, his scrutiny long and slow; male appreciation burning in the depths of eyes. My cheeks heated as I came to stand before him; the silence feeling a little too long. I cleared my throat which knocked him out of his trance.

"You look beautiful."

My smile was automatic. "Thank you."

He tilted his head to one side. "Maybe we should stay here? I don't want to share you with anyone. Either that or I take you back to mine and we, you know… *do* stuff," he said with a suggestive smile.

A zoo of butterflies suddenly went crazy in my stomach. Those words made me as nervous as a kitten.

Noah cocked an eyebrow as he waited for my response.

"Maybe we should?" I said, sounding much more confident than I felt.

He shot me a look that said it all, but I was struggling to concentrate; my insides twisting.

Those penetrating eyes narrowed.

"I think I'll feed you first," he responded, his tone deep and raspy.

He shoved off the car, uncurling his body, and dragged open the passenger side door.

"After you," he said motioning for me to climb in. It appeared he was going all out gentleman again tonight. My tension evaporated and I slowly started to recover my confidence.

"Where are you taking me then?" I questioned as he joined me in the front. I moved back slightly as he leaned his large body over mine and dragged the seatbelt over me, securing it. His eyes lingered on my legs as I crossed them.

"You're staring Noah," I grinned, the opposite of offended.

A muscle in his jaw flexed before he choked out a laugh, leaning back into his own seat and shooting me a pointed look, "I'm a man Lucy, we have carnal urges and besides, I'm enjoying the view."

Noah's eyes trailed across my breasts and down my body. His smile was cheeky and I released a chuckle of my own.

After a three-beat silence, he readied himself to start the car, checking the gearstick and adjusting the rear-view mirror.

"I thought we'd drive into Scarborough. They have a restaurant I like there. Do you like Greek?"

I'd never really tried much Greek food but I loved kebabs and felt thrilled that he was taking me to a place which would be oozing with his culture. Well, half of it anyway.

"Sounds good."

Noah started the car and pulled down the driveway and out onto the road. The radio was on, but the volume was low. It added to the atmosphere and relaxed me further.

"How's Vee?" I questioned.

"She's good. Let's hope she doesn't get jealous when she realises that I have another woman in my life."

Warmth bloomed in my belly at the thought of being that other woman in his life.

We spent the journey into Scarborough discussing various topics. One of the main conversations was about Moses Wallis and the suspected dog-fighting group. If that was in fact what was happening, we still had no solid proof.

Everything had gone quiet. It was a relief, as the thought of Noah being involved in something which was potentially quite dangerous, made my heart thud in my chest. It did not sit well with me. The men they were thinking of challenging were criminals after all.

"Don't you think you should just call the police and let them handle it?" I said, worry lacing my words.

Noah shot me a look before explaining. "They don't seem to take crimes like this that seriously, ones that concern dogs and shit."

He was probably right. I remembered the call I'd made to lodge the surgeries suspicions and the woman on the phone who sounded like she couldn't care less.

I decided to question him though, he sounded like he knew more than he was letting on.

"How do you know? They might do if we give them the medical records of the injured stray dogs we've had in the surgery."

The car growled as Noah sped up to overtake a tractor.

"There was a working puppy farm in the area and the RSPCA were involved. A guy who works for me has family that work for that organisation."

"Alex?" I said with a frown.

Noah shot me a look. "Yes. Well, his cousin said the police did jack shit about it until they were forced to get involved."

I soaked up what he was saying and it started to make sense.

"So, if we tip them off, they may not even go to the scene, but if we call it in as an emergency call, they have to attend. It's policy."

So that was the plan and it made perfect sense now. I just wished there was another way.

"Well, what can I do to help? I don't want to be useless."

We were now in Scarborough and it was busy. Noah was focused on finding a parking space.

"Noah?" I prompted as he at last found one big enough for his car.

"I don't want you anywhere near it."

"Why not?" I questioned.

"We're dealing with some dangerous people Lucy, proper lowlifes; not to mentioned aggressive animals. You could get hurt. I'll need to be one hundred percent focused and if I'm worrying about you, I won't be."

His explanation made me feel precious and I felt some of that hurt I'd experienced at being left out of things disappear. My heart was dancing in my chest. This *had* to be what love felt like. It was unpredictable and *overwhelming* but I embraced the feeling. I wondered if Noah felt the same way or if it was all just a show to try and get me into bed. The one that got away and all that. I pushed away the miserable thought. I needed to remain on my guard, just in case. Maybe I'd read the situation completely wrong. It wouldn't be the first time. My thoughts dashed back to David before I shook them away.

I pursed my lips, annoyed with myself for thinking that way. When had I become so jaded? Again, David popped in there, having my brother smack me in the mouth probably had something to do with my additional dose of wariness.

I eyed Noah's profile as he pulled on the handbrake.

"To be honest, there is no way of knowing if it is going down or not. I haven't seen or heard anything about Wallis for a while."

"Maybe it's finished with now or they could be running them in another village?" I suggested.

"We'll stay low and keep an ear out. It's all we can do at the minute."

The sweep of his gaze was protective and I nodded my understanding.

Breaking eye contact, I turned to climb out of the car but Noah put a restraining hand on my arm.

"Hold on," he instructed before releasing me and leaving the vehicle. My eyes monitored him with a smile as he strode around the front of the car and then opened my door for me. Who would have thought that Noah had such manners? Our eyes tangled as he helped me down from the cab.

He had managed to find a car parking space behind the restaurant, I could see The Laughing Greek sign on the side of the building.

After locking the car, Noah grabbed my hand and we set off walking toward the entrance. The heels of Natalie's boots clicked across the pavement almost in time with my pulse. I was buzzing.

* * *

The restaurant was busy, but luckily Noah had booked a booth in one of the corners where it was more private.

He asked if I wanted to try a mixture of dishes and made a few helpful suggestions. It was my first time in a Greek restaurant after all. The theme and décor of the place screamed Mediterranean. It was bursting with positive energy and spicy smells. I felt like I was on holiday.

After perusing the vast menu, we went for a Meze platter as a starter and for our mains, we both had the chicken Souvlaki.

Dinner was *delicious* and the conversation flowed naturally between us. I didn't feel nervous or uncomfortable. It was like I'd known him my entire life which I had, sort of. When we'd first sat down, I'd felt a little tongue-tied but the feeling soon vanished as Noah launched into a variety of different subjects. Mostly about Greek cuisine and his time in Cyprus with his father.

Whilst we were waiting for our deserts, Noah drew the focus of our discussion toward my family, plunging me back into my past, but he didn't mention David. I was grateful for that as I still wasn't' ready to deal with that particular, unresolved nightmare.

"So, you look like your mother," Noah stated, batting my confession back at me as a young pretty waitress gathered our plates. She was a teenager but had rather large breasts which she intentionally pointed in Noah's direction. I hid my smile; that type of female behaviour around Noah was something I would have to get used to.

I eyed his perfect face whilst thanking the semi-swooning girl as she replenished our drinks. Noah had that kind of physical appeal that made you have thoughts that should be kept in the bedroom. Pure sin and sexual energy hummed from him. When we'd first walked into the restaurant, most female eyes had traced his movements. Noah had such an aura of confidence and had always entered a room as if he expected an applause.

When we were alone again, I replied to Noah's question. "Yes, very similar."

He leaned back in his chair, regarding me with a thoughtful expression. "She's beautiful then." The compliment created a wide smile and my cheeks heated.

"You blush so prettily," Noah pointed out with a grin. My stomach somersaulted as I recalled his comment about something else, he thought I'd do 'prettily'.

Leaning back into the seat, I took a sip of water, watching him over the rim of the glass. "How about you? Do you look like your father?"

Noah rolled his shoulders, shuffling. I hoped I hadn't made him feel uncomfortable.

"I suppose I have his colouring but we don't look alike. He's also much shorter than me." Of course, he would be. There weren't many men out there the size of Noah, he was huge.

"I tilted my head and regarded him; my brows threaded. "Where do you think you get your height from then?"

Noah exhaled and quirked his head to one side.

"My grandad was a big guy, so I guess my dad's dad," he revealed in a deep, warm voice and I suddenly had the urge to dig deeper.

"Do you miss him? Your dad I mean?" my voice had dipped to a whisper.

Noah shrugged. "Not really. It's always been like this. Dad working away for most of the year. It's just a routine that we all got used to and if I'm honest, we're not that close. I'm closer to my mum and Natalie."

He then placed his hands on the table and threaded his fingers. He had such strong confident hands.

"What about you? Do you miss your mother?" He must have seen me gulp as he followed this question with, "You don't have to answer if it makes you feel…" he let the words trail off.

I pinched my bottom lip with my teeth as I decided how to answer.

"Honestly Lucy, we can talk about something else."

"No, its fine," I reassured him. To be honest, Noah was probably the *only* person I felt I *could* talk to about my mother.

I inhaled and regarded him with what I hoped was a neutral expression. Noah still looked unconvinced.

"At first, I'd felt shocked, followed by denial, I suppose. I kept telling myself that she'd come back but of course she never did. We were in touch briefly at the beginning but her replies weren't very consistent and the whole backward, forward thing started to make me feel worse, confused. You know, mixed messages and all that."

"So, what then? What type of coping strategy did you use?" Noah put in, genuinely interested in my depressing past.

"I put it to the back of my mind I suppose, didn't deal with it. What else could I do. I couldn't get closure as mum stopped taking my calls. So, I never got an explanation as to why she left me, or should I say, us. I wondered if it was my fault. I'd not been that helpful at home during my early teens."

"I can't imagine she left because of you. What was her relationship like with David?"

"What do you mean?"

"Did he use controlling type of behaviour with her?"

My brow wrinkled as I thought back. There had been rows between mum and David. The blood started to chill in my veins. Had David hurt my mother in the past? Was that another reason she left?

The thought was too painful and I did what I did best, I pushed it to the back of my mind.

"They used to argue," I replied truthfully.

"I imagine there is more to her leaving than just running off with another guy Lucy. Maybe in time, when you have your own place and independence you should try and speak to your father about it. It could be more complicated and you deserve to know the truth. You said it yourself. Closure. If you don't get that, you'll never be able to heal and move past it."

I nodded, it hurt, but what Noah was saying was right and my hiding from it, hadn't really corrected anything.

"I did try and speak to my father about it, but it was so painful for him. He said that my mum hadn't been a well woman. She could be impulsive, and at times told lies."

Noah's strong jawline squared. "Wasn't well in what way?"

A myriad of memories flooded my thoughts.

"I was told she had behavioural issues. Erratic behaviour. I'm not sure whether I believe that or not. I don't really remember her like that."

"Did you know the guy she ran off with?"

"No, they were childhood sweethearts. I heard my auntie say so one night, when she thought I wasn't listening."

His eyes flickered as I mentioned childhood sweethearts. Was that what we were now? I gave myself a silent talking to, I needed to stop getting ahead of myself.

I spoke a bit more about my mother and the months after she'd left. Noah took everything in, he didn't try to interrupt me or finish my sentences; he just listened. It was encouraging. It felt nice to be with someone who was genuinely interested in me, in what I had to say. I could count the number of dates I'd had on one hand but, most guys were just waiting for their turn to talk. Active listening at its best.

I flinched slightly as Noah stretched out his hands and placed them over mine. The gesture one of support and understanding and I smiled shyly across at him. How had I gotten this boy so wrong in high school?

"Anyway, I try not to over analyse it all. I have thought about getting back in contact with her again but haven't had the guts. The thought of more rejection and all that."

Noah nodded but didn't comment further. My skin felt extra sensitive where he touched me; his thumb moving over the back of my hand; that stoking sensation, teasing me. It was crazy as I now *loved* it when he touched me; gooey inside didn't even begin to describe the volume of emotion I was experiencing.

Our ice creams arrived and Noah withdrew his hand; it suddenly felt like I'd lost a limb; pathetic I know. One would have thought I had been starved of human contact for years and in a way, I suppose I had been.

We sampled each other's desserts. Noah actually fed me from his spoon across the table; like you see couples do in romantic movies. Luckily, I didn't dribble any down my chin.

My whole evening was heading toward that picture perfect zone. Even considering I'd spoken about my family. It was like sharing a bit of my backstory had lifted a portion of stress away.

"Do you think your parents love each other?" I questioned Noah as he finished off his ice cream. He lifted his head, those dark eyes tangling with mine.

"In a weird long-distance way, I suppose. But it works. When dad comes home, they're all over each other. Absence makes the heart grow fonder and all that bollocks I suppose."

His reply was interesting, but I had never understood long distance relationships. Melanie, who I'd shared a house with during University had spent most of the time crying about her boyfriend; a med student who was studying at the opposite side of the country.

What's the point in seeing someone and trying to build up a relationship when you're never together? It's not the same just phoning each other and Zoom isn't ideal either. Without being able to touch them, smell them...

"I would hate it." The statement was out there before I could stop it and the atmosphere at the table changed.

Noah's eyes narrowed slightly, a strange expression flittering across his face before he contained it. "What? A long-distance relationship?" he questioned, seeking clarity. There were now deep grooves on his forehead.

I placed my spoon down without breaking eye contact. "Yes."

Noah lowered his own cutlery and stretched his massive arms behind his head, stating

"You'd struggle as an army wife then."

I almost didn't register his comment, I was too busy admiring the view. The guy radiated that soldier vibe, especially with those bulging biceps.

I pursed my lips in thought before replying. "I don't know how they do it. Surely, they get lonely being back home by themselves?"

The direction of the conversation still felt fairly normal, but I could feel a hidden edge to it. I wondered if I was channelling this or if this was coming from Noah. Maybe it was because we were talking about the army and he had been kicked out. I imagined he'd still feel sore about that.

Noah dropped his arms again. As usual, Mr Fidget.

"It depends, not if they live on the base," he pointed out in an even tone.

I still wrinkled my nose at that one. I wasn't buying it.

"But what do they do on an army base?"

Folding his arms, he cocked a brow at me. "Some *work* on the base. There are women in the army Lucy. Some take an interest and help to raise money and shit. Others just indulge themselves in the social side of things."

My eyebrows inched toward my hairline. I was surprised by his response. "So, there is a social scene at least. I can't imagine what type though, aren't most bases in the middle of nowhere?"

He smiled, his even white teeth flashing, like he was enjoying my ignorance. "You'd be surprised. The social scene can get pretty wild in the army. Women are the worst."

I sat up in my seat, now extremely interested. Maybe life in the army wasn't that dull. Although, I could talk. It wasn't like I was Miss Excitement anyway. Other than the last couple of weeks, I'd felt more like a couch potato.

"In what way?"

His reply amused me.

"Misbehaving," he delivered with one of those looks that suggested something erotic.

My shyness kicked in and I fleetingly glanced away. "I see."

As I turned back, Noah delivered one of his smirks.

"You can lose the horrified expression. We're not talking debauchery Lucy. They just know how to have a good time."

We sat in silence for a few beats; our gazes remaining locked; both drinking each other in, and I felt a sudden need to be closer to him. The table now an unwelcomed barrier. Knowing people were most likely watching us, we couldn't really do anything anyway.

"I still don't think it would be for me," I put out there truthfully.

Noah shook his head, disagreeing with me before he said, "You'd be fine if you were with me."

Cocky much I thought, playfully rolling my eyes. Recovering, I replied. "Hmm, I'm not sure, and anyway. You're not even in the army now."

Noah's expression suddenly twisted and my hands itched, tension shooting up my spine. Had I said too much, pointing out that he was no longer in the army so carelessly? He now watched me with hooded eyes before he said in a flat voice,

"No, I'm not but..." his voice trailed off.

Butterflies kicked off again in my stomach. "But?"

He dragged a hand down his face before scrubbing at his chin with his fingers; almost as if he was attempting to clear his head. This added a dose of confusion into the mix and I watched wide-eyed as Noah straightened his shoulders before saying, "I have some news actually."

The way he delivered this line was as if he hadn't made up his mind that he was going to say anything, but then just decided to go for it. My curiosity brimmed to life.

Swallowing, I leaned back in my seat; giving Noah my wholehearted attention.

"I received an email from my old commanding officer," he paused and my breath hitched.

The silence stretched.

"They got him. The guy I reported for molesting that girl."

His words delivered a punch of relief to my stomach and the breath I'd been holding slowly seeped between my lips, allowing my lungs to deflate.

I lifted an unsteady hand to my chest.

"That's great news Noah."

He smiled but it didn't quite reach his eyes. "It is good news."

I felt my face relax.

Noah's expression remained a mystery. He didn't look that happy about it which was strange. A thought sliced into me. I could feel another 'but' coming on.

He was now watching me with a strange expression, as if he was looking for the answer to a question that he hoped to find on my face. There was a flutter in my stomach.

My brow threaded. “So, how did they catch him?”

Noah shifted again and drummed his fingers on the table lightly, retaining eye contact.

“Someone managed to film him on their phone on two separate occasions.”

My stomach suddenly rumbled which was odd considering the amount of food I’d consumed.

“So, did your old boss contact you?”

“Yes, I got an email the other night. The army made a full apology and wiped my record. They also reinstated my stripes.”

My eyes roamed over the beautiful angular lines of his face as I was so pleased for him. “Noah, that’s brilliant. Why don’t you look pleased about it?”

He cleared his throat but his eyes remained glued to mine. “They’ve offered me my old job back.”

My entire body stiffened as realisation filtered into me. My mouth suddenly felt dry but I didn’t take a sip of the water in case it came back up again.

“And they want you to come back?” Old memories of my mother’s abandonment raced into my thoughts like an unstoppable train. Needless to say, I did not welcome his next words.

“Yes.”

BOOM! The news came rushing toward me, fear of the unknown stabbing into me.

My blood circulation seemed to stop before draining away and puddling into my feet. I should have been filled with excitement and joy for him but I felt the total opposite. I risked a small smile. “I don’t really know what to say.”

“They’ve offered me the same job but with a higher rank and backpay into my army pension.”

My entire body stiffened. It was like there wasn’t enough oxygen in the room and I couldn’t think straight. Those butterflies now felt like a wrecking ball.

I swallowed some air and managed to choke out, “But that’s great,” lying, attempting to make my fake smile appear genuine.

Noah crossed his arms again; his expression shifting. He knew exactly how his words were affecting me.

“You *really* think so,” he questioned with an arched eyebrow. He was watching me with the most phenomenal intensity.

At that point it all felt too surreal. I couldn't bare my soul to him, not yet. It was too soon. What if he rejected me?

I rocked from side to side feeling claustrophobic. Was the room getting smaller?

"Yes." My voice was like a squeak. Another stirring of unease nibbled inside me and I felt physically sick. I imagined my nose growing like Pinocchio.

Noah suddenly seemed larger in his seat. He now wore one of his 'unimpressed' expressions.

"So why do you look like you're going to throw up Lucy?" he said in a grilling tone, gesturing toward me with a flick of his wrist.

Panic bled into me as I struggled to peel my tongue off the roof of my mouth. "It's just a shock I suppose. Thinking of you going away again." No, no no!

"I didn't say I was, yet," Noah responded in a severe voice. What the actual hell? His deep voice interrupted my inner rant,

I suddenly felt like crying. Was he toying with me? How the heck had our evening changed to this? Relentless doom started to orbit the area around me.

"Then why are we having this conversation, Noah?" I replied moodily.

"I'm testing the water I suppose." His face suddenly softened.

'So, he *was* toying with me' I thought, staring helplessly into his masculine, sharp face.

"Why?" Confusion sliced through me, catching me off guard.

"I wanted to see your reaction. See what you're thinking."

My pulse picked up. I had to be strong. Don't let this boy in. Not fully, not yet.

"Well, I suppose it's nothing to do with me Noah. You should do what's right for you," I said, blatantly lying through my teeth.

My reaction seemed to amuse him and he wore that look that used to annoy me so much.

"Wouldn't you miss me?"

Puffing out a breath, I leaned back in my seat, folding my own arms. It was funny really, when Noah crossed his arms, he looked strong and in control. When I did it, I looked defensive.

"I can't believe you're asking me that," I said as a delaying tactic, so I wouldn't have to admit anything.

He didn't like my side-step.

Noah bristled angrily and tension shot between us.

"For once in your life, give me a straight answer Lucy. No more fucking games," he bit out, his voice raised slightly.

He was angry and surprisingly, *so was I!*

"Of course, I *bloody* would," I shot back. My voice sharp, dripping with annoyance. After *everything* that had happened between us, how the hell could he be asking me that? Surely, he knew how I felt? How my feelings had changed toward him.

I darted a quick look around the room, hoping I hadn't drawn attention to us. Thankfully, everyone was still engrossed in their own business.

He opened his mouth to respond but was disturbed by Miss Big Boobs who appeared to remove our dirty dishes. Noah paid her no attention at all. His focus was all on me. The waitress must have felt the tension as she cleared the pots at light speed and shrunk away, awkwardly clearing her throat as she murmured something about the bill.

After she had gone, Noah's eyes were narrowed into slits. "Why don't you tell me not to go Lucy? Tell me how you really feel for once?"

A pause stretched between us as his eyes roamed over my face, almost desperate for the answer that I was too chicken shit to supply. I knew at that point what he was doing. What he needed from me.

My shoulders slumped and I felt like a balloon after someone had stuck a pin in it.

"I can't," I responded in a weak, miserable voice.

My reply antagonised him further and he shifted his bulk, leaning over the table, his stare piercing my retinas. His hands shot out and he took my fingers in his, before tugging my body forward. There was no escape, no hiding.

"Lucy?" he prompted sharply, and I snapped, stating in a lowered, harsh voice.

"What do you want me to say Noah? Beg you not to go back to doing something you love? Offer to come with you? Be an army girlfriend?"

"Yes, if that's how you feel," he shot back through clenched teeth. He was pissed off.

I leaned away from the angry energy that now bounced across the table.

"You need to do what's right for you." Surely that was the right thing to say, be the bigger person and all that? The thought drained away all my joy.

He hooked his chin at me. "And what's right for you?"

It felt like there were fingers closing around my throat.

"I don't know really. Saying here, getting a better job, finding a flat, I suppose." I knew I was rambling, blatantly attempting to steer away from saying the obvious. The thought of Noah leaving now was like taking a bullet.

"That's bullshit day to day crap. You *know* what I'm talking about."

The bill arrived and Noah shot the girl a look that could have melted glass. She almost dissolved where she stood.

"I'm only telling you what I want," I volleyed back.

Noah snorted, reminding me of a bull before it charges. "Yes, and what else?"

"I don't know what you mean," I parried.

He went for the jugular. "You can continue to skate around the issue, but we both know what you want. You want me, Lucy."

Slumping back into my seat, I closed my eyes and leaned back.

"Can we just talk about something else?" Only a scream could express my true feelings at that point. I needed to escape from the chaos of emotion this conversation was creating. All sorts of thoughts were firing through me.

Noah paid the bill and I dashed to the toilet.

Whilst washing my hands I stared at my reflection, my cheeks were flushed. I had imagined I'd look pale and drawn, feeling the way I did.

We walked together to Noah's truck in silence. I was itching to speak but I felt so uncertain; terrified of my feelings. Of exposing myself.

Noah was right, I *was* a coward. Something twisted deep down in my stomach.

Still playing the gentleman, Noah assisted me up into the truck, watching me with an assessing stare.

Once we were both inside the cab, we sat in silence; both staring out of the windscreen into the car park before Noah turned toward me.

"I need to know how you feel Lucy." His tone was measured and encouraging and goose bumps shot across my skin.

I knew what he wanted me to say, but I felt like I was swimming in unchartered waters. The cold hand of dread was wrapped around my throat at the thought of rejection.

"*Tell me*," Noah urged. It was still a tone that brooked no argument.

And those gates I had kept closed for so long *burst* open. I twisted in my seat, my eyes clashing with his. I was breaking my own rules, I knew that, but I didn't care. I had to get it off my chest. The sensations I felt as I offloaded were intense but a thick fog started to lift.

"*Fine*. I'll *tell* you how I feel; what I think about the thought of you leaving. I feel like you've pretty much torn me in two to be quite honest. What can I say Noah, you've won! You did it. You *finally* got under my skin," I panted, pausing to catch my breath. The words were ejected from my mouth at light speed.

His stare was intense. "Go on."

Licking my lips to moisten them I then spilled my all.

"I suppose it started at school. I was drawn to you, to your strength and it made me feel weak and non-virtuous. You were the *opposite* of the type of person I expected myself to be attracted to. You knocked me out of my comfort zone. So, I did hide. Purposefully stayed away and didn't give you the time of day. I was too busy seeing the bad side of you that I never looked for any good. But I was wrong and I know that now."

A beat of silence passed and I scrunched my hands into fists.

"I guess you light me up, make me feel something; alive I suppose." I hated that I sounded like a cliché but it was true, Noah Savvas had awakened me somehow. "It's all head spinning kind of stuff. You've made me realise that I want a new direction in my life. Something different, a new adventure, away from that stifling connection with church life and suffocating family members."

I paused for a minute, realising that I was prattling on and Noah was just sitting there in silence.

"Sorry, I'm rambling now."

He grinned. "Ramble away. I could listen to your voice all day and not get bored."

Feeling a whoosh of relief, I then delivered the sucker punch, searching his beautiful face. The light caught his eyes and highlighted those green flecks I loved so much.

"I want you, Noah."

I paused to catch my breath and my heart swelled in my chest.

"And I think I'm in love with you."

Fourteen

Through my entire speech, Noah's eyes *never* left mine, not even to blink. He didn't try to interrupt or pull a face; he just sat there quietly, watching me, *absorbing* what I had to say. His expression was impassive but I didn't regret that last sentence which contained those three special words. It was relief to hear them out loud. I *was* in love with him and that feeling was now too strong to deny.

The silence stretched between and I watched as Noah closed his eyes briefly and drew in a large breath, his broad chest expanding with air.

I opened my mouth to speak but hesitated as, without warning, Noah moved; leaning over the central console and sliding his hands under my armpits. He turned my body and dragged me backwards onto his lap. His corded thighs were rock hard under the softness of my bottom and he pushed my hair back off my face so he could see me clearly. His dark brown eyes, drinking in my features. I placed my hands loosely on his shoulders.

"Finally," Noah drew out. "I've *always* known it, Lucy. Knew it would come to this once you'd came to your senses."

He paused momentarily before shooting me a pointed look. "You do realise I've felt that way since fucking high school."

"Really?" I said, hating how lame my voice sounded.

"Yes, really." His tone was now more forceful.

My pulse skyrocketed at his words, the amount of joy I felt at that moment should have suffocated me.

Noah Savvas *loved* me? I was loved?

My eyes searched his face, looking for a sign that he was playing with me. Still partly shocked that a man like Noah could *ever* love someone like me. Low self-esteem was my middle name after all.

Taking in the stubborn jut of his perfect Cypriot chin. He was deadly serious. I could see the truth reflected in every part of his face.

"I love you," he said slowly, making each word count.

"You love me?" I echoed. Needing to hear them again and again.

He smiled warmly, shifting the hand that had touched my hair and tracing his fingers down my spine. "Yes," he purred.

The blood in my veins started to sing.

The past was the past, but I couldn't stop myself from asking. "So why did you treat me so badly at school? I thought you hated me or something."

Both his arms were now around my waist as I sat there sideways. My legs tangling with his in the foot well. My dress had risen up and my tight-clad thighs were showing but I didn't care.

Noah shrugged as he pondered my question.

"As I said before. Self-preservation. I knew you weren't ready for me. Not then. I guess I wasn't really ready for anything myself either. Raging testosterone and all that other bullshit of puberty. I know I was a dick to you and I'm sorry. It's a boy thing, isn't it? Treat the girl you fancy like shit and she'll never know."

That is exactly what Natalie had said. My cheeks heated under his watchful stare.

"I remember every time you blushed, I wanted to kiss that unmistakable hot patch of skin in an apology."

He moved a hand and touched my face again, affectionately. His eyes darkened.

"I don't think I will *ever* forgive myself for hurting something so beautiful."

Those fingers wrapped around my waist flexed against my spine, bringing our bodies closer and he brushed his lips gently over my mouth before resting his forehead against mine. Noah's eyes closed again and he released another, deep meaningful breath. Almost as if he felt some type of relief himself. His masculine scent was in my nostrils, titillating my senses.

"I want to hear you tell me not to go back into the army Lucy. Be selfish for once in your life. Believe me when I say, it feels good."

He then opened his eyes, our noses almost touching; gazes tangling again as I said in a firm, strong voice.

"Don't go. I don't want you to go Noah. *Stay with me*. Stay and let's see where this goes." My tone was fairly commanding, I was impressed with myself. The slight curve to Noah's mouth suggested he was too.

He drew his head back before he said. "I'll stay.

I wanted to jump from the truck and do cartwheels of joy around the car park.

"Really? You'd do that for me?"

He quirked his head before relying. "No."

Wrinkling my nose, I frowned. "What do you mean?"

"I'm staying for *both* of us. It's what I want. I never intended going back into the army."

I felt like the rug had been pulled out from under me.

"I'm confused. The way you told me suggested..."

He smiled, looking pleased with himself. "Yes, I did it on purpose to draw you out of your safe zone; that fucking ivory castle you've been hiding in."

Realisation about his sly moves hit home. The sod.

"Noah Savvas! You, sneaky son of a..." I shot out, punching him on the shoulder.

He reared back with a grin. "Easy?"

...Gun!" I ended. I refused to allow him to force me down the bad language route. He already made me question my faith.

The air in the cab lifted, the tension draining away.

"You should see your face," Noah chuckled.

I shot him my best glare. "I could kill you." My whole body was seething and I slapped him on the leg for added measure.

"And there are the fireworks. Now you truly are worthy of your red-haired status. With bells on," Noah teased.

Huffing I wiggled in an attempt to move off his lap, pushing against his chest but he kept his arms around my waist, caging me.

"I actually thought you were saying goodbye," I grumbled.

His lip curled. "I know, that was the point. And now you know how that made you feel. I wanted to shake you out of that prim façade you project," he purred, the sneaky so-and-so.

Of course, he had a point. Now my feelings were out in the open I felt better, less tense. Like there were now no secrets between us. "I suppose so, you underhanded demon."

He regarded me with a macho, primitive expression. "And you better stop moving like that or we'll have another issue on our hands."

I stopped immediately, as I felt *exactly* what he was talking about against my backside. I shot him a cheeky look for good measure. No longer embarrassed.

Noah brushed his lips against mine again before he pulled back, his face now serious.

He then delivered a speech of his own.

"The saying you never know what you've got until you've lost it makes perfect sense to me now. My life didn't really kick off again until the day your car broke down. I remember Tom spoke about you in the pub one night. It was the night I found out you were back home. He was banging on about how he was intending asking you out. I almost lamped the fucker. But then I told myself not to panic, knowing that I would get to you first. I was determined to see you, get under your skin. Find out if that thing between us at school was still there. When I realised you were the girl in the car I had gone to rescue, it all made sense. I know it sounds stupid, considering that I don't believe in a higher power, but it felt like fate."

I drank in those words, devoured them like I'd been trapped in the desert without water for years. Opposites attract and all that. I was shy and reserved. I needed strength in my partner, someone that could encourage me to step out of the box like Noah did.

We stared into each other's eyes. Connected at last. Electricity crackling between us.

I couldn't wait to see where things went with Noah.

* * *

The drive back was pleasant. My whole body was alive with pleasure and contentment. We spoke about various subjects. We discussed Christmas and the New Year and how we would spend this time together.

I did refer back to the matter with Moses Wallis but Noah changed the subject, that discussion now out of bounds for me it seemed.

As Noah pulled the car into the driveway of his parent's house, he cut the engine, released his belt and climbed out.

He walked me to the door. It was dark but the light had been left on outside.

The soft glow from the lamp was draped over us as I stood and looked up into Noah's striking features. He was watching me with a fondness I had never experienced. I felt truly loved for the first time in my life.

"So where do we go from here?" I said up into his face.

He circled my waist and pulled my body against his, forcing me to crane my neck further to retain eye contact. I could feel he was still hard against my stomach and I draped my arms loosely around his neck, standing on my tiptoes.

"I guess we take it a step at a time, but we still need to make 'us' official I think." My body trembled against his. He was so solid and that familiar wave of lust appeared. This time I didn't feel any shame and I embraced that feeling.

"Us?" Part of my brain wasn't listening as I stared up at him dreamily.

"Yes us. Tomorrow, I'm going to introduce you to my friends," Noah exclaimed proudly. His words puzzled me as I'd already met them, unless he had another stash of buddies.

"You mean the ones I met properly at the wedding?" I questioned smoothly.

"Yes."

I cocked my head pointing out, "But I've already met them."

His next words lit me up even more; excitement pooling into my stomach.

"Not as my girlfriend you haven't." His eyes appeared almost golden.

My grin widened, it must have been the meatiest of smiles and I replied with confidence. "Sounds good to me, boyfriend."

Noah chuckled; that deep throaty tone making my toes curl. "I feel like I'm at high school again. Does it feel strange to you?"

"What?" I said, caressing the back of his neck with my fingertips.

His gaze was welded to my face. "Calling me your boyfriend?"

"No. It feels pretty right to me." So did all the sexual scenarios which were circling my thoughts.

I felt elated knowing that Noah Savvas *would* be my first lover. I wondered what it would feel like to lose control in his strong arms. Pretty amazing I imagined. Sex with Noah would no doubt be earth moving stuff, considering how strong our mutual attraction was.

And it would be good. I knew he'd take care of me.

Noah was a man, not some fumbling teenager. I was totally clueless about sex and having Noah as my teacher made my insides melt.

I drifted out of my thoughts as Noah lifted his hands to cup my face, whispering, "At last we're on the same page," before lowering his head and taking my mouth in a passionate kiss. I groaned in utter abandonment; thoroughly enjoying that flare of sexual excitement I felt as his mouth took control.

And that must have been what true happiness felt like. I was complete at last.

* * *

On Christmas Eve, David came to the house. Noah's family had suggested I stop looking for flats until after the holiday period. I eventually agreed and graciously accepted their invitation to spend both Christmas and New Year with them.

It was Christmas Eve and Noah was out for drinks with the boys.

Natalie answered the door and ushered David into the kitchen before checking to establish if I wanted to speak with him. I did. She gave me one of those looks that said, 'yell if you need me', but I knew I'd be safe. Yes, David had lashed out and lost control but I couldn't imagine it ever happening again and I wasn't afraid of him. He'd messed up. He was only human after all. I had decided to forgive him days ago, but I would *never* go back to the house. David had taken a part of me that I would *never* get back. I wasn't the same girl.

My brother was in the kitchen, staring out of the French windows into the garden with his hands in the pockets of his chinos. He'd lost weight.

"Hello David," I said in a calm, soft voice. He turned and my resolve to be firm almost evaporated on the spot. He was pale, his face strained, and he looked ill. The tendons on his neck appeared to be more pronounced and my heart squeezed.

"Lucy. You look well." His gaze glanced over me briefly, his expression less intense than I remembered. I read his look as being something to expect from a brother to a sister and I felt an injection of relief.

I smiled thinly. "I'm sorry to say it but you don't. You look shocking David."

He exhaled as he held himself there, his body rigid. "What do you expect? I've been going out of my mind with worry," he replied, his voice shaking slightly.

"You should have texted me sooner."

His expression changed from tired to pained, "I thought you'd just ignore me anyway. You had every right to."

I suddenly felt nauseous.

"I wouldn't do that. That's not who I am David," I responded in a truthful voice.

A silence stretched between us and I pushed my hands into the pockets of my jeans.

David looked at the ceiling, his face a mixture of emotions; none easy to describe. He then lowered his head and looked me in the eye.

"I'm sorry Lucy. For what I did, how I treated you."

I released a sigh of frustration, this strained situation had been left too long and had now festered. We'd shared the same womb at the end of the day; that same pain when mum had left.

I gave him a levelling look, stating, "I know and I believe you, David." And I did. Remorse was written along every uncomfortable grove on his face.

His face changed and he suddenly looked like a lost little boy. "Will you come home then? Dad was asking about you. We miss you."

I left it a moment, the unanswered question out there, floating before us like a massive decision.

"No David."

He dashed a hand down his jaw, I noticed he hadn't shaved; his ginger stubble was bright on his face.

"It will *never* happen again Lucy, I promise. I've been going to the Doctor to try and sort my head out. I lost my way. I know that now."

"Well, that's good and I'm pleased for you but I'm not coming home. I'm going to find a flat to rent."

His shoulders slumped in defeat.

"So, you're leaving home and it's all my fault?" he questioned in a pained voice. That raw sound made my insides twist.

I shook my head and took a step further into the kitchen, pulling my cardigan further against my body.

"It isn't your fault. To be honest I haven't been happy since I've been back. I found my independence at university and I've struggled. Irrespective of what happened that night. I actually want to get a place. I need my own space."

I was telling the truth. There were several factors as to why I didn't want to go back to that house and they weren't all David related.

I offered to make my brother a coffee, to break bread and all that but he declined, saying how he needed to prepare for the Carol Service which was taking place on Christmas Day.

We made our peace in a roundabout way. The feeling between us was still strained, but better than nothing and I told him I'd visit dad in between Christmas and New Year.

David still left the house with his tail between his legs, an awkward air about him but what could you do? He'd hit me and there was no taking that back, from his point of view anyway. I just hoped he realised my forgiveness was for real. Time was the only healer from that point onwards.

I thoroughly enjoyed Christmas Day, we opened presents, played games, drank and ate until I thought I would explode; it really did feel like I was part of a real family again. Noah and Natalie were like a double act winding each other or their mother up, it was fun to see, and it made me see just how much I had missed out on. It had *never* been like that with my family, even when my mum and dad were supposedly happy.

I'd bought Noah a new leather tool belt and had his initials engraved onto it and he bought me a beautiful necklace. It was white gold with a pendant that held both of our birthstones combined. I would *never* take it off.

As promised, in between Christmas and New Year, I went to see my father. He made me a coffee and we sat and spoke about this and that, mainly about where I saw myself living. He offered to help me financially, but I knew he couldn't really afford it.

My relationship with my brother and father was by no means repaired, but I felt better.

In respect of the dog fighting syndicate, everything had remained quiet over the holiday period. No dogs had been brought into the surgery. It suggested that things may have calmed down, either that or they had moved on somewhere else.

It still left a sour taste in my mouth, like a bitter pill. Unfinished business. Noah felt the same way, especially when we were reminded of it every time we saw Vee. Poor love.

She was such a sweetie. She and Noah were inseparable. During the times Noah and I were cosied up on the sofa or laying on the bed in his room she'd push between us. It was playful but there was a definite marking the territory vibe.

* * *

Around a week later, whilst we were taking the Christmas tree trimmings down, Noah called me and explained that Connor had received a tip off from one of the locals; a guy who bred Akita's. The tip off was about Wallis.

It turned out that Moses Wallis had been away in Ireland for Christmas with his dad's family, hence the reason for the dog fighting business going quiet. Connor had been told Wallis was back and that a fight was being put together for the following weekend. The informant had explained that Wallis had harassed him about selling him an Akita and how he'd become aggressive when he'd refused. This had led to said chap making a few enquiries of his own and faking an interest in enrolling one of his dogs in one of the fights.

Between them, the boys hatched the plan to catch Wallis in the act and call the police. The thought of things going wrong worried me, but *nothing* I said would change Noah's mind. They would take matters into their own hands to ensure the police raided at the right time.

Noah had a point of course. The police couldn't do anything without evidence.

After our brief conversation about it, Noah had shut me down again and explained that everything was in hand.

My nights from that point on were pretty much sleepless.

* * *

The weekend of the alleged fight came. It was Saturday and I was in the process of closing the surgery when Tom's car shot into the car park, spraying pebbles everywhere. The fact that he was driving fast sent a shard of alarm into me; Tom Wade usually drove like an old lady. Something was off.

He clambered out of his Volvo, and yanked open the back door before foraging inside. I pulled the door wide, straining to see. What on earth was he doing?

My eyes widened as he withdrew an animal from his backseat. It was another dog and it was completely limp. Was it dead?

"What's happened?"

"I've got another injured dog. Mrs Haunch saw it in her garden last night but was too scared to go out. She found it almost lifeless in her flower bed this morning and called Ella.

"Why Ella?" I questioned, puzzled as to how she had become involved.

"She does their gardening and was the closest."

As we entered the building, I assessed the animal.

"The blood has clotted but the wounds look fresh, come on; bring him into room two, I've just finished sanitising in there," I suggested, wanting to help.

And that was my first time in assisting a vet whilst we attempted to save the life of an injured animal. Tom had to put it to sleep in the end as it didn't regain consciousness and was in a bad way. It was the first dead animal I had seen, apart from the occasional badger or fox at the side of the road. I managed to hold back the tears, but it was so sad. Forever the professional Tom was unfazed.

As Tom prepared the dog for cremation and I cleaned the table, my brain was racing. Connor had been told the fight was tonight but it must have happened already. Unless it was going on over two nights?

I pushed away the thought and climbed into my car, checking my phone for messages. Should I contact Noah and tell him? I knew he and the boys were going to the farm tonight in an attempt to close things down. If the fight had already taken place, they'd be wasting their time.

As I was about to start the engine, my phone rang. It was Harlow.

Her words were rushed. "Are you with Noah, Lucy?"

"No. Why?" I fired back.

"Shit. Look, I imagine the guys are probably on their way to the farm right now, but we need to stop them. The fight has already happened, it was purposefully brought forward to Thursday."

Harlow's words confirmed my suspicions.

"I thought so. Tom just found another injured dog with fresh wounds. So, the guys will be wasting their time then," I pointed out calmly.

Her next words knocked me into action. "There's more to consider than that."

My thoughts were scrambled, I was totally lost. "What? What do you mean?"

"Wallis; I think he may have somehow got wind of what the guys were planning and so they brought the fight forwards on purpose. Wallis and his mates may be waiting for them when they get there. Like a trap type of thing."

My heart skipped a beat at the thought of Noah being hurt somehow.

"How do you know?" I shouted into my phone.

"I don't for definite but my stepmother said she'd heard something in the pub. I overheard her talking to my dad about it."

"Really?"

"Yes. She didn't mention Connor, Noah or Nate's names, she just said a 'group of lads' and how she'd heard they were going to confront Wallis and his gang. What if Wallis knows that and wants to kick the shit out of them to send a message?"

"But surely the guys can handle themselves?" I questioned.

"What if they're outnumbered?" Harlow volleyed back. She had a point.

I dragged a hand across my chin, feeling out of my depth. "Have you tried to call Connor?"

Harlow was panicking, I could hear it in her tone and I shared that feeling entirely.

"I've called *all* of them, their phones all just go to voicemail. If they are on their way and travelling through the village, phone signal is really bad out there."

I pursed my lips, trying to think of the best option.

"Are you sure of what you heard?"

"No, not really, I couldn't hear that well. But surely, it's better to be safe than sorry?"

"I agree, we've got to warn them, just in case. Where are you?"

"I'm at the farm, I'm closer to Sinnington than Natalie's house. I have a car, but I don't drive."

Harlow knew I was living in Noah's old room and must have thought I was there.

I corrected her, "I'm at the surgery and so I'm not that far. I have my car. I'll drive over there now and warn them."

The silence felt thick before she quickly put in.

"OK, sounds good. But be careful Lucy."

"I will."

I didn't even run back into the practice for backup. I wasn't thinking straight, I just had to get to Noah. If anything happened to him, I couldn't bear it.

I started the engine and shoved the car into gear.

Switching my car to hands free, I attempted to call Noah's phone but got nothing.

I needed Noah to be safe and knew at that point, that I'd do *anything* in my power to protect him.

Fifteen

I identified Noah's Nissan Navara. The thing was huge and the total opposite of discreet. It was parked up a side road, just around the corner from the farm and I drove my car adjacent to it and peered inside. As suspected, the cab was empty, so I pulled my car up in front of it, parked and dragged the handbrake on.

Withdrawing my phone, I then pushed my bag into the foot-well of the passenger seat.

After briefly checking for messages, of which there were none, I evil-eyed the empty bars which revealed there was no phone signal. The swirly buffering icon appeared, continuously searching on a loop. One of the downsides of living in the middle of nowhere.

I was still dressed in my work uniform, which wasn't the most practical of armours, so I covered it with my coat and pocketed my phone.

There was a chill in the air and a distinctive smell of the country.

I made my way past Noah's car in a half-run half-trot. Anxiety gnawing at my guts.

As I rounded the corner and walked carefully in through the battered gates into the farm, it appeared deserted. There were no cars to be seen, *nothing*. There was also an eerie silence. Maybe Wallis hadn't set anything up after all? The speed of my heart slowly started to decrease, the beat becoming less frantic.

The large barn where the 'security' man (and I use that term loosely) had appeared weeks ago was closed, and my eyes scanned the yard searching for Noah.

SLAM!

I almost jumped off my feet and plastered myself against the boundary wall as a car door slammed in the distance. The echo of the sound suggested it came from *behind* the main barn and my pulse sped up.

To add to my terror, I was grabbed from behind, a solid hand covering my mouth and nose. It was Noah's body; I was used to that chiselled shape of him now and relief pooled into me, replacing that initial surge of panic.

"Don't make a sound Lucy, OK?"

His hand remained in place but he moved his fingers off my nose, which allowed me to breathe. I inhaled greedily nodding my head to signal I understood. Noah carried me over to the first barn, the one with the roof and door missing. His arm was tight where it was wrapped around my body.

When we were inside, he released me and I spun around to face him. The pleasure I felt at seeing him was short-lived. I wasn't in the good books.

He was angry, his face pulled taunt.

"What the hell are you doing here?" he growled in a deep, hushed voice.

Of course, he didn't know what I had to say.

"I came to warn you. We missed the fight, it happened earlier in the week. Harlow thinks Wallis got wind of the plan and that they may be waiting for you," I babbled, my lips almost tripping over the words.

Noah cocked his head to one side, regarding me through a veil of annoyance.

"I know," he replied with brooding confidence.

I frowned. "How?"

"Because there was no one in there when I arrived. Just the aftermath," he replied.

"Oh goodness, can I see?" My eyes were wide as morbid curiosity bubbled to the surface.

Noah shook his head. "Not a good idea, it's not nice Lucy," he informed me, moving away to glance out of the barn; checking to see we were still alone. Once he was satisfied, he moved back toward me, his walk almost predatory.

I leaned back against the rotting barn wall, needing something solid to hold me up. My limbs felt numb but anxiety ran through the rest of my body like a river of dread.

"So, if there's evidence in there, we should call the police now," I suggested, searching his face for the answer.

Noah pursed his lips before replying. "I've tried, but there's no signal here. And Wallis just arrived a few minutes ago. He's in there now, three others are with him. I imagine they're here to clean up. We need to get the police here now really."

"What if they're not here to clean up? Maybe they're waiting for you?"

"Well, there's that too. Although I'm not so sure. They have chemicals with them," Noah pointed out before adding, "Maybe they're here to do both?" he huffed before dragging a hand of frustration down his face. Almost as if he was trying to wake himself up.

His words resulted in a slither of alarm to snake up my spine and my mouth hung open like a fish.

"But there aren't any cars? How did they get here?"

"There must be another door into the barn. I think they're parked around the other side."

My heart almost skipped a beat thinking of the noise of the car door I had heard. "So, you think they're just here to clean up, that there's no threat to you?"

He paused before replying.

"Either way, it doesn't really matter now as they've lost the element of surprise."

Adrenaline jetting into me. "Well, we need to do something," I panted pushing off the wall to move past him. Noah grabbed my upper arm, spinning me back quite forcefully.

I looked up in confusion, my head a mush of confused thoughts as I struggled to process what was happening.

"*We,* don't need to do anything, you need to get back in your fucking car. The guys should be here any minute," he growled, his fingers firm against my skin.

His comment rattled me but inside, I knew he was right.

My shoulders dropped and he eyed me thoughtfully as I submitted in defeat. He still continued to glare at me, his body a tower of protective strength. A force to be reckoned with.

Looking up, I watching him through my lashes. "What are you doing to do? Will you fight them all?" I began again, my voice scratchy.

Noah's expression shifted as he arched an eyebrow. "Whilst your faith in me is charming, Lucy. I am one man. I'm not fucking Rambo." He tugged me further toward his strong body, "I am a normal, flesh and blood guy."

I almost snorted at his words, as there was nothing *normal* about Noah. It appeared my idea of a baptism of fire wasn't' going to work.

He held me against his solid body, the warmth from his chest seeping into my own skin. "Maybe I could help?" I said miserably, feeling like a tiny waste of time. "I've got a good kick on me," I boasted with a half-smile.

He wasn't' amused. "For the love of God Lucy, please just do as you're told. Connor and Nate will be here any minute. We'll handle it."

I tugged at my arms and he released me. My head drooping in defeat as I stepped back from him, away from the safety of his body. I felt so useless.

"Fine, I'll go back to my car," I said in a small voice.

As I spoke, Connor's pocket started to vibrate and he dragged his gaze away, his forehead scrunched. We both realised at the same time that miraculously, his phone was ringing.

"Shit, I must have picked up some signal in here," he whispered.

Noah withdrew his phone to identify the caller.

"It's Connor, go Lucy. Now." He shot out, motioning toward the exit with a flick of his hand as he turned away to take the call. As I left the barn, I could hear Noah talking faintly in a rapid, hushed voice.

As I walked out into the now semi-darkness, I stole a nervous glance at those large doors into the main barn, suddenly overwhelmed with the urge to see inside; to witness what had happened there. To make it real.

There was a narrow gap in the wood of the panelled surface; just next to the area Noah had pushed me against that night.

Shooting a glance at the barn which held Noah, I shuffled over on quiet feet and pushed my face close to the gap. I'd just take a peek and then go.

I couldn't really see much. The section of the barn I could see looked empty. I recalled the noise of the car door. Maybe Wallis and the other low life scum had left now?

Again, a dart of fear jetted into me as for the second time in minutes, I was tackled from behind and dragged against a large body; only this time it *wasn't* Noah. The hand that slid over my mouth was dirty and sticky and my stomach lurched as I fought against the rock-like hold. My yell was muffled.

I was roughly manhandled into the main barn, my feet dragging against the ground and I attempted to jerk myself away. My assailant was squeezing the air from my lungs, he held me that tightly.

My vision was compromised as my eyes were watering. Part of my hair was trapped between my back and the man's chest. Pin pricks scattered across my scalp at the tug on my hair; the pain was immense.

I could hear muffled voices before I was released, or should I say dropped to the ground like a dead weight. My hands shot out to break my fall.

"Look what I found? This barn does has a mouse after all," the stranger behind me said. I had yet to see his face but I recognised his voice.

Pushing up onto my knees, I shook the hair from my face, my skull was literally throbbing. There was a metallic odour in the air which was mixed in with that wet dog hair smell and something else I couldn't identify.

The smell I didn't recognise was bad, you could tell. Like how you imagined death would smell.

The violence of emotions was absolute chaos. Fight or flight kicked in and I attempted to stand but my assailant pushed a hand on my shoulder and I sank back down to my knees again.

Struggling to put my strong face on, I lifted my head and directed a glare at the other three men; the big one in the middle was the guy from the surgery and I almost had a heart attack on the spot. Thoughts of shouting for Noah were wiped away. Visions of Noah on the ground with these four men beating him up, kept any idea of involving him at bay. I sure hoped the guys arrived soon. Strength in numbers and all that.

"Carrots, I'd recognise that hair anywhere," the man I assumed to be Wallis said as he walked closer to me. I glared up at him. He really was a mean looking thug.

He had blue surgical gloves on, looking more like a serial killer than a surgeon. I kept my focus on him, I didn't want to look around at my surroundings in case I saw something I would regret seeing. The source of that smell for a start.

"You know her?" one of his henchmen said in disbelief. He was a smaller stocky guy and he was holding a mop. So, they *were* tidying the place up.

"She works at that practice where I teethed Kiza's meds from."

Kiza, I assumed would be the name of his dog. A champion fighter I imagined. Poor thing.

A million thoughts swan around my head; what would they do with me? Surely, they weren't murderers? Shit, I did not appreciate *that* thought. Tremors of distress pumped through me. I suddenly felt like I'd made the biggest mistake of my life by not getting into my car. I should have listened to Noah.

The guy at my back walked around me to join the others and my gaze darted to his face. It *was* the man we'd seen last time. The 'money man', Noah had called him.

"She was here the other week making out with her boyfriend against the wall. They were going at it pretty hard. Gave me a boner that lasted all night. She was almost riding him," he sneered. I felt heat burst through my cheeks. His chin was angular, sharp almost.

"Was she," Wallis replied, itching his must-have-been-punched-many-times-nose.

"Yep. As you said, you'd remember that hair anywhere."

I had never felt any desire to dye my hair in the past but at that moment, I regretted that I hadn't.

"So, where is the boyfriend now?" Wallis questioned, in a voice as rough as the harshest of sandpapers.

Adrenaline surged through me and I felt a sick feeling in my stomach. How I'd love to wretch all over their dirty, probably bloodstained boots.

My lips felt dry and my throat was like the desert. I opened my mouth, willing sound to come out but it was a struggle.

"Well?" he bit down at me, his face darkening with impatience.

Biting back a sob I blurted. "He isn't here," I managed not to stutter. I just hoped he believed me.

"Really?" he said, his face suggesting he didn't buy the lie easily.

He glanced around before barking out instructions. "Go and check the cars and then have a look around. I'll finish up in here."

They all nodded and snapped to attention. The stocky guy stopped, propped the mop against the side of the barn wall before turning back. "What are you going to do with her?" he questioned with a flick of his head. I couldn't be sure, but I thought I identified a trace of concern in his tone. I didn't know whether to be more alarmed by this or not. Was the man worried Wallis *would* do something to me or worried that he *wouldn't*, 'tying up loose ends' so to speak? I sure prayed that Wallis didn't consider me a loose end.

"We're just going to have a little chat and then I'll let her go," Wallis said, removing the gloves and dropping them into a bucket next to the discarded prop.

The stocky man revealed how he felt about that.

"Are you fucking nuts? She'll tell someone!"

A twisted expression materialised on the face of the man directly in front of me. It wasn't nice.

"No, she won't. By the time I'm finished, she'll keep her pretty mouth closed for the rest of her life."

A jelly-like feeling shot through my legs as full-on terror kicked in.

"Please, I won't say anything. I don't even know what you're doing here," I panted out the lie.

Wallis wasn't impressed. "You can stop with the female hysterics. This isn't a scene from Breaking Bad. We're not going to fucking kill you."

I was surprised a criminal could look as offended as he did, but Wallis was blatantly annoyed by my reaction to his threat.

I frowned. "But the dogs?" He was still responsible for death.

He rolled his eyes and shrugged his wide shoulders in a careless manner.

"They're mutts, not fucking people," he bit out as if that made it perfectly OK. The guy certainly had a twisted view of things.

His tone then turned grim. "We don't kill people, but we do fuck them up. So, keep that in mind," he warned gravely.

Wallis moved his gaze away and darted a look at his buddies before flicking his head with a dismissive motion.

"Go on then, fuck off and check outside. See if we have anymore company. I'll deal with this."

That lightheaded feeling I'd experienced started to fade as a jet of relief shot into me. So, we were going to have a chat? I could deal with that. My limbs stopped quivering.

The others left, leaving me alone with Wallis.

"Stand up," he demanded, crossing his arms over his chest.

I did as he instructed and we circled each other; my eyes warily watching him. We stopped and he took a step toward me, getting in my face. Clearly trying to intimidate me.

"So, tell me what the fuck you're doing here? And don't say you're here by accident because we heard talk in the village that a group of locals were going to try and interfere."

So it was true, they had been warned. Breathing hard through my nose, I glared up at him, and endeavouring to pull myself together I managed to say. "I was out for a walk actually." I was impressed at the amount of sass I'd generated.

I continued to stare him down. Don't show him any weakness or he'll feed it back to you.

"In the middle of nowhere. You *fucking* liar."

I flinched as he growled the words. It was like I was suddenly looking death in the face and full-on panic resurfaced. He looked sickeningly pleased with himself that he'd managed to shake me up.

Wallis then boomed down at me.

"Do you know who I am? Do you have any fucking idea—?"

I didn't actually, not really; I thought to myself ruefully. I knew he was a crazy, sick dog killer and that was about it.

Wallis stopped mid-sentence, distracted; his eyes darting behind me. My back was now facing the door I'd been dragged in through and his gaze was drawn there.

Everything then went into slow motion and I lost all coherent thought; my mind a scramble.

My arm was grabbed and I was swung away from Wallis by what could only be Noah. After dragging me behind his large body, he released me and I fell backward, managing to jam my hands out to cushion my fall. I jarred my wrist as I landed on my backside; pain vibrated up my spine.

Looking up, my mouth fell open as Noah's large fist hit Wallis straight in the face; catching him directly on the nose. His shoulders were bunched as he put his entire weight behind that punch. The crunch of bones knocking together, echoed through my ears.

There was suddenly a ringing sound and all I could focus on was the two men as Wallis retaliated and launched himself at the bigger man with all his might. Noah had to be about a head taller and was carrying more weight but he still stumbled.

They brawling men went at each other, wrestling, jabbing at each other's stomachs, torsos; pretty much anywhere they could get at. Noah fell back slightly and Wallis broke away, almost falling to the ground. Blood oozed from his nose and my stomach lurched at such a gruesome sight.

I shuffled backward on my bottom on the filthy ground as the pair went at it again and Wallis lunged forward, driving his shoulder into Noah's stomach which brought them both down onto the ground beside me. I rolled to the side, away from their thrashing limbs. Grunts and growls erupting into the space.

After a couple of minutes of climbing on top of each other, they separated and pushed to their feet.

"You've got guts coming here, you fucking cunt," Wallis spat out, rubbing his sleeve against his nose, covering it in blood. I noticed there was also a cut above his eye.

"I know where you live mate and I'll fucking end you and your little bitch." Wallis roared flicking his head toward me.

His words had the desired effect and then some, Noah growled, his whole body enraged, fury pouring from his shoulders.

"Not if I end you first, you fucking pussy."

The two men circled each other in a fighting stance before Noah charged and grabbed a fist full of Wallis's hair, yanking him forward and smashing another fist into his face again. It actually hit him in the throat and generated an anguished bark/choke as Wallis clutched as his neck.

Relentlessly, Noah drew back his arm and punched him in the stomach. This knocked Wallis to his knees before he reared back, his face an open target.

Noah shot a look behind him, I'd never seen him look so fierce. I knew from his expression that he was partly ashamed that I was witnessing him in this murderous headspace.

Turning back to Wallis, my mouth dropped open as Noah lifted the weakened man up to his feet by his T-shirt and full-on head butted him in him the face. The thud was so loud you could almost feel it. Wallis dropped to the ground making a guttural sound, he wasn't out cold but he was dazed, his hands covering his face.

Other noises fell into the mix, car doors, shouting. Bad language. This appeared to be coming from outside and I thought I heard Connor shout.

A flurry of emotions rocked me; relief, despair, fear.

My hand suddenly touched something soft and sticky beside me and that mist started to clear. I didn't dare look. My focus remained on Noah. Straightening, the victor dashed a hand down his face, his large chest heaving with exertion. Animalistic danger pulsated through Noah's hard frame.

I'd never been afraid of him before, but at that moment I should have been. His face was pulled taunt with murderous fury, to the point where I feared for the other man's life.

I drew my gaze away from the ghost of the man I knew. There was blood; *everywhere*. That sticky fuzz was still by my hand and I touched it with the skin of my palm, suddenly needing to identify it. My wrist was still throbbing; my whole being recoiling in disgust.

After a deep breath, I twisted my head and peered down.

Noah was speaking to me, telling me not to look and to take his hand, but I couldn't stop myself.

By my hand there was a paw and two soulless brown eyes, almost looking up at me. The open, lifeless eyes from the fallen body of a dead animal. It even still had its collar on. I rubbed my hands together viciously and shoved away, shuffling back on my bottom, jabbing the floor with my feet.

I could hear screaming, the vibration of the sound shaking my body and I clawed at my neck with my fingers. The building was spinning, the scene before me barely visible now.

That cry echoed around the building and it wasn't until Noah shook my shoulder, that I realised the voice was mine. The pitch was ripped from the very back of my throat. I couldn't breathe, I was suffocating and bitter tears stung my skin, like acid against my cheeks.

"No, no…"

Confusion, disbelief, pain…A pair of strong arms encircled my upper arms and started to pull me up but my legs felt like two bits of string.

"Lucy, get to the car, do you hear me. Now!" Noah's voice was firm but had little effect, his hands falling away as I managed to stand. I felt dazed as I looked around. There was so much blood; clumps of fur, and what I assumed were teeth on the floor around me. Three furry bodies were dumped in a pile, next to what appeared to be a skip. Flies were buzzing around the surface and I didn't need to look inside to know what it held. Nausea hit me, cruel and thick.

Connor suddenly appeared around the doorway in record time at the opposite end of the building. It was the same door Wallis's goons had disappeared through.

As he spotted us, he cocked his head. "You good in here?" he shouted.

Noah's hand curled around my arm again to stop me from falling before bellowing over his shoulder.

"Yes, fine. Deal with the others," Noah yelled back.

"It's done. The Police are on their way," Connor informed him, glancing briefly at me before disappearing.

I could feel an acrid taste in my mouth and I bent forwards, ejecting the contents of my stomach onto the crimson-stained floor of the barn. The motion of retching wracking my entire frame.

Noah moved to hold my hair back and I vomited again. I didn't feel embarrassed, there was much too much anxiety in my system to allow anything else in.

Wiping my mouth on the back of my hand, I twisted and looked up into Noah's face, his nose was bleeding and there were angry bruises on his jaw.

"You good now?" he said, smoothing my hair back, his eyes glued with concern to my face. I wasn't, what I had just witnessed would probably haunt me for a long time.

"Are you?" I batted back as I eyed his face.

He dashed a hand across his darkening jaw, smearing crimson across his cheek before he shot me a tight smile and glanced around. He too was tortured by what we saw.

Fury as I had never witnessed in a person suddenly infected his face again as he glanced towards the dogs. An exchange of understanding passed between us; what needed to be done.

Stepping back from him, I glanced over to where Wallis was attempting to push to his feet, an inferno shooting through me. I was on fire, I had never experienced rage like it. I wanted to kick him in the stomach.

I watched Noah's as he strode away and grabbed Wallis from his fallen position. Dragging his half-limp body over to the pile of dead bodies. Lifeless animals, thrown into a heap with no regard or respect for their lives. The cruelty of it was painful to view.

Noah had Wallis by the scruff of his blood-stained T-shirt, his other hand in his hair and he pushed his face into the pungent remains of the dogs he was responsible for killing.

Wallis fought against Noah's hold but he couldn't break free. Foamy drool ran down his beaten face.

Briefly forcing him to face the animal carnage he had caused, Noah then dragged Wallis's face back up; his hand still in his hair and he growled.

"You twisted, sick fuck..." before releasing his hold, pulling back his arm and sending another punch into Wallis's already badly beaten jaw, knocking him out cold. He went down like a sack of potatoes.

As Wallis thudded to the ground, Noah spat on the floor next to his battered body. Signalling his disrespect. I fleetingly remembered he had done that to David.

I heard sirens increasing in volume outside and I wiped my hands down my tunic. I must have looked a sight, dirty tear stained with sick down my top.

You reap what you sow came to mind as I watched Wallis's still body.

Dizziness hit me again and I swayed slightly before Noah turned and lifted me into his arms. My own automatically circling his neck as he dragged me into the safety of his embrace. His heady smell was still there. It still comforted me; even thought I could sense the hint of sweat and blood cocktailed in there.

He carried me out of the barn and into the night air. As the cold hit me, I dragged in a huge breath. Everything was so much fresher.

There were cars parked, flashing lights and I spotted Connor and Nathan. Nate's face was a mess but Connor didn't have a hair out of place. Typical. Didn't *anything* affect the guy? He was obviously an experienced brawler.

The police were there and I saw the stocky guy was in handcuffs and in the process of being led away.

Nathan was making a statement with a brooding Connor standing beside him. As he saw us, he drew away and approached us. His dark gaze assessing Noah's injuries.

"Hell Noah, you look fucked up. You must be losing your touch," Connor said cockily. My goodness, was now the right time for the big dick thing, again a term Melanie used when her brothers were trying to best each other.

Noah was still holding me close to his chest and he glanced down. "Whatever, I had a fucking distraction. Where's yours?"

"At home, safe," Connor replied with a smug smile.

"Which is where mine should have fucking been!" Noah boomed, annoyance pouring from him.

"You need to keep a leash on that one."

I ignored Connor's Neanderthal, 'belonged in the dark ages' comment as guilt bled into me. I should have just left like Noah had instructed. I could feel his aggressive stance, he held me quite rigidly in his arms. Yes, he had saved me, but I was obviously still in trouble.

The thought that I had let him down raced through me and a tide of misery washed into my conscience.

The water works were back. Tears fell down my face and my entire body stared shaking in his arms.

"Easy Lucy, it's OK. You're safe now." Noah asked, drawing me tighter against him. Liquid seeping from me.

"I thought you were going to kill him," I sobbed.

His eyes softened. "I'm sorry if I scared you. And I'm sorry you had to see me like that."

I shook my head and tried to appear dismissive, as if I didn't care about that. "It's OK."

Shooting us both a God-give-me-strength-look, Connor rolled his eyes before scoffing. "Good luck with that one bro." Obviously uncomfortable around crying females. I wondered how he'd have felt if it had been Harlow in there. He'd probably have killed someone.

Shooting one last glance between us he strode off. I'd have shot him a dirty look if I'd had the energy.

We all had to give statements to the police, I did so in between bouts of crying before Noah took control and basically told the policewoman that I'd had enough and that he was taking me home. It was definitely said in a 'whether you like it or not' tone. He was so commanding and manly, to be honest; he probably had the woman in the palm of his hand anyway. I saw the sly looks she shot his way whilst supposedly taking my statement.

Noah assisted me over to where his car was still parked. My eyes were gritty but I managed to doze off on the way back home (well, my temporary home). After pulling into the driveway and parking the car, Noah placed a reassuring arm around my shoulders and followed me into his parent's house.

"We'll drive back and collect your car tomorrow, when you've had some sleep."

"OK," I smiled.

As we walked toward the stairs, Natalie was on her way down with a guy behind her. "What the hell happened to you?" she said to Noah, her nose wrinkled in horror.

Natalie and her 'guest' moved to the side to allow us to pass. "I'll fill you in later Nat. I can see you're busy," he part-sneered as he gestured toward the nervous looking guy. She grinned at him and gave us a finger tipped wave before setting off toward the front door. Said guy following her like a nervous puppy.

We both went upstairs and Noah ran me a bath. The whole time we were mostly silent. Just an occasional instruction from Noah and a thank you here and there from me.

I didn't resist when Noah started to help me undress. There wasn't anything sexual about it. He was *helping* me. His face was impassive as he lifted my naked body into the water. His breath did catch in his throat slightly as I turned, standing before him. I didn't feel any need to cover myself. I lowered myself under the barrier of the bubbles and he turned away. He then left me to it, asking me to shout if I needed anything.

After my bath, I walked into the bedroom I was using to find him sat on the bed texting on his phone.

My hair was wrapped in a turban and my body a towel. *Just* a towel. I was now suddenly very aware of my nakedness which was odd considering Noah had now seen everything anyway. My skin was flushed from the heat of the water and my body omitted a coconut smell, which was of course much more appealing than vomit, blood and grime.

Noah looked up as I entered, taking in my form, his reaction was instantaneous; the darkness of his tanned skin actually flushed. Clearing his throat, he briefly looked away and pocketed his phone.

"How do you feel?" he said, shoving up off the bed as I came to stand before him. I felt so tiny.

"Better now thank you."

"You almost gave me a fucking heart attack Lucy. When I saw you weren't at your car, I fucking lost it."

"I know, and I'm sorry. I just wanted to see what had happened."

He exhaled sharply. "Where has this sudden brave streak come from?" Noah questioned, his deep eyes drilling into mine.

"You said it yourself. I've been too sheltered from the harsher stuff. I wanted to try to be tougher. See how cruel the world really is. You know, seize the day."

Noah scowled. "Tonight certainly wasn't a, 'seize the day' moment and that wasn't being tough Lucy. That was plain fucking stupidity."

Of course he had a point.

My shoulders slumped. "I know. And I'm really sorry."

There was a beat of silence as his eyes roamed over my face. I could see a mixture of relief and anxiety.

Changing the subject, I noted he'd washed his face and his hair was wet. "Does your face hurt?" He'd cleaned himself up but he was still badly bruised.

He rolled his shoulders like he needed to remove a knot. "Can't feel a thing, to be honest."

Tilting my head to the side to regard him further I said almost vacantly. "Will they send him to prison do you think?"

Noah chuckled but there was little humour in it. "Absolutely. For a long time, I would have thought and the fact that he attacked you, will add to his sentence."

My brows knitted. "But he didn't, not really."

Noah moved back a step and folded his arms not breaking eye contact. "Nope, but he could have if I hadn't showed up when I did and anyway, that's the version I gave to the police."

I sighed. "Noah." He'd pretty much just confessed he'd lied. OK then, over-exaggerated.

"What? I didn't lie, I embellished the truth. I told you, turn the other cheek and I don't co-exist. I have no shame lying my arse off if it gets that prick inside for longer."

I smiled, he had a point.

"Anyway, I don't want you to spend a minute longer thinking of the screwed up shit you saw tonight," Noah said, his tone commanding. Shoving his hands into the pockets of his grubby jeans, he then shot me a pointed look. "No more foolish thoughts of being the hero. You don't have to be tough now you've got me."

His words pumped nice thoughts around my system and I grinned again and took a step forward, closing what little space there was between us.

My skin fizzed as he withdrew his hands and ran his finger-tips up and down my arms, warming the goose flesh which had suddenly appeared.

"I kind of like you in one piece," he whispered down at me.

"I really do love you Noah, you know that, don't you." I said, my voice full of confidence. I no longer felt shy saying it.

Noah's face warmed. "I know. And I love you, you beautiful, unpredictable girl."

He closed his eyes briefly, sighing. "You really will be the death of me."

There was a moments silence as he dropped his hands.

"I should go," he said, his voice husky. I could see the desire evident in his gaze as it flittered over my scantily clad body. It appeared the restraint he'd had in the bathroom had gone.

A thought suddenly occurred and I answered that craving inside me.

"Do you want to stay the night, here with me?"

He exhaled sharply. Sexual frustration oozed from him and he arched a sexy brow.

"Again, not a good idea Lucy. I don't think I could keep my hands off you a second night."

And there it was, I knew at last that I was ready. I needed this boy with every part of my body. Wanted him to take me through those unchartered waters. I wanted to be as close to him as I could possibly be in that most intimate way. For Noah Savvas to be my first.

"Then don't," I replied in a husky tone of my own. My voice thick with a provocative element.

He looked pained, like he was fighting himself and I relished that shudder that wracked his large form.

We were so close, our bodies leaning into one another, almost doing the talking for us.

"I want you, Noah. All of you." I was done with taking it slow and I moved to place a hand on his chest. Sexual heat rioted through me.

His fingers lifted to close gently over my wrist, stopping my movements. He was at war with himself. Being punished by both his head and his body as they fought for supremacy. "I can't believe I'm going to fucking say this but, no. You've been through another trauma tonight and it isn't the right time."

He pulled my hand away, lowering it to my side. His warm breath fanned my face.

His expression turned serious. "Our first time won't be that straightforward," his tone was terse.

My frown deepened. "I know you won't hurt me."

His beautiful mouth tugged into a smile and he quirked an eyebrow. "I'll inevitably hurt you Lucy. That's what happens the first time. Surely, you've read books and shit?"

I nodded before asking. "Does it bother you that I'm a virgin?"

He shook his head slowly, his eyes on my face. "Of course not. We all were once."

Running my gaze over his large frame I inhaled, taking in his scent and it added fuel to my fantasies.

He seemed to read my thoughts. "There's also the difference in our sizes."

My brow creased. "Do you think that will be a problem?"

Promise flared between us and he shook his head.

"No. Don't get me wrong, when it happens it will be perfect. But I want to do it right, take it slow. You're not ready, *especially* not after what you witnessed tonight.

"I guess you're right."

Noah gave me one of those cocky looks of his. "Of course, I am. I'm *always* right."

I released a puff of air. "You're also *always* an arrogant sod."

His smile widened. "Again, you're not wrong"

Suddenly changing the subject, I blurted. "I suppose you've been with loads of girls."

He screwed his eyes closed and dropped his head. “Lucy. Not really a topic for discussion.”

I shrugged nonchalantly. “I just wondered.”

He opened his eyes and shot me a pensive stare. “Too many, but past lovers are a no-go area I think.”

Contemplating these words, I wondered why on earth I’d asked. I knew whatever answer he gave me would hurt. Although I knew he’d gone without sex for quite a while; how long did he say, six weeks?

“OK. I don’t really want to know anyway,” I confessed, reason suddenly kicking in.

Noah stretched his shoulders. “And I use the term lovers loosely. It was just sex really, one-night stands and shit.”

A worrying thought suddenly chewed into me. “What if I’m not very good at it?”

He released his gentle hold on my wrist and closed that small space between us, slipping his hands around my waist and tugging my body into his. The towel and his clothes were the only barrier between our two forms.

He lowered his dark head, his hair still damp. “You have nothing to worry about. We have chemistry which is off the fucking chart. Sex between us will be amazing.”

“Really?” I questioned, searching his face for that reassurance.

His fingers were massaging the bottom of my back through the terry cloth. “Trust me, and there are feelings involved so it will be so much more.”

“I’m just totally inexperienced. I’ve only ever kissed a couple of boys.”

“Well, fuck me, I’m looking forward to teaching you all I know.”

A jet of excitement shot through me. Noah had spoken to me this way before, but now it seemed much more real.

“I am ready you know. I know how I feel.”

His hands dropped and fondled my bottom through the towel. “Me too and it will be worth the wait.”

Heat pooled between my legs. I had no knickers on, he probably wasn’t aware of how close he was. I released a panted breath. “Really?”

His eyes flared as he took in my bodies’ reaction to where he’d placed those strong fingers. “Abso-fucking-lutely.” Noah said with such surety that I believed him.

My mouth curled in a shy smile. “OK then. I suppose I should get into my PJs and get to bed.”

"Yes, and I should go whilst I still have a small amount of control. The fact that you're still wearing that towel is a miracle."

"I could always flash you, give you a taste of the good stuff?"

"Hmm, don't push it."

"OK, I'll behave," I laughed.

"Gets some rest, tomorrow we're going looking at flats for you, remember."

Noah then lowered his head and kissed me with such tenderness and thoroughness that I was almost breathless. He *stole* the air from my lungs. My breasts tightened as his hands moved lower and slid under the towel and over my bare backside, cupping my bottom cheeks and drawing me up onto my tip toes.

I heard the hitch of breath as he discovered I had no underwear on and he ground himself against my stomach, creating a delicious friction. I ached everywhere for his touch. As I felt Noah's erection, lust pumped through me. It was intense and exciting and I embraced it and shoved my fingers into his hair. Noah growled as I pulled his mouth further against mine and drank greedily from his lips. The attraction I felt went into overdrive.

Noah palmed my backside, needing the flesh there, and then I was free.

He released me and stepped back, his breathing irregular and my arms dropped to my sides. Dashing a hand down his bruised face, he gave himself a moment to recover from our kiss. I placed a hand against my chest as I too struggled for control.

The bed loomed beside us; beckoning us both.

The atmosphere calmed but there was still a crackle in the air.

"As I said, sex will be amazing between us Lucy, but we don't need to rush it. We have plenty of time."

Noah's eyes then probed mine, his expression determined.

"You're every orgasm will belong to me."

Before I could react, Noah then planted a soft kiss on my lips and readjusted my towel, ensuring it was still in place.

"Thank you again for saving me," I whispered.

A serious expression fell into place. "You're welcome."

"And I don't just mean tonight, Noah."

Understanding crossed his face and we shared a silent moment before he said. "Ditto."

And the boy I had given my heart to left the room, taking part of me with him.

I threw myself onto the bed, my entire body on fire. I touched my lips which were tingling and a further jet of excitement pumped through me. Noah's hands had been on my bare backside and I wondered how his fingers would feel between my legs.

I didn't regret the direction of my thoughts, this wasn't a sordid, guilty thing between us. We were in love, it was *real*, scary yet immensely satisfying. I felt safe and cherished. Noah's strength brought out the best in me. Gone was the shy little mouse who was afraid of her own shadow. I was slowly growing into someone I could be proud of. A wallflower that had lived in the shadows but was slowly creeping forward into the light.

And this time, I wasn't alone. Noah Savvas, my bully, my tormentor, was now my first love.

It was like we had both overcome stuff from our pasts and now the future together would only get brighter. Two broken souls that were whole again.

A new, exciting journey together was unwritten.

And I for one, couldn't wait for what came next.

EPILOGUE

Around Two Years Later

"Why do they call it a dog?" Max Walker suddenly chomped out with his mouthful. You could only just make out what he was saying after his last, overindulgent bite. "It looks fuck all like one."

The hotdog he was clutching was almost as big as his arm. He took another *massive* bite. Everyone watched with varying expressions as a jet of ketchup shot out of the end of the bun and onto his chest; the liquid soaking his tee. It looked like he'd been shot. He attempted to rub the blob away with his fingers, actually making it worse.

"Didn't your mother teach you it's rude to speak with your mouthful; you're the dog you scruffy twat," Connor volleyed back with an unimpressed glower.

"Please let's not talk about dogs," Nathan added with a been-there-done-that-face.

"It's mystery meat. They use dog parts as a filler," Ella teased with a straight face. Her words could have been seen as insensitive, considering what had happened in the village a few years ago, but everyone took it the way it was intended, as a joke.

The whole group were silently watching him to see his reaction when the penny dropped. He wasn't the brightest of people.

Horrified would be the best way to describe it.

Everyone groaned as his tongue shot forward and ousted some chewed food from his mouth.

"You're kidding that's disgusting!" It fell onto his knee with a plop and he dropped the bun-encased sausage next to it in alarm.

"That's not the only thing that's disgusting Max," Harlow added with a grossed-out expression.

Ella who was sitting with her boyfriend, shuffled backward between Ryan's legs with her own gasp of horror. "And I was joking, you moron!"

A blob of discarded sausage had narrowly missed her foot. "These sliders are Calvin Klein, dickhead!"

We were at the beach in Scarborough by the North Shore. It was a beautiful summer's day in August and it was the first time we had all been together as a group that year.

Sitting on the warm sand and soaking in the rays, we were doing what we usually did during our annual get-togethers. Hanging out, chilling, catching up, putting the world to rights, *and* each other.

I leaned my head back against Noah's huge bare chest, his male musky scent was mingled with salt water from the sea. The boys had been for a swim whilst the girls engaged in some essential girl talk.

Most of our chat had been about our relationships, the stuff we had done and the stuff we hadn't. Harlow and Ella had been only too keen to share tips they had picked up from their healthy sex lives. I'd chipped in occasionally, but certainly hadn't shared as much. They were at different stages in their relationships and had started to experiment with the kinkier side of things. I inwardly cringed when Harlow reported that Connor had slapped her bottom during sex one night and how she'd had *loved* it. The thought made my eyes smart.

With Ella, it was an 'anything' goes arrangement. To be honest, there probably wasn't anything she *hadn't* done. Tricky to get your head around, although I didn't overthink the subject. Ryan was such a cool cucumber and he certainly didn't look like he'd be into the things she spoke about. This was the first time I'd seen him out of a suit. I had him saved into my phone under MR SERIOUS.

Connor was MR MOODY, Nathan; THE RIDDLER (nothing to do with batman you see, more to do with the amount of girls he'd slept with) and I'd finally changed Noah from SATAN to NOAH. The girls were also saved under their given names.

I pushed away the image of what Ella had described earlier, not even sure how the position she spoke about would work. I transferred my mind back to my own sex life.

My relationship with Noah was far from vanilla but we hadn't gone down the fetish route yet. Definitely no toe sucking for me thank you. I didn't mind occasional biting and having my hands pinned over my head. Noah and I liked to experiment, but we were perfectly happy with the regular stuff too. We just fit perfectly, both emotionally and physically.

Said boy nuzzled my shoulder and a shiver flittered across my semi-naked body that had *nothing* to do with the sea breeze. I was wearing a black bikini and Noah hadn't been able to keep his eyes off me. I was playing with him on purpose, taunting him with what he couldn't have. Not at that moment anyway when we were surrounded by our friends.

"So how are your studies going Harlow?" I asked brightly. Harlow had moved to live with her father and Connor on her father's farm whilst she studied at Scarborough University. She aimed to become a primary school teacher.

She and Connor were *inseparable* now and I wondered fleetingly if they'd eventually have kids and settle down. Although she *was* the baby of us all and so it wouldn't be any time soon. I could imagine that Connor as a father would be extremely strict. He was the most possessive out of all the boys.

Harlow was sitting next to him with one bare leg draped across his and he had one hand placed on her creamy, perfectly shaped thigh.

Harlow's bikini was red with white spots and when we'd first arrived, she'd drawn pretty much every guy on the beach's attention. I'd caught a few cheeky looks my way which gave me a bit of a boost, but *nothing* compared to the reception she got. You could see Connor bristling with annoyance as they walked together across the sand; his hand draped possessively over her shoulder. A gesture which screamed 'hands off'. Noah had also noticed the looks I'd received and he too had dished out the deadeye here and there. I loved how protective Noah was. Connor's version came across a little too aggressive for my liking, but Harlow took great pleasure in it.

I shook my thoughts back as I realised Harlow was now answering my question. "It's going great thanks, Lucy. How are things with you at the practice?"

I was now a trainee vet nurse, working closely with Jay and Tom (who were now an item by the way – they'd kept that one a secret), I was on day release and spent one day at college and the rest of the time working on practical tasks at the surgery, and I *loved* it.

My thoughts darted back to Tom. Everyone was so happy when they found out about Jay and Tom. He and Jay were perfect together. They talked shop most of the time but they were still cute and madly in love. It turned out that Tom even had a fun side, something else he'd kept under wraps. He was now a fully trained vet and pretty much ran the surgery in the village.

I glanced fleetingly around the group. We were all feeling relaxed and sitting in a circle on towels laid directly onto the sand. Max had tidied up the mess he'd made and had now joined his brother Kyle on the sand, working on their tans. They were both almost as white as me and seemed to reflect the sun rather than soak it up.

I pondered Harlow's question about my job.

"I'm getting there. Tom's been a great help," I replied with a grin. I twitched as Noah placed a kiss on my shoulder and drew me further against him.

"You're doing more than OK Lucy," Noah whispered against the cuff of my ear, causing warmth to pool into my stomach. He was so encouraging after I'd decided to change the path of my career.

Over the last couple of years, our relationship had gone from strength to strength.

I now had my own flat in Scalby, the next village to the church and Noah and I either stayed at mine or at his place above his garage. We were together in *every* sense of the word.

Noah had taken my virginity with gentle tenderness and was a skilful lover, teaching me and guiding me slowly before I'd found my own way. I remember that initial discomfort before white hot pleasure had streaked through me. Noah had stripped away my shyness layer by layer and I was now gradually coming into my own. Getting to know my own body, my likes and my dislikes and let me tell you, there weren't many dislikes. Not even the rough sex Noah seemed to favour, which was *sensational*. He was half Cypriot at the end of the day and men from the med were wild and passionate. I'd embraced *everything* he had taught me and had experimented with a few ideas of my own. Noah definitely liked to be the one in control though, but if I felt the mood to take the lead. I took it. With bells on.

The banter continued to flow between us. Our friendship group was tight. The main topic of discussion was the holiday we were all planning together for the October half term. After aligning our diaries, we'd decided to fly out to Tenerife to stay in Ryan's Lane's deluxe villa. It had eight bedrooms, a cinema room, a gym (much to Connor and Noah's delight) and a *huge* swimming pool.

Ryan now ran the family business selling farming equipment and was minted. Ella was also successful in her own right, being the Director of a landscaping company. Connor was still of course a farmer, but pretty much ran the show, his stepdad Mike, Harlow's father, having stepped down last year after he'd slipped a disc in his back. He was OK, he just had to take it easier these days.

"About time," Ryan suddenly said, glancing past my shoulder. Noah and I both twisted to see Nathan and his latest lay (not my words of course, I was far too nice to say that about another member of my sex). He had been with this one for around three days which was probably his longest relationship. A personal best.

“Where the hell have you been shithead? You got my text about the beer I take it?”

Kyle and Max sprung to life at the word beer, their tans suddenly forgotten.

Nathan and ‘question mark’ (as we had yet to learn her name) approached our circle and Ella and Ryan moved over to allow room for another couple. Nate dropped a carrier bag with beer into the centre of us all. It sank into the sand next to a large bag of crisps, a black sack containing empties, and part of Max’s regurgitated burger bun. There was also part of a sandcastle that the girls and I had built before Max had decided to stand on it.

“Soz, we got held up. Believe me, you don’t want to know the details,” he explained with a glint in his eye. Everybody groaned, we all knew *exactly* what had kept him. The guy was a walking talking sex addict.

“This is, Janet,” Nate began as they both lowered themselves to sit directly on the sand, not having brought a towel. Noah started to nuzzle my neck, totally switched off from the group and I ran my fingers down his strong legs which almost enveloped each of mine. Our skin was so very different in contrast; I was white and freckled, and Noah was tanned and flawless; apart from the smattering of black hair. I loved our differences, we were unique in so many ways.

“Do you want a drink, Janet?” Nathan offered. He wore cut-off jeans and a tank top.

“Janey,” the girl corrected him. OMG, he couldn’t even get her name right. I didn’t feel that sorry for her as she probably didn’t care. Like his brother, Nathan Lane’s wealth was a big draw to members of my sex, as well as his reputation in the sack.

Janet aka Janey was tall and curvy with brown hair which was tied up in a messy bun, showing off her long graceful neck. Her bikini was shark grey. After getting her name wrong, Nathan grinned mischievously at her before placing an arm around her shoulders.

Connor divvied out the beers, throwing one over to Nathan and another to Ryan, before helping himself. I felt Noah shake his head from behind me, him being the designated driver of the day.

Kyle grabbed two beers and handed one to Max before they pushed to their feet.

“We’re going for food. We need some dirty meat,” Kyle announced stretching. His stomach was already turning pink. The brothers occasionally talked for each other, one of those creepy twin things.

Everyone else settled down and then Harlow squeaked as Connor lifted her and dragged her so she was half sitting on his lap. She placed an arm around his shoulders and he kissed her nose. To say he was such an aggressive, scary presence, they looked as cute as kittens together. I wondered if their parents knew they were in a relationship, considering they lived in the same house. Surely that wouldn't have been that easy to hide. They were all over each other.

"So, what were you guys talking about?" Nathan said, his eyes shifting around the circle.

"The holiday," Ryan replied as he played with Ella's hair. It used to be much shorter but she had grown it; it was now like a wave of chocolate silk.

"Cool," Nate shot back at his brother.

"Oh, what holiday is this, maybe I could come," Janey put in, suddenly animated, opening the bottle of Hooch she had in her hand.

Nathan's colour drained away and he shot us a quick warning look from beside her. "Ah, err, you know… that film, The Holiday, Kate Winslet and…" Nate lied. It was comical really as I imagined he'd *never* even seen that movie.

"Jude Law," I interjected, coming to his rescue. He shot me a smile of thanks before turning to Janey.

"Oh, I like that movie. Jack Black looks amazing in it," she giggled.

"Do me a favour babe. Run over and grab me a burger, I'm fucking starving," Nathan said before leaning over to plant a kiss on her lips.

Janey rolled her eyes as he gave her a five pound note, doing exactly as he'd asked.

We watched as she set off across the sand.

"You're such a bellend," Connor said when Janey had gone.

"Hopefully there's a *massive* queue and it keeps her busy for a bit," Nathan replied, two boyish dimples appearing on his cheeks.

"If you don't want to see her, why bring her here?" Ella questioned as she snuggled into Ryan.

"She's fucking crazy," Nathan replied with a tired expression. Maybe she'd kept him up half the night?

He lifted his muscled arms and pulled his tee up to reveal his tanned torso; one with several scratch marks across it.

We all sat up and paid attention, even Noah lifted his head. "What the fuck bro?"

Nathan grimaced and then glanced down at his skin. "Oh yeah, she's *wild* man. Anything goes."

Ryan snorted. "Too much for you to handle you mean."

I smiled, recognising that the playful 'taking the piss out of each other' banter was close.

"Honest to God, you might be right. I'm knackered. She's ground me down. I'm not sure that there's anything left down there to be frank."

Connor snorted, encouraging a darted 'behave yourself' look from Harlow.

"There wasn't much to start with, so Milly Taylor said."

Nate crossed his legs and necked his beer before shooting Connor a curious look over the rim of the bottle.

"Who?" he questioned with a cheeky grin. Of course, he wouldn't remember *all* their names, there was only just enough space in Nathan's head for his huge ego. I'd never met anyone so full of themself. Even Noah wasn't *that* bad.

"Fuck me, Nathan. Do you know the number of women you've slept with?" Ella said, rolling her eyes.

"Do you the number of women you've slept with?" Nate batted back.

This was a regular theme as Ella was a tomboy. Someone usually snuck the lesbian joke in there at some point. It was a fairly weak attack, considering she was sprawled between the tanned thighs of her boyfriend. Ryan even looked immaculate in board shorts. He probably ironed all his clothing; or had 'the help' do it for him.

From the look on his face, he wasn't impressed by his brother's comment about his girlfriend.

"How about you wind your neck in Nathan, before I beat the shit out of you?"

"It's fine Ryan. It was a piss poor comeback anyway. Do STD's mean anything to you Nathan?" she grinned.

"Funny. Anyway, she's just a booty call that's got ahead of herself."

Noah shifted from behind me.

"Talking of booty calls Connor, I think during our work out tomorrow we need to have a little chat," Noah suddenly said in a gruff voice. I turned to glance up into his perfect face and he winked at me. A silent code to say he was playing.

Connor cleared his throat, suddenly looking uncomfortable and Harlow flicked her gaze between the two men before slipping off his knee.

"Really? You're bringing that up here?" Connor said, an awkward pitch to his tone.

"*That* has a name and yes, Nat and I had quite the heart to heart the other night," Noah said as he started to run his fingers up and down my legs; the touch a sweet tickle.

"Fucking great timing. You're such a wanker." Connor huffed, stealing a glance at his girlfriend's expression.

Harlow blanked him and caught my look of confusion before uncurling herself from her boyfriend. She didn't look upset, not really and I wondered what was going on. Whatever it was, all three of them knew something.

I shot Ella a look, from her expression she was also in the know.

Nathan started to laugh. "You are so busted motherfucker. I wondered when *that* would come out."

"So, you're the one who's been running his mouth off then?" Connor accused, rolling his massive shoulders. His sleeve of tattoos adding to that sense of danger.

Nathan grinned, his expression taunting as he pushed his beer into the sand so it wouldn't spill and lifted his hands, palms flat to say I surrender.

"Nope, not me. I like my face too much the way it is." His reply suggested he was still wary of Connor. I knew they'd come to blows in the past as Noah had told me how Nathan had gotten his scar.

Connor shot Nathan a brooding look as Harlow pushed herself to her feet.

"I'm going to get us some chips Con. Sounds like you've got some explaining to do and so you'll do better with something in your stomach." And off she went, leaving an ashen-faced Connor to stew. It was the most uncomfortable I'd *ever* seen him.

"Yeah Con, you'll do better with something in your stomach," Nathan parried with a cheeky wicked grin. They guy definitely liked living dangerously. I couldn't tell whether Connor was joining in or genuinely pissed off. He had the most unreadable face of the group and he was the most unpredictable. And talking about unpredictable, his face darkened.

"How about I put my fist in yours?" Connor shot back in warning, his eyes narrowing.

A cocktail of voices from laughter to gasps to calming coos erupted from the group.

"We're just fucking with you Connor. I think someone needs another dose of ketamine," Noah replied, managing to bite his lip, sensing that he was about to go too far but somehow not being able to stop.

"I don't take ketamine you cheeky fucker," Connor growled back.

“Isn’t that what they use to tranq horses?” Nate questioned with a fake innocent expression. These guys had a death wish. “It probably wouldn’t work on Connor.”

“And you can fuck off dipshit. At least my dick hasn’t fallen off,” Connor shot back, glaring between the two men. Sticking one of his own insults in there.

I suddenly found my voice. Noah now wasn’t paying attention; he was too busy touching the freckled areas on my legs. He’d once told me he’d count them all. And he had, *several* times. He especially liked the ones that were located in my most intimate places. There was no hiding from Noah now, he knew his way around my body as well as I did.

Reining in the lustful direction of my thoughts, I asked for clarity on the matter, feeling a bit out of the loop.

“What’s going on?” I said, looking around the group. Ella and Ryan were whispering and I couldn’t make out what they were saying.

No one answered and so I gently elbowed Noah in the ribs and he huffed, stopped his tickling and wrapped his arms around my shoulders.

“I’ll let Connor tell the story,” Noah said, his voice directed over at said person.

“You’re such a bitch, Savvas. That was fucking *ages* ago and if your big mouth has put me in the dog house, I’ll get my own back,” Connor said with dark promise.

I twisted to see Noah’s grin. “What goes around comes around bro.”

Connor snorted. “That’s the best threat you can come up with, that’s just embarrassing,” he volleyed.

Noah shrugged carelessly. “Your highest score on Grand Theft Auto, is what’s embarrassing, mate.”

Their banter was all over the show, it was making me dizzy and I clapped my hands together to try and draw attention. “Err hello, can someone please tell me what you all know that I don’t?”

Noah had alluded that it had something to do with his sister, and Connor. And then it clicked.

“Oh. So, Natalie and Connor had a thing,” I put in, answering my own question.

I shifted to the side of Noah and took a swig of beer.

“Yep. Turns out big dick here was boning my sister for three months,” Noah announced.

Ryan cleared his throat and Ella laughed.

"As I said, fucking ages ago," Connor snarled moodily, refusing to apologise for something that happened in the past.

"I take it Harlow knows," I put in there with a double take, checking to see where she was in the queue.

It was hard to tell as she was near the front but there was a group of guys surrounding her. They'd stopped their game of football and had flocked to her like dogs to the tastiest bone. Thankfully, Connor couldn't see as he had his back to her. A good thing considering his current temper.

"Yes, she *fucking* knows. We don't have any secrets. It happened before we got together. Nat and I cooled things week's before Har got to the farm. And it was amicable before you fucking start Noah. We never made each other any promises."

Connor's voice had dipped, he wasn't happy. Noah needed to shut it down before he flipped. Something he did on and off, especially when he was off his medication. And no, he wasn't on ketamine!

"OK, calm down. I'll take your word for it," Noah said as I shifted to sit beside him, moving off the towel. The sand bit into my backside.

Connor shot Noah a grim look.

"If I don't get any tonight, I'll have myself a little visit with Lucy and chat about your past. You fucking man-whore."

Noah held his hands up in surrender. "I apologise. Just pointing out that you broke the code man."

"The code?" I questioned, needing to get that seed Connor had just planted about Noah with other girls out of my head. I knew he'd been with loads of girls before me, but not anymore. I nudged Noah, wanting to know what he meant by 'the code'. It hadn't been easy getting in with these guys; they were so close-knit and had shared so much more together before I had come onto the scene. I still felt like an outsider, at times.

"Yeah, no sisters or brothers or exes. It's against the rules."

"Fucking hell," Nate suddenly said under his breath with a wobble. "Time, I went for a piss I think."

He ran for the hills as both Ryan and Ella exchanged awkward glances. I wasn't sure what that story was about but something was off. It was like a large jigsaw puzzle that I'd never solve. Maybe there was some past animosity from Tom due to

Ryan getting with his sister. I shook off the thought. Whatever it was appeared to be between Ella and the Lane boys. Interesting.

The twins suddenly appeared back and resumed their earlier position, both with their faces buried in cheeseburger.

"I think perhaps you want to go and find your date Connor. Harlow appears to be dripping in boys," I said with a smile, hooking my chin behind him.

He cast me a dark look before turning to glare in the distance toward Harlow who was still standing by the burger bar. Guys swarming around her like bees to honey. She appeared to be smiling but wasn't being overly flirty. I did see her dart a nervous glance toward us. Probably checking that Connor couldn't see.

Turning back toward us he bit out, "Motherfuckers," under his breath before shoving to his feet. He dusted the sand off his shorts before cracking his knuckles. Oh dear.

"Keep your fists to yourself Connor," Noah warned with a serious tone. "That's Alex and his mates, they're harmless enough."

Alex still worked for Noah and he was such a funny, skinny thing, no threat at all really. Noah was protective of his staff.

Connor shot him a lopsided smile and flexed his tattooed arm.

"Don't worry, I'll leave him the use of his fingers so he can still work," he said. He then winked and if I hadn't been sat down, I would fallen down. Playful was not something you saw in Connor, especially when other guys were coming onto his girlfriend. No sir, where Harlow and other men were concerned, the guy had no sense of humour. I eyed his broad back as he marched away. Wondering about his torturous back story. Something I wasn't fully aware of.

"I must say I never thought I'd see the day Connor became a sappy fucker," Max blurted out, beer running down his chin. He definitely wasn't the most attractive of the group.

"I'd love to hear you say that to his face," Noah grinned, throwing me a wink.

We all chatted about Connor and his mood swings, behind his back, but in a supportive way. You definitely couldn't have those types of discussions with him present.

Connor and Harlow eventually returned with chips and re-joined the group; Harlow fed Connor one by one. They were chips at the end of the day, but it still looked sexual somehow. They were covered in ketchup and I smiled to myself as Connor drew one of Harlow's fingers into his mouth and sucked off some of the sauce.

I cleared my throat which drew Connor's attention up.

"Where's Nate?" he said with a frown, flicking a look around the area.

"Pissed off with his tail between his legs," Ella put in whilst snuggling towards Ryan. He had his hands around her and was stoking her bared midriff. She wore a bikini top, but denim shorts on the bottom half. Her legs were long and thin.

"So, the villa," Connor put in with a bored expression; he soon tired of that back-and-forth thing.

"One or two weeks?" Ryan questioned, pushing his aviator sunglasses up onto his head and looking at Connor directly. I knew there had been some animosity in the past between them; in fact, most guys surrounding me had had some type of run-in with Connor, he was angst encapsulated. Connor also struggled with his hearing in one ear and he had a bit of a chip on his shoulder about it. Noah had said that his dad used to do horrible things to him. The small amount of backstory I knew made sense, considering how abrasive he acted most of the time.

Everyone started talking about the villa and flight times and who would have what room.

"Ella and I will be in the master bedroom of course. The rest of you fuckers can fight it out between yourselves," Ryan declared.

It was his house at the end of the day. Ella beamed at him; her hair was almost to her waist now although she pretty much always wore it back. We had become quite close; Ella, Harlow and I. I was also good friends with Noah's sister Natalie but I considered them a different set of friends. It was funny really as I hadn't thought about that until now. If Natalie and Connor used to sleep together, no wonder she and Harlow weren't close. I remember Nat saying bitchy comments about Connor's girlfriend on and off. Something about her being spoiled and too into her looks. I'd batted them off of course as I didn't do mean.

As everyone chipped in about the holiday, I relaxed back into Noah. His warmth enveloped me. The sun had gone behind the clouds and when it disappeared, it was quite cold; we were in Yorkshire on the East Coast at the end of the day.

Life was going well.

I was happy; my issues with my dad and David had been settled amicably. I saw both occasionally for coffee and told them about my work and plans for the future. Noah and David actually managed to stay civil, but you could almost taste the atmosphere between them. The less amount of time they spent together the better really.

I occasionally went to church to see David's service and I still had my faith, but I kept this just for me.

The last few years had been an adventure. From my return from University, breaking down and being reintroduced to my school nemesis. Bringing down a dog syndicate, having to leave home and becoming independent. Becoming a mummy to a dog (Vee was still a big part of our life together). Not to forget my change in career.

Life in Yorkshire was interesting and today love in Yorkshire surrounded me.

But most importantly, I had found *myself*. It took one annoying, beautiful bastard to bring her back to life, but she was back and here to stay for good.

I no longer felt like a weakling that didn't have a voice and would stand up for myself if I needed to. I still didn't like conflict, but I rarely had to deal with it. Noah was always the one to stand in front of me, shield the blow.

And to finish things off, a certain cherry on the top, I had found *true* love. It was still a funny one to get your head around. Considering the man had actually been right in front of me all those years, hiding in plain sight.

Life with Noah wasn't perfect; there were bumps in the road along the way, each one we overcame, cementing what we had even more.

I loved him with all my heart and knew this was returned in spades. Noah couldn't do enough for me.

He was beautiful, caring, protective, and kind and he was *mine*. My fallen angel.

Our love for each other was wild, and impulsive at times, but it was real, passionate, and above all else… fierce.

THE END

In memory of all my dogs, past and present that have left their paw prints across my heart.

Love in Norfolk Series, COMING SOON…

Boundaries – Book One

Falling – Book Two

Savage – Book Three

Printed in Great Britain
by Amazon

32907193R00136